TOWARD THE SUNRISING

BOOKS BY GILBERT MORRIS

Through a Glass Darkly

THE HOUSE OF WINSLOW SERIES

1. The Honorable Imposter
2. The Captive Bride
3. The Indentured Heart
4. The Gentle Rebel
5. The Saintly Buccaneer
6. The Holy Warrior
7. The Reluctant Bridegroom
8. The Last Confederate
9. The Dixie Widow
10. The Wounded Yankee
11. The Union Belle
12. The Final Adversary
13. The Crossed Sabres
14. The Valiant Gunman
15. The Gallant Outlaw
16. The Jeweled Spur
17. The Yukon Queen
18. The Rough Rider
19. The Iron Lady
20. The Silver Star
21. The Shadow Portrait
22. The White Hunter
23. The Flying Cavalier
24. The Glorious Prodigal

THE LIBERTY BELL

1. Sound the Trumpet
2. Song in a Strange Land
3. Tread Upon the Lion
4. Arrow of the Almighty
5. Wind From the Wilderness
6. The Right Hand of God
7. Command the Sun

CHENEY DUVALL, M.D.
(with Lynn Morris)

1. The Stars for a Light
2. Shadow of the Mountains
3. A City Not Forsaken
4. Toward the Sunrising
5. Secret Place of Thunder
6. In the Twilight, in the Evening
7. Island of the Innocent
8. Driven With the Wind

THE SPIRIT OF APPALACHIA
(with Aaron McCarver)

1. Over the Misty Mountains
2. Beyond the Quiet Hills
3. Among the King's Soldiers
4. Beneath the Mockingbird's Wings

TIME NAVIGATORS
(for Young Teens)

1. Dangerous Voyage
2. Vanishing Clues

TOWARD THE SUNRISING

LYNN MORRIS & GILBERT MORRIS

BETHANY HOUSE PUBLISHERS
MINNEAPOLIS, MINNESOTA 55438

Published by Bethany House Publishers
A Ministry of Bethany Fellowship International
11400 Hampshire Avenue South
Minneapolis, Minnesota 55438
www.bethanyhouse.com

Printed in the United States of America by
Bethany Press International, Minneapolis, Minnesota 55438

Library of Congress Cataloging-in-Publication Data

Morris, Lynn.
    Toward the sunrising / Lynn Morris and Gilbert Morris.
        p. cm. — (Cheney Duvall, M.D. ; 4)

    1. Duvall, Cheney (Fictitious character)—Fiction. 2. Women physicians—South Carolina—Charleston—Fiction. 3. Reconstruction—South Carolina—Charleston—Fiction. 4. Charleston (S.C.)—History—Fiction. I. Morris, Gilbert. II. Title. III. Series: Morris, Lynn. Cheney Duvall, M.D. ; 4.
PS3563.08742T69   1996
813'.54—dc20   95–43937
ISBN 1–55661–425–X   CIP

This book is for all of us who have seen,
in the deep secret woods and the sudden glades,
glimpses of the Gray Riders,
and because we, in our dreams,
sometimes hear King Phillip's sudden hoofbeats,
and hear his boys' wild cries
borne on the hot South wind.

GILBERT MORRIS & LYNN MORRIS are a father/daughter writing team who combine Gilbert's strength of great story plots and adventure with Lynn's research skills and character development. Together they form a powerful duo!

Lynn has also written a solo novel, *The Balcony*, in the PORTRAITS contemporary romance series with Bethany House. She and her daughter live near her parents in Alabama.

AND when the men of Israel turned again,
The men of Benjamin were amazed:
For they saw that evil was come upon them.

THUS they enclosed the Benjamites round about,
And chased them,
And trode them down with ease
Over against Gibeah
Toward the sunrising.

IN those days there was no king in Israel:
Every man did that which was right in his own eyes.

Judges 20:41, 43; 21:25

CONTENTS

STRANGERS AND

❖ P·A·R·T O·N·E ❖

SOJOURNERS

The land shall not be sold for ever:
for the land is mine;
for ye are strangers and sojourners
with me.

Leviticus 25:23

1

MANHATTAN GUNNER

The Atlas Strong Shoulder Mason jar exploded into hundreds of gray-green shards.

"You killed it," Shiloh observed.

Ignoring him, Cheney Duvall lifted the Colt .44 six-shot with both hands, closed one eye, and took a long, even breath. Five small explosions sounded, and five tin cans flew into the air.

"Good shootin', Doc!" Shiloh declared. "With a little more practice you'll be almost as good as me."

"I'm already as good as you at target shooting," Cheney said smugly. "Now I want to ride Stocking and learn to shoot from a moving horse."

Shiloh Irons blew out an exasperated breath, propped his hands on his hips, and turned to her. Even though she was a tall woman, Cheney threw her head back to look up at him. Shiloh was six four, and his face was shadowed by his black Stetson hat. "Now, Doc—"

"Yes, Shiloh?" she interrupted with exaggerated sweetness, and fluttered her eyelashes.

Shiloh grinned. "I dunno, I musta gone crazy there for a minute. I was actually going to try to talk you out of something. But, don't worry, I'm okay now. I'll go set up the cans while you reload and get mounted up."

Cheney watched him as he turned and ambled toward the two sawhorses and two-by-four that served as a platform for their targets. He walked tall, and though his appearance was jarring in the jaded city of Manhattan, no one ever laughed at him. Today, in his black wool shirt, faded denims, long canvas duster,

13

and black hat, he looked slightly dangerous. His .44 was in a holster at his hip.

Lifting her heavy green velvet skirt just enough to clear the snow, Cheney went back to the stand of bare, spiky trees behind her, where the horses were tied. Close by them was parked a carriage, a magnificent barouche pulled by two night-black horses. The coachman had folded the barouche top down, so the two women seated inside could see the shooting clearly. Victoria Elizabeth Steen de Lancie and Jane Anne Blue sat on the red velvet seats facing each other, with luxurious furs on their laps and embracing their shoulders.

"You're quite good, Dr. Duvall," Mrs. Blue said shyly as Cheney neared the carriage. "I had no idea you were such an expert . . . um . . . shooter? Shootist?"

"Gunner," Victoria offered slyly.

Cheney laughed, laid the gun down on the barouche step, and pulled off her gloves. An immaculate footman stepped forward, bowed, took the gloves, and retreated a discreet distance as Cheney began to reload. Unlocking the breech, she placed the tiny cartridges with fulminate of mercury in the six chambers, then fit the percussion caps over the nipples of the chambers. Closing the breech with a businesslike snap, she began to load the powder and ball.

"Your hands are dirty, Cheney," Victoria said disapprovingly. "Why don't you let Will or David do that for you?"

"Because, Victoria, reloading quickly and efficiently is a skill, just as shooting straight is a skill. I want to know how to do it, and I want to do it well." Cheney retrieved her gloves and mounted Stocking, placing the gun in the specially made saddle holster that matched her gleaming leather sidesaddle. Shiloh had given her both the gun and the holster for Christmas four days earlier.

Stocking gave a welcoming whinny and wheeled. He tried to break into a trot, but Cheney expertly held his head as she went back out toward the targets. Shiloh came up and held the horse's bridle for a moment as he instructed Cheney.

Jane Anne Blue's eyes warmed as she watched. "She looks

wonderful, doesn't she? She's so vivacious and strong."

"Yes, she is," Victoria admitted. "I've never known anyone like her."

Cheney and Stocking made quite a picture in the open field with the virgin snow as a carpet and the light blue winter sky a ceiling. Cheney was wearing a dark green riding habit, and the nipped-in waistline of the rather masculine jacket made her waist look impossibly small. Her auburn hair was tidily tucked into a black net snood beneath her black hat, which was a smaller version of a man's top hat, and a black net veil floated behind her. She wore soft black leather riding boots, but no spur, for Cheney maintained that if a good rider had a good horse, a spur was unnecessary.

Her horse, Stocking, and Shiloh's horse, Sock, were matched geldings. Both were glossy chocolate brown, sturdy Standard-breds, almost sixteen hands high. Shiloh and Cheney could tell them apart easily, but to the unfamiliar eye the only difference between the two was that Stocking had a white marking up to his knee on his off hind leg, and Sock had a white mark up to his hock on his near hind leg.

"Doc, don't blow Stocking's head off," Shiloh was pleading.

"Oh, for heaven's sake! What do you think I'm going to do, sight between his ears?" Cheney pulled the gun out of the sheath and pointed it toward the sky. "Seriously, please tell me what to do. You know I always do what you tell me."

"Joke, right?" Shiloh settled his hat more firmly on his head and patted Stocking's neck soothingly. "First thing I gotta tell you is that Stocking might be used to hearing gunshots, but he's not used to them going off right behind his head. He might bolt."

"No, he won't. He might spook, but he won't bolt."

"Uh . . . just be ready. Now. Hitting a target from a moving horse isn't the same as sighting carefully from a strong stance. But you've got a really good eye, Doc, and I think you'll probably be as good at this as you are at everything else you do."

"Why, thank you." Cheney was always surprised and pleased at Shiloh's offhanded compliments.

"Welcome." He looked up at her and smiled, a careless, easy-going smile that made the "V" scar under his left eye stand out in relief. His teeth were white and even, his eyes a mild corn-flower blue, and whenever he smiled at people they generally couldn't help smiling back, as Cheney did now. "Here's what you do," he went on. "Just pretend, kinda, that you're pointing your index finger at the target. Only it'll be the gun, you see. That's all."

"That's . . . all?" Cheney said doubtfully, eyeing the neat row of six tin cans a few feet away.

"That's all for targeting," Shiloh replied. "Only other things you hafta worry about are cocking the hammer, pulling the trig-ger, holding the reins, guiding the horse, not shooting the horse, not shooting yourself, not shooting anybody else, keeping the horse from bolting, not falling off the horse . . ." His words faded as he headed for the carriage in the grove, well behind and away from Cheney and Stocking.

"Ladies, mind if I hide back here with you?" Shiloh asked Victoria and Jane Anne, tipping his hat.

Jane Anne's brown eyes were round with vague alarm, but Victoria sniffed haughtily. "Nonsense! She can do it, and you know it."

"But . . . what *is* she doing?" Jane Anne asked timidly.

"I'm sure I don't know," Victoria replied, "but I do know that she won't leave here until she can do it, and do it well."

"You're right about that, Mrs. de Lancie," Shiloh nodded. "The Doc's got more heart than most men I've known."

"Yes, heart," Victoria repeated softly. "I had nothing but a black hole in my soul until Cheney led me to Jesus. We've both learned a lot in the last few months about just how strong, and pure, a heart can be when it belongs completely to the Lord."

Shiloh looked and listened curiously as Victoria spoke so gently. Her demeanor was always coolly graceful. When she spoke of the Lord, he had noticed, her icy beauty seemed to take on an unearthly quality. Shiloh suddenly recalled a picture from his childhood—of two children crossing a bridge on a dark night. Victoria de Lancie, for a moment, looked like the lady angel who guarded those lost children.

Cheney had been letting Stocking trot around to work off some of his high spirits. Now she wheeled the horse around to the right of the targets, then set him on a trot past the makeshift table. Almost nonchalantly she pointed the gun and shot. Immediately Stocking reared and screamed, then tried to bolt. Still controlling him, Cheney allowed the horse to run a short way past the targets, where she turned him and urged him back at a dancing, nervous trot. When she neared the table, again she shot, and again he took off. This time Stocking was facing the carriage and headed for it at a dead run.

"Tea?" Victoria asked politely.

"Yes, thanks," Shiloh nodded. A footman materialized with a silver flask and a plain white china cup and saucer and poured the steaming tea for Shiloh. He sniffed in appreciation.

Jane Anne Blue's eyes were, if possible, rounder and bigger than before, and she was having difficulty breathing. It seemed that the ground shook as the huge horse thundered toward them. Cheney looked very small as she clung to his back.

"Er . . . um . . ." Jane Anne mumbled.

Cheney pulled the horse up sharply and turned him while Victoria gave Jane Anne a sympathetic look. "She's much too good a horsewoman for that, Jane Anne dear," she declared.

"Right," Shiloh said with feeling. "She might shoot us, but she won't let the horse run over us."

As Cheney and Stocking continued their crazy, noisy dance out in the snowy field, Victoria, Shiloh, and Jane Anne watched with enjoyment and talked desultorily of the weather, Cheney's skills as a "gunner," as Victoria insisted on calling it, and the recent cholera epidemic in New York.

"About a thousand people got it," Shiloh said, "and four hundred and ninety-four died."

"Dreadful," Victoria said and shuddered.

"Not nearly as bad as the '49 epidemic." He shrugged. "Over ten thousand cases. Five thousand seventeen died."

"Are you certain it's over?" Jane Anne asked.

"Yes, certain. Haven't had a new case since November eighteenth." Shiloh had worked as senior hospital steward in the cholera hospital and had proved so competent and effective that he had acted as an advisor to the eminent attending doctors and the Metropolitan Board of Health. He had no formal medical training, but had worked in the field hospitals in the War Between the States, and had been Cheney's medical assistant since April 1865.

"What are you going to do now, Shiloh?" Victoria asked quietly. The question was addressed to him, but her eyes and thoughts were on Cheney Duvall, who rode wildly in the field before them.

He turned to her and grinned. "Dunno. Need another footman?"

Victoria laughed, a quiet, tinkling laughter that was very ladylike. "I think not! I have ten, you know! Besides, I'd never be able to find a match to your height or the size of your calves."

"Victoria!" Jane Anne Blue was shocked. "Victoria, really!"

"Why, Jane Anne, you know one must have footmen in matching pairs," Victoria said mischievously. Her blue eyes twinkled so outrageously that even shy, reserved Jane Anne Blue recovered.

"Oh . . . oh, of course. I always demand that of all my footmen," she managed to retort. "And my butlers, and my maid-servants, and my hawkers, and my household troops, and my . . . gaffers, and . . ."

Victoria, Shiloh, and Jane Anne all began to laugh so loudly that Cheney turned to look at them curiously. Then she turned Stocking determinedly for another run. She had taken three shots, and the horse was just calming down a bit.

Shiloh glanced at Cheney, then studied the two women seated in the luxurious barouche. Three women less likely to be friends would be hard to find. Immensely wealthy and from one of the oldest families in New York, Victoria was a member in good standing of Polite Society, with silvery blond hair, blue eyes, and the kind of aura that spoke "expensive," without the vulgarity of words.

Jane Anne Blue, on the other hand, was not at all striking,

though she was certainly not unattractive. Her rich, curly brown hair was pulled back severely into a bun at the nape of her neck, but her expressive brown eyes and thin, girlish figure were more accurate indications of the kind of woman she was. As the head of the Behring Memorial Orphanage, she and Victoria—who was the patroness—had grown to be fast friends.

And then, of course, there was Cheney, who was nothing like either Victoria or Jane Anne. At twenty-five, she was complacently unmarried and financially independent, a woman courageous enough to have become a doctor and uncaring enough of public opinion to be proud of it.

As he thought about the orphanage that Linde Behring had founded in New York, Shiloh finally answered Victoria's question. "I've been thinking about going back to Charleston," he said. He had grown up at the Behring sisters' first orphanage there. Before she died, Linde Behring had told him that there were some items in Charleston that belonged to him. It was time for him to retrieve them.

Victoria's left eyebrow arched the tiniest bit, and then she turned to watch Cheney. "That may be a good idea, Shiloh, but you must take Cheney with you. Make her go. One need only glance at her to see that she's bored and restless. She needs to do something new."

"Yeah," Shiloh grunted. "You're speaking of that Cheney over there, right? *Make* her do this; *take* her there?"

"I shall recommend that she go," Victoria maintained with an air of finality that amused Shiloh greatly. The two women had an entwined history and were especially close, but Shiloh Irons knew a thing or two more about Cheney Duvall, M.D., than Victoria de Lancie did. "And what is so amusing, Mr. Irons?" she asked him frostily.

He began to answer her, but at that moment Cheney fired again, and a tin can ricocheted up into the sky. "Good shot!" Shiloh said. "Doc's gonna be as good shooting from the hip as Dev Buchanan is with a horsewhip!"

"D-Dev . . . Buchanan—?"

Shiloh turned, half-repentant, and almost made an apology

to Jane Anne Blue for the rather crude remark. But what he perceived was that it was Victoria de Lancie who looked pale, her eyes wide and dark, and Jane Anne was merely looking at her sympathetically. Within a second Victoria again looked polite and interested, and Jane Anne dropped her eyes. In that brief moment, however, Shiloh learned something very interesting about Victoria Elizabeth Steen de Lancie and Dev Buchanan.

Devlin Buchanan had been a part of the Duvall family since he was six years old. Richard and Irene Duvall, Cheney's parents, had taken Dev and his ailing mother under their protection when Cheney was an infant. Cheney and Dev had been educated by the same tutor until Cheney was twelve and Dev was eighteen. Then the Duvalls had sent Dev to medical school in England, and he was now a highly respected, internationally known physician.

Shiloh knew that when Cheney had graduated from medical school, Buchanan had asked her to marry him. He had surmised, from chance remarks made by Cheney's father, that she had truly been in love with the practice of medicine at the time; she had not said yes, but neither had she said no. Evidently she had asked Buchanan to wait until she had established herself in her chosen profession before she committed herself to marriage and a family.

This seemed to Shiloh to be a rather ephemeral and uncertain commitment. Cheney and Buchanan had practiced together in recent months and were undoubtedly close, but as far as Shiloh could see, neither of them seemed to be working toward a more solid relationship. Certainly, there had been no talk of setting a date, as far as he knew. Still, the strong bond between the Duvalls and Devlin Buchanan was unmistakable to an intelligent observer.

Shiloh Iron's particular gift of perception was part of his nature, unbidden and unstrained, and, at times like these, unwanted. In those few telling moments he had seen much more of Victoria de Lancie's feelings about Devlin Buchanan than he really wanted to know. Buchanan had horsewhipped a scoundrel who had insulted Victoria and Cheney, and then had immediately gone to England. Shiloh had assumed that this was to avoid any scandal resulting from the horsewhipping, though no word of it had ever been breathed to others by the persons involved. Besides that, Buchanan had a much-sought-after position at Guy's Hospital in London, and had only been in New York on a leave of absence.

When he saw the instant of hopeless longing on Victoria de Lancie's face as she breathed his name, however, Shiloh began to wonder if Devlin Buchanan might have left New York for another, more complicated reason. Ruefully he thought, *Hope I don't have to know all about that, either.*

Glancing from Victoria's closed face to Shiloh's averted one, Jane Anne returned to an earlier, less difficult topic. "Are you really going to Charleston, Mr. Irons?" she asked quietly. "Charleston, South Carolina?"

"Yes, ma'am," Shiloh answered. He searched her face. "Why?"

"It's just that . . . that . . ." Jane Anne swallowed hard, then she turned and searched the far distance with her warm brown eyes. "I . . . I think that Allan—my husband, Allan—might possibly be in Charleston."

Shiloh's even features hardened, and his eyes narrowed. "Want me to find him and bust his head for you?"

The words hung in the cold, still air as Cheney thundered up at a fast gallop. Stocking reared and pranced close to the carriage, his breath steaming out of his nostrils in a cloud. Cheney's cheeks were bright coral, her sea green eyes flashed, and she smiled exultantly. "I got two, Shiloh! Not bad, do you think?"

She dismounted expertly, and the coachman came and led Stocking away. Cheney stared shrewdly at her three companions. Shiloh looked grim, Victoria distant, and Jane Anne unhappy.

"What?" Cheney demanded.

An uncomfortable silence reigned for a few moments, and then Victoria rolled her eyes. "Shiloh's going to Charleston; Jane Anne thinks Allan may be there, and Shiloh wants to find him and bust his head. I, personally, am leaning to Shiloh's point of view. What do you think, Cheney?"

Cheney gave Shiloh an odd look. "Why, I think I might go to Charleston too."

Shiloh turned to meet Cheney's gaze, and though his expression didn't change, his eyes softened almost imperceptibly. A current passed between them, a certain recognition, and a mutual acknowledgment that their paths, once again, lay together.

★ ★ ★ ★

Twilight overtook Manhattan Island quickly in the bleak month of December, lasting only fleeting minutes before darkness. Cheney, Victoria, and Jane Anne had sat talking, huddled under the warm ermines and minks, for far too long. Now Shiloh and Cheney were going back to Duvall Court in freezing darkness.

It seemed not to bother the two, however, for they rode slowly, looking up at the star-frosted sky and speaking in lazy, quiet tones.

"Are you really going with me to Charleston, Doc?" Shiloh asked nonchalantly.

"Yes, I really am," Cheney answered. "And you really are not going to find Allan Blue and bash his head in. I will make certain of that."

Shiloh stirred restlessly and jerked Sock's reins a bit, uncharacteristic gestures for him. He said nothing, but Cheney could sense his anger. *Be honest,* she chided herself. *I'm angry, too. But Jane Anne isn't, so I have to be at least as charitable as she is.*

Eight years ago Allan and Jane Anne Blue had been happily married, with a seven-year-old son and a baby girl named Laura. Allan was a clerk; Jane Anne had been teaching at a girls' academy but had been dismissed because she was expecting. One night when Laura was two months old, Allan had wrapped a piece of hard candy in linen for her to suck on.

In the middle of the night, the rats had come.

Laura was bitten several times, got very ill, and almost died from an impossibly high fever. She lived, but her brain was damaged, and within two weeks Allan, Jane Anne, and seven-year-old Jeremy Blue realized that Baby Laura would always be just that—a baby. One night Allan Blue walked out of the shabby tenement apartment and never came back.

"Actually," Cheney went on uncertainly, "I was thinking of taking a trip to New Orleans to visit my great-aunts. A stopover in Charleston would be perfect; Father and I were just this morning discussing some urgent business he has there. But it's almost impossible for him to get away right now. He's right in the middle of putting in the steel processing plant." Richard Duvall had decided to expand Duvall's Iron Foundry to make steel with the new Bessemer processing method.

"Yes? What's in Charleston?" Shiloh asked with interest. Cheney was relieved as he visibly relaxed into his normal, easy seat on the big horse.

"Oh, Father was being a gentleman and thinking everyone else was, too," Cheney grumbled. "Now he's got a mess with one of his biggest customers, who happens to be in Charleston. Dallas Farm and Supply is the name of it. Mr. Dallas was doing quite a brisk business with Duvall's before the war, in both tools and pig iron. When the war came, Father, of course, had to comply with the blockade and cut him off. After Appomattox, Father contacted several of his really good Southern customers—five of them, I think—and told them that in order to help them recover, he'd supply them at cost, plus ten percent to cover shipping. Mr. Dallas took Father up on his offer. Now it's almost 1867—over a year and a half later—and he's still taking him up on his offer, for thousands of dollars a month."

With a small sigh Shiloh said, "There was no paperwork, I guess. An open-ended agreement, between gentlemen."

"Well, four of them took him up on his offer, got started again within a year, and now they're gold-plated customers again!" Cheney protested.

"Okay, okay, Doc!" Shiloh said, and Cheney could hear the smile in his voice. "I'm not the ungentlemanly bounder from Charleston here!"

"True," Cheney replied smartly. "You're the bounder from Charleston, but you are a gentleman."

"True, and don't you forget it."

"Don't you forget it if we should happen to find Allan Blue."

Shiloh stiffened slightly and looked away. Cheney sighed. She knew her words would have this effect on him, but she had to make certain that Shiloh would be able to keep his temper, assuming that by some miracle Allan Blue was still alive, in Charleston, and they found him. Shiloh was normally an easygoing man, but he could be frightening when he lost his temper. And he was never very patient with men he thought were contemptible. Still, Cheney felt a little forlorn that she had nagged him about it again.

Restlessly Shiloh took out his gold pocket watch, a gift from Cheney on a long-ago and faraway Christmas, and popped it open.

When Johnny comes marching home again, Hurrah! Hurrah! The silvery sound of the tune emanating from the timepiece brought vivid memories—sights, sounds, and even smells to both Cheney and Shiloh. Suddenly Shiloh smiled in the darkness. "This'll be the first time I've gone home in about eight years." He snapped the watch shut. "I'm glad you're coming with me, Doc."

I suppose he does think of Charleston as home, Cheney reflected. *I suppose even an orphanage, if you were left there as a little baby, can seem like home. . . .*

Shiloh had been abandoned at the Behring Orphanage in a crate marked "Shiloh Ironworks." Thinking of Shiloh being an orphan always made Cheney feel a little sad, even though Shiloh was matter-of-fact about it. Suddenly she realized, *Well, of course! How can I be so blind? That's why he hates Allan Blue so much . . . a man who abandoned his family!*

Turning to him, she said in a low voice, "I'm glad I'm coming to Charleston, too, Shiloh. I . . . I want . . . you to know that . . . that . . . I . . ."

He turned to face her directly, and she could almost feel the heat of his gaze. Taking a deep breath, she turned to look

24

straight ahead. "I'd miss you. That's all."

He kept watching her, waiting . . . but she said nothing else. Finally he turned away and said lightly, "You sure would. What would you do without me, Doc?"

"You don't know," Cheney said quickly and quietly.

Shiloh thought she had misspoken, that she meant to say, "I don't know." Upon reflection, however, he decided that perhaps she knew what she said, after all.

2

FOREBODINGS AND ILL OMENS

Shiloh came home to Charleston on Friday the thirteenth of January, 1867. Not being a superstitious man, he didn't think that arriving on this dark, cold, rainy day was particularly foreboding. He did, however, find the ruins of what had once been the Northeastern Railroad Depot an ill omen.

Cheney and Shiloh had decided that he would travel by train and bring the horses, Sock and Stocking, while Cheney and her companion, Rissy, would travel to Charleston by steamer.

Good thing, he reflected grimly as he rode Sock and led Stocking past the pile of rubble that had once been a fine brick rail station. *Trip took two solid weeks—and calling it a "trip by railroad" was sure a joke....* As soon as Shiloh was south of Philadelphia, the railroad lines had proved to be scarce and the routes torturous. Few lines had survived the ravages of war and few had been repaired. Four nights Shiloh had traveled on horseback. Outside of Charleston, two trestles had not yet been rebuilt, and the ferries were scanty and in frightful condition. The trip had been exhausting and depressing.

All day long he walked the streets of his hometown. Earthworks still stood, forlorn reminders of an invader not repelled. Pieces of guns and ammunition, pockmarked and rusty, littered the batteries. The outline of Fort Sumter was barely visible out in the harbor; only a part of one wall still remained, and the rest was merely a pile of blasted brick. Many of the fine homes along the South Battery showed shell damage. In Shiloh's mind Charleston had always been like a lovely, warm, vital woman. Now she was suffering from a slow, wasting disease that had turned her wan and pallid, a sad ash gray wraith of her former self.

Shiloh stood on Meeting Street beside a huge hole that had been dug in the middle of the street for no apparent reason and stared at St. Michael's steeple, visible above the bare January branches of the trees that lined the quiet residential street. Most curious of all, and inexplicably depressing to him, was the sight of this majestic steeple. It was still painted black, although no Union gunners squinted to train upon it now.

Out of the corner of his eye he saw a hurrying figure and turned to look. It was a woman, dressed in black, with a patched gray cloak. The hood was pulled close over her face, and she looked neither to the right nor to the left. She hurried past Shiloh almost at a run.

That's it, he thought with sudden realization. *That's one reason the whole city looks so odd and dreary. There aren't any ladies! Is she the first one I've seen?*

Shiloh thought hard for a moment. He had seen hundreds of soldiers in blue everywhere. He'd seen many, many Negro men and boys. But he couldn't remember seeing any women, not even colored women.

He sighed and continued his walk north. *I always thought Charleston had the prettiest ladies in the world. They all seemed to have such pretty skin, and hair . . . bright eyes and soft voices. . . . Guess now they're afraid to come out and just walk around like they used to. . . .*

His hotel room was welcoming. A fire blazed in the marble fireplace, and a blank-faced Negro man in a white tunic brought him a cold supper and hot, strong coffee. He went to bed early, because Cheney and Rissy would arrive in Charleston sometime tomorrow. Shiloh didn't want them down at the docks alone, even in daylight, so he decided to be there at dawn, and wait.

★   ★   ★   ★

The steamship *Bostonian* waded into Charleston Harbor at ten o'clock on Saturday morning. The only two passengers standing on the deck, braving the bitter winter wind, were Cheney Duvall and her companion, Rissy Clarkson. Rissy was as tall as Cheney, but sturdier-looking, with long, well-formed arms and legs. Her features were strong, her eyes wise and watchful. The color of her skin was a rich coffee brown. Born exactly one month before Cheney, Rissy in many ways felt as if she were ages older.

After they passed Fort Sumter, Cheney squinted her eyes and said, "There's Shiloh."

Rissy muttered, "You cain't see him from this far out, 'cause I cain't see him from this far out."

"It's Shiloh," Cheney replied sturdily.

And it was. As they neared the wharves on the South Battery, his tall form, with the long duster gusting behind him, became clear to Rissy. Many other men walked along or loitered on the wharves, but Shiloh stood unmoving, his arms crossed, looking out to sea.

He slowly walked along the wharves, following the ship until he came to the pier where the *Bostonian* passengers would disembark. Cheney hurried down the ramp, but Rissy clamped a strong cocoa-colored hand on her arm and hissed, "Don't you be a-runnin' down there after him! You ack like you ain't seen him for a month!"

"It's been two weeks," Cheney protested but descended more slowly.

"Hullo, Doc. Hullo, Rissy," he greeted them. Then, as he took Cheney's hand to assist her, he bent and brushed a kiss on it.

"My goodness!" Cheney flushed, and her eyes danced. "How long have you been here? Are these the famous Southern manners I keep hearing about?"

"Yes, ma'am," he replied, his blue eyes sparkling. "You're really in the South now."

"Oh happy day," Rissy muttered.

"Go over there." Shiloh waved to the street. "Sock and Stocking and a carriage are waiting for you. I'll get your luggage. How many men do I need?"

"Six," Cheney called back over her shoulder.

Shiloh groaned and headed toward the mound of luggage that stevedores were already piling on the docks. It seemed there were lots of cheap carpetbags, but he knew Cheney Duvall's massive brass-trimmed trunks a mile away.

"I think you're 'bout as glad to see them horses as you are Mistuh Arns," Rissy said. Cheney was talking to Sock and Stocking, patting them and fussing with their harness. "And your gloves is dirty now." Cheney ignored her, and Rissy unobtrusively slid up and gave them some grapes she had saved from the fruit basket in her stateroom.

Shiloh returned, along with five other men, all carrying huge trunks. With some difficulty they managed to load them into the small carriage, but then Cheney and Rissy had to sit in front with Shiloh on the driver's seat.

"You wanna sit on my lap, Doc?" Shiloh teased as the carriage started toward town. "Maybe we'll get a little more attention that way."

For once Rissy didn't fuss at Shiloh's flirting. "Blue skies! Ain't these men never seed a lady before?" All the men everywhere—soldiers, Negroes, young boys, and one or two gentlemen in top hats—stared curiously at the carriage. The men in top hats touched the brims as the carriage went by.

"Um . . . you and the Doc look so fine this morning, Rissy," Shiloh answered gallantly. "Guess all these gentlemen are just enjoying the view." *Probably haven't seen pretty young women in new, expensive clothes since about 1861*, he added mentally. *And a well-dressed young colored woman—that they've probably never seen.* He decided to keep these thoughts to himself. Rissy and Cheney would find out the meaning of this attention soon enough.

Cheney was wearing a traveling suit of rust-colored wool, with a touch of white lace at the high collar. Gold-braid frogs adorned the front of the jacket and the skirt all the way to the hem, with ornate golden buttons neatly fitting through the loops. Her jacket was long and gathered in the back with three gold buttons at the top of the gathers, and the fullness of the jacket fit neatly over the slight bustle in her skirt. Her hat was a businesslike low-crowned brown velvet, with the same gold braid as a hat-band and a single gold frog on the right. A small emerald pin was centered in the frog, with a rosette of white netting surrounding it. Rissy had managed to arrange Cheney's hair in smooth ringlets cascading down to her shoulders in the back.

Rissy's clothes, though not as expensive as Cheney's, were of fine quality. Her skirt and jacket were of gray wool, trimmed in dark green, with a snowy white lace jabot at her throat. A full cape with a hood, with a large golden tassel hanging from the point of the hood, was pulled close about her. She shivered as the Atlantic's long icy fingers of wind brushed over them.

"Where are we going?" Cheney asked, turning her head from side to side eagerly. The wind had brought out the color in her cheeks and made her eyes a bright sea green.

"Planter's Hotel," Shiloh replied. "It's not the biggest place, or the finest . . . I suppose the Mills House Hotel was, but it looks like every bluebelly in Charleston chipped away at it." Cheney looked at him quizzically, and he shrugged. "General Beauregard's headquarters, it was. They shelled it."

"Still, I don't see too much shell damage overall," Cheney observed. "I suppose Charleston fared better than Atlanta or Richmond."

"Yeah." The word was muffled, but Shiloh sat up straighter and smiled. "Anyway, I'm glad the Planter's is still there. When I was a kid, I always dreamed of staying in the Planter's Hotel. That's where all the big planters stayed when they came to town, and they always gathered in the restaurant. They looked so important, with their big cigars and their fine boots and their gold watch chains. . . ."

"Well?" Cheney said pointedly.

Shiloh looked at the three cigars neatly lined up in his shirt pocket, his shiny black cavalry boots, and the gold watch chain attached to a belt loop and leading into his pants pocket and grinned sheepishly. "I fit right in, huh? 'Cept I don't have a plantation. . . ."

Planter's Hotel was a discreet three-story building on Church Street. No sign adorned the front of the hotel, for it was one of those exclusive local establishments that disdained advertisement. It was distinctive, however, because the second and third stories abutted out over the first, and it was fronted with exquisite wrought-iron work. The hotel, like everything else in Charleston, was prohibitively expensive. The owner managed to make a fairly good profit from the restaurant, which was one of the best in town, and offered fare ranging in price from cheap to outrageous.

The lobby was tiny, but the red carpet was unworn and the desk was dark mahogany with a rich shine. To the left, delicious smells and low voices wafted from the restaurant. It was ten-thirty in the morning, which meant that the morning coffee break was in full swing. To the right was another sizable room that contained a bar but also served food.

"Good morning, Mr. Irons," the bespectacled clerk said in a soft drawl. His brown hair was plastered down, and Cheney could smell macassar oil as she neared him.

"Good morning, Mr. Barlow. These are the two ladies who will be needing the rooms I reserved."

Mr. Barlow's eyes grew round behind his tiny square spectacles. "I . . . I . . . beg your pardon? But . . . but . . . this isn't possible! There must be some mistake!"

"A mistake, huh? Then I guess you musta made it!" Shiloh frowned, placed his big hands palm down on the counter, and leaned far over.

Mr. Barlow became extremely nervous, and he dropped his pencil stub. Disappearing behind the tall counter, he finally popped up against the back wall. It seemed that he had to take two steps backward to retrieve his little pencil.

"I'm sure there must be a mistake," he repeated faintly. "Surely you don't mean that one of the rooms you reserved is for this colored woman?" Taking out a white handkerchief, he dabbed at his upper lip.

Shiloh looked upward and muttered to himself, "I can't believe I didn't think of this. . . ."

Rissy crossed her arms and frowned darkly but said nothing.

Cheney said very slowly, "Perhaps you don't understand, Mr. Barlow. My—companion—is to have a room adjoining

31

mine. A room just like mine. A room that costs the same as mine, and will be paid for, in gold, just like mine."

Mr. Barlow, still at a safe distance, shook his head. "I'm sorry, ma'am. We have perfectly suitable servants' quarters in the back, and they have their own dining arrangements."

"But..."

Shiloh laid his hand on her arm and shook his head. "Doc, Rissy, I'm sorry. But never mind. I'll find us something else."

"What?" Cheney demanded. "Won't we have the same problem wherever we go?"

"Uh..." Shiloh hesitated, then said mockingly, "Interested in buying a house in Charleston, Doc?"

"Maybe I will," Rissy put in, and Mr. Barlow's eyebrows shot up.

"Maybe I'll buy this stupid hotel," Cheney added.

"I think not," a deep voice said behind them. "I'm the owner of this stupid hotel, and I don't wish to sell it."

Cheney, Shiloh, and Rissy turned in unison to see a young couple standing behind them. The man was slightly built, about thirty years old, and dressed in a black suit and vest. The woman was tiny, girlish, about twenty, with lustrous chestnut brown hair and dark eyes. She was looking up at Shiloh, and her eyes shone.

"I'm Gard Granger," the man said shortly and made a stiff bow. Cheney noticed that his right hand wore a tight-fitting black leather glove and hung useless at his side.

Mr. Barlow began spluttering, "Mr. Granger, I'm sorry. We're having a problem, and I was just—"

"Never mind, Barlow. I see what the problem is." His dark eyes flashed on Cheney, then Rissy. "Give them the rooms."

"What? Her too?"

Granger ignored Mr. Barlow and said to Cheney in his curt manner, "This is my sister, Juliet Granger. She is your rescuer, ma'am. Now, if you will excuse me..." With that, he turned and disappeared through a door by the side of the desk. Mr. Barlow disappeared, too.

"You must excuse my brother. He ... he means well." Juliet

Granger spoke in a voice so soft it was almost a whisper. Dropping her eyes shyly, she murmured, "I hope you have a nice stay."

Cheney had recovered by now and introduced herself and Rissy. When she introduced Shiloh, he bowed and kissed Juliet Granger's gloved hand. "It's an honor and a pleasure to meet you, Miss Granger. Thank you for coming to the aid of these ladies. I was feeling pretty clumsy."

Cheney eyed Shiloh with ill humor as Juliet Granger glanced up at him, blushing furiously. Her hand seemed to linger in his for a few moments longer than was strictly necessary.

Rissy stepped up and politely said, "Thank you, ma'am."

"You're welcome. I . . ." Mr. Barlow had reappeared behind the desk, looking confused. Juliet went on hurriedly, "Here is Mr. Barlow to check you in, Miss Duvall. I'm sure you'll excuse me." With a last quick glance at Shiloh, she hurried toward the door through which Gard Granger had disappeared.

★ ★ ★ ★

"Those Grangers are strange," Cheney commented.

"At least you have the rooms," Shiloh replied. "To tell the truth, I'm not sure what we could have done if they hadn't shown up."

Giving him a curious look, Cheney asked carefully, "Would you have left with Rissy and me? You wouldn't have had to, you know."

With a careless shrug he said, "Doesn't matter now, does it?"

They were walking north along Church Street. The morning had been dark and rainy and cold, and Cheney and Rissy had taken a long, restful nap as soon as they got settled in. Cheney woke up precisely at noon, but Rissy slept soundly on. Just as Cheney began to grow restless, Shiloh appeared to take her for a walk.

"It's odd," Cheney commented. "All the biggest, finest houses here are along the waterfront. Exactly the opposite of New York."

Shiloh laughed. "That's sure the truth! Everything here's exactly the opposite of New York, Doc."

Cheney looked around with a critical eye. They were on the outskirts of the business district, but it was a dreary area and seemed almost abandoned. Many of the small shops were empty and boarded up, and some of the ones that were open had pitifully low stock. One side of the street was warehouses, and most of them were empty, with doors sagging sadly open. The only people they saw were soldiers, laughing and jostling each other on the narrow sidewalk so they wouldn't have to walk on the muddy street, and Negroes sitting on the sidewalks or in the doorways of the abandoned shops. Many of the soldiers watched Cheney with too much familiarity, and some of them made rude gestures and remarks—after she and Shiloh had passed. All of them watched Shiloh carefully out of the corner of their eyes and gave him a wide berth.

Horses sounded behind them, and Cheney and Shiloh turned to look. Soldiers stopped too and lined the sidewalk, craning their necks for a better view.

A splendid military company rounded the corner from a side street. The leader was on a great white horse, and behind him were two color bearers, one flying a black flag with a diagonal white stripe, and one flying a guidon, a small triangle of sky blue with no design.

As soon as the company of about twenty horsemen had come around the corner, the leader called out a sharp command. As a unit, the company escalated to a canter, and at the same time seemed to shift over to the side of the street—the sidewalk side.

"Uh-oh," Shiloh muttered and tried to pull Cheney back, but she was straining to see the gorgeously arrayed troops and impatiently shook her arm loose from his grip.

Far down the street they heard loud shouts and some curses, and the soldiers on the sidewalk began jumping back against the storefronts one by one, looking like a line of falling dominoes. Cheney didn't notice, however, as her gaze was transfixed on the man who led the horsemen. Shiloh rasped, "Doc . . ."

It was too late.

The horsemen thundered past, and mud splashed up in big, wet splotches on Cheney's skirt. Still she didn't notice; as the leader of the company had passed by, his eyes had locked on Cheney for long seconds. She stared up at him, her eyes wide.

Shiloh stepped up, murmuring something apologetic, and Cheney looked first down the street at the angry, mud-covered Federal soldiers, then down at her skirt. Then she began to laugh.

At the same time, a sharp command split the air, and it seemed that the horses of the company came to a dead standstill. Shiloh looked up curiously, but Cheney was still giggling as she watched the soldiers, some of them with mud all the way up on their hats, as they grumbled and brushed and dabbed.

Looking back up at Shiloh, Cheney saw the intent look on his face and followed his gaze back up the street. Three soldiers, the leader in front and two behind, were walking—almost marching—up the sidewalk. The soldiers in blue moved aside for them but muttered blackly as they passed. Some made obscene gestures behind their backs. The marchers looked neither to the right nor the left.

"This might be trouble," Shiloh muttered. "Listen, Doc—"

"No, wait," Cheney insisted. She wanted to see what the grandly dressed soldiers were going to do.

They were wearing uniforms she had never seen before. Their tunics were gray, with three rows of gold buttons in ruler-straight columns down the front. Two white belts crossed their chests, bandolier-style, with a big silver buckle, polished to a flashing sheen, in the middle of the "X." Their breeches were spotless white and tucked into mirror-shined cavalry boots. Instead of hats, they wore white "shakos"—a stiff, cylindrical hat with a short visor, a strap that came precisely below the lips, and a plume in the front. The leader of the troop, who marched in front, had a tall black plume on his hat, a gold insignia on his shoulders and cuffs, and cavalry officer's boots that reached midthigh. A saber hung at his side.

He walked directly up to Cheney and came to a stiff halt, with the two behind him in perfect step. Removing his shako, he made a low bow, and the two soldiers behind him did the same. "Ma'am, I am Cadet Captain Shadrach Forrest Luxton of the Citadel. I would not impose upon you in this manner, without a proper introduction, but it is necessary that I offer you my gravest apologies."

Cheney was speechless. Cadet Captain Shadrach Forrest Luxton was over six feet tall, and by his stern demeanor she somehow expected him to have a deep, booming voice. Instead it was rather high, though not feminine—a clear tenor. And the young man could not have been more than eighteen years old.

He was looking at Cheney expectantly, but she simply couldn't manage to speak. Unperturbed, he went on smoothly, "I assure you that I was unaware that there was a lady on this street, ma'am. Please accept my sincerest regrets for the damage done to your person by my troops." His blue-gray eyes went down to the large mud-spots on Cheney's dress.

Cheney recovered some sense and sensibility. At this point, it would be proper for Shiloh to introduce her and then himself. She looked up at him expectantly and was taken aback at the expression on his face. His blue eyes were wide with disbelief and were fixed on Shadrach Luxton's face. He seemed to have forgotten that she was there.

After a moment Cheney despaired of being introduced by Shiloh. Extending her hand to the young captain, she said, "Sir, I am Dr. Cheney Duvall. I accept your apology, and thank you for your attentions. Please don't concern yourself with my dress. The show was worth it."

A hint of a smile played around Luxton's mouth. His eyes began to glow. "Miss Duvall, it would be my great pleasure if you would attend one of our parade drills so you may see a real show. I would ask for the honor of escorting you, but . . ." He gave Shiloh a meaningful look.

Shiloh demanded in a strangled voice, "What did you say your name was?"

Shadrach's expression changed from curious expectancy to surprise, and then to amused recognition. "I am Shadrach For-

36

rest Luxton, sir. Perhaps you are acquainted with my half brother."

"Your . . . your half brother?" Shiloh repeated stupidly.

"Yes, sir," Shadrach answered, seeming to enjoy Shiloh's reaction immensely. "My half brother is Lieutenant General Nathan Bedford Forrest."

3

THE GUARD

"I'm not even sure who General Nathan Bedford Forrest is," Cheney grumbled.

Rissy's eyes narrowed to slits. Looking straight ahead, her profile as cold as an Egyptian statue, she muttered, "I've heard of that one. Back in the war, the papers said he was a woman-whippin', baby-stealin' slaver."

"What!" Her eyebrows arched high with surprise, Cheney turned to face Rissy. Stocking and the buggy seemed to wobble a moment as the reins were temporarily slack. "But . . . but Rissy," Cheney said tentatively, "Shiloh told me he rode with General Forrest for three years. He . . . he seemed proud of it."

Now Rissy's eyebrows shot up in surprise, but Rissy always recovered quickly. Her eyes still straight ahead, her mouth twitched slightly as she spoke. "Papers said that Gi'n'ral Forrest and his men burned colored soldiers alive. Sounds lak a lotta trouble to go to, doesn't it? Whippin' all the women and stealin' all the babies—where do you think they stole 'em *to*?—and buildin' crosses to burn all the colored soldiers on. I always wondered when they had time to fight the war. I'll hafta ask Mistuh Arns 'bout all that."

Cheney snapped the reins and made the usual buggy driver's clicking noise in her cheek. Stocking obediently went into a casual trot. "Perhaps I'll find out all about it this afternoon. Shiloh and I are invited to lunch—or dinner—with Shadrach Forrest Luxton, General Forrest's half brother."

"Well, is it lunch or dinner?" Rissy demanded, assessing Cheney's clothing with a professional eye.

"Apparently there is no such thing as 'lunch' in Charleston," Cheney replied smugly. "One has 'dinner' in the daytime, from two until four, and 'supper' late at night."

"No wonder the white folks here take naps all the afternoon! Eatin' from two 'til four! You ain't doin' no such thing! I'd hafta get two more folk to help me heave you into the bed!"

"But, Rissy, it's the custom," Cheney teased. "I must be polite, and those two men will certainly only talk about the war. I'll have to be quiet and eat. A lot." Slender and lithe, Cheney had been the same size since she was eighteen years old, and Rissy knew it. But when Cheney ate a large meal, Rissy had to loosen her corset, and sometimes let out a stitch or two in her skirts or tight-fitting jackets. This made Cheney irritable, which in turn made Rissy irritable.

"Awright, Miss Cheney, you go right ahead," Rissy retorted. "And tonight I'll jist cut a hole in a bed sheet and throw it over your head, 'cause you sure won't have nothin' else to wear!"

This sparring went on as Cheney drove the buggy north on Concord Street, which followed the Cooper River up the east side of the city. Mr. Barlow, while eyeing Rissy with suspicion, had given Cheney directions to Dallas Farm and Supply politely enough. Deftly directing Stocking in a left turn onto Charlotte Street, Cheney at once saw the sign ahead. While most of the other commercial buildings on the street seemed empty and shabby, Dallas Farm and Supply had a brand-new, crisply painted white sign with red lettering. It hung from a massive wrought-iron bracket and was framed with delicate curlicues. As the buggy drew near to the door of the three-story brick building, Cheney noticed the word "Vess" cleverly formed in the ornate wrought ironwork beneath the sign.

As Cheney pulled the buggy up to the front door, two men ran from an alley nearby and took hold of Stocking's harness. Ragged, their faces pinched with cold, they looked beseechingly up at Cheney. "Hold yo' buggy for a quarter, ma'am?" Cheney was horrified to see that one of them had no shoes, only ra[g]s wrapped around his feet.

"Come assist my friend and me down," Cheney or[dered]. "Then watch the buggy while I conduct my business, [I'll] pay you when we return."

A smile lurked in Rissy's kohl-dark eyes. There was a perfectly good hitching post standing in front of the store, and Cheney Duvall rarely waited for assistance in getting out of a buggy. There were soldiers in blue patrolling the street, so no one would dare lay a hand on the carriage or the horse. But those two men, Rissy was certain, had just earned themselves a silver dollar apiece.

Both of the men were older and grizzled. At Cheney's peremptory words, they looked at each other and nodded, and the one with shoes seemed to be elected to help Cheney and Rissy down. Wiping his hands repeatedly on his thin cotton trousers, he gingerly offered one to Rissy and dropped his eyes as she alighted. Rissy, in her blue skirt with three snowy petticoats and matching blue wool jacket, was dressed as fine as any white lady he'd ever seen, and he bowed deferentially to her—just in case.

His pinched mouth tightened as Cheney took his hand. Her dress was rather plain: a silvery-gray wool with somber black velvet trim along the hem and cuffs. The matching wool mantle she wore, however, was lined with silver satin and was richly decorated, with black velvet ribbon forming a complicated insignia along the flowing hem. Lining the hem was a five-inch gathered black Austrian lace. Her hat was black velvet—a V-shaped curve that fit closely along the crown of her head, with the point of the "V" low on her forehead. The same black lace was gathered into a full ruffle in the back. As the man was thinking of the richness of these ladies' clothing, Cheney was thinking how very cold his hand was.

A brass bell jangled happily as Rissy and Cheney entered ⁀ Farm and Supply. Stopping just inside the door, the ⁀ked around. At first glance, the mass of tools and ⁀nfused Cheney's eye so that the huge room ⁀niky metal jungle. After a few seconds she ⁀ were on the left, heavy implements ⁀yed in a semicircle centered around ⁀ implements were in bins and shelves ⁀ marine supplies took up the right wall. ⁀ow," she murmured to Rissy and moved over to look more closely at it. The unmistakable Duvall Iron Shield was forged on the blade.

A jolly-looking man with long, wavy red hair came to greet them. He was older, perhaps sixty, but was still thick and sturdy. Her father had told Cheney that Alexander Dallas had been a blacksmith for thirty-five years before he opened his store. "Good morning, ma'am," the man drawled courteously. "I am Alexander Dallas. How may I be of assistance to you today?"

Cheney pointed. "How much is this plow?"

Dallas gave her a strange look, eyeing her rich mantle and fine leather gloves. Then his eyes dropped, and the jovial note in his voice faded. "That's . . . that's a Duvall plow, ma'am. The finest plow made in the world. It's forty-five dollars." His hand strayed over to the grip of the plow and caressed the polished wood absently. Duvall plows were cast as a single piece for strength and durability, and the oak grips were sanded to a satiny finish, then varnished four times. Heavy leather covers were also made specially to fit the handgrips, and if one used and replaced the grips, a Duvall plow would last several lifetimes. Duvall's Tools and Implements was, at this time, selling this plow to Alexander Dallas for four dollars, plus forty cents for shipping.

Her nostrils flaring white, Cheney drew in a sharp breath and glanced at the woman standing close beside her. Rissy's eyes had narrowed dangerously, and with deliberate slowness she swiveled her head to look around the semicircle of heavy implements. Nine more plows were displayed, and all of them were Duvall's.

Cheney turned back to Alexander Dallas, who still did not meet her eyes. "That seems an exorbitant price for this plow, Mr. Dallas, no matter how wonderful it is," she said with acid sweetness. "Do you sell many of them at that price?"

"Yes, ma'am," he mumbled, gripping the plow with more force. His huge fire-scarred knuckles turned white. "And . . . um . . . credit is available, you see. . . ."

"At what rate?" Cheney asked, her temper growing more evident with each word. "Oh, never mind! I'm sure it's only about sixty or seventy percent!"

"Yes, ma'am." The words were almost a sigh.

Cheney couldn't understand this old pirate's humility. "Mr. Dallas," she said in an ominous tone, "my name is Cheney Duvall. My father's name is Richard Duvall, of Duvall's Tools and Implements."

His massive head snapped up, and his expression was one of bewilderment. Moments of silence stretched out as he seemed to search Cheney's face for—what, she couldn't imagine. Finally he made a half shrug, held out his hand, and mumbled uncertainly, "Well, ma'am, it's truly a pleasure and an honor to meet you. Thank you for visiting the store. Is . . . is there anything else I can help you with, ma'am?"

Cheney blew out a noisy, exasperated breath and looked at Rissy. If Alexander Dallas was feigning this total lack of guile, he was an actor good enough for the stage. Cheney could see the same puzzlement mirrored in Rissy's eyes, and Cheney decided she must be right in her feelings toward this man. Rissy was generally a very shrewd judge of character, while Cheney usually trusted all people upon meeting them, if they had nice manners.

Cheney started to speak, but two men, talking in low tones, came through the door behind the store's counter. Dallas turned around and, with one hesitant look back at Cheney, called, "Vess! Come here! This lady might want to meet you."

Now Cheney was totally mystified and watched in silence as the two men came around the counter to where Cheney, Rissy, and Alexander Dallas were standing in an uncomfortable little knot.

Both of them were big men, tall and powerfully built. Their skin was like polished ebony, and both of them had unusual eyes, almost Oriental, slightly up-tilted. One was wearing a blacksmith's apron and removed heavy leather gauntlets to wipe his hands carefully as he neared the two women. He was older, Cheney observed, with gray generously sprinkled in his hair and pronounced crow's-feet at the corners of his eyes.

The younger man was dressed in a black suit with a red-and-gray striped waistcoat. The suit was shiny, and Cheney saw that the knees of the breeches were discreetly patched, but it was clean and pressed. She looked up into the men's faces and knew immediately that they were father and son. Out of the corner of her eye she saw Rissy make an uneasy movement with her hands, and Cheney glanced at her quickly. Rissy was staring up at the young man, her eyes wide.

"This . . . this is Vess, ma'am—I mean, Miss Duvall," Dallas said uncomfortably. "Vess, this is Miss Cheney Duvall. It's her family that owns Duvall's Foundry."

Vess, the older man, nodded slightly and looked down at his hands, but didn't offer one to Cheney. "Ma'am, it's real nice to meet you. I allus use Duvall's pig iron. I allus said it's the purest and the sweetest."

Now Cheney was completely nonplused. *They seem to think this is some kind of social call . . . and how can pig iron be pure and sweet?* Rissy's sharp elbow jabbing in Cheney's ribs cleared her mind a bit. "Yes, I'm sure—Vess," she managed to say. "And this is Rissy Clarkson."

Pointedly Rissy offered her hand to the young man, who took it quickly. "I'm Luke Alexander, Miss Clarkson. Miss Duvall. I'm Vess's son. It's a pleasure to meet you."

His voice was deep and as warm and rich as a slow-moving river in summertime. Rissy, for once, was quiet and merely looked up at him.

The tableau was frozen for an instant: Vess and Alexander Dallas watched Cheney curiously; Cheney was looking at Rissy with surprise; Rissy and Luke Alexander were only looking at each other.

When she recovered, Cheney cleared her throat and said, in a gentler tone than she'd used since she entered Dallas Farm and Supply, "Mr. Dallas, there is some business I would like to discuss with you. Perhaps we might go into your office?"

Now the three men glanced at each other, Dallas and Vess blankly, Luke wary and watchful. Dallas nodded obediently and said, "This way, please, Miss Duvall."

At Cheney's uncertain glance at Rissy, Luke Alexander said, "Don't worry. I'll take care of Miss Clarkson, Miss Duvall."

Rissy was still looking up at him, smiling slightly. She nodded without looking at Cheney, so Cheney followed Mr. Dallas to the back of the store and into a tiny, sparsely furnished office.

Seating Cheney in the single straight-backed chair that was centered exactly in front of the desk, he took his place behind the desk and looked at Cheney, his expression still mystified.

"Mr. Dallas, I have come here, at my father's request, to see exactly how your store is progressing," Cheney said in a businesslike, though not an unkind, tone. "It seems to me that you are doing fairly well, so I require an explanation as to the manner in which you are conducting business with my father's company. It may not be illegal, but it is unethical and certainly ungentlemanly."

Alexander Dallas's eyes crinkled with confusion, and Cheney waited. He took a long, deep breath and looked off into the far distance. Finally his expression cleared somewhat, and he met Cheney's severe gaze squarely for the first time. "Ma'am, I think the first thing I oughta tell you is that I don't own Dallas Farm and Supply anymore. And that's why I don't have the foggiest notion of what you're talking about. But still, whatever it is, I am sorry. Real sorry."

Cheney was silent, and then her expression softened. "Yes, you are, aren't you? All right then. Would you mind telling me all about it?"

Dallas's gaze darted uncomfortably around the room and down at the desk. The top of the desk was completely bare, except for a replica of a birdcage, about six inches tall, in one corner. It was painted white, with tiny lacing surrounding the hanging loop at the top, and so delicate that Cheney could hardly believe it was made of iron.

Alexander Dallas ran one finger down a side piece of the birdcage. "There's not much to tell you, Miss Duvall," he answered quietly. "During the war I did most of my business with the Confederate States of America. When the Union troops finally got in, they took everything I had—said it was 'Rebel supplies and armaments.' "

He glanced up at Cheney, who nodded with understanding. His voice grew stronger, with the merest tinge of bitterness roughening it. "They took the plows and the spoons and the kettles, and even Vess's decorative wrought-iron pieces. This place was stripped down to the walls. All I had left was a pile of Confederate notes—which were worth more when you used them for kindling—and a big debt from the Confederate States of America. Which, as you prob'ly know, is going to be repudiated, or they ain't going to let South Carolina be in the United States anymore." His mouth twisted wryly. "Which was—I thought—the reason we fought the war anyway. But none of that matters now, I guess."

"I know it must've been hard for you, Mr. Dallas. I apologize for my rudeness before," Cheney said quietly. "So you had to sell the store?"

"Yes, ma'am. Just sold the name, really, was all it was. And Vess. He's the only reason I still have food to eat and clothes to wear."

"What do you mean?"

Alexander Dallas smiled, and it was affectionate and sad at the same time. "Vess, he's been doing wrought iron for Dallas's ever since I opened the store, you see. And his wrought ironwork is the best, the finest you've ever seen. It's more like he's an artist, you know?"

"I've noticed a lot of beautiful ironwork in the city," Cheney began but stopped as Dallas began nodding vigorously.

"That's his. Almost all of it's his." His eyes went to the delicate birdcage. "Anyway, when this company from Pennsylvania wanted to buy Dallas Farm and Supply in April 1865, Vess said he wouldn't work for anyone but me—which is a lie, since he hasn't worked for me since 1850, anyway. He just has—been with me for a long time. So this company, see, upped their price a little, and told me I could run the store, and offered me a pretty good salary." He sighed deeply, and his voice dropped. "I don't even run the store, you know. Luke does that. He's a whole lot book-smarter than I am, and he gets paid a fair wage, I guess."

Cheney thought carefully, then asked, "You say the company that bought Dallas's is in Pennsylvania? Who is your contact?"

Dallas shrugged and looked around the office rather help-lessly. "It's some lawyer fellow, a Pennsylvania lawyer, who represents this company. He came down one time, when he closed the purchase, and all the rest of the stuff we do is by mail."

"I need his name, and that of the company that owns Dallas's now, Mr. Dallas," Cheney said firmly.

"Forgot that fella's name," Dallas murmured, his naive blue gaze roaming around the room. "Need to ask Luke. But I know the name of the company that owns Dallas's—and lots of other stuff in this town, too, you can bet. It's Guardian Investments, Limited. We all call it 'The Guard.'"

4

THE POOR AND THE STRANGER

"*God has blessed you with a generous heart, Shiloh,*" he remembered Miss Behring telling him before she died. "*Your body is very strong, and by that you will know that a heart strong in love and generosity will never wither and grow bitter and full of grief.*"

"Then she talked about my death," he whispered. "*Remember, Shiloh! For the Lord has shown me now that your body will be strong, and hard, and muscled, even until the day you die, and it is His reminder to you that your strength comes from Him.*"

"Scared me," he said quietly, and Sock pricked up his ears. "All the times I've almost been killed, and her telling me that scared me more than anything. . . ."

With a dismissive shake of his shoulders, he searched the deep, quiet woods around him. The road to Behring's Corner was deserted. Although the air was cold, damp, and gray, the bleakness did not depress him. He felt lighthearted, and in spite of his efforts to suppress it, his anticipation was deepening into excitement.

For many years now Shiloh had been reconciled to the fact that he had no family, no history, no physical or emotional ties to this earth. As Miss Linde Behring had said, it had not made him bitter and full of regrets. Instead, he had come to an understanding that he was free to live and die as he pleased—and it had pleased him to find that the men and women whose lives he had touched found him generous and caring. He had chosen to be that kind of man.

But now he was turning a corner, and his life was going to change. At the Behring Orphanage was a piece of his history, and with a history comes an obligation, and with obligation comes the weight of care. This sober thought did not lessen Shiloh's exhilaration.

The small, arched bridge over the creek was still intact, he saw with relief. Behring's Creek was not deep, but it flowed swiftly, about saddle-skirt high, and was icy cold in January. In the quiet, Sock's hooves echoed hollowly over the cypress planks. Massive, ancient trees overhung the road on the other side of the bridge, and Spanish moss brushed Shiloh's face with damp, dead caresses.

Around one more corner in the muddy red road, and Behring Orphanage came into sight. A two-story cypress house, raised four feet to defy the occasional flood of the Ashley River, it was freshly whitewashed and the grounds neatly manicured.

Shiloh smiled slightly as he thought of how the Behring Orphanage had come to be in such a nice home, on some of the most fertile bottomland along the river. A man named William Manigault, whose ancestors had been among the first settlers of Charles Town, built himself a huge Georgian mansion six miles directly north of this house, his first home. A devout Christian man, Manigault had, as his land holdings grew from a few acres to hundreds of thousands of acres, faithfully sectioned off corners of his lands. These corners he had either given away or he had given the proceeds from the cotton away to the poor and needy. His old house plus the triangle-shaped corner of his land, consisting of about a hundred acres, he gave to the three Behring sisters for their orphanage.

Shiloh easily remembered the "Manigault Scripture," carved into an oak plaque and mounted over the front door of the house where he had grown up. *And when ye reap the harvest of your land, thou shalt not wholly reap the corners of thy field, neither shalt thou gather the gleanings of thy harvest. And thou shalt not glean thy vineyard, neither shalt thou gather every grape of thy vineyard; thou shalt leave them for the poor and the stranger: I am the Lord your God.*

"Leviticus 19:9–10," Shiloh murmured to Sock. He was one of the poor strangers who had lived by William Manigault's generosity—a man Shiloh had never met. But the land was called

Behring's Corner, and the creek was called Behring's Creek. Their names, too, would always be remembered.

Dismounting, he looped Sock's reins around the old iron post and ring, ran up the steps, and knocked softly on the door. No children were in sight, but he could hear faint cries in high voices and gleeful laughter far off behind the house. The grounds of the Behring Orphanage had many wonderful places to play.

Miss Behring answered the door. "Shiloh!" Her round, pink face lit up, and she stood on tiptoe to throw her plump arms around Shiloh's broad shoulders. Impulsively he picked her up and whirled her around, and she kicked and giggled like a young girl and didn't protest for him to put her down.

The youngest Behring sister, she was now about forty-five, he guessed. Short and tending to plumpness, she was still as neat as a pin. Gray streaks shone in her brown hair, but her eyes, deep blue pools of laughter, were exactly the same.

"Come in, come in!" she cried rather breathlessly when he set her down. "I have been so excited to see you!" Her German accent became more pronounced, and her grammar a bit careless, when she was excited. "All of the children are in the back, playing, and it's good. I want to talk to you."

Shiloh had been with her oldest sister when she died, and he had planned carefully what to say to this Miss Behring. The story Miss Linde had told him was personal and private and concerned only him, so he was determined not to betray Miss Linde's confidence. Even her two sisters had not known Miss Linde's secret.

"I'm sorry about Miss Linde," he said as she took his hand and led him into the quiet, warm house. "But I want to tell you that she was happy and at peace when she died."

Miss Behring led him into the drawing room, a cheery place with tall windows and a comfortable horsehair sofa, two overstuffed armchairs with hassocks, and four rocking chairs gathered about a smallish cast-iron fireplace with an elaborate wrought-iron mantelpiece. The faltering winter sunlight made the room golden, and memories flooded over Shiloh so strongly he could barely breathe. Seating himself in the same rocking chair he had loved so much as a child, he took a long, deep breath.

"I know, Shiloh," Miss Behring was saying. "Linde's home now, and though my grief was heavy when I first got your letter, now I believe that the Lord blessed her when He took her so young. Jesus has blessed us with the best of life's gifts," she sighed, "but there is a part of us that longs always to be with Him, and that waits with joy for that day."

"Not all of us look forward to it that much, Miss Behring," Shiloh said lightly, "but Miss Linde did."

Miss Behring nodded and settled comfortably into the rocking chair by Shiloh. "That is all I need to know about Linde, Shiloh. So let us talk about you. You were in the war, yes?"

"Yes, ma'am," he nodded. "I was in Huntsville, Alabama, when it started. I joined up in 1861 and went all the way to Appomattox."

"We prayed for you. The Lord brought you to our remembrance often. But He told Linde that you were all right, and that you would not die."

Shiloh gave her a mystified look. His fate had been, and still was, so strangely tangled with Miss Linde Behring.

Smiling beatifically, Miss Behring nodded. "You were always one of her favorites, Shiloh. Even though she did not show it. Did you know this?"

Shiloh thought of his childhood, of the older Miss Behring's gaunt, rather severe face, framing laughing blue eyes. Sometimes those watchful eyes had been inexplicably sad when they rested on him. He remembered her voice, cool and kind, and how he had known, even as a small boy, that somehow her feelings toward him were different. Never in word or deed did she differentiate between the children—but Shiloh had known. He had always known.

"Yes, I guess I did," he finally replied. "And before she died, she told me so, in so many words." *And told me why*, he thought. *And I'm glad—so glad!—that it only made me love her more, in-*

50

stead of making me . . . bitter, like she said. . . . "Linde," she said, "it means 'bitter.' "

Miss Linde Behring had been up late the night of November 2, 1843, and had heard footsteps on the porch and muffled sounds at the door. ". . . I waited, for I must not deal with those who must leave their children to strangers. Only God can do that," she had said.

Minutes later she had found a baby boy in a crate stamped "Shiloh Ironworks." This she told her two sisters and Shiloh. What she did not tell anyone—never told anyone, except Shiloh, before she died—was that also in the crate were three items: a scarf, and a jar or statue, and gold. She never told Shiloh how much gold, and he didn't ask, or care.

Miss Linde Behring had been twenty-two years old, plain, poor, and had known only a life of selfless giving. She had taken the gold and run off with a man. Five months later she returned to her sisters, and not a word had been spoken of it until, in that hot, bare room in Manhattan, she told Shiloh what she had done and asked his forgiveness. The scarf and statue, constant grievous reminders of her guilt, she had left in a box at the orphanage in Charleston.

"Linde left something here for you," Miss Behring said softly, her kind blue eyes watching expressions flit across Shiloh's face. "You know that, hmm? It is up in the attic, in the crate."

Wordlessly Shiloh went down the hallway and pulled down the folding stairwell to the attic. Warm air and a dry, dusty smell wafted over his face as he climbed up. The attic was lit, because the cypress siding above the ceiling was not battened, leaving wide cracks. In Charleston it was much more important to have ventilation in the roof for steamy, hot weather than to insulate against the indifferent South Carolina winters.

With surprise Shiloh saw lined up against the walls dozens of boxes, all shapes and sizes, neatly tied up with string. Looking closely at one, he saw a name on it, one he did not recognize. His eyes softening, he realized that each box must hold the odd tatters of the stories of dozens of children such as he: baby clothing, perhaps, or bits of blankets, or shoes. But there was only one crate. Bending over painfully, he saw the impersonal black block letters: SHILOH IRONWORKS. *My namesake*, he thought, his emotions so jumbled he took a moment to sternly suppress them into silence.

Inside was a flat box, about ten inches square, wrapped in brown paper and tied, not with string, but with an old, faded ribbon. As he gently picked up the box, dust motes flew up and danced for a few short moments. A fine powder rose from the ribbon when he ran his finger across it. *Must have been black velvet*, he thought sadly. He had never seen Miss Linde wear a ribbon of any kind.

His impulse was to tear open the box immediately, but, swallowing hard, he took it back downstairs without opening it.

"I . . . I guess this is mine," he said. "It doesn't have my name on it, but it was in the crate."

"Yes, Linde left that for you, Shiloh," Miss Behring answered. He searched her face carefully, and she met his eyes openly, with absolutely no hint of curiosity or longing. They held each other's gaze for long moments, and then they smiled at each other with complete, mutual understanding.

"I'd . . . I'd kinda like to leave the crate here, Miss Behring," he said, his voice so soft she could barely hear it.

"Yes, I understand," she nodded. "This is your home, and will always be your home."

They rocked in silence for a while. Shiloh loved that about all three of the Behring sisters. They were the most comfortable people in the world to enjoy quietness with.

Rising, Shiloh kicked the small, cheerful fire and knelt to fuss with the poker, stirring the coals and encouraging the flames. The sharp fragrance of burnt pine invaded the room. "May I ask you something, Miss Behring?"

"Anything."

"Do you . . . do you remember anything about the night I was left here?"

Miss Behring's rocker squeaked in a slow, solid rhythm. "Mmm . . . I was asleep, then, you know. Linde was awake."

"Yes," he said with only a hint of dryness. "I knew that." Rising, he propped an elbow on the corner of the mantel and traced a wrought-iron curlicue with his finger.

"There was a big storm. Earlier, before you came."

"A storm? I didn't know that."

"Yes. It was a strange storm—like the big, noisy storms we have here in summer—only it was November. A sudden and violent storm, with thunder and lightning and hard rain, and then hail. It lasted from early afternoon until late that night. I woke up, twice, because of the great thunder. . . . I think that is why Linde was still up. That, and because the Lord Jesus knew you were coming, and someone must be up to take care of you."

Shiloh half smiled as he stared blindly down at the mantel. Jesus Christ was Miss Behring's close personal friend, and she always spoke of Him as if He were in the next room, and might join them at any time. *Which He might*, Shiloh thought uneasily.

Miss Behring giggled. "I wanted to name you Thor Hammerson."

"What!"

"Don't be so horrified," she said mischievously. "You were such a big baby, so strong, so unafraid. And besides, you are lucky. My middle sister wanted to name you *Sturm von Drang*." She pronounced it "Shterm von Drankg," with the peculiar German roll of *r*'s.

"What!" he barked again.

His blue eyes were indeed stormy, and as she looked at him, tall and Nordic and powerfully built, one tiny corner of her mind wondered if her sister may have been closer to his name than they thought. Vague remembrances of her childhood in the Prussian city of Linz flitted through her mind . . . *tall men, blond and blue-eyed and grim, with spiked helmets and great jackboots* . . .

Bringing herself back to the present, Miss Behring casually laid her head back on the chair and closed her eyes, but her wide, bright grin escaped. "Yes, after *Sturm und Drang*. 'Storm and Stress.' A well-known German drama, eighteenth century," she recited. "It has much action and high emotions, and is about man's revolt against society."

Shiloh blew out an exasperated breath. "No offense, Miss Behring, but how did I get lucky enough not to be named Thor or Storm?"

The smile slowly faded from her face as she rocked. "Linde was holding you, looking down into your face . . . and you, as young as you were, were very still and seemed to watch her. She said, 'No. He will not be named any such ridiculous things. Shiloh . . . In the Bible, it means 'place of rest.' We will name him Shiloh. I think that maybe this boy will be a place of rest for people sometimes . . . and we will pray that he will find his own 'place to rest.' "

Shiloh was silent for a long time. Then he sank back into the rocking chair by Miss Behring's side and took her soft, warm hand. "May I ask you one more thing, Miss Behring?"

"Of course."

"What is your first name?"

She turned to him then, and the light in her eyes was like the tranquil Caribbean Sea that Shiloh had fallen in love with on his journey to Panama. With startling clarity, he suddenly remembered—*envisioned*—many sweet, warm dreams he had had of that sea, forgotten upon waking, lost in his memory until now, as he looked deep into Miss Behring's eyes.

"My name is Etta," she said. "It means 'happy.' "

5

SHADRACH FORREST LUXTON OF THE CITADEL

"Mistuh Shadrach Forrest Luxton sends his sincerest compliments, ma'am," the black steward said solemnly as he bowed from the waist, "and awaits yore pleasure downstairs." He disappeared, and Cheney heard his discreet knock at Shiloh's room down the hall and then his respectful murmur repeated. Shiloh had returned from the Behring Orphanage only twenty minutes ago, and Cheney was relieved to hear him make an affirmative mumble to the steward.

"I'm going down, Rissy," Cheney said firmly, giving herself one last head-to-toe appraisal in the floor-length mirror.

"You orter make them men wait," Rissy grumbled. "You's s'posed to make men wait for you." With practiced jabs she pushed hairpins tighter into the French twist at the nape of Cheney's slender neck.

"But I don't want to fidget around here for fifteen minutes," Cheney argued. "I'm ready now, and I'm going down now."

Rissy sighed heavily and loudly but obediently held out Cheney's shawl. Turning, Cheney extended her arms, and Rissy draped the glimmering Madras over one arm, pulled it down to a graceful curve below Cheney's waist, then draped it over the other arm. Cheney had changed into a dark green silk dress, one that Rissy had approved for the strange custom of having the largest and most sociable meal in the middle of the day. Authoritatively Rissy had ordered that Cheney may not show any *décolletage*—which Rissy pronounced very nearly correctly—but she might show her neck and a little bit of shoulders. The plain green silk trimmed with a modest cream lace fit Cheney's waist and hips tightly, with a small bow in the back and only a hint of a bustle.

"You wear this here shawl, now," Rissy said sternly.

"I don't understand why," Cheney teased. "It's so sheer, it doesn't actually cover anything! And besides, I have to let it droop like this, don't I?"

"Hmph!" was all Rissy deigned to retort.

Cheney hurried to the door, but before she disappeared she looked back uncertainly. "Rissy, have you—what kind of . . ."

"You g'wan down, you're in such a big hurry, Miss," Rissy said, making shooing motions with her hands. "I eat in the kitchen, with the other servants, and we prob'ly git better food than you white folks. And I got some company comin' for *lunch*," she added with relish.

Satisfied, Cheney whirled and very nearly knocked Shiloh down. "Oh! Here you are!" she exclaimed.

One of Shiloh's eyebrows arched upward. "You're excited about having dinner with him, aren't you?" He offered her his arm.

Cheney grabbed it and almost overmatched his long strides as they headed for the stairs. "Yes, he's interesting," she replied. "But what I really found interesting was your reaction to him." Her sidelong gaze slid upward to his face.

"Huh? What do you mean?"

Shrugging, Cheney answered in a low voice, "I've just never seen you show so much—emotion—as when you saw him, and found out who he is."

Shiloh frowned but said nothing more. They had reached the ground floor, and Shadrach Forrest Luxton stood by the door in the lobby, quiet and unmoving, but certainly not unobtrusive.

His uniform was not as striking, perhaps, as the parade drill uniform Cheney had first seen him in, but she would have noted him in a crowd anytime, anywhere. His tunic was gray wool, with the same three rows of twinkling gold buttons as at their previous meeting, but no insignia. Instead of the bandolier belts, today he wore a single black one from right shoulder to left hip, with a black belt around his waist and gray breeches. His thigh-high cavalry boots were impeccably shined, and the saber at his side was in a silver sheath. A gray shako, with the same distinctive full black plume, was under his arm, and he wore spotless white leather gauntlets. For the first time, Cheney noticed his thick, wavy black hair, and that his shoulders were very broad, so broad they were almost disproportionate to his slim frame.

To her surprise, he snapped to attention and saluted Shiloh smartly. "Sir!" he exclaimed, in his distinctive tenor voice. "Begging your pardon, sir, I was unaware before that you were an officer."

Cheney glanced at Shiloh, who looked uncomfortable. "Relax," he murmured. He did return the salute. "I was a noncom, just a sergeant. And besides, I'm not in any army anymore. And we're inside."

Mystified, Cheney looked Shiloh up and down as he shifted uneasily from one foot to the other. He was wearing a simple black linen shirt and gray breeches tucked into his cavalry boots. She had seen the clothing before and knew vaguely that Confederates had worn gray—but now the significance of the yellow stripe down the side of his breeches became clear to her.

Shadrach Luxton relaxed his stance, though his posture was naturally stiff and erect, and grinned. "Doesn't matter, sir. We still always salute the colors. The gray, that is." He turned to Cheney expectantly. With a little hesitation she offered him her hand, which he kissed. His touch was firm, and she could feel the warmth of his lips through her thin lace mitt. Cheney blushed. She was having trouble adjusting to the extravagant courtliness of the men in this town.

"Miss Duvall, thank you again for agreeing to dine with me and Mr. Irons. You honor us. May I?" Shadrach offered her his arm, and with Shiloh on her other side, Cheney was most gallantly escorted into the Planter's Restaurant.

The room was larger than Cheney first thought. Each table had a large plant shielding it, or a wooden planter along one or two sides. In this way, the room gave an appearance and feeling of intimacy. The carpet was red, and the tables were set with three white tablecloths. The top tablecloth was removed after soup, the next after the main course, and the last after dessert, so that no offending stains or crumbs from the last course remained. All of the utensils and saltcellars were of highly polished silver. One side of the room was lined with windows, and the muted winter sun made the light in the room soft and gentle.

A Negro waiter in a double-breasted red coat appeared and, with a slight bow to Shadrach, led them to a round table by the windows. After Cheney was seated, the men sat down and Shadrach looked up at the waiter, who stood silently by. "Afternoon, Eli," Shadrach said courteously. "You know what I want." He looked inquiringly, first at Cheney, then Shiloh, until they nodded consent. Turning back to Eli, he went on with satisfaction, "Then all of us will have the same."

Cheney looked around the room with curiosity. Seven Federal soldiers sat at a big table together, slightly apart from the rest of the tables. Three men, one businessman in a top hat and two men dressed in clothes that were clean but very old and patched, ate alone. Only one other woman was in the room, obviously with her husband. She was wearing a wide hoop skirt, black wool shawl, old black bonnet, and neatly darned black mitts. Cheney's clothing—the newest fashion from Paris—must have been strange to the woman's eyes, but she looked Cheney up and down with reluctant admiration and envy.

"It will be a few minutes, Miss Duvall," Shadrach informed her. "The first course is she-crab soup, and it's made fresh."

"Good," Shiloh said with relish. "It's been years since I've had a good she-crab soup. And—" he observed the discreet elegance of the room with satisfaction—"I'll bet it's really good here."

"The best," Shadrach nodded. At Cheney's uncertain expression he explained, "I think you'll like it, Miss Duvall. It's one of the dishes Charleston is famous for. And even if you don't, we'll have shrimp and grits, fried chicken and rice, cornbread and biscuits and, I hope, some fresh tomatoes. This time of year, they're only hothouse"—he shrugged disdainfully—"but they're still pretty good."

"My goodness!" Cheney exclaimed. "Charleston takes its

dinners very seriously, it seems!"

"Oh yes, ma'am," he answered with a peculiar glint in his eyes. "We take everything—particularly ourselves—very seriously."

He shot a sly glance at Shiloh, who returned it, but the exchange puzzled Cheney a bit. She had not yet seen that people from Charleston not only thought Charleston was the center of the world—particularly below Broad Street—they seemed to be almost unaware of any other world. Except as it affected Charleston, of course.

"Never mind," Shadrach said, smiling at Cheney. "You'll find out everything you want to know about Charleston while you're visiting us. I, on the other hand, have never had the privilege of visiting New York. Please tell me all about it, and yourself, Miss Duvall." His expression as he looked at her made Cheney self-conscious. Shadrach Forrest Luxton was very mature for his age, and his demeanor was that of a much older man. His skin was an attractive olive color, and smooth as a girl's, but his eyes were sharp and penetrating.

"I'm sorry, I can't do that, Mr. Luxton," she said, shaking her head.

"I beg your pardon, ma'am? Certainly I meant no offense. . . ."

Cheney smiled brilliantly first at Shadrach, then at Shiloh. "Oh no, of course not. I just meant that I think Shiloh might positively burst unless you two men talk about your brother—and I have a feeling that you, possibly, may feel the same way."

Both of the men laughed quietly but exchanged guilty glances. Shadrach said to Cheney, "What a prize! An insightful woman, and one who doesn't wish to talk about herself!"

"I just want to eat," Cheney retorted mischievously.

"And an honest woman!" Shadrach added warmly.

Shiloh seemed unable to take his eyes from the young man's face, and whenever Shadrach spoke, disbelief flitted across Shiloh's face over and over again. "It's almost uncanny. . . ." he muttered.

"See? I told you," Cheney murmured softly.

Shadrach turned to Shiloh and became solemn. "You're only the second man I've met here who knows him," he said quietly. "He reacts the same way. I must look very much like him."

"It's . . . it's not so much your looks," Shiloh said, almost to himself. "You're so much younger than he is—but your voice . . ." He took a deep breath. "You sound just like him, except, of course, your *words* don't sound like his."

"What in the world does that mean?" Cheney asked.

The silent waiter, Eli, reappeared with china plates, silverware, and red linen napkins. A young boy, also in a red coat, brought iced sweet tea garnished with a sprig of fresh mint, and a sweetgrass basket with a red linen napkin covering it. The rich smell of hot biscuits and cornbread was as heavy as the steam rising from the cunningly woven basket.

"Before we go on, may I say grace?" Shadrach asked casually. Without waiting for an answer, he bowed his head and said, "Thank you, Lord Jesus, for this food, this time, and these friends to share it with. Amen."

"Now that," Shiloh grinned, "didn't sound like your brother."

"I know that!" Shadrach exclaimed with an answering grin. "He's a blue-deviled heathen, isn't he, Mr. Irons?"

"He sure is! Puts us plain old heathens to shame!" Shiloh seemed proud of this.

"Excuse me," Cheney interrupted firmly, though she didn't stop buttering her square of cornbread. "I'll allow you two men to talk all night about General Forrest, but first please give me a little background." She gave Shadrach an embarrassed look. "I'm aware that your brother is quite famous, but—I was in medical school during the entire war, you see—and I—" She made a little helpless gesture with her butter knife.

"The Doc was pretty busy in school in Philadelphia," Shiloh defended her. "Medical school's tough."

"No, no, it's I who must apologize, ma'am," Shadrach said remorsefully. "I didn't realize until just now—I should have been calling you Dr. Duvall."

"No," Cheney smiled, "please call me Cheney."

Shiloh was surprised. Normally Cheney was not so free in either giving or taking first names. He recovered, though, and quickly added, "And call me Shiloh and I'll call you Shadrach. Now about General Forrest . . ."

"Oh yes, let's get back to something important," Cheney teased.

Again both Shadrach and Shiloh looked rather sheepish, but Cheney pointedly took a huge bite of cornbread and nodded. Shiloh gave her a grateful look. "I was wondering—" he began.

At the same time Shadrach turned to him and said, "I was wondering . . ."

Again all three of them laughed, and Cheney marveled to herself at the animation—almost excitement—these two men showed as they spoke of, or tried to speak of, General Nathan Bedford Forrest. *He must be an extraordinary man*, she reflected. *I've never even imagined Shiloh so . . . eager, so energized . . . he's usually so . . . careless, easygoing. . . .*

"You're my guest, you go first," Shadrach was saying generously.

"I was just hoping you'd tell me something about General Forrest," Shiloh answered. "Before the war, you know, about . . . him, his family—I mean, your family."

Shadrach looked chagrined. "But I want to talk about the war. I hardly know anything about it, or him, except what I've read in the papers."

"Take turns," Cheney advised, amused at their stubborn little-boy expressions. "We have time, and I've grown very curious myself. Especially since we've talked all around him for half an hour now, and neither of you have told me anything about him."

"Now you first," Shiloh said with a grin.

"Okay," Shadrach said obediently. His blue-gray eyes grew rather dreamy and far-focused. "He is only my half brother, you see. He was already twenty-seven, and married with two children, when I was born. And I haven't seen him since the beginning of the war, in 1861. I was only twelve then. . . ."

"Then he's in for a big surprise when he sees you again,"

Shiloh murmured, again searching Shadrach's features closely. "You must look exactly like he did when he was your age."

Shadrach focused and nodded at Shiloh. "Our mother says that since Bedford's twin sister, Fannie, died, God gave him another twin, nearly thirty years later. That's me," he finished proudly.

"I didn't know he had a twin sister!" Shiloh exclaimed.

"My mother was first married to Mr. William Forrest, and they had eleven children," Shadrach explained. "Bedford was the eldest, and he was just fifteen when Mr. Forrest died. Bedford took care of Mother and all of his brothers and sisters. When Bedford was twenty, the whole family, Mother included, was struck down with fever. Two of his brothers and all three of his sisters, including Fannie, died. Bedford almost did," he said in a low voice, "but Mother says that God must want to keep Bedford alive awful bad."

"That's the truth," Shiloh agreed vigorously. "There's no man walking around that's had more chances to get dead!"

This made Cheney laugh, and both Shiloh and Shadrach looked at her blankly. They had forgotten her, she saw, and she determined to be quiet from then on. This was no particular generosity on her part. The eagerness with which Shiloh and Shadrach spoke was affecting her too, and her curiosity about General Forrest was truly piqued.

"Go on, Shadrach," she encouraged him. "I really want to hear more about your brother—I mean, your half brother."

"It's all right, Dr.—Cheney," he replied gravely. "It's an honor to be called his brother, and I lie about it whenever I can."

"You can," Shiloh said ruefully. "No one would ever know." He sounded almost jealous.

With a shrewd look at Shiloh's wistful expression, Shadrach went on, "Well, Mother married my father six years after Mr. Forrest's death. I have two brothers and a sister—I'm the youngest—and Bedford has always treated us just as he has his own brothers. In fact, just as he does his own son."

"So your father doesn't take it amiss that your mother named you after her first husband?" Cheney asked gently.

"He never did," Shadrach answered readily. "Father died when I was sixteen. But he loved my mother very much, and he always said that all of the good things in all of her children were from her, anyway. My brother Joseph is very much like him, and Father said he was blessed by that, but that I was doubly blessed to be all the good things that Bedford is, along with the good things that Mother is." He turned to Shiloh then, and for the first time he looked his age. "But . . . I don't think I'm really much like Bedford . . . am I?"

Shiloh considered him carefully before answering. "That's kind of a hard thing to say. General Forrest—" He shook his head. "There is no one like him. You look like him, you're built like him, and you sure sound exactly like him, and you—your—you look proud—and—stern, like he does. . . ."

Cheney suddenly realized how difficult it was for men to speak to each other of these personal things. *Women do it easily—endlessly!—but men seemed to be embarrassed.* Carefully she filed this bit of information away.

Shadrach was listening closely, avidly, so Shiloh made himself continue, "But you're not like him, not like I knew him." Shadrach's face fell, and his wide shoulders drooped just a bit.

"But you have to realize, Shadrach," Shiloh added, "that we were at war, and your brother—" he shot Cheney a cautious look, then seemed to shrug it off—"your brother," he repeated defiantly, "is a man of war. All I know of him was when we were fighting—and killing. And General Forrest is the fiercest fighter I've ever seen or ever hope to see. He's got more courage than any man alive or dead. He's fearless, and relentless, and deadly, and even strong men are afraid of him."

Shadrach sat straighter in his chair, his shoulders again becoming ruler-lined, and his blue-gray eyes began to glint as Shiloh spoke. For long moments the two men looked at each other, and Cheney, too, was caught in the strange spell that was spun by words spoken of General Nathan Bedford Forrest. It seemed that as Shiloh spoke, he had somehow conjured up this man—this leader of men—and some of his power was felt by the three.

"So, you see, that's all I know of him," Shiloh said, breaking the silence. "The soldier, the general. I've always wondered about the man. All of us did . . . because we never knew him. We would have followed him anywhere, fought against anything—because we knew he would fight with us, and lead us back out again—but we never really knew him." A depth of regret that Cheney never thought she would hear from Shiloh was painfully evident in his quiet words.

Shadrach grimaced, and now, in his turn, pain was evident on his face. "He's a complex man, hard to know and hard to understand. I suppose my mother knows him best, but she's like him, you know. She can't put it into words."

"Excuse me," Cheney said softly. "But you never explained to me—what is it about General Forrest? Does he have some sort of . . . speech difficulty? Or impairment?" Cheney was very interested in this because she had suffered from terrible stuttering as a child.

To her surprise, Shadrach and Shiloh burst out laughing, and the uncanny aura of reverence dissipated. Cheney was almost disappointed and frowned. "What's so funny? I didn't mean to be rude, or amusing! I am a doctor, you know, and I—"

"It's okay, Doc," Shiloh said with some repentance. "Let me explain. It's just that—Shadrach, here, like I've said, sounds just like General Forrest, but . . ." He gave the younger man an inquiring look.

Shadrach nodded. "Yes, Bedford sent all of us to good schools. He sent me here, to the South Carolina Military Academy—of course, we all call it the Citadel—in 1862, when I was thirteen. His brothers, Jesse and Bill and John and Aaron, were too old by the time Bedford had the means to do this, but he sent his youngest brother Jeffrey to Colonel R. L. B. Lawton's Academy in Memphis, and all of us Luxtons to whatever good school we wanted. Even my sister, Molly."

His voice kind, he told Cheney, "My brother, you see, had no formal education at all. He taught himself to read. But his speech is backwoods Tennessee, with a Mississippi twang thrown in for good measure." Again his voice was full of pride.

"Nice people call it 'border idiom,' but mostly it's just ignorant country. It doesn't bother Bedford, or my mother, though."

"No wonder," Shiloh maintained solidly. "I think General Forrest is probably the smartest man I've ever met. And a lot of times I think, with the way he talks, that he's . . . he's . . . there's a word for it, but I can't think of it." Shiloh looked frustrated but went on with determination. "He's making fun of how people make fun of him."

"Self-parody," Cheney suggested.

Shiloh snapped his fingers. "That's it!"

"What are you talking about?" Shadrach demanded impatiently.

"Like . . . like . . . 'Git thar fustest with the mostest,'" Shiloh quoted.

"He never said that," Shadrach scoffed.

"Of course he didn't," Shiloh agreed, his blue eyes sparkling. "But a rumor was going around that that line was his entire war strategy. So after that, whenever anyone asked him about strategy or tactics, his eyes would look like knife-points, and he'd mutter, 'Git thar fustest with the mostest.'" He turned to Cheney, and she thought again that she had never seen him so animated. "It was a double-double-cross, you see?"

"No, I'm afraid I don't," she said apologetically.

Shiloh barely waited for her to finish speaking. "First, because General Forrest's speech was never that bad in the first place, and anyone who was really smart and paying attention would realize this. And second—mostly—" he shot Shadrach a look of high humor—"because we never got there first, and we hardly ever—only twice I can think of—had the most. All of us old hands used to say, after that saying started going around, that the Old Man was doing it on purpose. Attacking entrenched positions or garrisons, you know, and letting us know how lucky we were if the odds were only eight to five."

"That's what I've heard," Shadrach said in an awed whisper.

"It's the truth," Shiloh insisted.

Cheney, now mollified, addressed Shadrach in an attempt to turn the conversation to him. "So, Shadrach, I notice that your speech is very polished. And you eat in the Continental manner—were you educated in England, by any chance?"

Shadrach grinned. "No, ma'am—I mean, Cheney. I'm just like Bedford that way, too. Left-handed."

"Huh?" Shiloh interrupted. "He's left-handed?"

At this point Cheney, with finality, despaired of this dinner including any subject whatsoever that did not revolve around Nathan Bedford Forrest.

"Yes—well, he was," Shadrach amended. "But when he was just a child, some man told him it was a 'sinister preference.' So he taught himself to use his right hand as well as his left."

" 'Sinister preference,' " Shiloh repeated, and his eyes glinted. "It fits him. I'm surprised he wanted to correct it."

"I tried to, myself," Shadrach sighed, "but I couldn't do it. Not as strong as he is, I guess."

"There is absolutely nothing wrong with left-handed people," Cheney declared. "Sinister preference, indeed! All it means to be left-handed is that you are left-handed."

"Except for General Forrest," Shiloh demurred. "But to be fair I have to say he's sinister with both hands."

"Ambidextrous sinisterness?" Shadrach ventured.

"That's right!" Shiloh said with a grunted laugh. "There's about fifteen dead men who could attest to the right hand, and about fifteen dead men who could swear to the left!"

"Shiloh!" Cheney was thoroughly shocked on several accounts. First about the topic, second about the numbers of dead men involved in the topic, but mostly about Shiloh's and Shadrach's gleeful enjoyment of the topic.

For once, Shiloh didn't defer to her. With a strange look he said in a cold voice, "It was war, Doc. You'll never understand, because you weren't there."

"But Shadrach wasn't there, either!" she snapped.

Shiloh and Shadrach exchanged meaningful looks, and there it was: they were men. They understood the peculiar dark exhilaration of war. Cheney bowed to this, even though by habit she wanted to protest. Her world, that of an educated physician, was a man's world, and she fought hard for acceptance into it.

But this was different. War was different.

"I'm sorry," she said softly. "Please go on."

"Thanks, Doc," Shiloh said, with obvious sincerity. Turning back to Shadrach, he asked, "You knew about his personal kills, then?"

"I heard," he nodded, "but I wasn't sure until now that it was true."

"It is true," Shiloh asserted. "We always said that Billy Yank shot twenty-nine horses out from under him—and he gave them back good as he got, plus one just to keep ahead of them." In an even voice he amended to Cheney, "General Forrest killed thirty men in the war. Personally. In hand-to-hand combat."

"Yes," she said dryly, "I understand. Fifteen with the left, and fifteen with the right." But she smiled to take the acid out of her words, and Shiloh smiled back. And Cheney became aware of her own unique, particularly feminine brand of exhilaration.

6

A Night and a Day in Gray

Charleston's famous she-crab soup finally arrived, hot and fragrant and creamy. Cheney fully intended to take two polite sips, but it was so delicious she ate the entire bowl and wished for more—until the shrimp and rice and fried chicken, and juicy, firm tomatoes with big dollops of rich mayonnaise on top arrived. All three of the party ate hungrily, with appreciation, but Shiloh and Shadrach never stopped talking about General Forrest.

In a moment when Shadrach and Shiloh were both chewing, Cheney broke in. "Tell us about a battle, Shiloh," she said eagerly. "You never tell me anything about the war."

Shiloh looked at Shadrach and rolled his eyes. "Uh-oh. You know what it's like to tell girls about the war!" Shadrach didn't, but he looked boyishly grateful at Shiloh's easy inclusion. Shiloh went on, "You know, when men talk about the war, they want to know about the numbers, and the artillery, and the ground, and the order of battle."

"Yes," Shadrach agreed cautiously.

Shiloh frowned darkly at Cheney, who made a face at him. "Girls," he pronounced with feigned disgust, then went on in a high falsetto, "How did you feel? What did General Forrest look like? Were you scared? What was General Forrest wearing? Did you cry? Was General Forrest wearing a sword?"

"So," Cheney said complacently. "What did he wear?"

"See?" Shiloh said with a glance at Shadrach, then he turned and answered Cheney obediently. "Usually in hot weather he laid his tunic across his saddle and went in his shirtsleeves. And he wore a canvas duster—like mine, you know?—in cold weather."

"Yes," Cheney nodded, "I know. Go on."

But Shiloh's eyes turned to Shadrach, and he kept his gaze fixed on him as he said, "That duster . . . On the second day of fighting at Fort Donelson, General Pillow asked Forrest to take out a gun emplacement, up on a hill. Two big guns."

Shadrach drew in a sharp breath, but Shiloh kept speaking in a low tone.

"So Colonel Forrest led the charge. They killed his horse, so he rushed them on foot . . . and me and another boy in his escort, about my size, lost our horses in the same volley, and managed to keep up with him." He drew a deep breath and closed his eyes for a minute. "We captured the guns, but the gunners . . . we couldn't capture any of them alive. They lay in heaps about their guns, and their blood froze black in the snow. . . ."

Opening his eyes, he trained them steadily back on Shadrach. "After we got back to camp, Colonel Forrest took off that duster, looked close at it, laughed, and growled, "Reckon it's dead." Then he tossed it to his aide, Captain Strange, and told him to throw it away. But he didn't."

Shiloh's voice grew so quiet Shadrach and Cheney had to strain to hear him. "Captain Strange took that duster and had it cleaned, and kept it in a box. Sometimes in camp at night, he'd bring it out, and General Forrest would pretend not to know. We'd hold it up to the campfire and look at it . . . and count the fifteen bullet holes in it. Fifteen," he repeated, as if he still couldn't believe it.

"That's impossible," Cheney whispered. Shadrach drew in a sharp breath.

"Yes, it is," Shiloh quietly agreed, "but it's true. I was there. I saw."

All three of them stared into space, and the waiters came and took up a tablecloth and brought hot coffee and pecan pie. Shiloh, Cheney, and Shadrach didn't notice for a while.

Finally Cheney shook herself slightly, and Shiloh and Shadrach looked at her. "Well, Shiloh, you have succeeded in telling me what he didn't wear," she said mischievously, picking fat pecans methodically off the top of her pie and eating them one by one. "Getting important information out of you is very diffi-cult."

Shadrach grinned, and Shiloh shook his head resignedly. "Okay, you win. See, General Forrest, like I said, started out going around in his shirtsleeves 'cause he didn't really care about parading around in gold braid and stars. But then that all changed, and he started wearing full dress uniform almost all the time."

"Oh?" Cheney asked. "What changed him?"

"Three reasons," Shiloh said. "First, he did it 'cause he noticed that all of us looked for him all the time. In battle, whole companies would falter if they couldn't see him.

"Then he did it, because whenever he was trying to prevent the further 'effusion of blood' "—he winked at Cheney—"the enemy always wanted to see him before they'd surrender. Just him. Early in the war, they'd ask about the numbers, you know?" Shiloh turned to Shadrach, who nodded. "But then they just wanted to see him. So he always made sure he had his tunic . . . even though it did stay across his saddle in hot weather."

"Yes," Shadrach grinned. "Mother always said she couldn't keep a coat and tie on Bedford."

"But what was the other reason?" Cheney demanded.

"You'll like this one," Shiloh snorted. "We used to make jokes about his needing a cart and a mule just for his trunks—not to his face," he added hastily. "But the ladies made over him—! They were always giving him new tunics and sashes and gauntlets and capes and even boots!"

Shadrach laughed. "Ladies always did take to him."

"Always," Shiloh maintained. "I hafta tell you, every one of his men was young, and we were all good-looking, like me." He waited for Cheney's inevitable outburst, then continued, "And General Forrest was forty years old when the war started! Didn't matter to the ladies, though. Didn't rub off much, either, we found out. They didn't want to mess around with the pack, only the leader."

"I'll bet," Cheney muttered darkly, and Shadrach shot her a quick, shrewd glance.

Turning back to Shiloh, he asked in a too-casual tone, "Did Bedford pay much attention to the ladies?"

"Nah," Shiloh shrugged easily. "Except . . . maybe one lady . . ." Two curious gazes burned into him, but Shiloh was silent and reflective for long moments.

"I'll tell you about Murfreesboro, Doc," Shiloh finally said quietly. "And about this one lady that General Forrest did notice." Shadrach and Cheney barely moved as Shiloh told them the story.

"It was July of '62," he said in a faraway voice. "All we'd really done so far was figure out, at Fort Donelson, that we were gonna follow Lieutenant-Colonel Nathan Bedford Forrest before we'd follow any general, and then we decided it again after fighting a rearguard action at Shiloh.

"There were about a thousand of us. I'd made enough of a nuisance of myself 'til Colonel Forrest put me in his escort, just to shut me up, I think. So, anyway, we stuck real close to him, and that's how I kinda knew what was going on."

"Wait," Shadrach interrupted in a reverent whisper. "You mean you were in his escort?"

"Uh, yeah," Shiloh mumbled, "and so—"

Shadrach interrupted again, turning to Cheney. "Don't let him fool you, Cheney. My brother's bodyguard is almost as famous as he is. His escort—sixty-five of them—were noted, again and again, for giving account of themselves in battle as if they were a full regiment. They're known all over the South for their valor and personal sacrifice."

Cheney looked accusingly at Shiloh. "You never told me!"

Flushing a little, Shiloh shrugged and went on pointedly, "So—we were on a march, to wreck General Buell's line of communications."

Shadrach frowned. "Pretty high odds there, hmm? Thirty thousand to a thousand?"

"That's right," Shiloh agreed with relish, "and that's why Colonel Forrest only planned a raid, instead of a full offensive. See, that's what so many of the generals and leaders didn't understand. They thought he was just a reckless and daring raider.

71

But Nathan Bedford Forrest never made a gesture in his life. He was reckless—with his own person—but he was never reckless with his men. In fact, the one thing that made him madder than anything was the *useless* sacrifice of men. Whenever one of us went down, there better be a definite result as payment. When he was commanding, it was understood that every drop of our blood was gonna be paid for.

"So, after considering all the circumstances carefully, the way he always did, Colonel Forrest decided that if we could get to Murfreesboro and break the lines there, Buell would have some trouble getting all of his little bluebellied ducks in a row.

"Now, we rode a hundred and fifty miles from base, over the Cumberland Mountains, in the heat of July, with men in blue crawling around everywhere like a kicked-over anthill. And we were a brigade that was fairly untried in battle."

He turned to Cheney to explain: "Lieutenant-Colonel Forrest wanted us to fight with the infantry at Shiloh, but the 'West P'inters,' as he termed them, told him that cavalry weren't s'posed to do that."

Shadrach snorted, and Shiloh winked at him. "At Fort Donelson, Generals Floyd and Buckner and Pillow surrendered over ten thousand men, but Forrest told them—and he was just a green lieutenant-colonel then—that he couldn't and wouldn't do that. He told them that he had not come out to surrender. He swore that he'd take every man in that fort out, if they'd just let him, but they wouldn't listen to him. So he just shrugged and told them that he had promised the parents of his boys to look after them, and they weren't gonna die in some Yank prison camp. So we left."

Cheney gasped, "You left! Just like that? While ten thousand men stood around and surrendered?"

"Yep," Shiloh answered with a mixture of glee and sadness. "Our brigade took out another five hundred or so infantry on the backs of our horses, but the others thought they had to do whatever the generals told them. Like I said, that's when we all decided that we were gonna do whatever Bedford Forrest said. We didn't lose a man.

"Anyway, to get back to Murfreesboro: that's why we'd been with him since '61 but we really hadn't fought together as a brigade. Along the way we picked up Colonel Morrison's three hundred Partisan Rangers from Kingston and some companies of Tennesseans and Kentuckians under Major Baxter Smith. So Colonel Forrest had about fourteen hundred men under his command. But we didn't have any big guns. We scouted and found in Murfreesboro there were about fifteen hundred men: the Seventh Pennsylvania Cavalry; the Ninth Michigan; the Third Minnesota; and a Kentucky battery of four guns."

Cheney tore her eyes away from Shiloh for only a moment to glance at Shadrach. His face was completely blank as he strained to absorb every word that Shiloh uttered, and his eyes shone like stars. Cheney didn't know it, but her eyes glimmered, and her face was alight, too, as she listened.

"So there we went, charging off, a bunch of kids on our horses to trounce fifteen hundred veterans and four big guns. But we had Nathan Bedford Forrest leading us. Even if we were scared, we would have been shamed down to the ground to let him see it.

"About twenty miles from Murfreesboro we went through this little town called Woodbury," Shiloh continued and began to arrange the silverware and the saltcellar to show Shadrach the ground. "We got there at about eleven o'clock at night, and all the women were gathered out in the square, buzzing around like a swarm of stirred-up bees. They ran up to us—mostly to Colonel Forrest—and grabbed onto his stirrup sheaths, and clasped their hands together, and started crying out to him."

Cheney and Shadrach, if possible, leaned even closer to Shiloh. He was speaking in a clear voice, but they both felt they wanted to hold his words close until later, when they could turn them over and over and see General Nathan Bedford Forrest—and Sergeant Shiloh Irons—clearly, when they were alone and had time to remember.

"The provost marshal from Murfreesboro, one Captain Oliver Cromwell Rounds, had come galloping through Woodbury that day and had taken every man and boy over twelve years old to jail in Murfreesboro. Seems like this Captain Rounds had been a real terror in the countryside, to men and women both. Rebel partisans, he called the men in Woodbury, and I guess they were. But it was mostly old men and kids, and that made Colonel Forrest real mad, especially about the kids. He's funny about kids."

Shadrach nodded assent to this but impatiently motioned for Shiloh to continue.

"On top of that, the ladies in Woodbury told us that the Yankees had captured six Rebel soldiers and had decided that they were spies, and were going to hang all of 'em in the morning." He drew a long, hard breath as he remembered Forrest's wrath. "That made Colonel Forrest so mad we all got scared—and we were his men!"

Shadrach looked sympathetic, but Cheney scoffed, "Surely not, Shiloh! You're exaggerating."

Both Shiloh and Shadrach shook their heads in an oddly identical gesture. "You can't imagine, Doc—" Shiloh said.

"You sure can't!" Shadrach breathed.

"So tell me," Cheney prompted, amused.

Shiloh thought, then grinned. "Forrest's temper is legendary. After a while—after you stopped worrying you were going to be killed—it got to be almost interesting. It was kinda . . . kinda . . . impersonal, like a force of nature—a typhoon, maybe.

"No man came nigh to him when he was mad. The only person in the world that ever calmed him down was your mother, Shadrach," Shiloh said, and Shadrach's expression grew gentle.

"She'd put her hands on those big shoulders and call his name, over and over again, and soon he'd be as docile as a kitten. But only her. We were scared even to get within hearing range of him, and not just 'cause his language blistered our ears so bad we thought they might catch on fire! Even his staff stayed out of bashin' range of those long arms when he was mad. And then you had to allow room for the flat of his saber, so we gave him a real wide berth! 'Bout twelve feet, if we could get it, and we slunk around pretty quiet even then!"

Shadrach and Cheney laughed, but Shadrach insisted, "Go on, Shiloh. What did you do?"

"We rode on to Murfreesboro," Shiloh answered, "and the first thing Colonel Forrest did—he was leading, of course—was ride right up to the jail with us, his escort. A full company was guarding the jail, but we came up on them so fast that they scattered like dandelion fluffs in the wind. Before they did"—Shiloh frowned fiercely—"they tried to shoot the six soldiers in the jail, but afterward one of the prisoners, a Captain James Paul, told me that they all flattened up against the wall so the guards couldn't angle their rifles right. So instead the guards set fire to the jail, took the keys, and ran off."

"You mean—" Cheney whispered.

"They tried to burn 'em alive," Shiloh said harshly. "Me and another boy bent back the bottoms of the cell bars, enough for them to crawl out flat on their bellies. Colonel Forrest came in, holding his saber in one hand and his pistol in the other, and he was like the devil himself. He looked around and asked me, 'You got it, boy?' I said, 'Yes, sir,' and he left. Captain Paul grinned and said, 'Glad I'm on his side, whoever he is.'"

"Smart man," Shadrach said smugly.

"Sure was," Shiloh nodded. "By the way, he was a spy, and a good one. We met up with him two or three more times, and I think he would have spied on Abraham Lincoln himself if Colonel Forrest had asked him to.

"So after we freed all the prisoners, we fought. We fought against cavalry, and infantry, and artillery. The Yanks had been having some kind of fuss, so they were separated into three camps. Colonel Forrest split us up into three companies, and we all fought on horseback, on foot, by hand, with rifles, with pistols, and, once, even with axes." He grinned. "Later, all of us swore that Colonel Forrest himself was leading our group, all the time—at the same time. All I know is, it seemed like he was everywhere where there was fighting, and he was always on the battle line."

"Always," Shadrach echoed softly.

"Always," Shiloh repeated firmly. "Always first in a charge—

usually outriding us—and always last in a rearguard action."

Cheney listened hard to the unfamiliar military words and the strange dark-and-light story and looked at Shadrach Forrest Luxton. In her mind a picture of General Nathan Bedford Forrest—a man she had never met, whose photograph she had never seen—began to crystallize. Cheney also found herself searching Shiloh Irons' comfortably familiar features with new eyes.

Shiloh shook himself slightly to continue. "Finally, after a night and a day of hard fighting, Colonel Forrest sent Duffield a little note, demanding his surrender of the Ninth Michigan. Now, Bedford Forrest never learned many technical military terms, but there were three phrases he learned, and he even taught himself to spell 'em right. He used 'em a lot."

"And they were—?" Cheney breathed.

"They were: 'I demand your unconditional surrender,' 'to prevent the further effusion of blood,' and . . .'"

" 'Or I will have every man put to the sword!' " Shadrach almost shouted.

"Right!" Then Shiloh went on in a careless drawl, "So Colonel Duffield read the little note and looked around at the mess we'd made of the cavalry and his Michigan infantry, and he surrendered.

"Then Colonel Forrest galloped on down the turnpike to Colonel Lester, of the Minnesotans, who'd been giving us a tough time. Forrest sent the same little note to him, and Lester asked to confer with Duffield. Now, Lester still had a brigade and the four guns, and we all figured that he was going to try to talk Duffield into un-surrendering. But Colonel Forrest let him go to Colonel Duffield anyway.

"So together they talked a lot about the little note—especially the part about the effusion of blood, some of which could possibly turn out to be their own. Then, together, they decided that they must prevent this terrible effusion."

Shiloh grinned as Cheney giggled. "But the little note, you see, gave 'em a real humane reason, a real noble reason, for their action. 'To prevent the further effusion of blood,' you know, meant their men's blood, too. Now some of those men told me afterward—kinda rudelike, I gotta say, and some of 'em were real loud—that they weren't as anxious to be saved as Colonel Duffield and Colonel Lester were to save them. But," Shiloh added magnanimously, "they hadn't read the little note."

When Shadrach and Cheney quieted down a bit, Shiloh went on, "Now, we were expecting anywhere from hundreds to thousands of reinforcements to come galloping up any minute, since Buell's army was scattered all over three states. So Colonel Forrest sent scouts out in every direction to find out who we could go send the little note to next.

"But this made the situation in Murfreesboro get kind of embarrassing. See, we had a hundred and fifty civilians to escort back to Woodbury along with twelve hundred rank-and-file prisoners to guard, and two colonels and a captain, oh yeah, and a stray general—T. T. Crittenden—and all their staffs—and a battery of four pieces, forty wagons, three hundred mules, and one hundred and fifty horses. There just wasn't enough left of Forrest's boys to worry with everything. But Bedford Forrest has no shame, and he wasn't about to lose any of those spoils, and he was as proud as a new papa at those guns!"

"What'd he do?" Shadrach asked eagerly.

"He separated out the Yank men from the officers," Shiloh said, "and told them if they'd move his guns, and drive his wagons, and herd his mules, and guard their own selves, he'd parole 'em at McMinnville."

"What happened?" Cheney demanded.

"Those bluebellies cheered Colonel Nathan Bedford Forrest, C.S.A.," Shiloh grinned, "and they went all the way to McMinnville with us, and then they went home. General Crittenden and Colonel Lester and Colonel Duffield and Captain Oliver Cromwell Rounds—who, I might add, we caught sleeping in a feather bed and was still standing around in his nightshirt—all looked kinda forlorn. I almost felt sorry for 'em," Shiloh said airily, "but not quite."

"But what about the woman?" Cheney prompted him.

"I was getting to that," Shiloh said indignantly. "While we

were trying to get the whole long wagon train moving, Colonel Forrest was on Roderick—one of his most famous mounts—and was in the square, telling everyone what to do and how to do it and where to go. It was confusing, and loud, and hot and dusty." Shiloh's voice dropped into a deep baritone, and his eyes softened to a mild sky-blue. "This lady came out of a house on the square."

Suddenly the whole room seemed to be quiet, and the silence was heavy. Cheney and Shadrach grew very still.

"She was stately, and gentle-featured, and had silver hair," Shiloh said in almost a singsong voice. "Her skirt was black, and it swept along the sidewalk as she walked toward Colonel Forrest. He saw her coming and got quiet, so we all got real quiet too. In one thin white hand she was carrying a little lace handkerchief and in the other a silver spoon.

" 'Colonel Forrest,' she asked, 'will you back your horse for me?'

"He lifted his hat, and with his heavy black hair falling down around his shoulders, bowed, and then pulled on Roderick's reins.

"That lady leaned over, scooped up a spoon of dust from the ground where Roderick had been pawing, and poured it carefully into the folds of her handkerchief. Without another word she bowed very low to Colonel Forrest and went back into her house, carrying her silver spoon and the little piece of bulging lace.

"Colonel Forrest watched her, and his face colored a little. Then he wheeled Roderick around and rode out of Murfreesboro at the head of the column. He didn't say much to anyone for the rest of the day, and he never mentioned that lady. But we all thought of her a lot. And I think he did too."

7

UNRATIFIED, UNRECONSTRUCTED, AND UNREPENTANT

"Doctah Cheney Duvall requests that you accomp'ny her to the telegraph office, Mistuh Arns," Rissy said with exquisite formality. Clasping her hands in front of her white apron, she waited patiently for his answer.

Shiloh glanced down the hall to Cheney's door, which was uninformatively closed. "Uh . . . she sick?" he asked in confusion. He was sleepy, not having drunk his first cup of coffee yet, and he could not quite comprehend this unusual etiquette. The Doc was perfectly capable of banging on the door herself and calling for him to come out; she had done it plenty of times, in several different locales and under varying circumstances.

Rissy rolled her eyes. "No, suh, she ain't sick, Mistuh Arns. But while I'm here, she ain't gonna go beatin' on no gentemmen's doors an' hollerin' like some wild child for them to come out."

Shaking his head slightly in a vain attempt to clear it, Shiloh answered, "Sure, I'll go with her. But I'll have to go rent another carriage, so it'll be about an hour or so."

"No need, Mistuh Arns. She wants to ride."

"All right. Half an hour, then?"

Rissy nodded and turned to go back to Cheney's room, which was all of twenty feet away.

"Rissy," Shiloh called.

"Yas suh?"

"Call me Shiloh," he grinned and ducked back into his room before Rissy could answer—negatively, of course. She always did.

Reentering Cheney's room, Rissy looked at her with pursed lips and narrowed eyes, then nodded with approval. Cheney's

79

black velvet riding habit was quite becoming. The very severity of it enhanced her strong, rather exotic good looks.

"When?" Cheney demanded impatiently, picking up a riding crop from an open trunk and swishing it through the air. She never whipped Stocking, of course, but she liked to carry the fine leather crop with the gold-trimmed handle, and gestured gracefully with it in lieu of the ever-present fan ladies were required to carry.

"Half an hour," Rissy replied, moving to straighten the disarray of the trunk.

"That was silly, Rissy," Cheney said absently, tapping the crop against her heavy skirt. "I could've gone to ask him."

"I know that," Rissy said, getting down on her knees. Meticulously she removed from the trunk parasols, shoes, reticules, gloves, small boxes of Chinoiserie and shagreen that held jewelry, and round hatboxes, then began replacing them neatly. All of Cheney's clothes Rissy had sheathed in perfumed linen drapes and hung in the Provence armoire looming against the wall. "But it don't look right."

"But, Rissy," Cheney argued, "you know there is absolutely nothing of an . . . um . . . improper—or, rather—romantic . . . um . . . I mean . . . anything that requires chaperonage going on between me and Shiloh," she finally finished, much less firmly than she meant to.

Rissy got back to her feet and turned to face Cheney. "I know that too, and I've wondered why not."

"What!"

"Niver mind," Rissy said blandly. "Now you jest sit down here and let me see can I figger out how to tame this wild hair down so's we can get that top hat on it."

Obediently Cheney sat. As Rissy struggled with her hair, Cheney brooded over the woman's cryptic words.

What is it that Shiloh and I share, exactly? she mused. *Rissy has been with the two of us more than anyone . . . and even she doesn't understand it.* Cheney met her own eyes in the mirror and the corners crinkled as she smiled to herself. *I don't even understand it! I wonder if Shiloh does. . . .*

She thought of how they'd been when they first met. Shiloh Irons had been more relaxed and less guarded then, even though it had been right after the war, in April of 1865, when it seemed he would have been more high-strung or less open and warm. Cheney's cheeks colored as she remembered kisses—two of them, both quite passionate—they had shared when they had traveled to Seattle, Washington, together on an arduous and dangerous journey.

So what happened? Cheney asked herself, but knew the answer even as she formed the question in her own mind. *Maeva Wilding happened, for one thing . . . and Devlin Buchanan, for the other. . . .*

When Shiloh, Cheney, and Rissy had journeyed to Arkansas to care for the people in the backwoods of Wolf County, it had seemed to Cheney that she and Shiloh were still—rather awkwardly on her part, rather casually on his—exploring the possibilities of a close relationship more than simple friendship and professional ties. *But then he met Maeva, and might have loved her, but she died, and Shiloh changed,* Cheney thought dully. *And I realized then that Shiloh is a—dangerous man. Not physically, of course,* she amended hastily to her reflection in the mirror. *Not physically threatening—well, all right, not to women, at least—but dangerous in other ways. . . . Everywhere we go, women fall all over themselves over Shiloh! And I am certainly not going to get in that long line!*

With this resolution Cheney drew herself erect with a jolt. Rissy watched the telltale expressions on Cheney's face. "Have you heard from Doctah Buchanan lately?" she asked politely.

Dev . . . Lord, I still think that You must mean for Dev and me to marry someday, she prayed decisively. Even as she repeated the familiar litany to herself, however, she became aware of the peace that the Lord gave her whenever she began to fret about getting married, and romance, and being an old maid. Her answer to these difficult questions had never been a definite *no* or *yes,* or any sudden vision of the future, but always she felt peace and comfort washing over her from Him, and then it truly didn't seem to matter much one way or the other. *He has a plan*

81

for me, Cheney thought gratefully, *and I'll find out about it in due season.*

Her thoughts went back to her well-beloved Dev. *We may not adore each other with a great, all-consuming passion—which does seem to make perfect idiots of people—but we are alike, and we do love each other deeply, and we know and understand each other so well. No mystery there to confound you . . . the way there is with Shiloh. . . .*

"You didn't answer my question," Rissy persisted. "Have you heard from Mistuh Dev lately?" Rissy was Devlin Buchanan's housekeeper when he was in residence in Manhattan.

"Um, yes, Rissy. I received a letter from him just before we left home," Cheney said absently, still staring blankly into the space in front of the mirror. "I suppose he's fine. His letter was mostly about new medical studies and discoveries."

"Hard to tell about him sometimes," Rissy said with an innocent air, "and easy to tell about him sometimes."

Cheney's eyes focused, and she turned to look up into Rissy's face. "You think so? He seems quite readable to me. Not like—"

"Mistuh Arns?" Rissy finished the sentence for her, then turned her firmly around and lifted the black felt hat with the floating black veil to pin on Cheney's hair. With sure movements she picked up a long, dangerous-looking hat pin with a diamond-studded head and worked it through the hat into the thick hair piled on the crown of Cheney's head. The hat was tilted slightly to the left, and Rissy had managed to secure a thick mass of auburn curls over Cheney's right shoulder. "Now Mistuh Arns, he's different."

"What do you mean?" Cheney asked eagerly.

Rissy's eyes flashed as she glanced at Cheney. "You think he's easy to know and that's all there is to it," she replied, then frowned. "But then it turns out that ain't all there is to it a-tall."

Now Cheney frowned. Rissy stepped back and narrowed her eyes. "Stand up," she ordered, and Cheney stood. Rissy got a clothes brush and began brushing the hem of Cheney's skirt.

"Rissy, about Shiloh—" Cheney began.

"He'll be here for you in just a minute," Rissy interrupted. "You ready?"

"Yes, but . . ."

Rissy stood and faced her squarely. "I don't know much more about him, Miss Cheney. Like I was saying before, it seems to me that you're the one who ought to, and you don't, do you?"

"No, I suppose I don't," Cheney sighed. "Yesterday, with Shadrach, I saw a side of him that I never suspected, never imagined."

Rissy nodded, then said in an unemotional voice, devoid of inflection, "I'd 'preciate it if you'd ask him a question for me sometime, Miss Cheney."

Cheney started, both at the request and at the peculiar tone of Rissy's voice. "What? I mean, of course, Rissy, but—what is it?"

"Ask him about Fort Pillow," she said in a monotone, her face expressionless.

"Fort Pillow? What's that?" Cheney asked, bewildered.

Rissy didn't answer, merely looked at her.

A soft knock sounded at the door. "Doc? You ready? Or you want me to go on down?"

Immediately Cheney brightened and said carelessly, "I'll ask him, Rissy. See you later. I'm ready, Shiloh!" She threw open the door, and Rissy was left alone.

★   ★   ★   ★

"What in the world is all this?" Cheney exclaimed.

"Must be draw day," Shiloh answered in a careful tone. He directed Sock a little closer to Cheney's horse.

Around them streamed hundreds, perhaps even thousands, of Negroes. All of them were on foot. Like a dark wave they parted around Sock and Stocking, then reformed into a packed mass in front of the horses. Sock and Stocking were unconcerned—this was no different from negotiating the jumbled streets of Manhattan—but Shiloh was concerned at the sheer number of people, including children, who passed so closely around the horses. The Negroes paid them little attention save

83

for their curious glances at Cheney, who was dressed so elegantly and whose seat on the big horse was easy and assured. One of the men, Cheney noted, glanced darkly at the riding crop she carried and gave her a wide berth. The implication astounded and unsettled her.

"Where's the telegraph office?" she demanded, eyeing an older man who ducked his head when she caught him staring at her, and scurried away almost in fear.

"There's one up on King Street. The one down by City Hall is only for military and governmental use these days." Casting a jaundiced eye around, Shiloh added, "I thought it'd be less trouble to go up on King Street, anyway. Didn't know it'd be draw day."

Cheney looked at him curiously. "What is draw day?"

"Your Bureau of Refugees, Freedmen, and Abandoned Lands at work." He was looking straight ahead, his even features expressionless. But the "V" scar under his eye seemed to stand out in relief as the skin around his eyes tightened imperceptibly. "Today must be draw day, the day they distribute. You know, clothes and shoes and rice and flour and seed and tools."

"The . . . the . . . Bureau of what?"

"The Freedmen's Bureau, Doc. The agency that Congress formed to help the slaves."

"Oh." Cheney looked around at the stream of humanity surging forward. "Can we go see?"

For the first time Shiloh turned to her. "Why?"

"I just want to see," Cheney insisted. "I wanted to ride, anyway, so I could see some of Charleston. What's wrong with that?"

"Nothing. Guess so," Shiloh said with uncharacteristic shortness and touched Sock lightly with his heels to maneuver slightly in front of Cheney. It removed him from conversation's reach.

Shiloh led Cheney north on Church Street to the City Market, but then—along with the crowd—took a sharp right instead of a left to King Street. They neared the docks, two riders and two mounts, a moving island alone in a stream of hurrying people. Cheney felt a little uneasy on the secondary streets, which were little better than muddy alleys hidden between the looming walls of warehouses, but soon they turned a corner onto the more generous expanse of Concord Street.

At the intersection of two anonymous side streets, long planks had been set up on sawhorses, and then covered with sheets. Four soldiers in blue sat at the tables with piles of lists and pieces of pencils. Two of the seated soldiers were young and smooth-faced, and they spoke matter-of-factly to the suppliants. Two of them, in stark contrast, were heavily bearded and carelessly uniformed and growled rudely to the Negroes. All of them concentrated diligently on marking the receipt ledgers in front of them. Cheney's tidy mind noted that the Negroes did not sign the receipts. Then she realized sadly that likely none of them could read or even write their own names. Until the war, it had been against the law in South Carolina for Negroes to be taught to read or write.

Behind the seated soldiers were carts. The horses had been unhitched, and the carts formed two lines of four, each stretching behind the tables. A dozen more soldiers stood behind the four seated men and received the pieces of paper the clerks impatiently tore from receipt books and thrust unseeing behind them. The soldiers would peruse the list, collect certain items from the carts, and return and hand them to the man or woman who stood waiting at either end of the table.

Shiloh and Cheney drew up their horses some distance away from the tables and carts and soldiers. The Negroes formed four long lines that streamed past them and around the corner and out of sight. They were quiet and orderly, not speaking too much among themselves. Anxious dark faces strained to see how much was piled in the carts, and to judge how far back they were from the tables.

"Shoes," Cheney whispered to herself, eyeing the carts, "and shovels and hoes and some plows . . . flour . . . no coats." Her voice dropped even more. It was cold, and most of the people wore no heavy outer clothing.

"Blankets," Shiloh muttered.

"Hmm?"

"Blankets," he repeated and pointed. "Those are blankets. Better than nothing." One of the last carts was piled high with neat gray squares of wool.

Even as Cheney watched, a young woman holding an infant, with three children crowded around her skirts, took a pile of blankets from a blank-faced soldier. Turning, she bent toward the children. The biggest child took a blanket and wrapped himself and the smallest in it, and the middle child took another. The woman wrapped herself and the baby in the third, smiled briefly down at her children behind her, and led them down the narrow side street that fronted the long tables.

"Looks like they could've given her four," Cheney observed scathingly.

Shiloh shrugged. He had recognized those small rectangles of wool. They were Confederate gray.

They watched for a while, Cheney studying the scene intently, Shiloh motionless and neutral.

"Ready?" Shiloh asked, and Cheney nodded.

He led her to the side street where the Negroes who had already received their "draw" were filing out. About twenty feet away from the draw tables was a small booth. It was simply a waist-high box with a frame, but it was curtained and swagged in the most outrageous shade of purple velvet Cheney had ever seen. No sign was posted on the booth.

"Right here! Right here, ladies and gentlemen!" cried the man behind the frame, shouting like a circus barker. Cheney, ignoring Shiloh's dark look, drew Stocking closer.

The man in the booth was sharp looking, with a long thin nose, a slash of a mouth, and slicked-back hair. He wore a somber black suit, but with a loud purple waistcoat and an impossibly large watch-fob hanging heavily at the end of a vulgar chain. It seemed to be a sunburst design, and had lettering on it, but Cheney couldn't read it. Curious men and women passed close by the booth, checking to see if he was giving something away.

"Here you go, ladies, thank you, remember the Union

League and the Republican Party," he pattered on mindlessly as he shuffled some items over the smudged purple-velveted top of the booth. "Yes, yes, here you go, thank you, remember the Union League and the Republican Party—and Mister Linkum!"

His eyes flickered up at Cheney as he spoke the dead president's name in a conscious jibe at the Negro dialect. He was giving them purple candles, Cheney saw, with the sunburst design worked in them in black wax. Some of the Negroes looked at the candles curiously, and at the man blankly, but they took the candles with a shrug. They needed light, too, in the long winter nights.

Cheney and Shiloh moved on, slowly and carefully. "What was that all about?" Cheney asked when they were past the lurid purple booth.

"Union League," Shiloh answered carelessly. "Surprised you haven't noticed them before, in New York. Teaching the poor ignorant coloreds how to vote, you know."

Cheney absorbed this; her ignorance of politics was beginning to appall her. "But—can Negroes vote here?"

"Not yet. But they will, I guess." He seemed to become aware of his short, uninformative answers and continued patiently, "That's part of the problem with Reconstruction, you see, Doc. Negro suffrage."

"Well, they can vote in New York, and they ought to be able to vote here."

"Yes, New York voted to give Negroes suffrage—but they tacked on a two-hundred and fifty buck filing fee."

"They . . . they did?"

"Yep," he replied without heat. "And Congressman Thaddeus Stevens of Pennsylvania is the most radical of the Republicans—"

"And one of the most outspoken supporters of Negroes," Cheney interrupted.

"Yep," Shiloh said again, his eyes fixed on her. "But Pennsylvania voted down Negro suffrage. So have Wisconsin, Minnesota, Connecticut, Nebraska, New Jersey, Ohio, and Michigan. And that just about names the members of Congress that are hollering long and loud about the South giving Negroes the vote. So the Union League was formed by them to come down here and assure that Negroes—even the completely illiterate ones—learn where it says "Republican" on a ballot to put their 'X' by."

Cheney blew out an exasperated breath and met his mild gaze with a frown. "Are you telling me, Shiloh, that you believe in slavery? That you believe in all these horrible lies that Negroes are not human, and don't have the same rights we do?"

Shiloh watched her gravely during this impassioned outburst. "No."

"What then?"

"I was just telling you about the Union League," he replied with no sign of reproof.

Cheney drew in a breath, then mumbled, "I'm sorry, Shiloh. I know you must think I'm stupid—"

"What?" Shiloh was startled, and he jerked his head around to stare at Cheney. "Never, Doc," he said firmly. "I never think that. You're one of the smartest women—no," he amended, "one of the smartest *people* I've ever known."

"Why . . . why . . . thank you, Shiloh," she fumbled, surprised at both the compliment and at Shiloh's vehemence.

"Welcome." His guarded blue eyes turned back straight ahead.

"But I don't understand anything that's going on here," Cheney persisted. "What . . . what kind of government is it here in Charleston right now, anyway? Who's in charge?" Sweeping her long, slender arm in an all-encompassing gesture, she went on, "Is Charleston under military rule—still—two years after the war?" Now that they were back on Market Street, the familiar sight of soldiers with rifles was everywhere.

Shiloh pointed to her to take a left on King Street as he explained succinctly, "Not surprising, you don't understand the politics, Doc. Ever since April of '65, the plan of Reconstruction of the rebel southern states has been up and down, back and forth. It changes whenever Congress comes into session, and then again when President Johnson gets the bills on his desk, and then again when Congress dismisses, and then again when Congress reconvenes."

He directed Cheney to the hitching rail in front of the plain square building with the Western Union sign over the door. Neither of them dismounted, and Cheney watched Shiloh's face closely as he finished, "But Charleston is different, anyway. It's always been treated differently—ever since those boys from the Citadel fired that first shot at Fort Sumter. . . ." His voice trailed off, then he focused again on Cheney's face. "Right now the city of Charleston is still under the same military jurisdiction it's been under since soldiers marched into the city in 1864. Looks like it's going to be for a while."

"But why?" Cheney asked.

For the first time that day she saw Shiloh's familiar grin, and his even white teeth flashed. "Because, Doc," he drawled outrageously, "our Constitution is un-ratified, our city is un-Reconstructed, and us Charlestonians are un-repentant."

★   ★   ★   ★

As they were returning to the hotel, Shiloh remarked blithely, "Must be nice to send a telegram to someone."

"What?" Cheney asked, mystified.

"Just never did, that's all. Never had anyone to send one to."

Little ripples of pity went through Cheney and made her throat constrict, but she swallowed hard and made herself be as light as Shiloh. "You can send me one," she teased, "any time."

"Wish I'd thought of that," he mumbled almost inaudibly.

Cheney didn't know what he meant, so she went on, "And this one wasn't very much fun, anyway. I just told Father what I'd learned about Guardian Investments, Limited, and gave him the name of that lawyer in Pennsylvania." She grew quiet for a minute, and her brow furrowed as she thought. "Shiloh— what—you mentioned some name—" She faltered and squinted her eyes. Shiloh waited until she turned to him. "Did I tell you that lawyer's name?"

"No," he replied, "just that he was in Pennsylvania." Cheney had related to him all that had happened at Dallas Farm and Supply.

"His name is John Pride Rounds," Cheney said half expectantly.

"Yeah?" Shiloh turned to her, now with interest. "I'll never forget that last name. You remember—he was the captain, with the Seventh Pennsylvania—"

"In Murfreesboro!"

"Yeah. Captain Oliver Cromwell Rounds," Shiloh repeated with the same disdainful curl of his lip as when he'd spoken of the man the previous day at dinner. "You think there's a connection?"

Cheney thought for a minute, then shrugged. "Probably. It's such an unusual name—in Pennsylvania. And if I remember my English history correctly, John Pride was one of Oliver Cromwell's best soldiers. But I suppose it really doesn't make any difference."

"No," Shiloh said quietly, "but it's funny."

"The coincidence?"

His eyes, shaded by the black Stetson, swept around him slowly, unseeingly, as he answered. "All of them," he finally said quietly. "The war . . . how it linked people's lives in such strange ways. . . ."

"And severed them," Cheney added.

They were both silent as they approached the hotel. Shiloh helped Cheney dismount. A man waited expectantly on the sidewalk, a little down the street from the entrance of the hotel, and took a hopeful half step toward them.

"Here you go, Jubal," Shiloh said, tossing the reins to him. "Take them to the livery and tend to them, okay?"

"Sure, sure, Mistuh Shiloh," the man said eagerly, showing large white teeth in an ear-splitting grin. "Be glad to." He was in rags, as Cheney expected, but he did have on worn boots and an old gray coat. Dark stripes showed where military insignia had been carefully removed. Shiloh flipped a coin in the air, which the man caught expertly and pocketed as he ran, leading Sock and Stocking.

Cheney and Shiloh entered the hotel, climbed the stairs, and went down the quiet hall. Wordlessly Shiloh took her hand, brushed a kiss on it, and hurried to his room.

"S-see you later," Cheney called uncertainly after him. She had wanted to ask him about lunch, but then she decided maybe it was best if she sent Rissy to invite him, after all. Sighing, she opened her door and entered her room, then stopped midstride with delight.

"Look, Rissy!" she called in the direction of the connecting door, which was open. "Look! Presents!"

Rissy stalked through the door, protesting. "Shut that there door, Miss Cheney! Ain't no need in standin' out in the hall shriekin' about it! Like I ain't been answerin' your door ever two minutes to some delivery boy!"

Cheney hurried over to the round table, set in front of the French doors that led to a tiny balcony. Her eyes were alight with surprise and pleasure. "What is it? Who are they from?"

Rissy crossed her arms and rumbled, "Do you think I opened them boxes and read your love letters?"

"Oh . . . no . . ." Cheney said absently. On the table were three boxes. One of them was a six-inch cube, one was a flat square, the third was tiny. Two of the boxes had ribbons around them, with small notes folded under the ribbons. Cheney picked up the cube, untied the knot impatiently, and opened the box. Inside was a perfect white orchid, set on a bed of dried rose petals.

"Oh!" she exclaimed. "Rissy, look! Isn't it beautiful!" With gentle fingers Cheney picked up the orchid and put it to her nose. "I never could resist doing that," she murmured softly, "even though I know very well they have no scent."

"I wonder who it's from," Rissy said scathingly, her arms still sturdily folded. "Reckon that note that's on the floor under your big foot might tell us?"

"I don't have big feet!" Cheney retorted automatically, but hastily she moved aside and scooped up the forgotten note. First she scanned the signature and smiled. "Shadrach Forrest Luxton," she told Rissy, who smiled a little herself.

At the top of the white parchment, in a firm but back-slanted script, was written:

Yes, Heaven is thine; but this
Is a world of sweets and sours;
Our flowers are merely—flowers . . .

"A poem—but I don't recognize it," Cheney muttered and hurriedly read the rest of the note.

Doctor Duvall,

Again allow me to express my gratitude for joining me and Mr. Irons at dinner. You are a most gracious and interesting dinner companion, and the fact that you are a lovely and intelligent lady increased my pleasure—and my appreciation— a hundredfold.

If I may again impose upon your good graces, I would be honored if you would attend a Special Drill of my Troops tomorrow morning. It would be my great pleasure to call for you at nine-thirty. The drill will last perhaps an hour, and then—I hope to be so very fortunate—I will request your company for the remainder of the morning. There is a place I would very much like to show you, and as Mr. Irons has assured me that you are an expert equestrienne, I believe you will enjoy the ride and—dare I?—the company.

Mr. Irons has already graciously assented to be my guest for the day. Your reply, Doctor Duvall, is most anxiously awaited at the Citadel, and I remain,

> *Most gratefully,*
> *Your obedient servant,*
> *Shadrach Forrest Luxton*
> *The Citadel*

"How charming!" Cheney exclaimed with real pleasure.

"What?" Rissy demanded, looking over her shoulder.

Absently Cheney handed the note back to Rissy and grabbed the next box, the flat square. This one had no ribbon or note, but when Cheney removed the top she saw that it contained a sheaf of especially fine notepaper that appeared to be trimmed in gold, a quantity of small envelopes, and a bar of sealing wax with gold flecks in it. One sheet of the paper was creased and placed on top of the sheets, and Cheney eagerly unfolded it. As she read, her eyes grew round with surprise.

Doctor Duvall—
Please accept this small gift with my hope that your stay at the Planter's Hotel will be a pleasant one.
                    Gard Granger

"Blue skies!" Cheney exclaimed. "I can't believe it!"

"What?" Rissy demanded, crowding Cheney as she strained to read the note. It was easy, because Gard Granger's handwriting was just as he spoke, and composed—plain, large, block capital letters.

"Hmph," Rissy grunted.

"It's very strange," Cheney mused. "Such a fine and expensive gift . . . I'm not sure . . ."

"Me neither," Rissy said solidly.

"Still . . ." Cheney thoughtfully laid aside the note. "He presents it as a sort of business gift." Impatiently she grabbed the third box, the smallest one, and by some whim read the note first. Then she was glad, because it was the best of all. It was written in Shiloh's clearly masculine, but curiously graceful, hand.

Cheney,
Please accept this small gift. I'm very glad you're here in Charleston with me.
Would you do me the honor of joining me for dinner? I have taken the liberty of reserving a quiet table at the restaurant. There is something I want to show you and something I want to tell you.
If it is your pleasure, I will call for you at eleven o'clock.
                    With thanks,
                    Your friend,
                    Shiloh

Cheney's face bloomed, and her eyes shone—but then she frowned down at the note. "Is this some kind of joke? I just saw him!"

"He didn't know you was gonna wake him up at dawn's crackin'," Rissy noted tersely. "He musta done this last night."

"Oh yes," Cheney said in a subdued voice. "Of course."

"Why don't you look at what's in the box, Miss Cheney?" Rissy suggested with a syrupy-sweet voice. "Or do you mebbe think somethin's gonna jump out at you?"

"No, of course not," Cheney huffed, "but this is just so unusual for Shiloh. I thought it might be a joke."

Rissy shook her head impatiently as Cheney hesitantly fingered the small box and fidgeted with the ribbon. It seemed to be a very old ribbon, because it was fragile and crackly, and black velvet dust puffed up in clouds around her fingers.

Inside the box was a single perfect pearl.

8

IN THE STUDY OF JUDGE GARTH GRANGER

Vess Alexander took a deep breath, said a short prayer, and walked up the cobblestone path. The last time he had been to this house he had not dared to come to the front door—but now Mrs. Eliza Deal Ramsey lived in the back, in the servants' quarters, and this house belonged to Judge Garth Granger, who was a protector of freedmen like Vess. On the big white door was a heavy knocker of brass made in the shape of a roaring lion's head. Firmly he banged it twice against the base and strained to hear the cadence of the footsteps behind the door.

Don't matter noway, he told himself sturdily. *Ain't gonna be easy whether it's Miz Ramsey or one of them marshals.*

The door was too thick to hear any footsteps, so Vess was surprised and relieved when Miss Juliet Granger opened it herself. He had met Miss Granger several times, when she accompanied her brother into Dallas Farm and Supply to buy marine supplies.

"Why, hello, Vess," she said in her almost-whisper. "Please come in. Did my father send for you?"

"Yes, ma'am," he answered, taking one step into the foyer and stopping. "He sent me an order, and I'm s'posed to be here at eleven."

"Then you're very prompt. Come into the drawing room, and I'll let him know you're here." Her skirts whispered across the polished oak floor, and Vess followed. She led him into a room with white walls, gold brocaded drapes, and furniture that looked as if no one had ever sat on it and no one ever would.

"Please wait here, Vess," Miss Granger instructed him and disappeared. Vess watched her leave, then listened. No heavy boots or coarse voices sounded in the quiet house.

I must be gittin' old, Vess thought wryly. *'Course it's draw day, and them marshals are at the draw, so they ain't got time to be here bossin' me around.* Of Judge Granger's four favorite marshals, two of them were all right, Vess supposed, but two of them were crude and impatient.

Judge Garth Granger, a brevet colonel from the Pennsylvania Quartermaster's Office, had been appointed provost tribune for the city of Charleston, and there were twenty provost marshals assigned to him. The Federal forces occupying the city were under the command of Brigadier General John Hatch, who was in charge of all military matters, but the provost tribune administered all Freedmen's Bureau matters. In the confusion of Presidential Reconstruction versus Congressional Reconstruction, both the military commander's job and the provost tribune's job had enlarged in scope. Finally it sifted down that the provost tribune would oversee all the goods and services provided to freedmen by the Bureau, and his tribunal was the sole recourse for any and all matters relating to labor disputes or any other cases of injustice against freedmen.

Vess knew and understood all these political shifts very well. *Judge Garth Granger, he's a powerful man*, he told himself with a half shrug. He had been brought before the seats of the mighty many times, and though he had not been a suppliant of any sort since 1850—quite the opposite, in fact—it used to make him nervous. These days it never did. Until today.

He looked around the room idly, though he had no wish to move or sit down. Over the white marble mantel was a portrait of a beautiful woman, and Vess sighed deeply as he realized who it was. *That's why you're uneasy. Funny the judge left that painting of her up there . . . mebbe it seems like to him too that this here's still her house.* It never occurred to Vess that this might be a cruel taunt: to leave a portrait of the former mistress of the house, when she was young and beautiful, hanging in a room which she now never entered except to clean. His mind didn't assess this, because his eyes, instead of dwelling on the portrait, were focused on the past.

Vess had spent his last day as a slave out in the garden of

this very house, and Mrs. Eliza Deal Ramsey was the reason he had been a free man for seventeen years. Vess suspected that Mrs. Ramsey knew this, and he also suspected that this knowledge filled her with rage and bitterness like nothing else in her life ever had.

'Cept maybe the judge takin' this house, and her havin' to hire on as the housekeeper, and live in the servants' cottage, he reflected with not one whisper of triumph. *Lord Jesus, I thank you from the bottom of this old heart.... Vengeance is mine, saith the Lord.... How you have brought the mighty low, and raised the lowly ones....*

"Vess?" Juliet Granger floated into the doorway.

"Yes, ma'am?"

"My father is nowhere to be found." She was a little upset, Vess could see, and he marveled at it. "I must apologize. Neither I nor Mrs. Ramsey had any idea he had left the house." Gliding over to him, she looked up. His face and eyes were downcast, a posture Negro men had to take in the presence of white ladies.

"Vess?"

"Yes, ma'am?" he answered, looking up.

"Won't you sit down and make yourself comfortable? I'm certain he will be back momentarily. I've never known him to miss an appointment."

"Thank you, ma'am," Vess responded quietly. "I'm comfortable. I'll wait."

Juliet Granger assessed the room with a knowing look. "No, I believe I'll show you into his study. You can be seated by his desk, and perhaps look over your papers ... are they drawings for some of your beautiful work?" She turned and went down the hall, and Vess followed obediently.

"Yes, ma'am. A fence and gate and window trim, and a table and chairs for the garden."

"Here we are." Opening a door at the end of the long hallway, she led Vess into a man's study with dark carpeting and dark furniture. Every wall, from floor to ceiling, was covered with books, all of uniform height and thickness. Curiously Vess noted that there were no spaces in the bookshelves. The books were lined up as solidly as stacked bales of cotton.

"Please, be seated here, Vess." Juliet Granger gestured gracefully toward a wooden chair in front of the almost-black expanse of the desk. "I wish I could look at your drawings, but my father says ladies need only worry about the inside of the house, not the outside. I'm certain they're lovely."

"Thank you, ma'am." Vess waited. He couldn't imagine seating himself while any lady, white or colored, was standing.

Juliet Granger gave him the gentlest of smiles and left the study, closing the door quietly behind her.

Vess sat down, finally, and looked about the room. The numerous books, instead of evoking the intimacy of a reading room, only made the study anonymous and boring. Unconsciously he studied the items on the desk for some clue to Judge Granger's personality. Vess had never met the man.

The only personal item—if one could call it that—on the judge's desk was a marble statue, finely carved and highly polished, of Blind Justice: a noblewoman, swathed in Grecian robes and blindfolded, holding a book in one hand and a set of scales in the other. *I know what they're gittin' at, makin' her blind*, Vess mused, *but I allus thought it'd be better if'n she could see and still be Justice.*

Carefully Vess averted his eyes from the view of the garden outside the single window. *Funny he sits with his back to the window* . . . When Vess realized that he had a strong notion to do just that, he made a conscious decision to exorcise this last old raggedy demon, once and for all. . . .

He was just another field nigger when he was a boy. He was different, though, and he was aware of it, though he never told anyone—not his parents, or friends, or his master, John James McKay. As a child, Vess was alert and observant and always mature for his age. Since Mas' McKay thumbed his nose at anybody telling him he couldn't teach his nigras to read, Vess started reading the Bible—at age three. By the time he was ten and picking cotton, he endured the torturous work and scorching days by praying constantly—and by his mental games.

If this tract is fourteen acres—and there's eighteen slaves—and eight of them pick one row an hour, and four of them pick two rows an hour, and six of them pick three rows an hour, how many pounds of cotton will we have at noon? At three? At sundown? How long will it take us to pick the tract?

In time Vess realized that he didn't always think in words. He began to visualize single images that sped into comprehension of a total picture at an unbelievable rate. Later Vess could, in the span of a few moments, take one glance at a house or garden, visualize the wrought-iron artistry he could create, and know the exact amount of pig iron—to the ounce—that he would need. He didn't calculate it. He just saw it.

Vess was a prodigy, though he still didn't know the word. For years Charlestonians had recognized that he possessed the peculiar genius of an artist. But no one knew except Vess—*and the good Lord above*—he thought warmly, of the great breadth of his mind. Though the power of Vess's thoughts and perceptions was almost supernatural, he was not at all articulate. He'd made no special attempt to be.

Because he was big and strong and smart, Mas' McKay had apprenticed him to the blacksmith when Vess was sixteen. When Vess was twenty-four, Alexander Dallas had bought him.

Thank you for Mistuh Dallas, he prayed for perhaps the ten thousandth time. *It was a long road for both of us, but we toiled on and both ended up walkin' with you ... Thank you, Lord Jesus. ...*

Vess had been a better blacksmith than Dallas, and it hadn't taken Dallas long to realize it. He had suggested Vess try some ornamental wrought iron—a simple gate—and within a year every person in Charleston who could afford it was at Dallas Farm and Supply placing orders for Vess to put on his hire badge and come see about their house or garden or office.

Unconsciously Vess felt in his waistcoat pocket. *Still there ... dunno why I worry about that blamed badge.* It was his hire badge, a simple square of thin copper with the imprint:

Ironwork
No. 1
1841

Vess smiled. Alexander Dallas had no use for the pretense of putting some big number like 101 on Vess's hire badge. "You're the only slave I got, and the only one I expect to have," Dallas had said in his rough way. "Ain't gonna fool me, nor you, nor no one else if I put some fancy number on it."

In 1850, after ten years of spectacular success of Vess's wrought ironwork, Mrs. Eliza Deal Ramsey had asked for Vess.

That garden, he thought with a pang, *right there it was, right where I'm lookin'. . . .*

"I want birdcages," she said in that quick, impatient way of hers, tapping her skirt lightly with a riding crop. Turning, Vess stole a quick look at her profile but dropped his eyes again cautiously before she caught him. She was beautiful, he guessed, but it was hard for him to judge white people, with their pale skin and sharp-angled faces and cold blood. Miz Ramsey had a polished crystal look and a hardness like a diamond. At twenty, she was married to a man almost three times her age.

"I want them six feet tall, painted white, with lots of lacy trim. There"—she jabbed the riding crop toward points along the shrubs bordering the walks—"and there—and there—here—"

"Miz Ramsey," Vess said as quietly as possible. "I cain't do no birdcages."

Though his gaze was lowered, Vess saw her turn very slowly and the riding crop become still. "What did you say, boy?" she asked in a frozen voice.

"The birds, they chew on the paint and on the bars, and it kills them," he explained patiently. "So I ain't never done no birdcages, ma'am. Instead, if you'll let me do you some drawings, I can show you where you can put a little gazebo right here, and I can even make one that'll look like a pretty little birdcage, and . . ."

"Boy," she stepped close, and Vess then looked up at her. He was calm, and composed, and did not flinch even though she was furious. "Are you deaf, and stupid too, you stupid nigra? I said I want birdcages!" She stamped her tiny, spurred riding boot. Twice.

Vess merely met her gaze, neither asking nor telling her anything. Clenching her teeth and her riding crop, her blue eyes spark-

ing with anger, she grated, "Are you going to do my birdcages, or not?"

"No, ma'am."

She stepped behind him and began hitting his bare legs with the riding crop. Over and over again the stiff leather swiped the air, until the back of Vess's legs stung all over. He was wearing ragged short pants and a loose cotton shirt, and she hit him twice across the back. But that must have been frustrating to her, because he felt the loose shirt tangle the blow. So she hit his calves a few more times.

Stepping back in front of him, breathing heavily, she rasped, "Now are you going to do my birdcages, boy?"

"No, ma'am." Vess answered in the same monotone as before, and though he was seething and filled with shame, he took care not to show it. His face, he felt, was stuck in granite. It was hard to move his mouth.

He met her eyes, however, and for many years afterward Vess had searched his own face curiously in the mirror to try and see what she saw there. There was nothing in this world that he could do, or would do, that could possibly hurt Eliza Deal Ramsey. Such things never fouled Vess's mind.

But ugly fear came over her doll-like features. Pressing her small white hand to her twisted red mouth, she took a faltering step backward. "Get out of here, and never come back," she whispered hoarsely.

Vess returned slowly to Dallas's store. Alexander Dallas took one look at Vess's face and instantly his eyes traveled up and down Vess's body. Then Dallas stepped—lightly, and quickly, for such a big man—around behind Vess. Vess remained mute and motionless. He sensed Dallas bending over a little, and Vess thought dully, Know you cain't see no red marks on my night skin. Then he felt the gentlest of touches on his back—on bare skin. Musta ripped my shirt, I guess.

Alexander Dallas came back around Vess, his mouth a thin line and his blue eyes filled with pain, and went to the back of the store, into his office, and said not one thing. For the first time in his life,

Vess went somewhere without letting his master know. He went home.

At dawn the next morning a subdued knock sounded on the door of Vess's cottage. Vess opened the door, and Alexander Dallas handed him his hire badge. "You're a free man, Vess," he said quietly. "You're under my name and my protection." Then he left. Vess had never been back to this house, until today.

The last dingy tatters of shame and pain dissipated from Vess's mind and heart. The room in which he was sitting materialized again in his vision. Suddenly Vess was conscious of the presence of Almighty God, heavy and strong and invigorating, in this sterile room. The corners of Vess's strange Oriental eyes crinkled into the familiar crow's-feet of laugh lines as he grinned widely, and he recalled a phrase he'd heard that stubborn old slave owner John James McKay say, years ago. Vess Alexander murmured happily, "My Abba, He is very fond of me."

★ ★ ★ ★

After some time of gazing with simple pleasure at the view of the garden outside, Vess decided to pull out his drawings and give them a last once-over. Judge Granger, he was almost certain, was going to want some Gothic horror of black octagonal bars an inch in diameter topped by long spikes. Vess's drawings were of a simple and elegant theme of circular white bars topped by shapes resembling arrow-tips, but with the tips and side-pieces of the arrows rounded and not sharp. *Glad I got that set of scales on the gate and small ones on the window-bars*, he thought with satisfaction. *Bet I've got him.*

As he started to lay out his drawings, he saw that because they were outsized they would disturb the papers on the judge's desk. Vess leaned over to push them farther away; then he decided that he'd better stack the three piles neatly, in the same order as they were, to the side. As he moved around the desk and looked at the three orderly piles of papers, his eyes suddenly—unbidden—focused on the contents of the papers.

Within seconds Vess knew the exact portent of the papers, and they ceased to be square white pieces of paper with com-

102

plicated markings on them. They were translated into fast-moving pictures in Vess's mind, with Judge Garth Granger—a man-shaped shadow—in the center of a complex web, a web of betrayal of trust and misuse of power. Vess Alexander did not know the word "embezzlement," but he did know stealing when he saw it, and he saw it all plainly.

With a heart now heavy, Vess decided to leave his drawings and go home, and pray that God Almighty would tell him what to do, and give him the strength to do it.

9

THEM CUSSIN' HORSY WOMEN

Cheney almost tripped as she hurried down the thickly carpeted enclosed stairwell, and pulled herself up sharply at the bright vision of herself *rolling* into the hotel lobby.

"Mr. Barlow would be quite shocked," she giggled to herself, "and I'm certain he would insist that there must be some mistake." Cheney knew she was being a little silly and slowed her pace down to a decorous walk. *It's amazing how lighthearted it can make a woman to receive three gifts from three attractive men*, she reflected happily.

Mr. Barlow looked up and nodded politely, his ever-present pencil stub in his hand. Then he did a very minimal double take, because Miss Duvall was looking particularly well this morning, with her cheeks flushed and her eyes bright.

"Mr. Barlow, I need to send a message to the Citadel," she said. "Would you be so kind as to assist me?"

"Certainly, Miss Duvall," he answered with a little more than his customary tepid politeness. She really was striking in that black velvet riding habit. "Messenger boys are always available at the Planter's."

Thoughtfully Cheney stared into space and tapped the envelope she held against the desk, not noticing as Mr. Barlow held out one hand for it. After a moment he picked up his little pencil again.

"Is Mr. Granger in?" she asked abruptly.

"Yes, ma'am," he answered, looking quizzically at her over the rims of his little square glasses.

Cheney waited for a moment, then went on impatiently, "Well, may I see him?"

"I . . . don't know."

Cheney sighed with exasperation and kept her voice even. "Let's begin again, Mr. Barlow. Will you please tell—that is, will you please go into Mr. Granger's office—now—and tell him that Dr. Cheney Duvall is at the desk, and would be most grateful if she could speak to him for a moment?"

"Oh. Um—I suppose—yes—I could do that."

With obvious reluctance Mr. Barlow disappeared. Running her fingers over the unshaped blob of gold-specked wax on the envelope, Cheney decided, *I must get some sort of seal . . . a nice one . . . and tell Mr. Barlow to hurry the boy to the Citadel . . . I'm sure Shadrach is waiting expectantly for a reply.*

After Cheney had opened her gifts and admired them for a while—Rissy sniffed that Cheney was "playin' with her toys"—she had sat down and written a note to Shiloh, accepting his dinner offer. Then—after a slight scuffle with Rissy as to the propriety of Cheney "gallopin' 'round this town with a bunch of gallopin' men"—Cheney had composed a rather more formal note of acceptance to Shadrach Luxton and hurried down to see about sending it. About Gard Granger she had been undecided until now.

"Mr. Granger says for you to come in, ma'am," Mr. Barlow's voice sounded from her right. He was standing at the door beside the desk, holding it open only slightly as if Cheney were invading some inner sanctum. His sallow cheeks had two red spots on them, but Cheney took no note of that.

As she swept by him, she handed him the note and murmured, "I appreciate your assistance, sir. Please see that this is delivered as quickly as possible."

Down a hall and straight ahead was Gard Granger's office, with the door standing open. Upon entering, Cheney cast a quick glance around the spacious room, which was masculine and functional. Gard Granger sat behind a no-nonsense rectangular banker's desk, which was untidy with high piles of papers and several serious-looking ledgers. Cheney reflected that the paperwork for the hotel business must be very cumbersome, indeed. Then she recalled that Shiloh had told her Gard Granger was harbor master of Charleston Harbor, and he—and the soldiers who policed the harbor, dubbed "Gard's Rangers"—had gained an unsavory reputation for ruthlessness in collecting the harbor fees, which were so high they were considered little short of robbery. Cheney dismissed the thought. Gard Granger, whoever he might be, had been kind to her.

Granger got to his feet, his face darkening. "Dr. Duvall. How may I be of assistance to you?"

He did not come around the desk, Cheney noted, or offer her a chair. Mentally she shrugged and replied, "Thank you kindly, but I require no assistance, Mr. Granger. Mr. Barlow is most helpful."

"Good." Granger waited impatiently.

Cheney took a step forward, closer to the desk. Gard Granger somehow, by some movement that she could not quite pin down, withdrew farther from her. "Mr. Granger, I just wanted to express my appreciation for the stationery you sent me. It is lovely, and exactly the kind of stationery I prefer, as opposed to lots of flowers and flourishes."

"Flowers and flourishes." Granger repeated the words as if they were alien; Russian, perhaps, or Javanese.

"Um—yes. I don't like . . . them . . . um . . . that is, on my writing papers. You understand. Obviously."

Gard Granger's dark, well-shaped eyebrows winged slightly over his eyes. "Do I?"

This is a very odd conversation, and he is quite handsome in a tragic, Byronic sort of way, Cheney thought. *And I am beginning to get a little unsettled.* Determined to retain her composure, Cheney nodded, a tiny graceful incline of her head. "Yes, I believe you do, Mr. Granger. The stationery is an exceptional gift. I felt that I must express my gratitude in person. So thank you, Mr. Granger. Good morning."

She turned back toward the door, expecting to hear a curt goodbye.

"Dr. Duvall, please . . ."

His voice was warm—tentative—human. Whirling in surprise, Cheney saw that he had extended the black-gloved right hand in a "stop" gesture, and immediately she catalogued; *He has large rotor movement from the shoulder—elbow bent slightly—prosthetic hand?—wonder if it's from a wound—the war—accident—?*

Cheney could not possibly have lingered on his right hand for even one second with her passing glance. Still, Gard Granger's dark eyes saw too much. Sometimes Gard Granger even saw things that were not there. He stiffened, his shoulders tightened up, and his face shut as securely as a slammed door. With rigid politeness and precise enunciation he said, "You are welcome, Dr. Duvall. Good morning."

★ ★ ★ ★

"Shiloh Arns is a man," Rissy maintained stubbornly, "so he ain't got no notion what his note means."

"He does too," Cheney asserted. "Even a man knows whether he means lunch or dinner."

"You don't," Rissy pointed out.

This stopped Cheney cold, and it took her a few moments to recover sufficiently to pick up the argument—after a fashion. "It doesn't matter anyway. What we're discussing is what I'm going to wear."

With exaggerated patience Rissy explained—again—"We dunno what you're gonna wear. 'Cause we dunno whether you're goin' to lunch or dinner."

"The note says dinner."

"Seems like nobody in this here town understands what that is," Rissy muttered ungraciously. "Give me that note."

"It says at eleven o'clock."

"It might be eleven at night, jest like dinner's s'posed to be."

"Rissy, you know he means eleven this morning," Cheney said desperately. "Can't I just wear this?"

"Doctah Cheney Duvall!" The note was thrust down violently. "You ain't gonna go into no nice rest'raunt wearin' no ridin' habit like them cussin' horsy women!"

Cheney was unclear as to the exact origin of this comparison, but she was quite certain about Rissy's tone. It couldn't have been more outraged if Cheney had suggested she go to dinner naked. "Then," she asked meekly, "what shall I wear, Rissy?"

Throwing the note down on the dressing table, Rissy trudged over to the armoire, grumbling in a dire monotone punctuated by occasional loud exclamations as she shuffled back and forth through the ghostly shapes hanging in the big dark expanse.

"Why is this so hard?" Cheney muttered to herself. "It's just Shiloh."

"Just Shiloh!" Rissy exclaimed indignantly, though the force of her words was muffled since she had her entire upper body stuck in the armoire.

Cheney took a few moments to revise her statement. *She's right . . . this is the first time since I've known Shiloh that he's . . . that we . . . that I . . .*

She cleared her throat and tried again. *This is the first time he's . . . formally requested . . . my company.* Irritably Cheney mentally poked and prodded at the laborious words.

"Here." Rissy's single word was filled with satisfaction and brooked no argument. The decision was made—Cheney's dove gray cashmere dress. It was modest, but not demure. The front of the dress did not plunge, but the neckline was cut wide so that it was almost, but not quite, off-the-shoulder. The hem was slightly longer in the back than in the front to form a small train. With the matching fringed shawl and a cameo it was perfect.

Cheney was barely dressed in time, because Rissy dawdled pointedly while Cheney obviously wanted to hurry. Of course Shiloh's knock sounded at precisely eleven.

"Here's your shawl," Rissy said resignedly.

"Thank you, Rissy." Impulsively Cheney kissed her cheek before dashing to the door. Rissy stood, her sturdy hand pressed against her cheek as she shook her head and watched Cheney whirl away.

Cheney and Shiloh said hellos again, and Cheney saw that Shiloh was carrying a box tied with the same kind of ribbon that was around her pearl box. The two didn't speak again until they were seated at a discreet table in the restaurant. Cheney looked around curiously and realized that Shiloh must have wanted to speak to her in as much privacy as he could get. The nine o'clock to ten-thirty coffee break men had already left, and the dinner people would not be arriving for another two and a half hours. The only persons in the restaurant were Gard Granger and a man who must certainly be his father, Cheney noted in passing, and both of them looked angry. They didn't look up at Cheney and Shiloh, and Cheney dismissed them from her thoughts as soon as she had passed by.

"Good morning, Eli," Shiloh greeted the waiter, who bowed. Eli never said anything, and suddenly Cheney wondered if he was capable of speaking. "We only want biscuits and gravy and sorghum and butter and fig syrup, Eli. And some buttermilk."

"Only?" Cheney laughed.

Shiloh looked chagrined. "Okay with you, Doc?"

"Sounds wonderful. I got up too early for breakfast."

This might have sounded odd to anyone but Shiloh, who knew that Cheney was normally a late riser. When she woke up early—as Shiloh knew only too well she had this morning—she was usually grumpy and certainly not hungry. "Okay, Eli," he nodded, and the silent waiter disappeared.

Cheney and Shiloh looked at each other. The silence stretched on until Cheney smiled uncertainly. "Thank you for my pearl," she said awkwardly. "It's just—it's perfect."

Shiloh's eyes crinkled, though he didn't smile. "I knew as soon as I found it that I would give it to you." His voice was low and caressing.

Cheney gulped, and her thoughts danced off into a hundred directions. She couldn't speak for a few moments, and Shiloh merely watched her gravely. Then, after a taking a deep breath, she quavered, "F-found it?"

Shiloh didn't answer the question. "I have something I want to tell you, Doc," he finally said.

"Y-yes? And something to show me?"

"Tell you first." He looked out the window onto the deserted street. "I got some things at the orphanage that belong to me. That is . . . they belong to . . . someone else," he stammered, "but . . . I mean . . . they're mine."

Cheney didn't understand a single word of this, and she was nonplused by Shiloh's speech. She had never, not once, heard him stumble over words in this way. So she remained quiet and waited.

He took a deep breath, his eyes still wandering around the outside. Then he said, "They were found with me, in the crate, when I was a baby. Then they . . . got lost, and . . . forgotten. I just now, for the first time, have seen them."

"Oh," Cheney breathed, "you mean they might have belonged to your parents? And you didn't know about them, or see them, until now?"

"Yes," Shiloh said with undisguised relief and looked back at her. "And I wanted you to know."

"I'm glad, Shiloh. I would like, very much, to know."

"Well . . . here." He thrust the flat box at her.

Cheney removed her gray kid gloves and untied the frail ribbon with care, casting a smile up at Shiloh as she did. He nodded.

Inside the box was a scarf, made of satin, with the finest, most delicate needlework Cheney had ever seen. She picked it up and gasped with surprise as it unfolded to a length of about six feet. It was two layers of red satin, and worked onto the top layer were tiny and intricate figures, embroidered with satin thread. Her eye was confused and darted back and forth across the red expanse. Black dragons, red lions, men, women, children, ships, blue seas, red and yellow flames, hot red suns, white moons . . .

"This is Oriental, of course," she said to Shiloh in a tone that implied he already knew it.

"Guess so." He shrugged helplessly.

"You . . . but . . . there is absolutely no possibility that either of your parents could have been Oriental," Cheney said quietly and rather sadly.

"Guess not."

"Then—whose is it?"

"I don't know. Nobody knows. They were just with me when the Behring sisters found me on the steps of the orphanage."

"They?" Cheney unfolded the scarf completely and saw the fish at the bottom of the box. "Fish?"

She took it out and turned it over and over. "What in the world is this?" she murmured so softly it was barely audible, and Shiloh didn't reply.

It was made in the shape of a most curious fish, about eight inches long and wrought of a thin piece of metal. The scales on the body and the fins were so minutely etched that when Cheney ran her finger across them, they actually did feel like fins and scales. But there were two very odd things about this fish. One was that the eyes were almond-shaped, with an epicanthic fold. The other was that the fish's belly was moveable; that is, a separate piece of round metal was cleverly mounted on the fish, so that it moved in a circle lightly and effortlessly at a touch—or when one moved the fish itself around. The round piece of metal had deep engravings on it—not Oriental characters, for Cheney had seen them once, but more like regular groups of tally marks.

"I have no earthly idea what this is," Cheney said flatly.

"Me neither," Shiloh agreed readily, "but it's Oriental, too, I guess. Got a funny-slanted eye."

Cheney stared at the fish for a moment, then laid it aside. It was an alien object, so inexplicable that no matter how long she stared at it and thought, she knew instinctively that she would not understand it. The scarf, however, might give her some clue, some indication, of the meaning of this little piece of Shiloh's past. But no matter how hard Cheney tried, the scarf remained mute. It was exquisite, by any standards, and Cheney wondered how long it would take to make all of those tiny stitches. "Years . . . years . . ."

"What?" Shiloh asked alertly.

"I'm sorry," Cheney said. "I wasn't aware that I spoke out loud." Shiloh settled back down to wait, and Cheney resumed her search of the scarf's detail. But her heart was beginning to grow heavy. *He thinks—hopes—I might be able to tell him something—meaningful—but I don't know any more about this than a stray cat. Oh, how I wish I knew something—anything!—about Oriental peoples and cultures. . . .*

It was no use. The images were too unfamiliar, too confusing to her Western eye and orderly mind. The profusion of strangely dressed people, fanciful animals, real animals, nightmare landscapes, and dream landscapes were a mere jumble to her. Some of the symbols appeared several times, such as a creature that was a dragon with a lion's head; some symbols, like the lion with the dragon's head, appeared only once; some of the symbols she could not decipher at all, such as the one that appeared over and over again that was either a sort of pointy cloud or a kind of round flame.

Slowly Cheney turned the scarf over and looked at the underside. The scarf was formed by sewing a plain piece of satin onto the embroidered pieces. Formed on the underside were clever pockets, with long flaps to fold over any objects inside and prevent them from falling out.

She looked up at Shiloh questioningly, and he nodded uneasily. "That's where I found the pearl. Sewn in."

"There was nothing else in the pockets?"

He dropped his eyes, which startled Cheney. "No," he said in a strange, careful voice. "I found nothing else in the pockets."

Cheney couldn't decipher these unfamiliar signals from Shiloh, so she ducked her head and searched the embroidery on the shawl again for long moments, though it was hopeless and she knew it.

Finally, looking back up at Shiloh, she shook her head sorrowfully. "I don't know what any of this means," she murmured, "if it means anything at all."

To her surprise, he smiled warmly. "It's okay, Doc. It means something, all right, but we've got plenty of time to find out what."

"Shiloh," she murmured, "I will pray for you, and ask the Lord Jesus to help us find out about your parents."

His clear blue eyes were as pleased as a young child's. "Why, thank you, Cheney."

Shiloh only called her by name in rare—extremely rare—moments of warmth and intimacy, and it unsettled her when he did. Now she dropped her eyes and took a deep, unsteady breath. Then she carefully folded the scarf, laid the fish in the box, placed the scarf on top, and closed the box. "Oriental . . . it's very strange. . . ."

"Yep."

She looked at him curiously. "How much do you know about the Orient?"

"Know it's there. Only reason I know that is because the Behring's educational scope was pretty wide-ranging."

"Well, the Orient . . ." Cheney frowned. "I'm not even sure what that is, exactly. I know it means China . . ."

"Uh—what else is there?"

"Well, there's Japan, and Siam, and . . . Korea . . . and . . . and . . . Burma . . . and probably some other ones that I don't know or can't remember."

Shiloh's eyes flickered down to the box on the table. "Oh. So these things could be from any of those countries?"

"Ye-es," Cheney answered cautiously. "But I only say that because I don't know anything about it. If we can find someone who's not as dumb as us about the Far East, then I bet they could take one look at these things and at least tell us what nationality or culture they are from."

"Think so?"

"I'm certain." Cheney thought for a minute. "Have you ever seen any Far Easterners around here?"

Shiloh laughed, and Cheney was glad. "Not hardly, Doc. Have you?"

"No. I've never even seen any in New York. The only ones I've heard of are the Chinese railroad workers in San Francisco."

"That doesn't help me much," Shiloh said lightly.

"Maybe not," Cheney said softly, "but it does tell you one thing, Shiloh."

"What's that?"

"That your belongings came here by sea."

10

SILVER SABERS IN THE SUN

Rissy called it her "LAPE-is luh-ZOO-lee" habit, although Cheney had pointedly pronounced it her "LAP-is LA-zhuh-li" outfit several times. Rissy either didn't listen or didn't care. Either way, the lapis lazuli riding habit was the most extravagant ensemble that Cheney Duvall owned.

As she studied her full-length reflection in the tilting mirror, Cheney noted with satisfaction that the luxuriant velvet looked dark purple when she turned this way, and dark blue when she turned the other way. The semiprecious stone that lent its name to the particular color reflected light in exactly the same way.

The jacket was fashioned in a way reminiscent of a man's cutaway: tight-fitting through the bodice, small lapels, short in the front and slightly longer in the back, with a double-notch cut. Her blouse was also similar to a man's shirt, with a turned-down collar, and she wore a simply tied black silk ascot. The buttons on the jacket and the stickpin in the ascot were made of the unusual lapis lazuli stone mounted on gold discs, with tiny irregular flecks of gold imbedded in the polished black-purple-blue surface of the stone.

The skirt was tightly gathered and full, naturally, as a riding habit must be. Cheney wore only one white petticoat underneath. The skirt also had lapis lazuli stones as buttons from the waist to the hem, placed on the side, where the skirt was deliberately slit. The bottom four buttons were intended to be unbuttoned, so that the full, lacy ruffles of the petticoat showed provocatively.

But what Cheney liked best about the outfit were the accessories. Instead of the usual black top hat with a gauzy black veil, her hat was made of the same material as the jacket and skirt, and was low-crowned and wide-brimmed. The left side was turned up, with a large round lapis lazuli stone pinning a sweep of black ostrich feathers. The feathers arched rakishly behind and over Cheney's left shoulder. The outfit was finished to perfection with leather gloves dyed the same color, with lapis lazuli buttons, and Cheney had even ordered special riding boots made of the softest kid glove leather, and had them dyed to match.

The reflection of Rissy's face behind her showed satisfaction, both at the clothes Cheney had chosen, and at the fact that Cheney had now kept Shiloh and Shadrach waiting for exactly eight minutes.

"I must go," Cheney said, snatching up her riding whip. "It's scandalous that I'm late this morning, because I might make Shadrach late for the drill."

"They'll wait for him," Rissy said sturdily, "jest like them two men'll wait for you."

Cheney had already reached the door when Rissy murmured, "Miss Cheney."

"Yes, Rissy?" Impatiently Cheney stopped and turned, her hand on the doorknob.

"You look beautiful."

Cheney's arched eyebrows shot up in surprise. "Why . . . why . . . thank you, Rissy." She lingered a moment, unsure of what else to say.

"G'wan now," Rissy muttered darkly. "Shame on you for bein' so late." Busily she turned her back to straighten the tiny dressing table.

Cheney hurried downstairs and rushed out the front door of the lobby without noticing Mr. Barlow. He stood behind the desk, his mouth slightly open as if he had intended to speak to her, but Cheney was gone before he could say a word.

Outside, Shiloh, clothed casually in a gray shirt, gray wool breeches, and canvas coat, lounged against the hitching post holding Stocking's and Sock's reins. In his usual stance, Shadrach stood at attention beside him in the splendid Citadel dress uniform. Behind him stood two flag bearers at formal attention.

When Cheney came out, Shiloh straightened and pulled off his Stetson, but Shadrach removed his white shako, placed it precisely under his arm, and bowed deeply, and the two cadets behind him mirrored his movements.

"Good morning, gentlemen," Cheney said, her voice rich with excitement. "What an honor! A military escort!"

"Good morning, Dr. Duvall, and thank you for joining us. Dr. Cheney Duvall, may I present to you Cadet Lieutenant Logan Manigault. Dr. Cheney Duvall." Shadrach turned a precise quarter-turn and gestured to a slim young man of about eighteen, with long, wavy blond hair.

"It is a pleasure to meet you, Mr. Manigault," Cheney recited, echoing Shadrach's formality. Shiloh had already informed her that cadets were addressed by "Mr." instead of by their rank, as one addressed a man in the regular army.

"Dr. Duvall," the cadet said in a low voice, as soft and lazy as the Charleston spring breeze, "it is my honor and my great pleasure to meet you." Of course he kissed her outstretched hand, and of course Cheney blushed. No matter how she prepared herself, it seemed she was doomed to turn red when men greeted her in this manner.

Shadrach, taking a precise step backward to reveal the other cadet behind him, went through the same formality a second time. "Dr. Duvall, may I present to you Cadet Private Maxcy Roddy. Dr. Cheney Duvall."

"I am very pleased to meet you, Mr. Roddy," Cheney said.

This boy, a stout sixteen-year-old, colored a little as he brushed her hand with a butterfly kiss, and Cheney immediately felt better. "It is my honor to meet you, Dr. Duvall," he said. He had short dark-blond hair, very light blue eyes, freckles, and would, when he got older, tend to plumpness. Now he was simply sturdy-looking.

"You must pardon me, gentlemen, for being late," Cheney said a little breathlessly. "Shall we go?"

"Mornin', Doc," Shiloh said as he helped her mount. "Remember me?" Carelessly he tossed her Stocking's reins and stood by the horse with his hands propped on his hips.

"You?" Cheney teased as she settled into her seat and arranged the reins. "Of course I remember you. You're the bounder from Charleston."

"The gentleman bounder," he noted as he swung easily into Sock's saddle, "and you look beautiful, Doc."

"Sure do," Shadrach grinned, and the other two boys nodded agreement.

"Th-thank you. All of you," she said, the color in her cheeks deepening.

Shadrach positioned his massive white horse between Cheney and Shiloh, and the two flag bearers fell into place behind and to each side of him. When they were positioned properly, walking down the street, Shadrach called in a low tone, "Half-step."

It seemed that the cadet's horses recognized the command, for all three of them broke into a spirited trot. Instinctively Cheney and Shiloh spurred their horses lightly, so that the formation was not broken. With great satisfaction Cheney noted that Shadrach Forrest Luxton had just paid her two distinct compliments: one, by not inquiring if she was capable of a quick trot, and the other by assuming that she and her horse were able to respond intelligently to a cavalry command. She smiled exultantly as they moved quickly along the streets.

The morning was cold but sunny for the first time since Cheney had arrived in Charleston. The sky was a high, distant blue with no clouds, and the sun was the palest of winter pastel yellows. As they wound through the streets, every person stopped and turned to watch them as they rode by. For the first time, Cheney noticed that Shadrach's horse was "gaited." Each step the great white stallion took was separate, and he brought his hooves up high against his girth, with the hocks of his back legs almost touching his stomach. His neck was arched so highly that his chin almost touched his chest. Cheney felt as if she were riding alongside a medieval knight.

Shadrach led them north of the business district to a residential section along King Street. The street was wide, with modest houses along one side and a tiny park on the other.

Round humps of earth bumped up oddly in the park—bombproof batteries facing due north. Generous stone promenades lined the street, with simple stone benches placed along it at regular intervals.

Cheney had wondered why the drill was not at the parade ground of the Citadel, but when they arrived she thought perhaps she knew. A sizable crowd was gathered, with a noticeable absence of soldiers in blue, and an equally noticeable number of men clad in bits and pieces of gray and butternut. Cheney did see—though everyone else seemed purposefully to keep their eyes away from the spot—four men outlined against the sky where they stood atop one of the bombproofs. Two rifle barrels drew slashed black lines against the sky. Because they were silhouetted against the light, they were simple outlines in black. But Cheney was certain they wore blue.

Shadrach seemed to read her thoughts. "This is a Special Drill, Cheney. Each Friday we drill at the Citadel, and it is open to the public. Our Special Drills are by invitation only."

"Then I am deeply honored to be invited to attend," Cheney said warmly.

He bowed slightly and led Shiloh and Cheney to the right and front of the crowd. "Dr. Duvall, Shiloh, please stay mounted right here," he instructed them and wheeled away.

Two blocks down the street were about eighty mounted cadets, already formed into four companies. When Shadrach and the flag bearers cantered up, they drew their swords and made a downward sweep in a salute. He responded, then turned toward the crowd. Long moments passed as he sat at the head of the column, his sword now drawn straight upward close to his chest, the thin silver line precisely in front of his face. Behind him the horsemen shifted slightly, dressing their lines. The lieutenant of each company inspected his troops as Shadrach sat motionless.

Cheney took a moment to survey the crowd. Children were beginning to clamber up onto the stone benches so they could see. Many men stood in the street, most of them close to buggies and carriages with women seated in them. The women, for the most part, wore black or dark blue or gray, and were semi-hidden in "Queen Victoria" bonnets. Because of the wide, stiff fronts closely framing the face, a woman could only look straight ahead. Many of the women's faces, Cheney noted uncomfortably, were turned toward her, and generally were disapproving.

She was the only woman mounted on a horse, although other men, mounted, were dotted here and there. On the other side of the crowd, Alexander Dallas sat on a sturdy brown mare. When he caught Cheney's eye, he took off his hat and swept it into a low bow. A handsome older man, standing by Dallas's mare, turned to look at Cheney. He was compact, with wide, rather stooped shoulders. His hair was thick, wavy silver gleaming in the sun, and he had a generous swath of a silver mustache. Cheney nodded, again conscious of the dark looks of the women, some of them with their gloved or mitted hands to their mouths as they turned to whisper to their neighbors.

Shrugging a little, she turned back to ask Shiloh, "Who are these people, exactly?"

"Charlestonians," he replied. "Looks like mostly the upper class families. Probably most of those cadets have parents here."

"Upper class?" Cheney repeated, casting a surprised glance over her shoulder. The shabby buggies and the outmoded fashions had given her a different impression.

Shiloh grinned down at her. "Not like Manhattan, Doc. Money's got nothing to do with class in Charleston. Only blood."

"Blood," Cheney repeated thoughtfully.

"Yep," he nodded. "Long lines of thin blue blood."

"Oh. Yes, I understand."

"Not like you. You're like the other pure breed of horses."

Cheney turned on him furiously. "What!"

Shiloh's eyes were innocent sky-blue. "You know, cold-blooded horses—like Clydesdales and Shires—have old, honorable bloodlines. They seem steady and very gentle, but they are extremely powerful."

"You listen to me, Shiloh Irons—"

"But the most ancient and noble breeds are hot-blooded, like Arabs and Thoroughbreds. They're more high-strung, but fiery and full of courage."

Comparing women to horses was insufferable—particularly in the preachy lecturing voice Shiloh was using—and Cheney was outraged. "That is the most vulgar compliment I've ever received!" she ranted.

"Welcome." He turned back to the front, unable to hide his grin. "Could you keep it down, Doc? They're getting ready to start."

Shadrach had sheathed his sword and held up his white-gauntleted right hand. He called out a command, unintelligible to Cheney, both because she knew no cavalry commands and because Shadrach's voice had deepened into that growl that military officers seemed always to use when commanding companies of men. Throughout the drill all Cheney could hear was "Hrr-ump! Harr-oom! Herrr-Honn!"

But soon she was no longer listening and only watched. The cadets marched slowly, the horses almost in step, close to the crowd. The horsemen went through several close-quarter steps, sometimes with their stirrups touching the next horseman on either side. Sabers flashed, and Cheney flinched because they were so close it seemed that they would slash each other, but of course they never did. Shadrach wheeled and called, and his horse seemed light and nimble, in spite of its enormous girth. His saber flashed high, pointed toward the sun, and his face was stern and proud.

The lines of men did quarter-turns one way, half-turns back, and then a full about-face, then back to the crowd. Again they dressed, splitting into vertical lines, while one line moved toward the crowd and the next went away from the crowd. The lines formed again, horizontally, and at a single word from Shadrach, they began to sidestep neatly, each horse in perfect step, each line precise, every other line going the opposite way.

Finally came Shadrach's hoarse call for a retreat back down the street, where they quickly reformed into companies, with

Shadrach at the head and his flag bearers now on either side of him.

Shadrach called out a harsh command, and the cadets and horses became quiet and still. Then, Shadrach's voice came on the clear winter air, high and carried by the wind.

"Men!" Shadrach stood up in his stirrups.

Shiloh jerked straight in the saddle. To him it looked and sounded like Nathan Bedford Forrest himself that faced the crowd.

"Sabers!" Shadrach drew his saber, and it flashed like a mirror as he thrust it directly in front of him. Behind him came the deadly whisper of sabers pulled from sheaths. A spiked forest faced the crowd.

"Charge!"

Eighty horsemen, with Shadrach thundering at the head, his flags flying, came at a full gallop toward the crowd. A shriek sounded, and loud gasps, but they were lost in the wild, high cries of the cadets, who came screaming. The sound froze the blood, and the sight took Cheney's breath away. Shiloh's hand came to her bridle, and he muttered something, but she couldn't hear and didn't see. The men rushing toward her filled her eyes and mind.

They came on, closer and closer, and Cheney wanted to shut her eyes but couldn't. Then—at the last possible second—Shadrach called out, "Halt!" His horse stopped immediately and reared in triumph. Behind him eighty horses came to a perfect "sliding stop," throwing up their heads, their hind legs collected and controlled underneath them.

The quiet was unnatural. It seemed that the entire crowd held its breath.

Only ten feet away from them, Shadrach directed his horse into a quarter-turn, so he was facing Shiloh and Cheney. Without a spoken command, the companies made the slight adjustment together, although their horses were still prancing a bit.

Shadrach, with a precise, stiff movement, brought his saber up to his face and called in his normal Forrest voice, "Salute." Each man behind him did the same.

They were saluting Shiloh.

Tears heated Cheney's eyes suddenly, but she didn't care. She turned slightly to look at him. He sat straight, impossibly erect, and his shoulders were very broad. His eyes burned with hot blue flames, and his nostrils were slightly flared. Then, in a gesture so tense and controlled it looked as if he were made of strong metal, Shiloh saluted.

"Sir." Shadrach uttered the one word but held the salute for a few eternal seconds. Then eighty sabers whistled down to the horses' right sides, and Shadrach called quietly, "Dismissed."

The applause and hurrahs were deafening, and the eighty cadets of the Citadel turned into rowdy boys with swords, waving them wildly over their heads, screaming the "Rebel yell" and laughing loudly.

Cheney, Shiloh, and Shadrach were still motionless. Then Shadrach turned his horse again precisely to face Cheney. A single tear had escaped down her cheek, but her face and eyes glowed. Shadrach rode two steps forward and thrust his saber toward her, at an angle so it was pointed slightly over her head.

Cheney never fathomed how she knew exactly what to do, but she did know. Deftly she removed one glove, nodded slightly, and tossed it high into the air. Three lapis lazuli stones glinted dully in the sun.

Shadrach speared it on the point of his saber, and it slid down the length of the curved blade as if it were an oiling cloth. Shadrach retrieved it, drawing it slowly up the length of the saber. He tucked the glove into his belt, made a deep bow to Cheney, and turned to ride away. The crowd scattered before him like chaff in the summer wind.

★   ★   ★   ★

The morning had been saluted, and it was past noon before Shiloh, Cheney, Shadrach, and his flag bearers could extricate themselves from the crowd. All the men wanted to talk to Shadrach and meet Shiloh, but they had a hard time of it because it seemed that large numbers of young women also had a word, or many words, to say to them. Logan Manigault and Maxcy

Roddy stayed absurdly close to Shadrach Forrest Luxton, even when he was on foot and mingling in a lively, happy crowd. Cheney wondered if this was hero worship, or if the three were simply very close friends. Later she found out that it was both, and still more than that.

Alexander Dallas came to greet Cheney immediately after the drill and brought with him the distinguished-looking gentleman with the silver hair whom Cheney had noticed earlier. He was a Dr. Langdon Van Dorn, and Cheney wanted to talk to him about the usual doctor things. But the crowd was too noisy, and the day too beautiful, and the atmosphere too jovial for a serious conversation. Almost immediately after their introduction he was spirited away and Cheney was left alone, for no women had been introduced to her, and Shadrach and Shiloh were surrounded.

To her vague surprise, she found that it didn't really matter to her. She patted and talked to Stocking for a while, and told him he was a very good horse not to have run away in terror while those men were heading toward him in a screaming gray horde.

Suddenly a little boy, towheaded and gregarious, appeared to ask if he could give Stocking an apple. In her customary way of conversing with children—except for Laura Blue—Cheney talked to the boy as if he were an adult, only smaller. He was pompously named St. Croix DeLoche and didn't seem to notice Cheney's awkwardness. A woman's petulant call made him take leave of her and Stocking, although it was a dawdling and reluctant withdrawal.

Finally Shiloh, Cheney, Shadrach, and his two shadows left, cantering north at a spirited trot through the outermost parts of the city. They followed the Ashley River and slowed to a walk along a wide dirt road skirted by acres of cotton fields, their spent remains a jumble of brown sticks in an untidy winter disarray. Harvest had passed, and the time for renewing the earth had not yet come.

"That was magnificent," was Cheney's simple comment to Shadrach.

He nodded, a dignified gesture of acknowledgment, and said, "Thank you, Cheney."

"No," Shiloh murmured. "Thank you."

"Yes," Cheney agreed.

Shadrach smiled.

The small company moved slowly. No fitful, freezing Atlantic gusts blew this far inland, and the sun now had the power to warm them. Shadrach directed them off the main road onto a secondary way that led into a deep, murky wood. The road, however, was broad and well traveled. Birds called, fussed, and sang, and the horses' trappings made comforting sounds of creaking leather and slight metal jingles. The woods smelled of rich black dirt, some swamp, and occasional wafts of pine and cedar.

"Your horse is splendid," Cheney sighed, watching the big white stallion moving along with his exaggerated ballet movements. "Did you gait him yourself?"

"No, he gaited his own self," Shadrach said earnestly, and on the other side of him Shiloh grinned. "My brother sent him to me, along with this saber." He patted the silver sheath at his side.

"Thought that must have been one of General Forrest's sabers," Shiloh said in a teasing voice, "since it's like a razor all the way down."

"Both sides." Logan Manigault's tones of cultured disapproval drifted up to them. "And Shadrach *will* sharpen it all the time."

"No, he doesn't," Maxcy Roddy piped up. "He makes me do it."

"That's right, Private," Shadrach grunted without looking back.

"But I don't understand," Cheney interposed. "I thought swords were supposed to be sharp."

"Cavalry sabers—only at the tip," Shadrach explained. "But Bedford didn't know that, so he always sharpened his."

Suddenly Shiloh recalled—relived—a shard of 1862: the last field of a sixty-mile-long road of blood as Forrest drove what was left of General Sooy Smith's armies in defeat and disarray before him. Vividly in colors of gray and blue, he saw himself standing by his dead horse, looking defiantly up at a Union cavalry soldier, who pointed a Colt .44 at his upturned face. Shiloh could remember only waiting as he stared up at him, still clutching his own empty revolver, hard. Then the scene changed to scarlet as General Forrest thundered by, and with an apparently easy left-handed back swipe, severed the Union soldier's head. Shiloh caught the falling, headless body, grabbed the revolver out of now-dead hands, mounted the horse, and rode off after General Forrest. He couldn't remember exactly what he was thinking then.

Shiloh could see and hear nothing for a few moments as he remembered. He stared off into the deep, private woods silently. Then a movement and a flash of red—real, not remembered—made him sit up straight and narrow his eyes.

"Shiloh?" Cheney said uncertainly. She was facing him and saw his vigilant stance, but Shadrach was turned away from him, talking to Cheney.

"Saw something . . ." he muttered, and suddenly Logan Manigault and Maxcy Roddy were rudely crowding Cheney and Stocking as they tried to move up on each side of Shadrach.

"Get back, you two," he ordered harshly. "There's a little tent town over there, you know that. Probably just some of the colored kids wandering around, and wanting to watch us, like everybody on this planet always does."

Cheney wondered at the weary exasperation of Shadrach's tone, but she was distracted by the thought of anyone sneaking around and watching them, and her anxious gaze never left Shiloh's stiff back.

Manigault and Roddy stubbornly ignored Shadrach's order and kept pushing and shoving—with their horses, that is—until Shiloh relaxed and turned back to face front, shrugging a little. "Don't see anything now," he said easily. "I think it was a man— or two—but maybe it's like Shadrach says, they were just curious."

"You big oaf, if your horse steps on my horse's foot I'm going to bust you down to private," Shadrach said irritably to Logan.

Cheney chuckled, partly with relief and partly in amusement. "That would be devastating, wouldn't it, Mr. Manigault?"

"Yes, ma'am, but if Shadrach was dead he couldn't bust me," Manigault said quietly.

"If you were dead instead of me, it'd make me even madder than if I was dead," Shadrach blustered, somewhat illogically. "And this is a dumb argument anyway, because nobody's going to die. You two are just showing off."

"Had some trouble, have you, Shadrach?" The careless tone of Shiloh's voice was belied by the glint in his blue eyes.

"Everyone has troubles," Shadrach shrugged.

"You're the only cadet who's had that kind of trouble, sir," Cadet Lieutenant Manigault said stubbornly.

"That's right," Private Roddy put in, and Shadrach half turned to frown at him. Roddy swallowed and added, "Sir."

"What trouble?" Cheney demanded.

"Twice Shadrach was attacked," Lieutenant Manigault told her in spite of Shadrach's impatient stop-it gesture. "One night in an alley off Church Street some men tried to pull him off his horse, but that big brute"—he gestured gracefully to Shadrach's horse—"reared up and stepped on their feet and bit two of them, and they left."

"They ran," Shadrach amended with satisfaction, "fast."

"And the other time?" Shiloh asked.

"He was on foot, leaving my house to go back to the Citadel," Logan Manigault said with deep bitterness and helpless regret, "and somebody beat him up. Bad. Dr. Van Dorn was afraid for a while that he wouldn't be able to see out of his right eye."

"That was six months ago, Logan," Shadrach said quietly. "Forget it."

"Who was it?" Shiloh demanded sharply.

Shadrach shrugged. "They hit me from behind with something. Dr. Van Dorn thought it might have been a rifle stock, because he found little wood splinters in my scalp. I never saw them. I never even knew how many there were."

Then Shiloh asked a question, in a careful tone, which

126

Cheney considered irrelevant—at first. "Does General Forrest know?"

Shadrach turned his body toward him, pulled himself straight, and shook his head precisely from one side to the other. "No, sir. He doesn't need to know. I can take care of myself. I can take care of my men. And I must do it alone."

Shiloh watched him carefully as he spoke, then nodded and relaxed. "Good enough," he murmured and turned to face ahead.

The cypress wilderness thinned, and the company mounted a slight rise overlooking wide clear fields for miles in every direction. Ahead of them the road went straight down, then across the nearest field in a straight line, and then climbed a gentle hill. At the top of the hill, silhouetted against the slate blue sky, was the uneven outline of some ruins.

Shadrach pointed. "That's where we're going," he told Cheney. "The old Roddy mansion."

"How beautiful, and how sad it looks," Cheney murmured. Then, with a bright-eyed glance at Shadrach, she said, "Can we run?"

He didn't answer, only flashed her a grin, and the company, as one, flew toward the old Roddy mansion at a reckless all-out gallop.

Close beside her, Cheney was more aware than ever of the massive girth and immense power of Shadrach's horse. Though he set the pace, his hoofbeats were slower, lower, and much louder than the other horses'. His white mane shimmered silver silken waves that glowed in the bright morning. His neck arched beautifully, and even at a gallop his steps were high and proud.

Cheney, bent low over her saddle and grasping her leg-lock desperately, turned to look at Shiloh and saw he was looking at her.

Both were smiling.

BETWEEN BLOOD
P·A·R·T T·W·O
AND BLOOD

If there arise a matter too hard
for thee in judgment,
between blood and blood,
between plea and plea, and
between stroke and stroke...

Deuteronomy 17:8

11

CHARADES

"It is gentle, and lonely, and medieval," Cheney murmured.

"It is all of that now," Shadrach agreed. "I come here often and think about such things."

The old Roddy mansion must have been magnificent once. Dual curving marble staircases, now gray and crumbling, climbed gracefully toward nothing. One corner of the side and front walls remained, with holes where, once upon a time, glass had glittered in eight-foot windows. Jagged teeth of pillars, all different sizes now, were lined across a portico almost buried in leaves and brown twigs and old dust. One massive chimney still stood, though darkened by fire and age, and even though it reached a tremendous height, single bricks had purposely been removed, leaving black cavities.

"It is beautiful," Shadrach said with determined lightness, "and it may be sad, but I don't think it is depressing. Do you, Cheney?"

"Oh no," she replied, shaking her head. "I like it very much."

Shadrach dismounted and took Stocking's bridle to steady him as Cheney dismounted. They decided to leave the horses untethered, and all five mounts companionably wandered into the murky depths of a nearby grove of live oak trees. The gray wisps of Spanish moss looked like ghost-lace for wraith-dresses, moving slightly in the chilly, damp drafts. The horses lowered their heads and began to graze, even though no luscious green was visible beneath the arms of the Augustan trees.

"I thought you'd like this place," Shadrach said with satisfaction, offering Cheney his arm. "Let's have lunch."

"Lunch?" Cheney teased. "I thought Charlestonians had no such thing."

"I'm not a son of Charleston, like Logan and Maxcy," Shadrach scoffed. "I'm an orphan of Charleston."

Shiloh, beside Cheney, made a funny, awkward movement, but the moment slipped by. Though Shadrach seemed to note Shiloh's odd second of discomfort, he continued easily, "I do understand that there is a world somewhere north of Broad Street where people have lunch. Not like Logan and Maxcy. They think 'lunch' is something you feed your horses."

"Aw, Shadrach," Maxcy groaned. Logan merely sniffed.

A round table was set up, with a snowy white tablecloth, in the center of what could have been the great hall. Beside it stood an old man, his skin the color of dark chocolate, in a white jacket. With delight Cheney moved to the table, looking at the enticing food covering it, and the men followed her.

"Dr. Cheney Duvall, may I present to you my servant and lifelong friend, Josiah," Shadrach said warmly. "Josiah, this is Dr. Cheney Duvall."

Cheney offered the small man her hand, which he solemnly bowed over. "Doctah Duvall, it's a real pleasure."

"The pleasure is mine, Josiah. Thank you for coming out here and preparing this for us."

"Happy to, ma'am," he said, smiling up at her. "Happy to."

"Shall we?" Shadrach held out a chair—a straight, plain wooden one—for Cheney. Then he seated himself, and Shiloh, Logan, and Maxcy sat down. As if by signal, all of them bowed their heads for Shadrach's prayer.

"Our Lord Jesus, we thank Thee for this place, and this food, and for Josiah and his labor of love. I am grateful for these, my friends, and ask that you watch over us, and protect us. Amen."

"I like your prayers, Shadrach," Cheney said simply.

"Me, too," Shiloh said, to Cheney's surprise.

"Me, too," Maxcy agreed. "Especially the short ones."

"Be quiet, Private," Lieutenant Logan Manigault ordered, though his eyes smiled. "Miss Duvall's going to think the Citadel is a company of idiots."

"That's impossible," Cheney asserted. "I think the Citadel

and the cadets are wonderful." The three cadets looked pleased, and Maxcy flushed.

Josiah was busily chipping ice from a big block in a tin bucket and filling glasses with lime-lemonade. Cheney turned to Shadrach. "I am a little surprised, after seeing the Federals so much in evidence, that the Citadel is still functional."

"That's only because of Captain Luxton," Logan said quickly before Shadrach could comment. "The bluebellies—pardon me, ma'am—the Union forces occupied the Citadel, first thing. All of our instructors were long gone, and there were only about a hundred of us left."

"I remember that the Citadel usually has four battalions," Shiloh said. "Seven or eight hundred cadets."

"Guess you know where they went," Shadrach said, his eyes searching the far distance. "I was the only one of rank left, and I couldn't go with them. . . ."

"Your brother?" Shiloh asked quietly.

"First my mother," Shadrach answered evenly. "Then my brother agreed with her. I reached fourteen right after our brother—that is, my half brother—Jeffrey was injured and captured. But we thought he had been killed. Bedford wrote me and told me that I would not join the army, that I was to remain at the Citadel."

"I was with them when Major Jeffrey died," Shiloh said. "He was a fine soldier and a good man."

"Yes."

"I lost my older brother LeGare at about the same time," Logan said, "and my father and mother told me that I couldn't join, either, until after I graduated from the Citadel."

"And my mother and father barely let me go to the Citadel anyway," Maxcy sighed. "Much less to fight for the Glorious Cause."

"You were just a kid," Logan declared. "Still are."

"I am not!"

"Such unusual names the men in Charleston have," Cheney interrupted the gathering storm. "I met a boy in town called 'St.

133

Croix DeLoche.' And 'Logan,' and 'LeGare' . . . I like them, though."

Shadrach grinned, " 'Unusual'—that's polite of you, Cheney. I'd never name a child of mine Citadel Por-Shay or Church Street Hu-Gee or Manigault St. Croix Rutledge Roddy—"

"At least," Logan interrupted in his languid manner, "our names aren't funny, dusty ol' Bible names like Meshach or Abednego."

Shadrach stood, frowning darkly. "Sir," he growled, "do not ever cast aspersions on my noble name. Any of them."

Logan jumped up, knocking over his chair, and drawled, "You, suh, have a funny name."

Then Maxcy, grinning like a true idiot, jumped up, and the three moved away from the table with careful steps. Josiah, standing close, rolled his eyes expressively, replaced Logan's chair, and began placing portions of the food on the three boys' plates.

"Shiloh . . ." Cheney murmured.

"Aw, Doc," he drawled. "They're just showin' off."

Sure enough, the three boys who were almost men started shoving each other and calling each other names like "Jezebel" and "Ma-her-shal-al-hash-baz" and "Sooey Huey Hu-gee" and "Seawall Mr. Mudwater" and "Logan Many-Vaults." Then Shadrach drew his saber, and a loud, confusing, triple mock sword fight ensued, ending when Shadrach swatted Maxcy's round behind.

Cheney and Shiloh were laughing, while Josiah stood behind them, shaking his head and trying to hide his grin.

They came back to the table, red-faced and breathing hard, and Shadrach trumpeted, "I won! I delivered the killing blow to Maxcy's posterior!"

"Gosh, Shadrach, she's a lady," Maxcy admonished him.

"I have heard the term," Cheney said innocently, "though it's only because I'm a doctor."

The boys began to eat while Josiah rumbled menacingly, "You boys ack like a bunch o' wild rootin' hogs. You ain't leavin' this table agin, or I'll take up the food. Now talk nice. This here's a real lady."

With chuckles quickly quelled by a stern look from Josiah, the three cadets assumed their former politeness and ate. The food was delicious, Cheney reflected, a perfect lunch. The cucumber sandwiches were lavishly slathered with rich mayonnaise, and the cucumbers were sliced wafer-thin and were liberally salted and peppered. Fresh apples, green with a peach blush, were expertly peeled and quartered by Josiah as the diners requested. Paper-thin slices of roasted beef, heavily spiced, were cut into diamond shapes and piled high on a platter. They drank thirstily of the tangy lime-lemonade and then had bon-bons with hot tea from silver flasks.

"Mmm, these bon-bons are sinful," Cheney said, licking melted chocolate from one finger. "Did you make these yourself, Josiah?"

"Yes, ma'am," he said modestly. "I'm glad you like 'em. I cain't hardly keep 'em aroun', with them eatin' pack o' rats at the Citydel. I hadda hide these in a boot box to git 'em outen there safe."

Shadrach, Cheney, and Shiloh all laughed, while Logan and Maxcy exchanged puzzled looks. Dr. Duvall had actually addressed the servant while they ate, as Shadrach sometimes did. Logan Manigault shrugged. Maybe ignoring the servants during a meal was a Charleston thing, too.

Cheney turned to Maxcy Roddy. "Mr. Roddy, Shadrach says this is the old Roddy mansion. I hope it was not your home?"

"No, ma'am," he answered, glancing at Shadrach as if for guidance. "This Mr. Roddy was my great-fifth-cousin. But my father is trying to reclaim this land."

This evidently was comprehensible to the men, but Cheney couldn't understand and, in her usual manner, questioned him directly. "Reclaim it? What exactly do you mean, Mr. Roddy?"

Maxcy Roddy took a long drink of lime-lemonade. His pale blue eyes were still focused on Shadrach, who gave no sign that Cheney could identify. As Maxcy explained to Cheney, he kept darting glances toward Shadrach, "Mr. Hamilton Roddy's slaves revolted and burned this house in 1842, Dr. Duvall. Mrs. Alana Manigault Roddy and her four children managed to escape, with the help of a small group of the house slaves. They moved to New Orleans. Now the Freedmen's Bureau is trying to say that these are abandoned Rebel lands, and there is talk of dividing all eight thousand acres among the freedmen." He shrugged. "The land, on record, belongs to Hamilton Roddy III, but he is a minor who lives in New Orleans. So my father is attempting to reestablish rights to the land for the Roddy family."

"Mr. Roddy was never found," Shadrach said in brittle voice. "And because of that slave insurrection the Citadel was founded."

Everyone, including Josiah, looked around the ruins, their thoughts upon the ghosts that lingered here. Cheney thought with a slight shiver that she wouldn't want to be here alone at night.

"I . . . I . . . just wondered about it," Cheney said awkwardly. "This is the only evidence of burning I've seen here. Not like Atlanta must be."

"Or Columbia, our capital," Logan said quickly. "Sherman burned it to the ground."

"But Sherman's greatest insult was to Charleston, you know," Shadrach said, his voice now a lyric tenor. "First he had the bad taste to declare Savannah, Georgia, too pretty to burn, but said Charleston was just a desolate ruin. Then he had the vulgar gall to ignore us and march right on up to Columbia and burn it as though it were important or something."

"Aw, Shadrach," Maxcy said, "you love Charleston and you know it, and I don't care what you say."

"Yes, I do," he said simply. "Even though I'm not sure Charleston loves me."

"Of course we do," Logan argued. "You're the reason we still have the Citadel and the Gray Cadets." He turned to Cheney and spoke with more animation than Cheney had yet seen from him. "Shadrach was the one who organized the leading men of Charleston and made them apply to General Hatch to reopen the Citadel."

"General Hatch isn't bad," Shadrach shrugged. "And I think he likes being the president."

"Only time the men have gotten together and asked the Yanks for anything," Logan went on, "and it's the only time General Hatch went against Judge Granger, who had an unholy fit. Said we'd be unruly and a bad influence, and that the Citadel was a rebel monument that needed to be torn down brick by brick." With relish he finished, "But General Hatch got his back up and politely informed Judge Granger that this was a military matter, not a Freedmen's Bureau matter, and that the Citadel would stay. Forever."

"As long as you and Maxcy and all of you fools behave yourselves," Shadrach said grimly. "Never forget. We have to be perfect gentlemen, upright in every sense, law-abiding and honest. And always, without fail, we must treat everyone—everyone—with respect."

"We remember, Shadrach," Maxcy said in a subdued voice. "Honest."

"Never forget," he said sternly.

Then he turned to Cheney with deliberation and said, "That is the most fetching riding habit I've ever seen, Cheney. You look stunning."

"Thank you so much," she smiled and touched the brim of her hat. "This is my most favorite hat, and I happen to know"—she made a small smug face at Shiloh—"that it is called a Hardee hat, named after your illustrious General William Joseph Hardee."

"Listen to that!" Shiloh groaned. "She knows who General Hardee is because of her little bonnet—but she'd never heard of General Nathan Bedford Forrest!"

Shadrach chuckled, but Maxcy and Roddy turned to Cheney with undisguised astonishment. "I didn't say I'd never heard of him!" she exclaimed. "I finally remembered because of something Rissy said—that I had heard of him, about Fort Pillow!"

A stunned silence greeted her teasing words, and Cheney drew back when she saw the looks on the men's faces. Logan Manigault's face grew white with anger; Maxcy Roddy looked as if he would burst into tears; Shadrach winced painfully; and Shiloh looked as sad as a maiden's funeral.

"It's okay, Doc," he said softly and gave her a little smile. "It's just—hard, when something like that is all that people remember about us. What did you hear about Fort Pillow?"

"I j-just remembered reading—some years back—that General Nathan Bedford Forrest had . . . had . . . conquered or overrun or whatever they call it—Fort Pillow."

"Massacred it," Shadrach said, clenching his jaw. "That's what they called it. They said that the fort surrendered, and Bedford went in anyway and massacred all the Negro soldiers and their women and children, and the white soldiers, too." He spoke evenly, but his eyes were narrowed with anger. "In 1864 a congressional committee pronounced that he was a criminal who was guilty of murder. They've never gotten around to arresting Bedford, although there's still much publicity concerning it."

"Oh," Cheney said in a small voice.

"Wish they would've asked me about it," Shiloh said tightly. All eyes homed in on him.

"I was there," he went on harshly. "Don't believe everything you read in the papers. I don't want to talk about it, but I'll tell you this: the commanding officer of Fort Pillow refused our terms, and there was no surrender. What happened after that was a battle. General Forrest said: 'War means fightin', and fightin' means killin'.' He never, ever gave us speeches about *dying* for the Glorious Cause. He taught us about *killing* for the Cause. And people got killed."

A long silence ensued. Everyone stared into space, and Cheney was frowning with so much concentration that her face hurt. This part of Shiloh—*the killing part*, she harshly named it to herself—was very difficult for her to understand.

"Let's play charades," Shiloh said suddenly.

Logan, Maxcy, and Shadrach brightened immediately, in the manner of young men brushing away distant sorrows.

"All . . . all right," Cheney agreed, desperately trying to recover.

Shiloh stood and propped his hands on his hips. "This is gonna be fun, Doc. You gotta help me."

"All right, I will," Cheney said with a weak smile. "Come here and tell me what it is."

"Nope. I can't tell you. It's a secret."

"But you can't keep it a secret from me, you goof! Not if I'm supposed to help you!" It seemed Cheney had fully recovered.

"Just do what I tell you, okay?" Shiloh grinned devilishly. "For once? It'll be fun, I promise you. We'll get to play with our guns," he wheedled.

"I thought you weren't supposed to play with guns," Maxcy said nervously.

"Be quiet, Private," Logan said in his bored aristocrat's voice, but he looked eager.

"Great!" Shadrach said excitedly. "I've noticed that you have a Colt six-shot. Can't I help you, Shiloh?"

Shiloh shook his head. "Nope, you gotta guess what we are. But we can shoot a little bit afterwhile if y'all want to."

"Of course we can!" Cheney said brightly. "Both Shiloh and I always carry plenty of powder and shot."

Logan and Maxcy regarded her with wonder. Unquestionably, there was no woman like Dr. Cheney Duvall in Charleston. Maybe not in all of South Carolina. Maybe not in the whole South.

"First charades, though," Shadrach ordered. "I just thought of a good one. But you two go first."

Shiloh fetched both his and Cheney's guns and checked them to make sure they weren't loaded. Then, carefully, he passed them to Shadrach. "Check 'em."

Shadrach repeated Shiloh's careful actions: he squinted into the barrel, cocked the breech, stared down the chambers, blew into them, and snapped the breech shut. Then he went through everything with the other gun. Logan and Maxcy watched him with envy. Cadets weren't allowed any sidearms. They only had sabers.

"Check," Shadrach said crisply, handing Cheney and Shiloh their guns.

"Doc"—Shiloh gave her a come-hither gesture—"Look, I'm just putting on the percussion caps. See?"

"Oh, I see," Cheney said with sudden understanding. "They'll make a noise, yes?"

"They'll pop, kinda loud. But you know they're not loaded, and you know neither of us is in any danger." Shiloh looked at her, frowning darkly.

Cheney's heart began to pulse a little faster, but her voice was calm. "Yes, I understand."

"Okay. You stand back there, about ten paces." Cheney obediently turned and went to where Shiloh had pointed. She faced the piece of wall that was left of the old mansion.

Shiloh stepped behind the wall. Shadrach, Logan, Maxcy, and Josiah gathered behind and to the left of him, so they had a clear view of both Cheney and Shiloh.

Shiloh's head popped around the wall. "Ready, everyone? Ready, Doc?"

"Yes," she called.

"Okay. Now start walking toward me, and take a shot at me with every other step you take. Got it?"

"Right!" Her heart began to pound. Cheney had shot her gun many times, at many inanimate objects, and it was always exhilarating and somewhat nerve-wracking. Pointing a gun at Shiloh—even though she knew it was not loaded—and pulling the trigger made her mouth dry and her palms wet. In spite of the cool dampness of the day, Cheney all at once felt heated and clammy.

"Go!"

Cheney took a step, raised the gun, cocked the hammer— and Shiloh leaned out from behind the wall and shot directly at her. The sound from the percussion cap was nothing like a real gunshot, but Cheney almost dropped flat to the ground in shock.

Instead, she shot at Shiloh's head and kept walking.

He returned the fire.

Cheney flinched visibly but took a steady step and shot.

Shiloh leaned around the wall and coldly shot at her.

140

Cheney shot, drawing ever closer to him. She had stopped breathing.

Shiloh shot.

Cheney shot.

Another.

Another.

Cheney had reached the wall. Shiloh stepped out in front of her, shot point-blank at her, dropped the gun, and put his hands up. "I—"

Cheney shot him.

"—surrender," he finished quietly.

Cheney's eyes widened. Then she dropped her gun from nerveless fingers and took a long, shuddering breath.

Shadrach's whisper sounded loud in the silence. "Fort Pillow."

Shiloh stood very close to Cheney. He smiled and took her two trembling hands and enclosed them in his warm, rough ones. "Yes," he whispered hoarsely, looking deep into her eyes. "Fort Pillow, and every other battle I ever saw. Thanks, Doc," he said in a voice as warm and soothing as a bath scented with lavender. "You were wonderful."

★ ★ ★ ★

When everyone recovered from Shiloh's charade, they returned to the table to thirstily drink more lime-lemonade, while Maxcy gobbled two more bon-bons. Only three were left.

"Leave those alone," Shadrach ordered sternly. "You'll get too chubby to ride your horse."

"You just want them all to yourself, Shadrach," Logan said, greedily snatching another one. "Admit it."

Shadrach grumbled, "Do all captains have to put up with this disorderly conduct?"

"Yes," Shiloh answered. "I made sure they did. It's a sergeant's job."

"Lieutenant's job," Logan Manigault said, though the words came out sticky and rather muddled.

"I want to see Shadrach's charade," Cheney decided. Another bon-bon had helped her to recover from the soul-wringing play in which she had just starred.

"I want to do Mr. Irons' charade," Maxcy said stoutly.

"You can't do that one, Maxcy," Shadrach explained patiently. "We already know what it is."

"But I want me and Dr. Duvall to shoot at each other," he said stubbornly.

"No you don't," Shiloh said smartly. "She's a dead-eye shot. Kilt me with the first shot, she would've."

Three pairs of young, envious, marveling eyes trained on her. Modestly she said, "Thank you, Shiloh."

"Welcome. Now, I want to see Shadrach's charade. I'm so good at this game," he said airily, "I can probably guess it before he does it."

"Nope," Shadrach said, unable to contain his grin. "And even if you do, keep it to yourself. You'll want to see it anyway."

He turned and gave a sharp whistle, and the ground shook as his horse came thundering up close; right into the great hall, and close by the table. The horse took no notice of anything or anyone but Shadrach and nuzzled his chest so affectionately Shadrach was almost knocked down. "Wait a minute," he said with mock irritation. "Get back, you big ninny."

To everyone's amusement, Sock and Stocking and Logan's and Maxcy's horses suddenly came herding up, too, which made Shadrach's horse so happy he knocked over two chairs and almost upset the table. Mass confusion reigned in the great hall of the Roddy mansion for a few moments. Josiah loudly offered advice to the five exasperated horse owners. Finally, with pieces of apple, they bribed and coaxed the horses into calming down and moving off a bit.

"All right, I'm ready," Shadrach said. "Watch."

He moved to the off side of the horse and put his shako on his head; only it was backward, with the strap dangling down his neck and the plume floating out behind. Then he mounted easily. This, of course, meant that he was facing backward. The horse never moved or even shifted his great, round hooves. Shadrach frowned blackly off into the distance, then leaned over

142

and grabbed a large hank of silver horse tail and pulled it up sharply. Drawing his saber, he pointed it forward—or backward, as it was. "Charge!" he shrieked. The horse, with a bored look, began to back up.

Shiloh, Cheney, Logan, and Maxcy were laughing so hard that guesses were impossible. Finally, with tears in his eyes, Shiloh managed to grunt, "Poor old Gen-Gen'ral B-Brax-ton B-Bragg! It was j-just all too confusing for h-him!"

Shadrach whooped and waved his sword in a big circle over his head. "Charge, you horsy coward! Coward horsy! Charge, I say!" The horse kept taking patient, careful steps backward.

Maxcy seemed to be having a most peculiar fit of the type normally called "conniptions," but Cheney decided he was trying to say something. With great effort he grunted, "No, it's the . . . Captain . . . his own . . . self! It's . . . the Troop Leader . . . of the . . . Left-Handed Backward Brigade!" Suddenly he sat down, rather hard, gulping great lumps of laughter.

"You're both right!" Shadrach shouted and jumped off the horse with one easy leap. The horse watched him with great, liquid, pitying eyes.

From a slight distance behind them, Josiah muttered to himself, "White folks sho' do play some funny games."

"They tortured me unmercifully, Doctor Cheney," Shadrach said sorrowfully. " 'Your bandolier goes the wrong way! Your saber's flappin' in the breeze on the wrong side! You're signaling with the wrong hand! Messes up our lines!' I had to learn how to do everything backward."

"Forward, you mean," Logan said, still chuckling.

"Maybe to you," Shadrach said with an exaggerated sigh. "Now you do one, Logan."

"I don't think—"

"That's an order," Shadrach said.

"Yes, sir," Logan sighed, then came to bow deeply in front of Cheney. "Dr. Duvall, I, too, am obliged to beg for your assistance."

"I'm not going to shoot at you, Mr. Manigault," Cheney asserted.

Logan grinned. He had nice, small, even white teeth, and a lazy smile that probably had already broken grown women's hearts. "I appreciate that, Dr. Duvall," he said smoothly. "What I require is—if I may—?"

He leaned over one inch. Cheney saw what he wanted and moved close to him so he could whisper. Giggling, she responded, "Of course. I shall be happy to render this assistance, sir." She turned to the other three, who were watching them curiously—Maxcy with a touch of envy—and said, "If you will excuse us, please, gentlemen." All three bowed.

Cheney and Logan Manigault went behind the ruined wall, Cheney bringing Stocking with her. Soon she returned, hatless, and turned her back to the other three men to watch.

Shiloh observed the straight line of her back, the pleasing set of her head and shoulders, her small waist. Then he looked at her hair. Smoothly coifed in a chignon, it seemed at first as black velvet. When she moved, the hidden fire-depths glinted. Her neck was slender and long, and the back of it was creamy white, with little tendrils of auburn hair delicately brushing it. Shiloh found he had an insane but strong impulse to step up behind her and caress the back of her neck and feel those soft curls.

Cheney reached up and, in an unconsciously feminine, sensual gesture, touched the back of her neck with two slender fingers. She found a dark curl, and with a long, slow movement she smoothed it out straight. Then it flowed back up into a soft wisp of curl.

For a moment Shiloh felt as if something had sucked the breath out of his powerful lungs. *I can read her mind—say things sometimes before she does—without trying; but surely she can't . . . read . . . feel . . . my touch. . . ?* Shiloh was so darkly bemused that he almost missed Logan Manigault's less-than-grand entrance.

He came around the wall, perched on Cheney's sidesaddle, swinging his free leg, with the single stirrup flapping. His other long leg angled up around the leg-lock, and he was assiduously polishing his boot with a handkerchief. He had pulled a thick strand of his long hair around and onto his top lip, and he kept it in place by mushing up his mouth. Humming a little ditty, he appeared to notice a spot on his saber-sheath, frowned, and began to polish it. Cheney's hat was perched on the very top of his head—it was, of course, much too small for him—and occasionally with one long-fingered hand he stroked the feathers that curled around his ear.

Again the four players shouted with laughter. Finally Shadrach managed to gasp out, "Got to be General George Armstrong Custer. Best-dressed soldier in any man's—or woman's—army!" This made Shiloh and Maxcy laugh even harder, and then Logan could no longer keep his careful pose. His mustache fell down, and—inadvertently—his leg came out as he laughed, and then he banged it against Stocking's side.

Now, Stocking was normally a patient horse, and he could carry a rider, either male or female, all day long. But a man sitting sideways on him in a lopsided saddle, and then kicking him with a heavy boot and a sharp spur was just too much. He bucked, once, with great deliberation, and then stood still. Logan Manigault sailed through the air. As he crashed to the ground, he rolled instinctively. But then he lay still—very still.

Cheney ran. She touched him, turned him over, and his face was red—but it was not from injury. He burst out laughing, and the other three men did, too. "Help me, please, doctor," he gasped, reaching up for her.

Cheney stood up, crossed her arms, frowned ferociously, and prodded him gently with her soft boot. "Perhaps," she said calmly, "I should've shot you after all, Mr. Manigault."

12

NIGHT WHISPERS

With unfettered joy the three cadets from the Citadel took Cheney's and Shiloh's guns and shot to pieces several tree limbs, massive old live oak branches that had fallen on the still-gracious Roddy grounds.

After all the powder and shot were gone, sword fights commenced. Cheney and Shiloh fought fiercely.

"Pax!" Cheney shouted angrily. "You're cheating, Shiloh! We're supposed to be practicing saber-thrusts, and that was clearly a broadsword swing!"

"All is fair in war, Cheney," Shiloh told her gravely. Almost as an afterthought he added, "And love."

Cheney said no more.

Then the horses and horsemen—Cheney and Stocking and Shiloh and Sock included—learned and practiced the close-quarter lateral half step that Shadrach taught them.

Dusk was gently cloaking the old Roddy mansion when everyone reluctantly agreed to break up the party. The air had grown wintry. Shiloh fetched Josiah's cart—it had been discreetly hidden away from the partygoers' eyes—and everyone helped load up the leftover food and the tables and chairs. Josiah started back for town while the riders wandered the grounds, crunching crackly brown leaves under their boots and saying their farewells to the day and the old ruin.

Cheney took the time to look around one last time and imprint this wonderful, haunted place in her memory forever. Shadrach and Shiloh stood apart, staring at the remains of the mansion in the waning light and talking quietly. Logan and Maxcy withdrew to a discreet distance but stayed behind Shadrach.

The five made their way back toward Charleston in the same military formation in which they had come. Beside Cheney, Shadrach's horse glimmered silver in the gathering darkness. "Shadrach," Cheney asked, "what is your horse's name?"

He answered softly, stroking the horse's muscular neck, "His name is Israfel."

Cheney started and turned to stare at him. "Israfel?" she repeated. "Of the poem by Edgar Allan Poe?"

"Yes," he answered, puzzled at her reaction. "I like his poetry very much. I put one stanza of the poem in the note I sent you." Then he quoted:

> "In Heaven a spirit doth dwell
> 'Whose heartstrings are a lute';
> None sing so wildly well
> As the angel Israfel . . ."

"Do you know the poem, Cheney?" he asked.

"I just recognized the name . . . Israfel," Cheney murmured thoughtfully. "But . . . I . . . it's rather a coincidence. . . ."

Shadrach waited patiently as she faltered. In the grayness he could see that Cheney searched Shiloh's face for some sign or reading, but finally she turned back to him. "I'm looking for a— friend," she said. "A man who is very fond of Edgar Allan Poe. I . . . we . . . I thought perhaps he might . . . be here. In Charleston."

"Yes?" Shadrach said politely.

"Yes." Cheney was uncomfortable, as she had just told a lie, but could not tell the truth. Jane Anne Blue had asked that Cheney be discreet, and not embarrass her husband in any way, or discuss their problems with anyone. Finally Cheney sighed and said simply, "I'm looking for a man named Allan Blue."

Behind her, even over the crickets and night whispers and horses' slow footfalls, Cheney heard Logan Manigault draw in a sharp breath, and Maxcy Roddy burst out, "Al—"

Shadrach made no sign, did not change his expression or tone, but managed to negate his two companion's telltale outbursts immediately. "Allan Blue," he repeated. "I have heard that name and know something of it. How well do you know Mr. Blue, Dr. Duvall?"

Cheney perceived the cool use of her title instead of her first name, and realized that Shadrach, too, was being discreet about something or someone. And now she must answer a perfectly reasonable question: How well did she know Allan Blue?

"I . . . I . . . " she faltered and shot Shiloh a despairing glance, but his profile, clean and clear even in the growing darkness, was impassive. He did not move or look at her. "Shadrach," she finally sighed, "I do not know him. I have never met him. And I am not at liberty to explain why, but I do need to talk to him."

Now Shadrach turned to search Shiloh's face, whose expression did not change. It was as if he could neither see nor hear the riders beside him. Shadrach turned back to Cheney. "Dr. Duvall, may I inquire if your business with this man is personal?" he asked in a judge's impartial tone.

"Yes. It is." Cheney knew this sounded very odd, but she could think of nothing else to say.

Shadrach turned to face forward, and Cheney glanced at him out of the corner of her eye. On the other side of Shadrach, Shiloh's profile was outlined in the darkness. The two—though they looked nothing alike—had expressions that were strangely identical, their mouths set tightly, their eyes narrowed. Finally Shadrach turned back to face Cheney. "Dr. Duvall, you say you are unable to break a confidence in inquiring about this man, and I respect that—and you. I, too, for reasons that I am not at liberty to divulge, am guarding a certain confidence."

Cheney heard a sigh of relief from behind her.

"Allan Blue is dead," Logan Manigault said complacently.

Now Shiloh turned sharply, though his expression was guarded. Cheney cried softly, "Oh no . . . Oh no! This is . . . this is . . ."

To their surprise, Shadrach barked, "Be silent, Lieutenant! This is none of your concern!" He turned to Cheney, his face grim. "Cheney, you need to speak to a man called Captain E. Allan Perry. He will, if he chooses, be able to tell you about Mr. Blue."

Cheney's mind was whirling, and her thoughts refused to order themselves properly, and torrents of pity washed over her at the thought of Jane Anne Blue's poor lost husband dying before he had a chance to know of his family. Tears burned her eyes, and she couldn't speak.

Shiloh, in a tight voice, finally muttered, "E. Allan Perry. I'm no genius, but wasn't that the name that Edgar Allan Poe used when he came to Charleston in 1827 and joined the army?"

Cheney grasped this, weakly. "But . . . that's right! What . . . what . . . are you saying, Shadrach. . . ?"

"I'm saying, Cheney," Shadrach said in a kindly tone, but painstakingly emphasizing each word, "that the man you need to speak to is a man called Captain E. Allan Perry. You will find him in the Van Dorn Memorial Hospital."

"But . . . in the . . . but . . ."

Cheney never finished her question.

A loud, familiar crack split the dusky air. Ahead of her Cheney saw a wet splatter of mud fly up.

Shiloh jerked, wheeled Sock, and raced off into the woods.

Shadrach kicked Israfel, and he thundered off behind Sock. Logan Manigault courageously reached out and tried to grab the horse's bridle and shouted, "No!" But Israfel disdainfully tossed his mighty head, and the force of it almost knocked Logan out of the saddle.

"Stay with her, Maxcy!" Logan ordered harshly, then followed behind Shadrach and disappeared into the falling darkness.

Cadet Private Maxcy Roddy jumped off his horse, moved around to Cheney, and grabbed Stocking's bridle, hard. "Dismount, Dr. Duvall," he ordered in a no-nonsense soldier's voice.

"Wha—"

"Dismount! Now!"

Cheney slid from the saddle. Now she and Maxcy Roddy stood between the two horses, in a secret and safe place. Cheney found Maxcy's sturdy presence as comforting as if he had been a grown, hardened veteran. Indeed, his features, in the failing light, looked as if he had aged much in the last few moments.

"Why?" Cheney whispered hoarsely. "Why would anyone shoot at us?"

"Not us." Maxcy's voice was rough. "At Captain Luxton."

"But why?" Cheney repeated helplessly. "Because he's from the Citadel?"

He turned to look at her. "Shadrach Forrest Luxton *is* the Citadel."

★   ★   ★   ★

Shiloh Irons rode headlong through the dangerous darkness, giving Sock his head to swerve sharply and avoid tree trunks that seemed to leap up in front of them. Much of this forest was pine, so the undergrowth was negligible, and the horse's steps were muted in thick, fragrant pine needle carpeting.

Behind him, Shiloh heard the unmistakable slow thunder of Shadrach's horse. Within two or three more strides, Shiloh's sharp ears picked out a startling snap of a twig that had been stepped on in front of him, and he also became aware of the noise of another horse behind Shadrach. With a grunted curse he slowed Sock down. Clear visions of three blind horsemen falling into a great tangle when they all either smashed into a tree, or each other, made him cautious.

Sock still trotted, and Shiloh heard the other two horses forming up in a line behind him. Then ahead and to his left he saw firelight, and he spurred Sock into another reckless gallop, with Shadrach and Logan close behind.

They burst into the very small clearing from which fire beckoned them. Ahead of them a man skidded to a stop, turned, and pointed a rifle at them. Three more men jumped up and grabbed at the unmistakable outline of a stand of muskets, and then Shiloh, Shadrach, and Logan, in a close line, faced four rifles. In the flickering firelight they could see that the men were Negroes, dressed in layers of rags, but they couldn't make out their faces. The rifles were held up to their eyes.

Shiloh's gun—somehow—was out. Lowering his left forearm to his saddle horn, he leaned negligently over his saddle, a deceptively casual pose that allowed him to aim clearly. He took

150

dead aim at another muscular Negro man who had come out of a ragged tent to the left of the four riflemen.

"The second shot that's fired," Shiloh said conversationally, "is going to kill you, mister."

The stillness and quietness that followed his calm words made all the men in the scene feel oddly self-conscious. Shiloh alone seemed relaxed and confident. Beside him Shadrach's eyes widened, but instantly the young captain recovered and made himself sit still and not move or turn to Shiloh. Logan jumped when Shiloh spoke, and then turned in astonishment, but even he recovered quickly. He was privately but still embarrassingly grateful—to God or himself or someone—that he did not blurt out his first thought: that Shiloh was acting like an idiot—because that gun was not loaded—because he and Shadrach and Maxcy had used up all the powder and shot . . .

"Me?" the man grunted and narrowed his eyes. "I ain't even armed." But he made a very slight motion to the four men, and though they did not lower their rifles, Shiloh, Shadrach, and Logan all sensed that their fingers had relaxed on the triggers.

"What you want?" the man demanded harshly. "What you think you're doin', ridin' in on a man's camp like this?"

"Someone shot a rifle at us back there," Shiloh answered reasonably. "We thought we'd better come see about it." His eyes were slits, and though his gun was trained on the big man who held no rifle, his gaze burned on the first man they had seen when they rode in—the one who was still out of breath. "You know anything about it?" Shiloh demanded, now with careless arrogance. "Yeah, you, mister. Noticed you came running in just ahead of us."

The man, who was wearing a bright red flannel shirt, muttered, "I wuz down to the crick fishin'."

"With a rifle?" Shiloh asked with a smile that never touched his eyes.

The big man whom Shiloh targeted took a step forward, his hands propped on his hips. "I'm Caleb Blood Roddy, and this heah's my land. I'm tired of you white men ridin' through heah and tearin' up our camp an' skeerin' our women and children!

You men's trespassin'! Trespassers kin git shot!"

The deep satin of Logan Manigault's voice had grown rough. "Caleb Blood! But you're no Roddy!"

Shadrach spoke, and his voice was calm and quiet. "Caleb Blood Roddy—I know who you are. Your father was hung for the murder of Hamilton Roddy, and now you take his name, and claim his land?"

"I know who you are, *Captain*," he spat. "With a murderin' brother like yours, you ain't got no call to be talkin' 'bout my daddy!"

The fire reflected oddly in the mirror of the clear gray depths of Shadrach's eyes. He drew his saber—slowly—and laid it across his saddle, and Shiloh noted with interest that the four armed men all flinched slightly, though Caleb Blood did not. *Oh, well,* he said to himself, *guess that's no worse a bluff than your empty gun, Irons. . . .*

"Tell your men to stand down, Blood," Shadrach ordered.

In the silence that followed, the click of Shiloh cocking the hammer of his gun sounded loud. Long moments passed.

"Ground those arms," Blood finally growled, his eyes never leaving Shadrach. Caleb Blood Roddy was a powerful man who moved quickly, and now he crossed his arms across his chest in a smooth, haughty gesture. His face was strong, his eyes flashing with dark lights, his full mouth compressed into a straight line as he faced Shadrach Forrest Luxton.

The men lowered their rifles but did not loose their grips. Pointedly Shiloh eased down the hammer of his gun and lowered it slightly to point to the ground, but he did not holster it.

"I don't want anyone to get hurt," Shadrach said evenly, "so we're going to take our leave."

"Think you better," Blood grunted, "before someone does git hurt." His tone left no doubt as to who he thought would be the injured party, but his eyes flickered fractionally toward Shiloh. Shiloh saw it. Shadrach saw it. And Blood knew it, too late.

Shadrach went on, his tone now laced with a quiet, deliberate menace. "But first I want to know if you hurt my servant."

Shiloh didn't comprehend this, but he didn't turn to look at Shadrach or change his expression. Quickly he reviewed the peripherals of the scene: the fire, with two squirrels and a rabbit hung on a wooden spit; barely visible tents and shelters gathered around; the child who had scurried into the darkness when they rode in; the three men, who had been squatting and eating some food laid out on a—that was it. They were eating diamond-shaped squares of roast beef. A bowl held green apples. A pitcher held lime-lemonade. A bucket held a big chunk of ice wrapped in white linen and packed in sawdust.

Shiloh pulled the gun halfway up.

Blood, seemingly unafraid, took another step forward. "Ain't nobody hurt yore poor little slave, *Forrest* boy. We ain't gonna hurt no Negroes, even if they are poor ignorants who don't know we been set free. My boys ast him for some food, and he give it to 'em, and then went on his way."

Shadrach appeared to consider this, his eyes taking in the scene. "Yes, Josiah would have given you the food, as I would have." Blood looked confused for a moment, and Shadrach's voice dropped until it was a barely audible monotone. "But Josiah would not have willingly given you my mother's silver bowl and crystal pitcher. You may keep the food—"

"We don't need your stinkin' charity!" Blood snarled.

Shadrach smiled, and it wasn't exactly pleasant, and he continued in the same tone as if the man had not spoken. "—but I hope you did not harm my servant, Blood. Or I will be back, and I will demand an accounting."

Blood's hands went down to his sides, and his fists clenched into big black lumps. The rifles came back up. Shiloh's gun came back up. Shadrach never moved. Logan's thin nostrils were white, and his long-fingered, sensitive right hand moved slowly to draw his saber and lay it across his saddle.

"Git outta here," Blood said in a deadly voice.

Shadrach seemed not to notice Blood's fury, or the four rifles that were pointed now only at him. "I want that silver bowl, and I want that crystal pitcher. Now."

Again the silence was overwhelming. The four riflemen, now

behind Blood, tightened their shoulders and shuffled their feet slightly apart, and one of them closed one eye as he sighted on Shadrach. Shiloh said to himself, *You might die, and you promised to take Caleb Blood Roddy with you . . . might be able to jump on him and break his neck real quick . . . if they shoot Shadrach first. . . .*

"You die second, Blood," he said again calmly.

To all of the men, hours and days passed, wheeling around them, the blood roaring in their ears, their hearts hammering.

Blood turned, stalked to the food, dumped the apples onto the ground, threw the lemonade to the side, and walked deliberately back to Shadrach's horse. Taking a stance in front of Israfel, he said, "You come down here and git these, *Forrest* boy. I ain't waitin' on no white man niver again."

"No," Shadrach said flatly. "You stole them. You hand them back to me, like a man."

Shiloh cocked the hammer of his useless gun again, but now his thoughts were savage and triumphant. *If we live I'll have to tell Shadrach . . . he's just like Bedford Forrest! Go ahead, Shadrach, make 'em drink the bitter cup, and then crunch the dregs and choke 'em down!*

With an inarticulate snarl, Blood thrust the bowl and the pitcher up to Shadrach, who took first the bowl and slowly turned to Logan to hand it to him. Logan, as if in an uneasy dream, sheathed his saber and took the shining silver bowl. Then, with maddening deliberation, Shadrach turned back to take the pitcher and held it out to Logan.

Blood stepped back, his face ugly. Shadrach sheathed his saber, then held out his hand toward Logan. Fumbling, he handed back the pitcher to Shadrach and clutched the big silver bowl to his chest.

Shadrach nodded to Blood, took up Israfel's reins, and began to back the big horse. Shiloh, still holding his gun at the ready, backed Sock, and Logan's horse backed in step with them. When they neared the tree line Shiloh whispered, "Take off. I'll cover."

Shadrach muttered out of the corner of his mouth, "Why don't I just point this crystal pitcher at them, and cover you? It would be just as good as that gun."

"Shadrach," Shiloh managed between gritted teeth, "turn that horse and run! That's an order!"

Logan dashed off, then Shadrach and Israfel turned and disappeared. Shiloh called out to the five men, now black man-shapes outlined in the lurid firelight, "I get real scared when I hear noises in the dark woods, boys! Sure hope I don't hear anything or see anything on the way back to Charleston! I might shoot first and look to see who I accidentally killed afterward!"

With that he wheeled his horse and disappeared from Caleb Blood Roddy's view.

13

HUNTERS

"Mount up, Dr. Duvall."

This time Cheney heeded Maxcy Roddy's orders without hesitating. Faintly they could hear riders coming through the woods, like faraway thunder from a gathering storm.

After assisting Cheney into her saddle, Maxcy mounted, drew his saber, laid it across his saddle, and maneuvered his horse around behind her. "I believe those riders we hear coming are Captain Luxton and Lieutenant Manigault and Mr. Irons," he said steadily, "but if they are not, I want you to ride fast and hard back to town, and don't stop."

Cheney considered him but could not see his features in the darkness. Her fear had become anger, and her stubbornness grew stronger every moment. *I will do no such thing!* was her first thought. Her nostrils flaring, her cheeks flushed, she grabbed the butt of her revolver. The cold, smooth ivory felt slippery, and she realized her palms were wet. She stared down at the gun, suddenly feeling frightened again. *And what am I going to do? Point this gun at—someone? Anyone? And shoot them? Just like that?*

Her head jerked up, and her eyes strained frantically to see the riders who were approaching. But she could see nothing except the outlines of the nearest trees, gray against black. The confused rumble and clatter of horses running through underbrush seemed to strike sharply against her eardrums, though she knew instinctively that they were still some distance off.

Then—with a relief that was almost laughable—she remembered that she had no powder and ball left. The cadets had used up every grain of gunpowder she and Shiloh had, and every single bullet. She smiled grimly and nodded acknowledgment to herself. It seemed that she had no choice—but that also meant that she had no decisions to make.

Taking a deep breath, she said, "I will do what you say, Mr. Roddy. But I will certainly return here with the sheriff as fast as I can."

He turned to face the woods, and now Cheney could see the boyishly full curves of his profile. His voice, however, was hoarse with a man's anger. "There is no sheriff, Dr. Duvall. There is no one you can go to who will help you or us. Just go to your hotel and wait."

The protest on Cheney's lips melted away. Argument and discussion were over, because the sound of horses crashing through the woods had grown louder. Cheney, still looking back at Maxcy Roddy, saw him grip his saber tighter and raise it slightly. Realizing that if she hesitated he would give Stocking the flat of it, she hunched down slightly and readied herself for headlong flight, her heart thudding.

Shadrach, with Logan and Shiloh close behind him, leapt out onto the road. Their horses reared and panted as they formed around Cheney and Maxcy.

"Good," Shadrach said to Maxcy, who nodded calmly and sheathed his sword.

Not another word was spoken. The horses flew down the deserted road, four dark shapes and Israfel's white shimmer leading. They did not slow the reckless pace until they reached the outskirts of Charleston, and the first tall gas lamp encircled them with fuzzy yellow light.

Still they traveled at a brisk trot, but Cheney was able to sit up. "What happened?" she gasped. As she spoke she felt a sharp stitch in her side and pressed her hand hard against it. Riding at a full gallop for miles in a sidesaddle was muscle-screaming, breath-grabbing work.

"Hunters," Shiloh said grimly. His eyes, narrowed almost to slits, scanned continually from side to side, and everything they passed—each soldier, each person, each dog, each shadow—was the object of his withering scrutiny. Cheney turned to Shadrach and saw again with a start that his expression, his alert and tense watchfulness, was oddly identical to Shiloh's.

Shadrach dropped back to say a few terse words to Maxcy Roddy. The young man saluted him and, without a backward glance at the others, cantered off onto a side street. Shiloh asked no questions, and Shadrach immediately moved back up beside Cheney, with Logan still following so closely behind that Cheney could occasionally feel the wet warmth from his horse's great breath. Suddenly she was cold, and her side hurt abominably. No one spoke until they reached the Planter's Hotel.

Shadrach dismounted and helped Cheney to dismount, while Shiloh handed the reins to Jubal, who had appeared as soon as the riders had approached. Shiloh spoke quietly to him, gesturing to the two horses. Cheney was mildly curious, but Shadrach was holding her hand between both of his and speaking to her.

"Dr. Duvall, please accept my gravest apologies," he said formally, but his voice was rough-edged with bitterness. "I am responsible for placing you in such danger. I didn't foresee it, but that is no excuse, and I ask your forgiveness."

"Captain Luxton," she replied, matching his austere dignity, "today was one of the most delightful and memorable days I have ever had. I feel I owe you gratitude, not forgiveness. But since you have asked me, I do freely forgive you, and I do most sincerely thank you."

He bent and kissed her hand, and again Cheney felt how warm and firm his lips were, and she was suddenly conscious of how very cold and achy her fingers were. He straightened, smiled sadly at her, and murmured, "Good night, Cheney."

Shiloh—in contrast—grabbed her elbow, hard, and hustled her into the hotel and up the stairs. He stood with grim impatience, his arms folded, until Rissy opened Cheney's door. "'Night, Doc," he grunted, turned on his heel, and went swiftly down the hall to his own door without waiting for her to say good-night or turning around to see her watching him.

★　★　★　★

Forty minutes later he passed the same streetlight, only now it was the last instead of the first. Spurring Sock into a smooth, controlled canter, he searched the darkness to his left and right. Trying to hear anything over a horse's footfalls was pointless, so he concentrated on perception and interpretation of the dim landscape. Catching a glimpse of ghostly white peeking delicately through the treetops, he nodded with satisfaction. The new moon was two days old, her winter white sphere only slightly dimmed on her west side. When she fully rose, her cold sterile smile would not allow the forest to keep his dark secret shadows.

He saw them before they called out to him and reined Sock so sharply the horse reared, protesting, his nose pointed toward the blue-black sky.

"Shiloh," Shadrach called simply, assuring Shiloh by his voice. They were dismounted on the side of the road to his left, holding their horses' reins and waiting. "Mount up," Shadrach ordered Logan and Maxcy. Shadrach took his place by Shiloh, with Logan and Maxcy behind.

Shiloh frowned and turned to face Shadrach with a taut jerk of his head. The planes of his angular face were sharply delineated, a black-and-white relief in the night's cool light. Shadrach merely turned and looked at him expressionlessly, but he lifted his chin up enough to show defiance.

Shiloh muttered a curse under his breath, then kicked Sock into a gallop. Smoothly Shadrach stayed up with him, and Logan and Maxcy followed easily.

They rode about a mile, when suddenly Shiloh reined Sock to a full stop again. "You should've gone back to check on Josiah," he said harshly.

"Maxcy did," Shadrach replied shortly, searching the road ahead. "He's shaken up and angry, but they didn't hurt him." He waited.

Shiloh glared at his profile for a moment, then spurred Sock forward. They rode perhaps a quarter of a mile before Shiloh halted again. "I've decided that I'm not going to let you do this, Shadrach. Go home." Without waiting for an answer, Shiloh rode on.

Shadrach did not trouble to give an answer. He quickly spurred Israfel and stayed up by Shiloh's side.

With an inarticulate growl Shiloh jerked Sock to a halt, then roughly turned him and backed him until he faced Shadrach. "Maybe you didn't hear me," he muttered.

"I heard you, sir," Shadrach replied without inflection. "To state the obvious, it is not your decision to make. I am going back to remedy this situation. You are going back. I see no reason why we should not go together."

"I don't need your help, Shadrach," Shiloh said in a level tone. "What are you going to do, run them through with those sabers?"

"What are you going to do?" Shadrach asked with only the slightest touch of sarcasm. "Shoot them all?"

"Gonna try not to," Shiloh rumbled. "What I am going to do is ride in, grab up Red Shirt by the scruff of his scrawny neck, and teach him some manners. Then I'm gonna talk to Caleb Blood and see if his disposition's improved any, or if I need to give him a lesson in manners, too."

Shadrach narrowed his eyes and looked Shiloh up and down. "Good plan—for four men," he said succinctly. "Let's go."

"No." Shiloh didn't move.

Shadrach's voice became laced with anger. "I knew you would do this. You should have known that *I* would."

Shiloh frowned darkly and clenched his jaw. The cat-slits of his eyes glittered occasionally when the new moon caught them. "I did know. I just didn't think it would be tonight."

Shadrach shrugged, a gesture of gentlemanly arrogance. "It is my duty. She was under my protection."

"Hardly," Shiloh retorted, his voice deepening with menace.

Shadrach showed no sign of wavering. His light-gray outline was slender, erect, proud. "She was my guest."

"Yeah? Well, she's my . . . my . . . doctor!" Shiloh thundered.

A few moments of stunned silence followed this explosion. Suddenly Shiloh grinned, just a little—and then threw back his head and laughed.

Shadrach laughed, Logan Manigault smiled in a tense and

watchful way, and Maxcy Roddy looked absurdly relieved. Shiloh Irons was a man to laugh *with*, certainly—but not one to laugh *at*, not at all.

"All right," Shadrach finally said, still chuckling deep in his throat, "she's your doctor. I'd ask her to be mine, too, if I needed one. So, Shiloh, let's go."

Shiloh took a long, slow breath and looked back over his shoulder at the road glowing around them, converging into darkness ahead of them. "I don't think so, Shadrach," he said quietly. "Not tonight. Let's all go back to the Citadel. I think we need to think this through first."

Lifting his chin slightly again as he considered, Shadrach finally nodded once, deliberately. "I agree, Shiloh, but only because you rode with my brother, and that tells me what kind of man you are."

Shiloh started Sock forward in a slow walk, and Shadrach turned alongside him. "You mean," Shiloh said deliberately, "you know I'm not a coward."

"Yes."

Shiloh shot him a dark look.

Shadrach continued, "I think I would know that, anyway. But since you rode with Bedford, I do not require a long acquaintance to be certain."

"Yeah," Shiloh said sardonically. "Thanks."

"You're welcome," Shadrach said graciously.

They rode on slowly in silence for a while. Then Logan spoke up, "Sir? I still think Mr. Irons' plan was an excellent one. We're here. Why don't we just go clean up that place tonight? I fail to understand the reason for a delay." His languid tones grew sharper with impatience.

Shadrach considered this, then turned to Shiloh. "Lieutenant Manigault has a point, Shiloh. I don't know that we can come up with a better plan. Why should we delay?" He frowned. "Don't misunderstand me—I know you're not afraid—and I'm certain you're perfectly capable of beating that renegade buck to a pulp. I think you could take Caleb Roddy with only a little more trouble. You're built, and you move as if you might be an excellent pugilist. We're here to back you up and lessen the chances that you might be obliged to shoot someone. Why not now?"

Shiloh seemed to ignore the questions. "What do you want to do, Shadrach? When you graduate from the Citadel?" he demanded impatiently.

Shadrach knew Shiloh's point already but would not concede. "I'm going into the army," he replied stubbornly.

"Yeah, thought so," Shiloh said, and Shadrach turned to look at him in surprise. Shiloh's voice had softened. "I had hoped and planned to be in the army too. I thought, when the war was over, that I'd sign up and maybe go out to Montana or Wyoming. . . ." He jerked his shoulders back in a defensive gesture. "Now, you know, I'll never be able to bear arms for my country again," he said with deliberate harshness.

"Yes," Shadrach said quietly. "I know. I have four half brothers and two brothers who would still be in the army right now if they could. I am the only one. . . ."

Shiloh looked straight ahead, unseeing. "Yes. It's in your blood, and your heart. It would be stupid to throw it away."

Now Shadrach squared his wide shoulders. "So I will not do anything stupid, Shiloh," he said through gritted teeth. "But we have suffered insult, and indignities, and worse, long enough."

"That's right," Logan said bitterly. "You have, certainly, Shadrach. And, Mr. Irons, my mother was—accosted and insulted—by some drunken bluebellies. She is not the only lady to suffer indignities on the streets of Charleston. We had no redress. None at all."

"So that's why I never see ladies on the streets," Shiloh muttered.

"That's right," Shadrach asserted, temper again stiffening his fluid voice. "We can do nothing, except advise them only to go out with extensive escort."

"Yeah," Shiloh scoffed, "like the Doc was escorted tonight."

"Exactly," Shadrach asserted. "Other things have happened, too."

"Tell me."

"Dr. Van Dorn's hospital," Maxcy offered. "The first one was burned down just before it was finished. We didn't know if it was because he refused to treat coloreds or bluebellies."

"Captain Perry," Shadrach said evenly, "was attacked in the same way I was. Hit from behind. That's why he's in the hospital. Other men—Confederates, usually officers—have been subjected to ill treatment. Insults, rocks thrown at them, anonymous threats."

"None of these things have been dealt with by the authorities," Shiloh stated, not asked.

"No. The Union soldiers police the streets, and they make certain that no murders or armed robberies take place in broad daylight right before their eyes," Shadrach answered scornfully. "Judge Garth Granger's sole purpose for being here seems to be to make us accursed Rebels and cotton snobs and would-be aristocrats pay—heavily, and in gold—for our sins."

"Don't discount your own importance, Captain Luxton," Logan said, his voice dripping with sarcasm. "Hating you seems to brighten Judge Granger's life considerably."

The moonlight had grown bright enough now for Shadrach to be able to make out Shiloh's features, and he could see Shiloh's firm mouth twist into a bitter smile as he asked, "He doesn't like you, Captain Luxton?"

"No, he doesn't," Shadrach replied mockingly. "I can't imagine why. Maybe it's because he hates anyone who wears anything gray. Or maybe it's because he's unable to remember my name, and he's embarrassed. Several times he's called me 'Mr. Forrest'—in a most peculiar tone, I must admit. Quite loud."

"One would think he's met your brother," Shiloh said gravely. "One would think he didn't like General Nathan Bedford Forrest, and that you, possibly, are so much like him that Judge Granger finds it difficult to separate the two in his mind."

Shadrach turned to Shiloh with his eyes lit up, his smile wide with delight. "You think that is possible?"

"I do," he said pointedly, "now."

Shadrach turned to face ahead. "Then I must be certain to thank Judge Granger for paying me the highest possible compliment," Shadrach said with satisfaction and looked up at the moon with a smile. Then he sighed and gazed unseeing ahead. The glow on the horizon that was the city of Charleston was getting close.

"Anyway," Shiloh shrugged, "I guess what you're telling me is that the bluebellies are the only authorities, and they aren't interested in policing any of our problems."

"No. For a year and a half now," Shadrach answered, "we've been ignoring all of it, hoping the tensions would lessen with time. They have not. And now—tonight—it seems that even women are in physical danger."

"He wasn't shooting at her, and you know it, Shadrach," Logan argued. "He was shooting at you."

"Yes, and he deliberately did not actually shoot me. We all know that, too. But it doesn't make any difference. This incident is intolerable, and I do not intend to be tolerant of it."

"Me either," Shiloh said evenly. "But I still say we have to figure out something else to do. None of you can afford to go openly riding in there and cause trouble with those Negroes, no matter what the provocation."

"Openly . . ." Shadrach repeated thoughtfully.

"What?" Shiloh asked.

"You can't afford to go in there alone," Shadrach said, rousing himself.

Shiloh grinned, and it was hard and cold. "Sure I can," he said with unnatural ease. "But, like I said, we'll think it over. Maybe something'll come to me."

Shadrach shrugged with apparent carelessness. "Those nigras will still be there."

"If they aren't," Shiloh said, his voice almost inaudible, "I'll find them."

14

THE WALKIN' AND THE TALKIN'

City Hall was teeming with bluecoats, as usual, and with Negro men, which was not usual. Vess Alexander grimaced as he walked down Meeting Street—not with apprehension, for he had felt his burden lifted as soon as he had set out on his difficult task this morning, but with displeasure. Caleb Blood Roddy was talking with the four provost marshals, and Caleb Blood Roddy always meant trouble. Vess heartily disapproved of his own son Luke's friendship with that angry and bitter young man.

Even as the distaste formed in his mouth, however, he realized that this group of muttering, gesturing men might be the distraction he needed in order to bypass the Freedmen's Bureau offices, which took up the entire first floor of City Hall. Brigadier General John Hatch's offices of the United States Army were on the second floor. No Negro ever had reason to be on the second floor. Vess smiled. *Lord's will is gonna be done*, he reminded himself. *All you gotta worry about is doin' the walkin' and the talkin'.*

"Judge Granger isn't going to see all of you," Sergeant Sonny Micari was saying in his terse voice to Caleb Blood and his men. Sergeant Micari always sounded angry. "You're a mob. I'll take one of you in. That's all."

At fifty Vess Alexander was still a big man, his shoulders wide and his chest thick, but he tried to make himself small and unremarkable as he slipped through the crowd. He made it all the way up the steps, holding on to the gracefully curved iron balustrade that he'd made. He stood on the open portico in front of the ten-foot high double doors. His hand was on the curved iron handle.

"Vess," a silky voice sounded behind him. "What a coinci-

165

dence. I was going to have to come to Dallas's to bring you a message from the judge. It appears that you saved me the trouble."

Corporal "Teach" Case was twenty years old and spoke as if he were a forty-five-year-old schoolteacher. Vess would have known that slightly pedantic voice anywhere. As he turned, he knew that Teach's curly brown hair would be crisp and shiny beneath his kepi, and he would be stroking his precise brown mustache.

"Good morning, Corporal," Vess said, pushing the door open and taking a half step in. "I'll stop by your office on my way out, since it 'pears you're kinda busy right now."

Vess almost made it inside.

"Vess," Teach said insistently, laying his immaculate white hand on Vess's sleeve. "Wait a minute. You're here to see the judge, are you not? About the work at the house?"

Vess sighed slightly, let go of the handle of the door, and turned all the way around to face Teach squarely. "No, sir," he said evenly. "I'm here to see General Hatch."

Teach's arched brows went slightly higher. "Oh? For what reason?"

Vess met his gaze squarely, while his mind raced. *God tole you two things 'bout this day and this job: Don't lie, and don't worry about what you say. So here goes, Lord . . .* He opened his mouth and fervently hoped that something resembling the English language would come out of it. It was, and was quite sensible and to the point. "I'm sorry, Corporal Case. It's something I gotta talk to General Hatch, himself, about. Just General Hatch, and no one else."

"Is that right?" Teach said speculatively. Vess watched him closely. He seemed to waver, and he stroked his fine pencil mustache and looked down. Vess waited.

"Teach, go ask if the judge'll see Caleb Blood! Again!" Sonny Micari's tense tones broke the weighty silence between the two men.

Teach shook his head, squinting his eyes very slightly, as if arousing himself from a daydream. Then he looked back up at

166

Vess, and his face closed. "In a minute, Sonny," he said evenly. "Right now Vess needs to talk to the judge. He's got some unfinished business with him. Left your drawings in his study two days ago, didn't you, Vess? But you didn't wait to see him? I think you need to apologize to Judge Granger. Don't you, Vess?"

Sonny Micari made an exasperated sound, gave Vess a dark look, and wheeled to go back down the steps toward the waiting crowd of sullen men.

Vess spoke again, and was surprised to hear that his own voice, normally so soft and kind, had a fine knife-edge to it. "No, I don't think I need to apologize to Judge Granger. All I need to do is see General Hatch."

Teach crossed his arms and said persuasively, "Now, Vess, you know that you are a colored man. . . ."

"Yas, suh," Vess said sweetly.

Teach Case almost smiled as he went on, "—and if you have a complaint, you know that it's the jurisdiction of the Freedmen's Bureau—not the United States Army. I'm afraid, as a provost marshal, that I couldn't allow you to bother General Hatch with some issue that is likely my responsibility. So I'll take you in to see Judge Granger."

But Vess now merely smiled without humor and said cryptically, "I b'lieve you're right, Corporal Case. I b'lieve you might be some responsible. So I'm going to take my leave now."

He went down the steps with dignified slowness, and Teach Case found, somewhat to his own surprise, that he let him go.

Vess turned to walk back north on Meeting Street, breathing deeply of the tangy, salted morning air. At the barred entrance to the small park across from City Hall, he noted for the first time a man—tall, tense, and motionless—watching Caleb Blood Roddy and his men as they spoke and sometimes shouted at the provost marshals. *'Pears I ain't the onliest one that watches Caleb Blood real close*, Vess thought dryly. *That tall fella looks like he's got some serious business with somebody.*

The tall man did not move or take his eyes off the group in front of City Hall, and Vess studied him with mild curiosity for a moment. He was as unobtrusive as a man could be who was well over six feet tall. Leaning negligently against one of the bare trees, he remained motionless, his face shadowed by a black western hat, a long canvas duster hiding telltale details about his clothing. But something about his posture and the hard line of his jaw made Vess reflect that he looked like a dangerous man.

As the stranger passed out of his view, Vess dismissed him and Caleb Blood Roddy from his mind and began to find pleasure in the crackly brown leaves that crunched under his feet, the invigorating chill of the morning breeze, the heavenly smell of the day's bread coming out of an oven somewhere nearby. The streets were private and silent. Vess did not review the words and moments that had passed between him and Judge Garth Granger's marshal. Now he would go to the telegraph office up on King Street and finish this task and shed his burden. God had shown him this at some point as he conversed with Teach Case. Humming, Vess walked sturdily, his muscular legs pumping with a steady rhythm, his broad back straight.

King Street and the Western Union office were deserted, except for a balding clerk with a green eye shade. Yawning painfully, he took Vess's printed message. When he saw the addressee, he blinked twice, then looked up at Vess quizzically. "This right, boy? You sure you know what you're doin'?"

"Yas, suh."

The clerk shrugged. "It's your twenty-nine cents, boy."

Vess paid him and, as he was leaving, saw two ladies preparing to enter the office. Vess snatched his slouch hat off and dropped his eyes as he held the door. To his surprise, one of the ladies took his arm in a strong grip. "Mistuh Alexander," she said in rich tones. "What a nice surprise! What you doin' heah?"

Vess looked up as Rissy Clarkson bodily hauled him out onto the plank sidewalk. "Doctah Duvall, Miss Rissy," he said, smiling with pleasure. "How nice to see you on this sunrisin'! I had a telegram to send, o' course," he replied impishly to Rissy. "Ain't never sent one in my life, so I figgered I better go ahead and git it over."

Cheney laughed, while Rissy scolded, "Why didn't you git Luke to do it for you? Or me?"

Now Cheney's eyes cut to Rissy, Vess noted, as if she were startled at her servant's familiarity with him. Quickly Dr. Duvall recovered, however, and smiled brilliantly up at him. "Rissy thinks I don't have sense enough to send a telegram by myself either, Mr. Alexander. Don't pay her any mind."

"That ain't true, Miss Cheney," Rissy said pointedly. "I know *Mistuh Alexander* is real smart, sure smart enough to send his own tellygrams." Cheney's eyes rolled, but Rissy turned to Vess, her mouth twitching and her dark eyes brimming with mirth. "Me an' Luke are comin' to your house for dinner tonight agin, you know, Mistuh Alexander. But please tell Miss Ona that I'll bring some food, and for her not to cook up the whole country."

"Won't do no good," he said with a boyish smile, fiddling with his hat. "Me an' Luke eat a lot."

"Good thing, too," Rissy sniffed. "Not like some people I know." She cast an accusatory eye on Cheney.

"It's too early for breakfast," Cheney said in a bored tone. "Is this place even open yet?"

"Yes, ma'am," Vess said gallantly and opened the door for them. He bowed as they passed by, and Rissy smiled. "See you tonight, Mistuh Alexander."

"It'll be mine and Ona's pleasure, Miss Rissy," he said warmly, "and Luke's."

★　★　★　★

"On the contrary, I do most certainly have the authority, Gard. In fact, I am the only person in this city with this authority, and this responsibility, and I do not take it lightly. Neither will you. You will carry out my orders, my ordinances, and my wishes as I have prescribed." Judge Garth Granger addressed his son as if he were a naughty, slightly slow child.

"But . . ." Gard began.

"I am assigning more Harbor Rangers to you, Gard." Judge Garth Granger acrimoniously repeated the words that opened their conversation. "There will be no more ships entering Charleston without paying the harbor fees."

Seated in the plain, straight wooden chair in front of the

empty desk, Gard Granger searched his father's face, so like and unlike his own. The fine, sensitive features, dark liquid eyes, and full mouth combined in the son to form—as Cheney had noted—a melancholy sensuality. In the father they had become stiff features, dark eyes that reflected neither inner nor outer light, and a mouth tightly reined into a straight slash, with deep lines from nose to the corners. His father's short, dark hair was streaked with iron gray.

"One thing that Charleston does not need," Gard retorted sarcastically, "is more of 'Gard's Rangers.' It's bad enough that those ruffians you've assigned to police the docks have been named after me! But now you're allowing them to roam the countryside and terrorize the fishermen in their own homes! Those are the *ships* you're so worried about escaping up the rivers: two-man fishing boats with their families' suppers the only cargo!"

Judge Granger's response to his son was characteristically and meticulously severe, relentlessly exact. "First, you do not know what Charleston needs, Gard. I, as provost tribune of the city of Charleston, make those decisions. Second, you do need more rangers, you have them, and you will put them to the use which I direct. Not a single craft will dock in Charleston harbor without paying the harbor fees. Third, you will not speak to me in that disrespectful tone."

Gard Granger stood so quickly and spoke so vehemently that his father flinched slightly. "All right, *Judge*," he enunciated with icy distaste, "First, I know you decide everything about Charleston—for good or for ill, mostly ill, I see. A fine example is the outrageous harbor fees you have set, and which I suspect end up in blue pockets, though I don't know it, and don't wish to know. Second, I will have nothing to do with the rangers except as they deliver the harbor reports and collections to me. Third, I will now stop talking to you at all—which will please us both." He wheeled and stalked to the door.

"Gard!" the judge called, but his son did not turn or hesitate. "You . . . you are insolent, and your loyalties are as twisted as that accursed right hand!"

Gard never looked back at his father, and the door slammed so violently that the judge thought it might fly off its hinges. Judge Granger hit his desk with the flat of one square hand. Slowly, with an iron will, he made himself calm down. Nothing, and no one, could make him as blindly, stupidly angry as his own son.

A knock sounded on the door, and Judge Granger was surprised to realize that he had no idea how long he had been sitting there, pressing his blunt fingertips to his temples, his eyes closed. He cleared his throat. "Yes?"

Teach Case opened the door and entered the judge's small, square, sterile office. Judge Granger had chosen this small office instead of a more spacious one with tall windows, and Teach had always believed that it was because this one was square, and the other one was rectangular and too brightly lit. Everything in this office was at precise right angles. The only item that might be termed "decor" was a set of brass scales on one corner of the judge's desk, which were always empty, and set precisely even.

Of Judge Granger's top four provost marshals, Teach was his favorite. "Judge, we have a slight problem out here, and I have some information that I believe I must impart to you immediately," Teach said piously. "May we come in?"

Granger nodded and motioned impatiently for the men to be seated. Sergeant Sonny Micari, as usual, looked stormy; George Wynn looked sullen; Billy Rand looked blank; and Teach looked immaculate and sprightly. Teach sat in the chair Gard had recently vacated, directly in front of the judge's desk, while the other men lounged on the divan and in the overstuffed leather chairs. Judge Granger frowned slightly but said nothing. They never came to attention and saluted him now, as they had done when he was a brevet colonel. Still, they should show a judge more respect.

The judge propped his elbows on the desk and tented his fingers, placing his fingertips precisely together. "Yes? What is the problem?"

Teach cast a quick look over his shoulder at Sergeant Sonny

Micari, who shrugged tightly. Micari—heavily handsome, with Italian features, a close-trimmed beard and mustache, and a fiery temper—despised having a baby-faced corporal take charge of what he considered his province. But Teach Case was the only one of the provost marshals who could talk sensibly to the pompous and inflated judge. Micari lost his temper whenever he tried to talk to Judge Granger, and that could be dangerous, so he grudgingly allowed Corporal Case to take charge in these situations. Teach wasn't a bad sort, at that. He always gave Micari his due.

Now Teach nodded and turned back to the judge. "Caleb Blood Roddy and his men are here. They say that last night some white men—including Shadrach Luxton—rode through their camp and bothered them." Teach anticipated the effect that the mention of Shadrach Forrest Luxton's name would have on the judge, and he braced himself.

The judge's face turned red, and the lines between his nose and mouth deepened into crevices. "That . . . Rebel! He's a criminal, and I ought to arrest him and send him to prison for the rest of his life!" he thundered. "Every time I turn around he's making more trouble!"

"Mmm, yes, sir," Teach said delicately, "but are you certain that it would be auspicious to do so at this time?"

"And why not?" the judge shouted.

"As you informed me yesterday, Judge Granger, it does appear that Congress has effectively seized control of the federal government, and that they will pass the new Reconstruction Act before they dismiss," Teach hummed. "Possibly by March, all ten Rebel states will be under total martial law."

The Reconstruction Act of 1867 that Congress was force-feeding to President Johnson would split the ten Rebel states, excluding Tennessee, into five military districts. Each would be under the command of an army general, backed by troops, who was granted full authority over judicial and civil functions. Each of these military governors would have police power, sole and unlimited, in his district. Rumor from Washington was that General Sickles, a dour, unhappy man who was a friend of Judge

Garth Granger, would be appointed to District 2—North and South Carolina. That this martial system was already in place and practiced in Charleston was due to the fact that Charleston was still considered the source of sedition, the hotbed of secession, and the center of rebellion.

"I am the law here, now!" Judge Granger blustered. "The only law!"

"Yes, sir. But in a couple of months nothing you do will be scrutinized, questioned, or reviewed in any way, by anyone." Teach shrugged, one shoulder slightly higher than the other, and averted his face slightly. "When all of the Southern states and cities are formally organized into our—your system, sir—you will be viewed as the standard by which all the governors and provost tribunes will measure their successes."

"What is your point, Corporal Case?" the judge asked, slightly mollified by the blatant flattery. "I only want to arrest that Forrest boy. If he was trespassing, and threatening the freedmen, then he should be arrested and tried."

"Er . . . um . . . yes, sir," Teach said cautiously, "but the next few months are crucial, are they not? If Charleston is quiet and peaceful, perhaps the need for military jurisdiction might be questioned. . . ."

After a few heavy moments the judge nodded imperiously. "Yes, I see. Then my decision is that we will retain the *status quo*." He waved his hand impatiently, dismissing the topic, the freedmen's grievances, and the rights of the citizens of Charleston with those judicial words. "What else?"

"Well, sir, there is a man who wishes to lodge a counter-complaint against Caleb Blood Roddy and one of his associates," Teach said, watching the judge's face carefully.

"Yes? So?"

"He maintains that one of Blood's men took a shot at him and his companions last night as they were returning from the Roddy mansion, and he . . ."

"Wait. Was this man in the company of that Forrest boy?" The judge seemed unable to comprehend that the Citadel cadet was not General Nathan Bedford Forrest himself, and Teach privately thought that the judge's hatred for the Rebel general was obsessive. The judge was not a man who was at all times in tight control, but neither was he normally a man to be so blindly, blatantly bent on personal revenge.

"Yes, sir," Teach answered uneasily. "His name is Shiloh Irons. A lady was accompanying the party at the time, so he and the cadets are particularly—wroth."

"I'm growing weary of this topic, Corporal Case," the judge said ominously. "What do you suggest I do? Arrest the freedmen? I will not! Tell this man to stay off the Hamilton Roddy lands, and that if he wanders about in the country in such company as that Forrest boy, then it is no wonder that the freedmen take potshots at him! Tell him to stay away from Forrest and leave the freedmen alone, and he might escape arrest for disturbing the peace!" The judge pounded on his desk, making Teach and the other three marshals jump. "This meeting is over! You're dismissed!"

Teach nervously stroked his mustache and cast a worried look over his shoulder at Sonny Micari, who shrugged uneasily. Teach turned back to the judge. "Sir—Judge—I'm afraid that there is one more—extremely important—problem that must be addressed."

The judge drew in a deep breath, closed his eyes, rubbed his temples for a moment, and then looked back at Teach Case with barely controlled impatience. "What is it?"

"Take a look at this, Judge." Teach flipped a yellow piece of paper across the spotless, empty desk.

Judge Granger read it and looked up at Teach in puzzlement. "What is this?"

Teach merely shrugged; the note was self-evident. Granger perused it again. It was a telegram, addressed to Brigadier General John Hatch. This time Judge Granger noted that it was directed to the general's home on Tradd Street—not addressed to City Hall—and was marked "Personal and Confidential."

It read:

174

General Hatch:

Information concerning theft of United States property has come into my possession STOP Vitally important that I turn this information over to you personally STOP Contact me at Dallas Farm and Supply Friday if you can STOP If not I will call on you at your home at 9:00 A.M. Saturday January 21 STOP

Vess Alexander

"I do not understand this," Judge Granger said stiffly. "What could Vess Alexander possibly know about any theft of United States property? Why would he not come to me with this?"

Teach Case's face became carefully smooth. "Judge, I can only think of one circumstance that would merit this peculiar action by Vess."

Judge Granger's strict noncommittal gaze rested on him for long, uncomfortable moments. The judge never permitted direct spoken reference to certain activities conducted by himself and his four provost marshals; indeed, that is why they all referred to themselves, among themselves, as "The Guard." All conversations relating to their private enterprises were couched in careful euphemisms. That was one reason Teach was always the spokesman. The other three marshals were compliant to the judge's whims but incapable of tactful speech.

As the judge looked at him, Teach wondered—again—how Judge Garth Granger, tyrannically righteous, geometrical, stiff and unbending as he wielded the law, with vicious animosity toward anyone he deemed ideologically impure, managed such mental duality as to justify his relentless gathering up of money that did not belong to him.

Finally the judge said in a dead tone, "Certain papers were on my desk last Tuesday. Vess was there . . . but he left before I returned from seeing Gard."

"Yes," Teach said patiently.

"But Vess could draw no logical conclusion from those papers," Granger went on harshly. "He's just a Negro." Judge Granger regarded all Negro men as wayward, careless children.

He never gave Negro women or children a second thought.

"Well . . . please consider, Judge," Teach said delicately. "It does appear that Vess has some information that he considers important and concrete. Does it not?"

"Perhaps," Granger said stiffly.

"What were the papers left on your desk, sir?" Teach said, mentally holding his breath. The judge might blast him for his impertinence, but even Judge Granger must see that this affected—and endangered—all five of them equally.

Judge Granger did see this with a jolt, so he answered Teach. "They . . . they were the counts from the last draw day—"

"From last month? The originals?" Teach asked sharply.

"Yes," Judge Granger said, "and the revised counts . . ."

"The doubled counts?"

"Yes. And the shipping orders," the judge finished. "Two of the warehouses are getting overcrowded, and I was selecting the least noticeable items for an extra shipment. But I cannot believe that Vess could tie those three items together."

"Perhaps we had better act upon the assumption that he did, sir," Teach said with deference. Turning to Sonny Micari, he said, "Can you take care of this, Sonny?"

"Right," Micari grunted. His heavy, olive features were controlled, but his full mouth twisted.

"Wait a minute, men," Judge Granger blustered. "I think we—all of us, The Guard—had better make the decision of what to do about this."

Teach merely looked at him. "And what, exactly, do you think we should do, Judge?"

Judge Granger searched the four men's faces in turn. He saw nothing there—no deference, no kinship, no emotion at all. He was beyond his scope, and he knew it. Judge Granger matriculated the most complex paper shuffles, but he did not know how to deal effectively, personally, with men. "No violence," he said, and despised the weakness of his voice.

Teach turned again to look at Sonny Micari and slowly arched his left eyebrow in a question.

Sonny Micari looked to George Wynn. About forty, Wynn

was a morose man of muddy humors. His brown hair was long and unkempt, as were his beard and mustache. A cigar, which always seemed to be a short, wet stub, was permanently stuck in his mouth, and he always had cigar ashes in the mess of his beard and down his uniform front. His only answer to Micari's unspoken question was a shrug and a ferocious puff of the stinking cigar.

Sonny Micari then turned to Billy Rand, who had reached the age of nineteen only last week. He had joined the army at thirteen. Rand was average on all accounts—average height, medium build, dirty-blond hair, clouded blue eyes. Unnoticeable at all times was this young man, except in battle. Rand had a peculiar mindless ferocity when he was in combat that Sonny Micari had never seen matched before or since the war, and Sonny Micari had stayed close behind Billy Rand for four solid years. Within hours after a bloody battle, Billy Rand again became colorless and disappeared into the background. Now he focused vaguely somewhere over Micari's left shoulder and said tonelessly, "I'll do whatever you say, Sarge."

"Teach." Micari turned back jerkily to address Teach Case, who knew Sonny was asking him a question. The stabbing sentences Sonny uttered, as if against his will, had to be interpreted. "I won't kill Vess," he said temperamentally, as if it was just entirely too much trouble. "What else?"

"I have an idea," Teach said. "Judge, with your permission?"

Judge Granger lifted his taut shoulders with disdain, so Teach went on, "Did you see the *Record* this morning, sir? No? There is an interesting announcement in it. Apparently a certain social club—I've heard that it is composed of the most notable and upstanding men of Charleston—will be parading at midnight on Friday night."

"What are you blabbering about, Corporal Case?" the judge demanded. "What does this have to do with anything?"

Teach Case's mild brown eyes flickered for only a moment, but he allowed the judge to see before continuing in the same quiet, reasonable tone. "The Knights of the White Rose will be parading at midnight, Judge. On Friday night. I believe this presents us with a singular opportunity to deal with Vess Alexander, does it not?"

Judge Garth Granger, though he was an intelligent man, had no gift such as Teach Case's cunning and inventiveness. Without the foggiest notion what Teach was getting at, he said with gruff politeness, "Go ahead, Corporal Case, since we all seem to be of the same mind."

"Do we?" Teach said brightly, but before the judge could respond, Teach had turned back to Sergeant Sonny Micari.

15

BY LOVE UNDONE

"Stop that yawnin'," Rissy ordered. "A bug's gwine to fly in yo' mouth."

"I can't help it, Rissy," Cheney said, snapping the reins to coax a brisker trot from Stocking. The rented buggy was ill-sprung and rickety, she noted with irritation, and Stocking didn't like it any more than Cheney did. "I didn't sleep much last night."

"I tole you 'bout gallopin' around with them gallopin' men like one o' them cussin' horsy women," Rissy said with smug satisfaction, pulling her cape closer around her sturdy frame to combat the stronger breeze from Stocking's trot. She and Cheney were both dressed in the same cold gray as the morning.

Wearily Cheney left the bait alone and became lost in thought. After their return to the hotel last night, and Shiloh's brusque good-night, Cheney had watched him return to his room. Only minutes later she had heard his unmistakable long, measured tread in the hallway. Cheney had hurried to the door and looked out just in time to see his back as he disappeared into the stairwell at the end of the hall.

He had not returned all night.

"This must be it," Cheney said, drawing the buggy to a halt.

"Why you think that?" Rissy asked dourly. "It don't look like much to me."

The building, a one-story clapboard, freshly whitewashed, was long and low and had no sign. Cheney looked up at the telltale longitudinal ventilator along the roof. All pavilion-style hospitals were constructed with the ventilator, an open space of about two feet just under the roof line. She noted with approval that this hospital had louvered shutters, which could be used to

179

regulate the temperature of the hospital while still allowing ventilation.

Situated along the shores of Colonial Lake, the hospital had cheerfully sparkling windows overlooking the still blue water. The lake would have been as eloquently pastoral as its name, except for the exotic palmettos dotted around that gave it an eccentric tropical look. In front of the hospital were well-tended grounds shaded with great trees. Stone benches were placed under many of them, and Cheney imagined that on warmer days the patients, dressed in white robes, with clean white bandages and immaculate, courteous doctors and soft-spoken attendants, soaked up the tranquillity and peace.

Suddenly Cheney realized that she longed to be a part of a hospital such as this, and reflected restlessly that she must soon go back to work. With surprise she found that the thought of returning to her nice little practice in Manhattan was flat and tasteless.

"This is it, Rissy," Cheney said again, pushing her introspection aside. "I'm certain. Are you coming with me?"

"You sure you won't wait for Mistuh Arns?" Rissy asked, laying her hand on Cheney's arm to stop her from getting out of the carriage.

"Rissy, he's probably in some stinking smoky saloon playing poker," Cheney said scathingly. "Besides, he has no interest in helping me find out about Mr. Allan Blue."

Rissy blew out an exasperated breath and looked straight ahead. Cheney hesitated, searching her Egyptian profile, the set and inexpressive calm of her face in repose. "Well?" Cheney finally said.

"I gotta tell you, Miss Cheney," Rissy said carefully and soberly, "I don't think we's gonna be real welcome in there."

Cheney was tired and grumpy, and her eyes were gritty from the cold wind. "Rissy, what is the matter with you?"

Rissy sighed, then turned to look at her squarely. "Niver mind. Let's go on in and get it over." She knew, all too well, when Cheney Duvall had gotten herself fixed and would not be moved.

"Good. Finally." Cheney and Rissy both descended lightly from the buggy, and Cheney tied the reins to the wooden hitching post.

They went up the walk to the hospital and mounted the steps to a small portico. By the double doors was a gleaming brass plaque:

VAN DORN MEMORIAL HOSPITAL
In Memoriam, Major General Earl Van Dorn, C.S.A.
Soldier of Valor,
By Danger Undaunted, By Love Undone
1820–1863
I shall see Him,
But not now,
I shall behold Him,
But not nigh. . . .
The Book of Numbers, 24:17

Cheney thought that the verse was a peculiar epitaph, but on reflection she realized that it was a beautifully fitting motto for a hospital. More than ever she longed to be able to secure a position—as a physician, a *respected* physician—at a hospital such as the Van Dorn Memorial Hospital.

She opened the door and sailed inside, with Rissy close behind her. It was, as she had pictured, light and airy, a long room with a wide aisle down the middle, and the beds—perhaps a hundred of them—on each side. The room was suffused with the warm smell of fire in a wood-burning stove and lye soap. Immediately she stopped and began to scan the faces of the men. *What am I looking for?* she asked herself impatiently. *I have no idea what Captain E. Allan Perry looks like. . . .*

The man in the first bed on the right looked up—with one eye, for the other was covered with a big smeary lumpy bandage—and hollered "Uh-oh!" so loudly that Cheney jumped slightly.

Behind her Rissy grimly muttered, "Uh-huh. Yep. Uh-huh."

Another man, three beds down on the left, stared at Cheney, then slowly pulled his sheet up with both hands, all the way up over his face, left it there, and crossed his hands over his stomach. A man sitting in a wheelchair a little farther down rolled his eyes and mumbled helplessly, "Aww . . . aww . . . pshaw!" and then, to Cheney's horror, fumbled himself to a standing position. He had one crutch and one leg.

Someone moaned loudly, "Oh no! It's a woman!"

Someone else wailed, "Worse than that! It's a *lady!*"

Cheney called out, "N-no, I'm not! I'm a doctor!"

"Oh yes she is too!" Rissy barked. Whatever it was that Rissy was attesting to, there was no doubting the ferocity of her defense. The two men in the beds on the left, closest to Rissy, looked positively frightened.

Much to everyone's relief, Dr. Langdon Van Dorn came striding down the aisle, stripping off a gory, bloody apron and rapidly buttoning up a cream-colored vest. Cheney only had time to put out her hand and begin, "Dr. Van . . ."

"Good mornin', Miss Duvall," he said cordially, taking her hand, touching her arm, and taking short, determined strides back toward the door. "How charmin' of you to call upon us."

Cheney found herself out on the portico. Exactly how she got there so quickly was quite inexplicable to her. "But . . . but Dr. Van Dorn, I . . . I . . ." In confusion she stopped and looked around to get her bearings, so to speak.

Dr. Langdon Van Dorn now kissed her hand—which he was still holding lightly in a perfunctory manner—and waited for her to recover. Cheney stared at him rather rudely. He was, as she had seen at the Citadel cadets' Special Drill, a very handsome older man, with even features. His shining silver hair, long and wavy, and his sweeping white mustache, carefully groomed, accentuated most dramatically his flashing dark eyes. The cream-colored vest, shirt, and breeches had no stain. A compact man, perhaps an inch shorter than Cheney, Van Dorn seemed not to be conscious of this. Neither was Cheney. His gallantry, coupled with his efficient whisking of her and Rissy out onto the porch, had quite unsettled her.

Clearing her throat, she fiddled with her reticule nervously, caught Rissy's frown, and made herself stand up straight and be still. "Dr. Van Dorn," she said clearly, "I am here to visit one of your patients. May I?" Gracefully she gestured toward the door.

"Miss Duvall," he said in an exquisite deep drawl, taking her arm and leading her slowly down the steps, "I do recall that Alexander Dallas told me that you are from New York. I believe the practices must be a little different there than here in Charleston. This is a Confederate veterans' hospital, ma'am."

Cheney found herself slowly—patiently—inexorably—being returned to her carriage. "But Dr. Van Dorn, I am a physician, you see," she said firmly. "Fully accredited by the Women's Medical College of Pennsylvania."

"Yes?" he said politely and blankly.

Cheney was halfway to her carriage. "Yes," she retorted with some exasperation and yanked her arm away from his gentle grip. He looked innocently surprised. She went on, "I have been working as a physician for two years now, Dr. Van Dorn. I have a modestly successful practice in Manhattan. Now, would you be so kind as to escort me back into the hospital?"

"No, ma'am," he said, smiling indulgently. "You really don't need to be in there, Miss Duvall. A hospital is no place for a lovely young lady like yourself."

Cheney searched his face with disbelief. "But . . . but . . . I just told you, I'm a physician!"

"I believe that must mean somethin' in New York that it does not mean here, Miss Duvall," he said again, his tone ever so gentle and respectful. "Here in Charleston, we do not subject our ladies to the distresses and rigors of attending sick people. We have men—physicians and nurses—who are dedicated servants of the medical profession. Now, why don't you and your mammy go on back to the hotel and rest?"

"Dr. Van Dorn," Cheney said, her tone ominous, "do you have a hearing impairment, sir? Perhaps I could examine you and determine if this is your problem. I told you, I am a trained physician—a dedicated physician! I have treated men and women—competently—with all sorts of illnesses and injuries! But right now all I want to do is speak to one of your patients! That's all!"

"I beg your pardon, Miss Duvall," he said, bowing slightly and speaking with seeming genuine regret, "but I cannot oblige you this. Women—I do most humbly beg your pardon, ma'am, I mean, ladies—do not frequent the hospital. Please accept my apologies, ma'am."

"But . . . But . . .." Cheney was almost speechless with anger. Behind Dr. Van Dorn, Rissy shook her head and frowned, and Cheney made herself take a deep, long breath. "Dr. Van Dorn, will you at least take a message to the patient with whom I wish to communicate?"

"And who might that be, Miss Duvall?" he asked, his finely featured face only now showing wariness.

"Captain E. Allan Perry."

His eyes flashed in their dark depths. "And how are you acquainted with Captain Perry, may I be so bold to inquire?"

"No, you may not be that bold," Cheney snapped.

"Then, Miss Duvall, again I must respectfully decline to oblige you. Good morning, ma'am." He bowed gracefully, turned, and went back into his hospital.

★　★　★　★

"Where the deuce have you been?" Cheney almost shouted.

"Huh?" Shiloh said before he could recover.

"All night!" Cheney finished.

Shiloh grinned, put his hands on each side of Cheney's waist, and squeezed lightly. "Were you worried about me, Doc? Miss me?"

Hastily Cheney stepped—almost jumped—backward. "I suppose you might as well come in," she grumbled. "At least you don't smell as if you've been in a saloon."

"Gosh, thanks, Doc," Shiloh said dryly and came into Cheney's hotel room. Grabbing the back of one of the wrought-iron chairs by the small round table, in a smooth motion he turned it around to face the fireplace. Cheney watched with disgruntled admiration; those chairs were heavy. She could barely wrench the other one out from underneath the table, and Shiloh hastily jumped up and pulled it around for her, close by his.

Then he seated himself, rested his elbows on his knees, and held his hands up to the merrily popping fire.

"Well?" Cheney demanded, seated stiffly. "Where have you been?"

"Wish I hadda been in a saloon," he grumbled. "Lot more fun."

"You shoulda been to the hospital with us," Rissy said, swooping through the connecting door. "Now that was some fun."

Draped across her arms was one of Cheney's ruffled underskirts, and the hot cottony scent of ironing followed Rissy into the room. Hanging the petticoat and carefully sheathing it, she put it in the armoire and came back to stand by Cheney's chair. Propping her fists on her hips, she glared accusingly first at Shiloh, then Cheney. Her point made, she returned to her room, making quite a production of leaving the door open.

Shiloh watched Rissy, his eyes lit with amusement, and asked Cheney, "Hospital? Did you go to Van Dorn's?"

"I did," Cheney painstakingly replied.

"Dr. Van Dorn didn't let you in, did he," Shiloh stated, staring into the fire.

"No he did not."

"Made you mad, didn't it."

"Yes it did."

"Still mad, aren't you."

"Yes I am."

"Okay, I'm scared." He stood and looked down at her, his eyes alight. "I better go."

"Sit down," Cheney ordered. "Dr. Van Dorn escaped, but you're not going to."

He sat back down, lounged back, and stuck his long legs out so his boots were close to the fire. "You sure look pretty today, Doc." His eyes cut toward her. "You're just pretty."

"Never mind that!" she said hastily. "We were talking about Dr. Van Dorn!"

"So you wanna tell me about it? Or just holler at me 'cause I was out all night?"

Cheney stared at his profile, admiring the way his trim eyebrow arched over the blue eye, the defiant "V" under it, and his straight, thin nose. Then she noticed faint smudges under his eye, and the light golden day's-growth of beard on his squared jaw. *He looks tired, but not—dissipated,* she thought reluctantly. *And he looks—tense—unusual for him . . . I wish he'd just tell me where he's been and what he's been doing!*

"Doc, I can't tell you where I've been and what I've been doing," he said in a low voice. Cheney jumped, and he gave her a sly, knowing glance. "You're just a girl," he went on, his mouth twitching. "You don't need to know about man stuff."

"What! Why, you . . . you . . ."

"Man," he said blandly.

"You . . . you . . . man!" she said as scathingly as she could, her eyes flashing. "I . . . I . . . I . . ."

"You're a woman," he said helpfully.

"Oh! You're . . . you . . . arrogant, insufferable—" Cheney broke off hastily and blinked. It occurred to her that she needed two favors from him, and that perhaps she ought to consider changing her approach slightly.

He was watching her, laughing at her, his eyes bright in spite of the weariness. She cleared her throat and made a tiny, graceful gesture, turning her palm upward. "I'm—pardon me," she said stiffly. "I didn't mean that you, personally, were arrogant and insufferable. Just men in general."

He cocked his eyebrow. "But I am a man, in general."

"I know that!" Cheney said with exasperation. "Will you just let me apologize?"

"Now I'm really scared," he went on.

"Be quiet! Can't you see I'm trying to ask you a favor?"

"Or two?"

"Yes!" she almost shouted. His mouth split wide in a grin, and Cheney reluctantly smiled back. It was hard not to. Then they both laughed, and she teased, "I demand that you do me two favors! Immediately!"

"Sure, Doc. How can I refuse such a polite request from a lady?"

"That's right, a lady," she said with mock arrogance, "and don't you forget it, you . . . you . . . man."

"I could never do that, Doc," he said lightly, which nonplused her a bit, but he went on. "So what you want me to do?"

Cheney considered and decided to ask him the easy one first. She rose and went across the expanse of the room to the bed. He watched her, admiring the strength in her walk—no Victorian mincing in Dr. Cheney Duvall—and her deft, purposeful movements. "Here, read this," she said, returning to her chair and handing him a telegram. "It's from Father. It was here when we got in last night. At least, when *I* got in last night."

He glanced at her, but now her eyes were twinkling a little, so he scanned the contents of the telegram:

> *Glad you're enjoying your little vacation darling STOP Tell Shiloh I hold him personally responsible for any damages you inflict just teasing STOP Contacted J. P. Rounds in Philadelphia no help at all STOP Dallas Farm and Supply bills paid with notes issued on: The Guardian Bank of Charleston STOP Would you and Shiloh check on this bank and find out if privately owned by The Guard STOP Love You, Love You, and your mother says Love You STOP*

Shiloh's eyes glowed with warmth as he read. Cheney was glad that her father had sent him a greeting, in such a personal voice, even though it was at her expense. Richard Duvall and Shiloh Irons seemed to be good friends. This made Cheney happy for both her father and Shiloh, who, for all his warmth and outgoing personality, was basically a loner.

"Well?" she asked softly, her thoughts unconsciously reflected in her voice and face. "Will you help me find out about the Guardian Bank? Or do you know of it already, Shiloh?"

He looked up at her and took a moment to search her expression with pleasure. "Sure, I'll help you, Doc. I've never heard of it, but we'll find it." Glancing back into the fire with concentration, he asked, "If a company opens a bank, they'll be registered, won't they? Even if it's a private bank?"

"Oh yes," she nodded. "The Board of Directors would be

required to register with the Department of the Treasury in order to issue notes."

"Good. Then we shouldn't have any problems."

"No . . . no . . . we shouldn't," Cheney said hesitantly. She was already thinking of the other favor she wanted to ask him.

"So what's the other favor, Doc?"

"I wish you wouldn't do that," she sighed almost inaudibly, and he pretended not to hear. Then she went on loudly, "Dr. Van Dorn won't let me in the hospital to see Captain Perry. His reasoning seems to have nothing to do with the fact that I'm a lady *doctor*," she said sarcastically, "only that I'm a *lady*."

Shiloh laughed. "Well, you couldn't get a job—except with Mr. Mercer and 'Mercer's Belles'—when you first graduated because you're a *female* doctor. Then, in Arkansas, nobody cared whether you were a female or a doctor; they just didn't like you because you were an educated Yankee. Then in Manhattan you had trouble because they thought you weren't a lady. Now, you've got troubles because you are a lady! You sure are a lot of trouble, Doc!"

"I know that," she snapped. "Will you help me, or not?"

He turned, withdrawing slightly from her, and kicked a log with his heavy boot. A fiery shower of sparks flew upward against the black of the chimney. "You want me to go see this Captain Perry?"

"Yes."

"And ask him about Allan Blue?" His voice grew tight.

"Yes," Cheney said, then added in a low voice, "please."

He stared into the fire, eyes narrowed slightly, and said nothing. In those quiet, tense moments Cheney saw with a jolt just how deep his animosity toward Allan Blue must be. *He's never hesitated for a moment when I've asked him for anything,* she realized. *I've never thought of it before . . . but he's never said no to me . . . in fact, I usually don't even have to ask him . . . for anything. . . .* She was unsure whether she found this revelation pleasurable or uncomfortable.

"Before I do this," he said carefully, "I want you to know that I don't give a fig for Allan Blue. Guess I'm saying I'm not very sympathetic to this cause, and I might not be the right man to go ask his friend about him."

Cheney sighed and dropped her eyes. She began to pleat her gray wool skirt between her fingers, and he turned to watch her gravely. When she spoke, her voice was faraway, dreamy, and she seemed—at first—not to address Shiloh's objections at all.

"When Mr. Blue left, Jane Anne received a letter the very next month. Well . . . it wasn't a letter. It was a plain envelope, with no return address, but one of the postmarks was Charleston, South Carolina. It had thirty-three cents inside it. That's all," she said, her voice roughened with pity. "The next month it was eighty-two cents. The next month it was eighteen cents. All of these letters had a Charleston postmark on them. Within a year Jane Anne was receiving one dollar, two dollars, sometimes five dollars, each month." She sighed deeply, her eyes still downcast. "And always with odd cents enclosed. Jane Anne said she had no doubt that Allan sent her every single cent he had that he didn't spend on food."

Shiloh grunted, with only a little less impatience than before. "So? Does he have people here? Why did he come here?"

Cheney looked up at him and smiled tremulously. "He has no relatives living at all. His mother died of consumption when he was eight, and his father died two years before he and Jane Anne were married. He was an only child."

Shiloh was silent, his eyes back on the fire, blank and unseeing. Cheney went on, "I don't know if you know this, but Edgar Allan Poe's life was much the same . . . and Jane Anne said that Allan loved everything Poe ever wrote. She said Allan was a man rather like Edgar Allan Poe . . . gentle, sad, and . . . hopelessly romantic." Cheney's dress was pleated precisely even between her fingers. She dropped the bit of material and began again. "In 1862 Jane Anne started receiving large amounts of money . . . and still the little bits of change. . . . Anyway, it was hundreds—even thousands—of dollars."

"What?" Shiloh asked, raising his head.

"Yes," Cheney said, her voice almost choked, "but they were Confederate greenbacks."

Shiloh made a jerky, impatient gesture with one rawboned hand. "Well, that's marvelous! Really helped Mrs. Blue—and Jeremy and Laura—a lot, in New York!"

"But, Shiloh," Cheney said quietly. "Don't you see? Allan Blue is not a stupid man—he knew that Jane Anne couldn't use that money! But he sent it to her anyway!"

Shiloh blew out an exasperated breath and turned his face away. Cheney waited and felt her eyes sting. Finally he turned back to her, and his features were settled into gentleness. "Yeah, well, that's sure a tragic and romantic and hopeless gesture," he said dryly, "so I kinda do—see your point." His eyes sharpened. "You're talking about Allan Blue like he's still alive. Logan Manigault said he was dead."

"Shadrach didn't," Cheney pointed out with heavy emphasis.

"True." He shrugged carelessly. He put his hands on his knees and pushed himself out of the chair. Cheney again realized how very weary he was, even though he only showed it obliquely, in unguarded movements like this. She stood, too, and faced him with a pleading look on her face, but said no more.

"I'll go see Captain Perry, Doc," he murmured, rubbing the back of his neck. "Tomorrow."

"I would appreciate it," she said with relief.

He stepped close to her—perilously close—and now he seemed indolent, loose-limbed. "Would you?" he asked. His face was thrown into shadow, but Cheney could see the lightness of his blue eyes.

"Y-yes. Th-thank you." She tried to back away, but it was impossible. The chair was already jabbing behind her knees.

Suddenly Shiloh reached up and awkwardly fingered an escaped curl of her hair. "I'll do anything for you, Doc. You know that."

They stood, still and close. Cheney's eyes, round and darkened to a smoky emerald green, were focused on the angular lines of his face. He looked only at her hair.

Then—jarringly—he was at the door, and Cheney blinked

190

several times. "Gotta go take a nap," he said, biting down on a yawn. "That okay with you, Doc?"

Cheney, gulping, sat back down suddenly, and hard. "Uh . . . umm . . . yes. Of course—that is—yes."

He opened the door and took a step outside.

"Shiloh?"

"Hmm?" He turned back.

"Thank you. For saying I . . . look pretty and . . . and . . . that I'm . . . pretty," she said with lame correctness.

"Welcome."

Then he was gone.

16

DOCTORS AND NURSES

"St. Anthony's fire." Shiloh whipped the reins with unnatural ferocity. Sock lunged, then pulled the buggy away from the Van Dorn Memorial Hospital at an alarmed trot.

"Oh no," Cheney murmured, then gave Shiloh an anxious once-over. "Did you touch anyone?"

"Yeah. Captain Perry, and he's got it."

"Did you wash?"

"With soap and water. No carbolic acid or chloride of lime around that I could see."

"Hurry," Cheney said tensely.

"Git on there, Sock!" Shiloh muttered and snapped the reins again. The horse obediently broke into a canter, which was difficult for him. The one-seat buggy was small and light, but since Sock was pulling it with Shiloh, Cheney, and Rissy riding, anything over a slow trot was hard work. Under the harness Sock's withers began to lather, and his breath turned into great fog-puffs on the cold morning air.

Rissy leaned over slightly to look at Shiloh, then studied Cheney. Shiloh looked grim, his jaw clenching occasionally. Cheney's face had paled, though the cold of the morning colored her high cheekbones prettily. The line of her back and the set of her shoulders were strained, as if by sitting stiffly she could hurry the small buggy.

"Whass St. Anthony's fire?" Rissy demanded.

"Erysipelas," Cheney answered automatically, her eyes searching the streets ahead.

Shiloh's mouth twitched, and he glanced sideways at Rissy over Cheney's head. Rissy winked solemnly at him. "Oh," she said. "Well, now I see why they calls it St. Anthony's fire. So what is it, Miss Doctah Cheney?"

"An acute febrile disease associated with intense edematous local inflammation of the skin and subcutaneous tissues."

"Oh," Rissy said again, ladling sarcasm. Cheney didn't notice, and Shiloh almost smiled, so Rissy went on, "Whass feburl?"

"Characterized by fever, or feverish," Cheney answered impatiently. "Shiloh, it's the next corner."

"Yes, Doc," he said obediently, making a face secretly at Rissy. The lines around his eyes had relaxed, she noted, but his hands gripped the reins so tightly that his knuckles were white. She grinned reassuringly back at him.

"So whass edeemitus?" Rissy asked innocently.

"Dropsy, or swelling. An abnormal excess accumulation of serous fluid in connective tissue or in a serous cavity," Cheney answered, her mind clearly far away from the words.

"Oh. So whass inflation?"

"Inflammation," Cheney said tightly. "Shiloh, watch out for those two men. Hurry up." Without taking her eyes from the street, she continued, "It's a local response to cellular injury marked by capillary dilatation, leukocytic infiltration, redness, heat, and pain."

"Yes, ma'am, I thought so," Rissy grunted. Still Cheney missed the mischief in her tone, and Rissy looked up at Shiloh's profile. "Did you know all that, Mistuh Arns?"

"Nope," he answered, a quick grin flitting across his face. "I just thought it was a sickness when you got fever, and your skin turns red, and you swell up."

"That's what I just said," Cheney snapped. "Shiloh, hurry up—you're letting Sock just dawdle along!"

"Doc, he's pulling hard already," Shiloh said gently. "It's all right. I'll scrub good when we get back to the room."

"And I want you to strip off all those clothes," Cheney muttered ominously.

Shiloh's left eyebrow shot up, and he opened his mouth, but when he caught a glimpse of Rissy's face he quickly pulled his expression back into a semblance of gravity. "Um . . . sure, Doc," he said meekly.

"Hmph," Rissy growled, low in her throat, and turned back to face straight ahead.

"Hurry!" Cheney cried.

★ ★ ★ ★

Two hours later Shiloh's quiet knock sounded on Cheney's door. Before Cheney could rise from the table by her French windows, Rissy sailed into Cheney's room and threw open the door. Shiloh was casual, his arms crossed, his legs far apart. His hair was still a little damp, and the stringent scent of carbolic acid still clung faintly to him. "Can I come in, Rissy?" he wheedled. "I'm all clean and pure now."

"Hmph," she grunted, stepping aside for him to enter. "Thass a matter fo' some speculatin'."

Cheney narrowed her eyes to look him up and down, and finally she sighed deeply. Then, with conscious effort, she cleared her face of anxiety and relaxed her posture. "Hello," she said uncomfortably. "Sit down, please."

Shiloh grinned easily as he lounged into the chair across from her. "Hey, Doc, you don't have to be embarrassed 'cause you were worried about me. St. Anthony's fire is no joke. I know. I wouldn't want you to get it."

"I'm not embarrassed," Cheney muttered, blushing.

Rissy rolled her eyes to high heaven, then propped her hands accusingly on her hips as she turned to Shiloh. "Where's them clothes?" she demanded.

"Huh? Oh. The ones that Doc insisted I strip off immediately," Shiloh said as innocently as a baby lamb. Rissy's eyes grew round with warning and hastily he went on, "Don't worry about them, Rissy. I'll take care of them later."

"Uh-huh. Whatcha gonna do wid 'em?"

"I dunno," Shiloh said carelessly. "I'll find a kettle or pot or something somewhere and soak 'em in a carbolic acid mixture. Then take 'em to a laundry."

"Uh-huh," Rissy said again accusingly. "I'd almost let you

do it, if'n I could be aroun' when you go down to the kitchen to 'splain to Miz Philomena 'bout how you need one o' her pots to wash yore britches in."

"Miz Philomena?" Shiloh repeated blankly.

"She's the cook," Rissy said smugly, "an' she'd fetch her a step stool to stand on whilst she beat you over the haid wid a big ol' rollin' pin. An' you'd stand still an' let her do it, too."

"Uh-oh," Shiloh said with vague alarm. "That kind of lady."

Cheney, recovered now, began to chuckle. "Maybe you'd better let Rissy handle this, Shiloh."

"Okay," he said with visible relief. "I don't think I want to go up against Miz Philomena." His eyes crinkled as he looked up at Rissy. "Thank you, Rissy, I would appreciate it. But listen—I wrapped the clothes up in a clean towel. Don't unwrap it, and don't handle the clothes. Just dump the . . . whole . . . thing . . . in . . ."

Rissy had drawn herself up to her full height, and her dark eyes flashed with menace. "I know you ain't tellin' me how to clean up after doctahs who been handlin' who knows what!" she barked. "Mistuh Dev and Miss Cheney would burn they doctorin' clothes and scrub they skin off! Hmph!" With that somewhat obtuse observation, she whirled and stalked out of the room, her head held as high as a queen's.

"Gosh," Shiloh said repentantly. "Does that mean she's gonna burn my clothes and scrub my skin off?"

"No, I don't think so," Cheney teased. "At least—maybe not. We'll hope not."

Shiloh held up his hands and turned them over, his face rueful. "If she does, we've got a good start on my hands. That carbolic acid is tough stuff." His hands were big and roughened. Four of the knuckles were permanently outsized from his prizefighting bouts. Now they were stained slightly yellow, and the skin underneath already looked chapped. "But it sure does work," he sighed.

Cheney leaned forward, resting her elbow on the table, and propped her chin on her hand. A Bible lay on the table in front of her, and she pushed it to the side but left it open. Shiloh glanced down at it and saw with a start that it was opened to the nineteenth chapter of Leviticus. The only Bible verses that Shiloh knew—the "Manigault Scripture," verses nine and ten—were underlined in heavy black ink in Cheney's Bible.

She was talking, and with an effort Shiloh raised his eyes to direct his attention to her. "Shiloh, you know, I've never even asked you, or talked to you about it. Now that I think of that hospital, and Dr. Van Dorn, I've realized how odd it is that you practice disinfection so faithfully. You always have. How is that, since most doctors not only don't believe in it, they actually discourage it? How did you learn?"

"I've been meaning to ask you about it," Shiloh said, sitting up a little straighter. "It is funny that we've never talked about it. See, I don't know any medical reasons why. The only reason I believe in 'disinfection' is 'cause of the Behring sisters."

"Yes?" Cheney asked curiously. "They studied medicine?"

"Nah. They studied cleanliness," he replied mischievously. "If they woulda studied medicine, they wouldn't have been so big on disinfection."

"Sad but true," Cheney said caustically. "But tell me. Just being clean didn't teach you about disinfection, about carbolic acid and chlorinated lime and procedures for prevention. How do you know all you do about such things?"

"This is gonna sound kinda funny," he drawled, "but it's all 'cause of smell." In spite of the carelessness of his words, he gave her an anxious glance.

Cheney frowned, then her face cleared and she almost laughed. "You have a very keen sense of smell, don't you? And 'laudable pus'—"

"Stinks to high tarnation!"

"I can't believe it," Cheney said softly. "Do you mean to tell me that because what almost all doctors swear is 'laudable pus' actually smells like rot that you figured out the efficacy of preventive disinfection?"

Shiloh, Cheney had observed in the past two years, was incredibly intuitive about sick people and simply knew instinctively how to make them feel better. He was an astute learner who could remember complicated prescriptives easily, and when Cheney taught him a medical principle, he was able to translate it into practice efficiently. But for an untrained medical attendant to learn, and believe in, and commonly practice the principles of disinfection—contrary to traditional, unquestioned medical teachings—was unheard of.

"It wasn't quite that big a jump," he finally said, frowning. "You really wanta know how I decided to use carbolic acid or chlorinated lime or whatever?"

"Yes, I really want to know. I think it's fascinating that you've reached this conclusion—the same conclusion that Dev Buchanan and I worked out painstakingly by studying and collating information from four studies made over the span of a decade, by four different doctors, in four different countries," she said sarcastically. "It took Dev two years to compile our findings and conclusions on disinfection, and it took me two months to go through his final report. So how did you find out?" She snapped her fingers. "Just like that?"

"Yeah," he grinned.

"You did not!"

"Okay, I'll tell you," he relented. He looked out the windows for a few moments. The day was pale gray and lifeless. The soldiers wore single-caped greatcoats as they hurried along the street, hunched over in a futile attempt to escape the bite of the wind. Inside Cheney's hotel room the fire was warm, and the room itself looked warm with its dark maroon carpet and drapes, and the rich patina of the mahogany four-poster bed and matching Provence armoire. The Planter's Hotel was sturdily built and well insulated, so that even though it fronted directly onto Church Street, all outside sounds were pleasantly muted.

"In the war, in the field hospitals," he said, still staring out at the cold-blooded day, "the doctors always wanted to be sure and operate within the first twenty-four hours. Called it the 'primary period.' They said that they wanted to avoid the 'irritative period,' when the infection showed itself. Then the 'laudable pus' would appear, and that's what the doctors said was the lin-

197

ing of the wound being expelled so that clean tissue could re-
place it and the wound could heal. Have I got it right so far?"
He looked back at her.

"Yes," Cheney said quietly. "Go on."

He shrugged disdainfully. "Well, that hardly ever happened.
I saw a lot of men with lots of 'laudable pus.'" Searching back
out the window as if for a clean vision, his mouth tightened and
his voice grew curt. "I don't know how many of them I saw—
the pus stopped, the wound dried up, and they'd get a terrifically
high fever. Then the doctors would use carbolic acid—after the
infection was spreading like fire all over them from their
wound."

"Did that do any good? Any of them? Can you estimate any
percentages?" Cheney asked quickly.

"Sure I can. At that stage it helped about zero percent of
them."

"Oh. Well, that definitely simplifies our scientific compila-
tion of percentages."

"You know, it's hard for me to believe sometimes that it's so
simple and clear to you, Doc. And all those doctors"—he shook
his head—"they slaved, and worked, and cried, and went without sleep and food, and started all over again. They cared, and
they hurt, and they did everything a man could do to take care
of their men. But they seemed to be blind about some things."

Cheney sighed and ran her slender fingers down the page of
her open Bible. The parchment made a pleasing rustle in the
quiet room. "I know that, Shiloh. I know."

"Sure you do," he said in a low voice. "Better than anyone,
because most doctors are just as stupidly blind about you."

She gave him a grateful look, but he went on quickly, "Anyway, here's how it looked to me." Ticking off on his long fingers,
he explained: "A man gets shot. There's a bullet, and gunpowder,
and dirt, and who knows what all in the wound. Then you dig
it out with a scalpel that's dirty. Then the wound gets all this
pus that smells dirty." He dropped his hands, an abrupt, helpless
gesture. "And then you get a raging infection. And then you die.
Nobody's ever explained to me what's the problem with just first

washing out an open wound with something clean! You better know, when I took that musket ball in my leg, I poured a whole bottle of carbolic acid into it before they could explain to me that it wouldn't do any good! And I never got a sign of infection!"

Cheney was surprised at his vehemence, but she kept her voice clinical and even. "All right. Suppose there's no problem with cleaning out a wound or open sore. Why carbolic acid?"

"Like I told you, because it smells clean!" he snapped. "It's not a perfumy smell, for sure, but it smells clean!" Suddenly his face was a picture of ludicrous surprise, as he saw Cheney hiding a smile behind her hand as he railed at her. Shiloh recovered quickly. "You got all that, you doctor you?" he ranted mockingly. "Who needs all that book larnin' when you've got a nose!"

"It isn't as easy for those of us who are obliged to do without your particular nose," Cheney said with admirable gravity. "You see, according to Rissy, Dev's fine nose is either stuck in a book, or else he is struggling and not succeeding to see past the end of it."

Shiloh began to chuckle, and Cheney had difficulty keeping a straight face as she continued, "Also in Rissy's judgment, my own personal nose is always either stuck up in the air, or pokin' into someplace it don't belong, or is gittin' bended out of shape. In any case, now you see why Dev and I had to learn the hard way. We didn't have your nose around to tell us what to do."

Now Shiloh was laughing, which always made Cheney laugh.

Rissy appeared in the hall doorway—she had left Cheney's door pointedly agape—and stuck her hands back on her hips. "I'm too embarrassed to even come in heah!" she fussed, yanking the door shut. "I heared you two laughin' like two peahens all the way down in the kitchen with Miz Philomena!" The door slammed with finality.

Shiloh and Cheney abruptly grew quiet. Then, with guilty glances at each other, they burst into laughter again.

After this merry interlude Shiloh returned to their previous, more sober, conversation. "Anyway, Doc, it's like I said. I never had anybody teach me anything about disinfection. It just seems to me like there's kind of a special—uncleanness—about sickness and infections, and somehow stuff like carbolic acid and chloride of lime and sodium hypochlorite just seem like they're more . . . like . . . cleansing, I guess you'd say."

Cheney sighed and rested her hand across the Bible that lay open between them. "It's funny you should say that, and it's funny that you should use those particular words. I was just reading in Leviticus all about the different kinds of skin diseases—they called them all 'plagues,' and God told them exactly how to differentiate between the contagious ones, which were called 'leprous' and 'unclean' and the noncontagious ones, which were pronounced 'clean.' The contagious, leprous plagues required specific 'cleansings,' and the noncontagious ones only required cleanliness." She glanced up at him. "Sounds very much like what you were just saying."

He shrugged, dismissing the subject. "Okay, Doc, it's your turn. You tell me how you know about disinfection."

Smiling faintly, she closed the Bible and propped her chin back on one hand. "I don't think I will."

"Huh?"

Cheney chewed on her lower lip for a moment, her eyes speculative. "I think I'll get Dev's study on it and let you read it. I think that would be better than my just telling you."

He thought for a few moments, then nodded. "Okay. But you have to help me if I can't get through the first two sentences."

"I'll help you if you need it. But I really don't think you will." Before he could answer, she sat up straighter and folded her arms on the table. "Now. Tell me about Captain Perry."

He shook his head. "Sorry, Doc. There's nothing to tell. I mean, I didn't talk to him." His voice was carefully even. "He got whacked in the back of the head a week ago with something wooden, probably a rifle stock. Wooden splinters in the abrasion. Concussion, but no depression in the skull. He was down at the docks, and a fisherman found him."

"Who did this to him, and why?"

Shiloh shrugged. "One of the stewards told me they think it

was probably Gard's Rangers. But nobody knows because Captain Perry hasn't been well enough to question. He was unconscious when the fisherman brought him to the hospital, and stayed unconscious for a long time."

"How long?" Cheney demanded.

"For about thirty-six hours. When he woke up he seemed to be recovering pretty well. He was dazed and confused, his vision was blurred, and of course he was weak. But he was regaining strength."

"Then he got erysipelas," Cheney said grimly.

"Yes. He was the third one to get it."

"How many have it now?"

"Eight. Out of fifty-eight patients." Shiloh's mouth twisted. "Dr. Van Dorn's doing exactly what we did in the field hospitals when it broke out. He's got them separated, in the back room. They paint the edges of the infection with iodine."

"Well, I suppose that's better than nothing."

Shiloh gave her a quick, hard-eyed look. "But, Doc, you and I know that it's not good enough. It's true, the iodine does keep the disease from spreading—on the patient. But . . ."

"But the attendants don't wash between patients," Cheney finished, her voice tight, "and so the disease is spread from patient to patient."

"That's right," he said harshly. "We had an outbreak of it at a field hospital in Atlanta, and the case mortality was about forty percent. I got to wondering: if it was something in the air, and we isolated the patients that already had St. Anthony's fire, how come other patients all over the place kept getting it? So I watched. After three days I saw that the nurses would treat the patients, then come back into the general ward and treat other patients. And almost every time, it'd be one of those men that would come down with it next." Narrowing his eyes as he stared into space he muttered, "It just seemed like common sense to me. But when I asked a doctor about it he told me to stick with givin' the men whiskey and emptyin' the slop pails, like a nurse was supposed to do."

"I'm so sorry, Shiloh," Cheney said softly.

He jerked his head around sharply, then consciously relaxed into his customary careless manner. "Aw, forget it, Doc," he drawled, his eyes softening. "After all, I haven't had to put up with nearly as much guff as you have. And about Captain Perry, he was feverish and drifting in and out of a light sleep. He woke up and looked at me, but I could tell that he didn't feel like talking. So I didn't say anything to him."

"You're right, of course," Cheney sighed. "It's just that—I was hoping to learn something—anything—about Allan Blue."

Shiloh was silent for a long time. He leaned back in the white wrought-iron chair that seemed too small and too ornate for him. Staring at his boots, he said in a faraway voice, "Well, Doc, I gotta tell you. Captain E. Allan Perry has like . . . big, girly, hazel eyes, and he's got those long, thick eyelashes. And his hair—it was dirty and matted and long—but you could tell it's that . . . unusual color . . . that color . . . like . . ."

"Like honey, and gold, and tawny streaks?" Cheney asked excitedly.

"Yeah."

"Like Laura Blue's?"

"Yeah," he said reluctantly. "Just like Laura Blue's."

17

COLD IN THE MIDNIGHT

"Look, Doc! I brought you a present." Shiloh Irons joined Cheney out on her tiny balcony and handed her a stiff piece of paper, rolled up into a neat cylinder.

"Good evening, Shiloh," she said pointedly. "It's almost midnight. I was beginning to think you'd miss the parade. What's this?" Cheney unrolled the ten-inch-by-twelve-inch paper, then looked up at Shiloh accusingly. "You stole this!"

"Sure did," he grinned.

The poster read:

TAKE NOTICE

Knights of the White Rose
—bearing the sign of the rose—

Will Assemble
Midnight, Friday, January 20th,
The Year of Our Lord 1867

"Dum spiro, spero"

"What's that mean?" Shiloh asked, pointing to the Latin words.

" 'While I breathe, I hope,' " Cheney answered, studying the cryptic poster.

The announcement, which had appeared in the Thursday and Friday editions of the *Charleston Record*, was dramatic and imperious. On Friday morning, when the soldiers and citizens of Charleston had begun their workday, signs with this notice were posted on the lampposts at the corners of Queen, Church, Chalmers, and Broad Streets, which seemed to indicate that the mysterious parade would take place in this two-block square.

Charlestonians, rebelling against the bleak and oppressive days, created an air of festivity for themselves, and by eleven-thirty on Friday night these four streets were thronged with men, women, families, and soldiers, shivering in the cold, but determined to hold their place and watch these knights, who-ever or whatever they may be. Hawkers walked up and down, selling hot toddies and hot lemonade and hot tea, cookies and hot bread and cheese. One enterprising young woman had made small rosebuds out of bits of white tissue paper and was selling them for a penny apiece.

Cheney frowned severely up at Shiloh, who was still grin-ning. "What do you know about these Knights of the White Rose, anyway?" she asked suspiciously. "And—thank you, I guess—but why bring me one of these posters?"

He shrugged, turned, and leaned down to rest his elbows on the wrought-iron railing. "I don't know anything about this, Doc, honest. In fact, that's why I was out there wandering around, to see if some people or something was outside this two-block area"—he waved a long, strong arm expressively—"forming up. But I didn't see anything that looked like a parade. Then, when I was fighting my way back to the hotel—there's a bunch of people out there—I had the idea of taking one of these posters." He gave her a sly glance. "To see who, if anybody, would try and stop me."

Cheney made a face at him and demanded. "So? Did any-one?"

"Nope."

"Then that only leaves the one question. Why do you give it to me? Why don't you keep it?"

He stood up straight and crossed his arms, looking down at her. He was wearing his black hat, and his eyes were shadowed, but she could clearly see his mouth in the stream of light from the gas lamps below. One corner of his lips turned up crookedly. " 'Cause, you're one of the Dark Angels of the Mystic Rose," he said airily. "Their trademark is white roses. Maybe I should be asking *you* about the Knights of the White Rose!"

This was a reference to Cheney and Victoria de Lancie, who had attended two of Shiloh's prizefights. Each time Victoria had carried a single long-stemmed white rose and supplied dozens of white roses with which to shower the victor—who in each case had been Shiloh Irons. One of the more sensational New York newspapers had sold many papers with mysterious references to, and drawings of, the two heavily veiled women they had dubbed "The Dark Angels of the Mystic Rose."

Cheney propped her hands on her hips and her face flushed. "Oh! Shiloh! Really, you are so—" Suddenly she stopped, turned, placed her hands with exaggerated fluttering movements on the railing, and smiled up at him in a syrupy way. "Oh, Shiloh, you're mistaken. The other Dark Angel had roses. I had a scalpel, remember? A long, glittering, sharp one."

"Oh, yeah," he grimaced with mock fear. "I forgot."

"Don't forge-et!" she twittered.

"I won't. I don't."

"And one other thing," she said, still speaking in a voice of highly exaggerated sweetness, "if you tell anyone about the Dark Angels of the Mystic Rose, I'm going to tell everyone that it's because your fighting nickname is 'The Sweet White Rose of Manhattan.'"

Shiloh, who had been dubbed "The Iron Man" when he was sixteen years old, flinched painfully. "Gosh, Doc, I swear to you I'll never tell."

"Good," she said in her normal voice. "And thank you for the memento. What do you suppose we'll be remembering?"

"Dunno. Nobody knows."

They stood watching the crowd below and staring curiously toward Chalmers Street. If the parade was conducted in the two-block square indicated by the placement of the signs, then the Planter's Hotel would be at the top right corner of the route.

"Look," Shiloh said and pointed south. "The streetlights are going out."

Cheney and Shiloh could see clearly almost two blocks away. They were above street level, and because the second floor of the hotel abutted out almost to the street, and the balconies al-

205

most overhung the street, their view was unobstructed straight down Church Street. Both of them had excellent eyesight and could see the two blocks down to Broad easily. The gas lamps had obviously been turned off along Broad and Chalmers, with the rest of the city a benevolent yellow glow hovering behind. Shiloh pointed again, directly across from the hotel, and Cheney immediately saw that the gas lamps were going out on Meeting Street, parallel to them, at the same time.

And then they came. A long column of men on horseback, four abreast, snaked up Church Street, led by a single man. They wore white hoods, with slits cut only for their eyes, and long shapeless white robes that covered even their boots. The horses were swathed completely in white, flowing down to their knees. As they rode slowly down the street, one Knight in formation directly behind the leader reached up a long, slender pole and inserted it into the gas lamp; he turned it very slightly, and the circle of yellow light disappeared. The man's horse never got out of step with the column.

"Looks like one of 'em is the streetlighter," Shiloh joked.

"Shh!" Cheney said, jabbing him in the side. It was like hitting her elbow on a stone.

"Why? The notice didn't command us to be quiet!" he hissed.

"But everyone is! Don't make a scene!"

The crowd had grown unnaturally subdued. Even children stood quietly by their parents. The hawkers' monotonous calls had stopped.

The column of white ghost-men and ghost-horses marched. The leader of the Knights of the White Rose reached the corner of Church Street, just past the Planter's Hotel, and stopped, facing north. Behind him, the column came close behind them, then stopped. The silence was eerie. Loud rustles of fabric and slight creaks of saddles sounded, and then each of the Knights thrust staves high in the air. The leader's stave flamed, and he wheeled his horse.

Impossibly, it seemed—for the four-man column looked tightly packed—the leader galloped down the middle of the col-

206

umn, with two columns on the right and two on the left. As he rode, the Knights touched their torches to his, and they flared into flame, and they in turn lit the torches of the men next to them. Suddenly Church Street was again lit, the scene flickering weirdly by the lurid lights of hundreds of small torches.

Now Cheney could see one detail of the costume; each man had a small device worked in black on his left shoulder. She couldn't see the device, of course, but she was certain it must be a white rose. Each horse, also, had the device on a back corner of his draping.

"Well," Shiloh drawled, "it 'pears they're all white men."

"Yes," Cheney retorted sarcastically, "and they all have white horses."

He winked down at her. "Their hands, Doc."

"Oh."

Not a single word was spoken by the Knights. Every so often a shrill whistle sounded, signaling the columns to countermarch or turn a corner. The riders kept perfectly still, holding the spitting torches, looking neither to the left nor right. In the stillness they marched and countermarched in the two-block area, crossing over in opposite directions on the cross streets, the lines never broken, with no end or beginning. One man—the one who had led the column up Church Street—stood still and motionless at the head of the street, and obviously the shrill whistle came from him, though no slash was made in his hood for his mouth.

Shiloh nodded toward him. "Must be another one at the head of Meeting Street. When he whistles, you can hear an echo, a split-second behind his."

He watched the marching and countermarching, precise and disciplined, with narrowed eyes, then looked back at the lone figure, obviously the leader, at the head of the street. Cheney followed his gaze. "This is some pretty fancy marchin'," he muttered to himself.

Cheney arched her eyebrows in speculation. "Looks like the precise military hand of Captain Shadrach Forrest Luxton, if you ask me. And that—Knight—could be he. Look at the width of his shoulders, but he's slender. There's certainly too many of them just to be the cadets from the Citadel."

"True."

"But," she went on, nodding her head in the direction of the motionless leader, "that horse is certainly not Israfel, that's obvious." She leaned over the balcony a little. "That's a chocolate . . . with a . . . with a . . . that's . . . that's Sock!"

Shiloh jerked upright. "What! What!"

Cheney, who was glaring at him accusingly, suddenly laughed. "For a minute I thought you'd been fooling me, that you were in on all this!" She waved her hand expressively out over the crowd. "That's Sock!"

"Well, that little—scoundrel!" Shiloh growled, propping his hands on his hips. "You're right!"

Cheney was laughing with delight at Shiloh's discomfort. Suddenly he grinned and pointed. "There's Stocking, too. They musta both joined the Knights of the White Rose at the same time."

"What! What!" Cheney leaned precariously over the balcony, straining to look at the throng of horses' legs on the street. Sure enough, a white stocking flashed, and Cheney stared accusingly at the rider. He didn't exactly move his head, but Cheney could have sworn he glanced up at her, and she was certain it was Logan Manigault.

"Those little scoundrels!" she snapped, unconsciously echoing Shiloh. "Shiloh, did they ask you?"

"Nope." He shook his head, still grinning. "Did they ask you?"

"No! Of course not!"

"Whatcha wanta do, Doc? Have 'em arrested and hung for horse thievin'?"

Cheney, frowning, started to answer, then suddenly flashed a grin up at him. "Yes!"

He shrugged, then went to the French doors leading back into Cheney's hotel room. "From what I hear, Judge Garth Granger would probably oblige you," he said darkly. "Guess I better go down to the livery. Betcha Israfel and Logan's horse are down there in Sock's and Stocking's stalls. Think I'll have me a talk with those boys after this is all over."

Cheney searched his face with a little anxiety, but his eyes were gleaming, and she relaxed. "You'd probably better. Probably poor little Mr. Roddy felt that he had to steal a horse, too, if Shadrach and Mr. Manigault did. You'd better make certain that that horse's owner can take a joke, too."

"Okay, Doc." He opened one of the French doors, then turned. "Listen, don't go anywhere, okay?"

Cheney frowned. "And where do you suppose I might go? At midnight?" As an afterthought she added hastily, "And why shouldn't I, if I want to?"

"Never mind," he muttered, waving his hand in a downward motion of dismissal. "I shoulda known better." Then he left.

Cheney turned back and watched the parade for a while. It was bitterly cold, and she clutched her warm gray wool cloak around her tightly. Then the tips of her ears got icy, and she pulled up the hood, shivering slightly.

Rissy came out onto the balcony. "Heah, drink this. If'n youse gonna stand out heah like a icicle you might as well git warmed up." She held out a large, thick white mug.

Cheney grabbed it greedily and took a long whiff of the delicious citrus-spice aroma, and the steam curling up from it bit hotly at the tip of her nose. "Mmm . . . apple cider."

"*Hot* apple cider," Rissy cautioned, "and youse s'posed to put it in yo' mouth, not stick yore nose in it." Whirling, she headed back into Cheney's hotel room but turned again. "And don't drink a big gulp of thet stuff right now! Iss too hot! Then you'll be grumpy tomorrow, wid a burned tongue!"

"Yes, Rissy," Cheney said meekly. "I'll be good."

"Doubt it," she grumbled, pulling the double doors shut.

Cheney turned back to watch the parade. The Knights looked as if they were going to march for quite a while. With interest she began to pick out faces in the crowd. She noticed a little boy, holding tightly to his mother's hands, his face lit with innocent delight. His mother's lips were pressed tightly together, and her eyes searched the riders. *Perhaps*, Cheney thought, *she's looking for her husband.* The soldiers in blue were holding their rifles at that position that was not exactly at the ready but neither was it careless—rifle butt propped on their hips, barrels pointed toward the sky. Most of them looked amused or interested, but a few of them looked wary and scanned the crowd continually for trouble. But the crowd of people was well-behaved, orderly, and quiet, Cheney observed. She also noted that there was not one Negro anywhere that she could see.

She caressed the steaming cup in both hands, warming her fingers. *Rissy didn't fuss about my not wearing gloves,* she thought idly. *She's been a little—not tense—kind of—keyed up today. Wonder why?* Again Cheney studied the crowd and thought about the absence of any Negro faces. Normally Negro men and boys were all over the streets of Charleston. Taking a cautious sip of the steaming cider, she burned her tongue.

The doors behind her creaked open, but Cheney didn't turn around.

"Miss Cheney? Could you come in heah, please?"

Cheney whirled in surprise. Rissy stood in the French doors, glancing behind her. When she looked at Cheney, her strong features were clouded with worry. Cheney hurried to her. "Of course, Rissy. What is it? What's wrong?"

They went into Cheney's room, and Rissy shut the doors, then glided to the connecting door that led into her adjoining room. "Please, in heah, Miss Cheney," she said, giving Cheney a pleading look over her shoulder. Cheney followed her, mystified.

Luke Alexander stood in Rissy's room. He looked huge, and undoubtedly he was uncomfortable. His head was dropped low, and he fidgeted with a wide-brimmed hat, turning it around and around between his long, black fingers.

Rissy stood close to him and turned back to Cheney. "Some friends of Luke's is real sick, Miss Cheney. He came to get me, but it sounds like they need a doctah. Will you come?"

Cheney never hesitated, not for a fraction of a second. "Of course. Who are these people?"

Luke Alexander looked up, and Cheney now saw that his unusual almond-shaped eyes, which he had kept hidden from her, were smoldering with resentment. "They're colored, Dr. Duvall," he said, his voice guttural. "I didn't ask Rissy to ask for your help."

Cheney faced him, her shoulders erect, her face wiped clean of all expression. "These people, they are ill?"

He nodded, once, then dropped his eyes again cautiously.

"They need a doctor?"

He nodded.

"I am a doctor, Mr. Alexander. That is not just what I *do*, that is what I *am*." She watched him, and after a moment he lifted his face, which was now cleared of resentment, but was carefully expressionless. After a moment he nodded once more.

"Good," she said briskly. "Now, I need to know some things, so that I can bring the right medicines. These people, are they old? Young? Children? How many are there?"

Alexander dropped his eyes again. "They're just old people, Dr. Duvall. An old couple."

"Yes? What are their symptoms?"

"Miss Lalie's got fever," he replied uneasily. He glanced at Rissy for support, and she nodded approvingly at him. "She's been sick a couple of days, I think. But Miss Lalie, she's sicker than Moody." He shrugged helplessly. "I don't know much more. Both of 'em has stuffy heads, and Moody's sneezing, hard, and a lot."

Cheney turned to go back to her room. "All right, Mr. Alexander. Wait here, please, while I get my medical bag packed." She hesitated, then turned back. "How did you get here?"

"I drove a cart into town," he said. "Dr. Duvall, Moody and Lalie live out in the swamps. You sure you wanna—"

"Yes," she interrupted. "If your cart can carry all three of us. My horse is—not available at the moment. And neither is my nurse."

"'Course, I'm comin'," Rissy said, glancing up at Luke, and Cheney was astonished at the warmth and affection in her eyes and voice. "I know I ain't no nurse like Mistuh Shiloh, but I can help you, Miss Cheney."

"Y-yes, of course you can, Rissy," Cheney stammered. Then she grew still, and frowned with concentration. "Where did you get my apple cider?"

"Down in the kitchen. They're stayin' open tonight 'cause of that spectickle." Rissy jerked her head toward the street, and Luke's hands tightened—jerked—on his hat. The brim crumpled.

"Go see if they have any plain apple juice, Rissy. Not with all this heavy spice added. If not, get some apples, about a dozen," Cheney ordered as she hurried back into her room. "Get two lemons and a jar of honey. And get some clear broth—a half gallon, if they have it. If not . . ."

"I'll git me some chickens and cook it up myself," Rissy called after her.

"Yes!" Cheney called from the other room.

Luke Alexander watched Cheney's back, then turned to look down at Rissy, and took her hands. "You're somethin', woman," he teased. "Done got Moody and Lalie a real doctor!"

Rissy smiled and stepped close to him. "The best doctah you ever saw," she murmured.

"Aw, she's just a white woman," he said mockingly, then bent to kiss her.

Rissy pushed him away with surprising strength and stalked to her door. "Miss Lalie and Mistuh Moody's gonna be thankin' the Lord for her before this night's over, Luke," she growled in a fierce whisper. "An' you better start doin' the same, right now! She ain't just doin' this for me, you know. She'd do it for you, or for anybody!"

"Would she?" He shrugged with open disdain.

"Yes, suh, she would! An' while I'm down in the kitchen, doin' somethin' useful, you jist git on back downstairs to thet buggy!" she huffed, still in the menacing whisper. "You ain't stayin' up here in my room like I'm some kinda fancy woman!" She flounced out the door, leaving it open.

Luke Alexander chuckled and shook his head. But he did obediently follow Rissy out the door.

★ ★ ★ ★

Moody and Lalie had influenza, as Cheney had suspected. Influenza was a sly illness, and capricious. Sometimes it attacked people in a form so mild it was much like a common cold, and sometimes it was devastating, and sometimes it was fatal. No prescriptive cured it.

Lalie had been sick for two days, and Moody was only now coming down with it. The little old man was terrified—not because he was getting sick—but because his wife was so ill. Cheney was completely unsuccessful in calming him down, because he seemed to be in complete awe of her; he even seemed to be positively afraid of her. Finally Rissy sat down with him at a crude wooden table and took his hand, and stroked it, and spoke softly to him.

The cabin had only one room and a dirt floor, which was meticulously covered with fresh pine needles and cedar rushes. Though the cabin was so old the cypress boards were blackened, it was spotlessly clean, with plain white curtains and white crockery that gleamed on the single shelf above the sink and pump. The rough wooden table had two rickety chairs. A black metal stand was in the fireplace, and four heavy black iron pots and pans were hanging on the wall. The bed, tucked into the corner of the tiny room, had clean sheets and a cheerful crazy quilt coverlet. Miss Lalie was in bed, though she tried to get up when Cheney came into the cabin. She was so tiny she looked like a little girl instead of a woman. Her fever was very high, and when she coughed it racked her body so savagely that she could barely breathe.

Cheney turned to Luke Alexander's hulking figure. He had been obliged to stoop to come in the cabin door, and his head seemed perilously close to the open crossbeams of the roof. "Mr. Alexander, you warm up some of that apple juice, just to where it's warm on your wrist—the way you do milk for a baby." Cheney ignored his blank look and went on issuing orders as unconcernedly as if he were her servant. "And heat up two cups of that chicken broth, get it hot. And, no, Rissy can't help you; she's going to have to help me."

She turned to Moody, who was calm now and sat watching Cheney with wide, dark eyes. Occasionally he sneezed, and his nose was running. His handkerchief was a large square of red flannel, and it was clean, Cheney noted with approval. "Mr. Moody, I want you to sit there and be quiet, and drink as much of that apple juice as you can get down. Then, when you can, drink all of the water you can get down." She looked at him closely.

"Yes, ma'am," he said obediently. "I will."

"Don't just drink when you're thirsty, Mr. Moody," Cheney went on. "Drink something all the time. Water or fruit juice. No coffee, but you may have weak tea, sweetened with lots of honey. But right now have apple juice."

"Yes, ma'am." He licked his lips and turned to watch Luke Alexander as he gently stirred the apple juice he had already poured into a big pot and had hung over the fire. The smell of fresh apples permeated the little cabin and mingled sweetly with the smell of the pine and cedar. "Could I hev some of it right now, Doctah?" he asked meekly. "It shore do smell heavenly!"

"Yes, it does," Cheney smiled. "Of course, as I said, have as much as you can hold."

He started to say something but sneezed instead. Cheney sighed. Tomorrow, probably, or maybe the next day, he would be as ill as his wife was right now. She turned to Rissy. "I'm going to make a whiskey toddy for Miss Lalie. After she drinks it, she'll start to sweat. We need to bathe her with lukewarm water and break this fever. Will you see if you can find a pail or a basin, and get some water, and wash her face and hands right now?"

"If it's from that pump, it's going to be icy," Rissy said doubtfully. "I'll have to heat it up a little."

"Yes, go ahead," Cheney said. She took off her heavy cloak and threw it carelessly onto the single empty chair at the table. Setting her businesslike black leather medical bag on the table, she took out a spotless white bibbed apron and put it on, fumbling with the wide ties at the back. Wordlessly Rissy stepped up and tied it into a big perky bow as Cheney started taking bottles out of the bag. She glanced at Moody, who sat with his head bowed, his gnarled black hands crumpled helplessly in his lap. "Are you all right, Mr. Moody?" she asked softly.

He looked up, and tears shimmered in his old eyes. "Why, shore enuff, Doctah Duvall. I'm gittin' better now, since you've come. I was just thankin' the Lord Jesus for sendin' you here. You're a miracle walkin', is what I think."

Rissy cast a triumphant glance over her shoulder at Luke, who looked suitably subdued.

"Oh no," Cheney smiled. "I'm just a doctor. But you keep right on praying, Mr. Moody. I'm glad that you know Jesus, because it is by His stripes we are healed. And that is how your wife will be healed, Mr. Moody. I promise."

★　★　★　★

"It's cold in this midnight," Rissy said, shivering.

"It's way past midnight," Cheney muttered, pulling her cloak closer around her. "I have no idea what time it is, but it must be three or four o'clock in the morning." She made a brisk clicking sound, then jerked the reins a little. Luke Alexander's horse was obedient and moved smartly along the dark, muddy road, though Cheney dared not coax him into a trot.

Lalie's fever had broken, and she had been able to drink an entire cup of the rich chicken broth. Cheney knew that she was not in any real danger, but the influenza was making her weak and miserable. She would begin to feel better, probably the very next day. Cheney had given very simple instructions to Moody on how to take care of his wife.

Then she had cautioned him in clear language that he would likely be as sick as Miss Lalie was by tomorrow or the next day. This upset him again, because he was afraid he wouldn't be able to take care of his wife. He was so distressed that Luke Alexander had gruffly offered to stay the remainder of the night and see how Miss Lalie was in the morning.

Cheney and Rissy had wearily decided to take the buggy and return to Charleston to try to get a few hours' sleep. Rissy would bring the buggy back to Luke in the morning, and Cheney promised to come back the next afternoon.

"You sure you know the way back, Miss Cheney?" Rissy asked hesitantly. "I sure wasn't watching when we came."

"You were watching Mr. Alexander," Cheney teased. "It was pretty obvious you didn't know or care where you were."

"Hmph," Rissy grunted, but without the usual heaviness. She turned to look straight ahead, and Cheney knew that she couldn't be teased or taunted into talking about it. Sighing, Cheney reflected, *I've seen Rissy flirt with men before, but not once has she ever given any of them the slightest indication that she'd seriously consider them for a minute. But this time . . . it looks as if she's really in love . . . now what does she think she's going to do about it?*

Cheney was surprised at how she was already mentally objecting strongly to Rissy's falling in love with Luke Alexander. She puzzled over it awhile, wondering why she was so against it. Then she shunted the uncomfortable thoughts aside.

The two women went slowly and cautiously along the narrow, dark road, both Cheney and Rissy searching the brooding woods on either side of the open cart. Moody and Lalie lived close to a small creek, a tiny crooked finger of the Cooper River, and near a small swamp. The land was low-lying, and most of the trees were great cypresses with long locks of ghostly Spanish moss hanging mournfully from their bare, spiky branches. The moon was lopsided, and though the night was clear they could not see many stars.

Cheney was not at all afraid. In fact, she usually liked night rides, even in cold weather. But she had gone past being tired, and was now fatigued, and that made her feel even more chilly than the cold night warranted. Her fingers and feet felt like ice, and she kept clenching her jaw tightly, until the ache reminded her to try to relax the tension in her body. But she knew that Rissy, though she would never admit it, was afraid, so she spoke to her in warm, reassuring tones.

"Now, see, up here, Rissy? You must remember, if you bring the buggy back tomorrow. Here's a crossroads, and we're taking a left. Then about a mile up is a side road that will take us back to the main road into Charleston. These are the only turns you'll have to make."

"So comin' back I'll take that right off the main road from town, then a right onto this road at the crossroads," Rissy said thoughtfully. "I'll 'member."

Soon they were almost to the main road leading into Charleston. Sudden hoofbeats sounded ahead, coming from the north, on the hard turnpike. Rissy grabbed Cheney's arm. "Don't git out on that road, Miss Cheney! Let them riders go on by!"

Cheney looked at her in surprise but immediately yanked back on the reins, and the horse came to an obedient, quick stop. "Well, I was hardly going to pull out in front of them," she said petulantly but kept her voice low. "But I suppose we can wait here and let them pass." Actually, she admitted to herself, the approaching horses were at an all-out gallop, which was odd for this time of night. They had seen no other riders or buggies on the road, either going to or returning from Moody's cabin. Maybe it was better if the riders, whoever they were, didn't see her and Rissy.

The horses, their hoofbeats fast and furious, pounded nearer and nearer. Rissy and Cheney sat perfectly still, and Cheney took Rissy's warm hand in one of hers. With her other hand Cheney kept a tight grip, with slight tension, on the reins, and the horse stood very still and stayed obligingly quiet, not stamping or tossing his head. Cheney liked Luke Alexander's horse and decided that she would tip one of the livery attendants generously to take especially good care of him when they returned.

The horsemen were very close—just around the bend of the small road, as a matter of fact. Cheney and Rissy could see nothing, for the thick woods grew close right up to the roadside, but they could hear the horses plainly.

"Hold up!" The loud grunt sounded close—very close—to Cheney and Rissy, and Rissy clasped Cheney's hand tightly. The road was perhaps only twenty feet away, but even on the main turnpike their view was obscured by trees. When the horses stopped, Cheney and Rissy could hear them panting and stamping impatiently. Now Cheney was glad that she had stopped; the riders could not, of course, see the buggy, either, unless they turned onto this small road.

"I gotta get this off. Hold up." The man's voice sounded hoarse with either excitement or anger, it was difficult to tell which.

"You're bleeding." This voice, a different one, was a bland, bloodless, monotone. Cheney jumped a little at the words, but Rissy grabbed her arm, a warning, and shook her head violently.

The first voice, low and as harsh as gravel, cursed for a few moments. "Take that stuff off, you idiots. Tear off a strip and gimme that!" The leather creaks of another man dismounting sounded in the night air, followed by the crisp crackle of fabric ripping.

Another voice—Cheney had already deduced that there were three horsemen—spoke up. This man's voice was deep, too, and curiously garbled, as if he had something in his mouth. ". . . snakebit, did you? . . . Hrrmph! . . . Gard still ain't gonna like it."

Cheney had heard about "Gard's Rangers," the rough soldiers who patrolled the docks and collected the harbor fees— sometimes at rifle point—from all vessels coming through the harbor. With disgust she thought these men must be some of the infamous Rangers, back from chasing some poor fisherman who had tried to escape the outrageous fees by fleeing up the winding Cooper River. Shiloh had told her that the Rangers rarely tried to follow the boats by water, because both the Ashley and Cooper Rivers had hundreds of tiny inlets and streams, and the bluebellies couldn't possibly know the rivers and swamps as well as the locals. But if the Rangers recognized a boat, and found out where the owner lived, they would go to the fisherman's shack and still collect the fees. Their methods were rumored to range from threats to outright beatings. Cheney breathed a tiny sound of disgust, and Rissy's hand tightened painfully on her arm.

"You—shut—up." Now the first man sounded cold and venomous. "Let's go."

The three horses' hoofbeats pounded off to the south and finally faded away into the night.

18

BY LONG FORBEARING

Cheney felt like a fool.

"Lord, I feel like a fool," she said out loud, and loudly.

But there it was.

By long forbearing is a prince persuaded, and a soft tongue breaketh the bone.

"I didn't even want to read Proverbs," she told the empty room.

But Cheney knew she was not speaking to an empty room; it was filled with a Presence that Cheney knew and loved, and though she heard no audible voice she heard a gentle, persistent whisper in her heart.

"All right, Lord," she muttered. "But I feel like a fool."

She dressed in her black velvet riding habit and immediately felt a little better. Impatiently she crammed her hair into a crocheted black snood, then placed the miniature top hat at the most businesslike angle, square on the crown of her head and slightly tilted forward. Snatching it off again, she tore off the cloudy black veil that floated delicately behind.

"I may have to talk soft," she announced, "but I don't have to look soft." Irritability was in her fingers as she tore the delicate black fabric. She reflected moodily that when Rissy returned from taking the buggy back to Luke Alexander, she would probably remind Cheney—several times, in imaginative ways—that Cheney was obviously unable to dress herself, or do other little things basic to life, without her. With jerky movements Cheney flung the hat back on her head and pinned it in place with a diamond hatpin, noting with a tinge of wicked satisfaction that the diamond was entirely too large and ostentatious for early morning.

Grabbing up her medical bag and riding crop, she stalked out of her hotel room, slamming the door violently.

In a moment she stalked back into her hotel room, threw down her medical bag, and again banged out of the room.

In another few moments she walked back into the room, picked up her Bible, and left, closing the door quietly behind her.

★　★　★　★

Staring undecidedly at the Van Dorn Memorial Hospital, Cheney murmured to Stocking, "Well, here we are. Now what?"

Her first impulse was to tie Stocking to the hitching post and go and wander pointedly and tragically out on the grounds by the lake. Surely Dr. Van Dorn would notice her and at least come out to speak with her. Then again, he might simply send one of the attendants to tell her to go home.

"Or he might call the police, or marshals, or whoever it is that's responsible for crazy ladies wandering around aimlessly in this town," Cheney grumbled. Stocking's ears pricked up, but he shifted her weight from one side to the other in a gentle movement as he stood quietly.

Cheney sighed. Even her horse was more patient than she.

With sudden determination she dismounted, hitched Stocking, and in long, strong strides walked up to the door of the hospital and knocked firmly.

After a long wait a young man, about eighteen years of age, with long brown hair and hound-dog eyes, cracked the door open one notch. When he saw Cheney he jumped. "Uhh . . . umm . . . uhh—" he stuttered, his eyes round and his thin cheeks flushing bright red.

"Good morning, sir," Cheney said, taking care to make her voice warm. "I am Doc—Miss Cheney Duvall."

"G-good-m . . . morning, Doc . . . Miss . . . ma'am," he stammered painfully.

Cheney smiled, very slightly. "And you are. . . ?"

"I'm . . . I'm . . . nobody," he said, his sad eyes searching desperately around for—something. Anything. "I mean, I'm just a nurse."

"I happen to think that nurses are quite important people," Cheney said with just the right touch of briskness. "May I ask your name, sir?"

He relaxed, just a little. She didn't look dangerous today. In fact, she looked pretty, and nice. "My name's John, ma'am. John Jamison." He was standing up straighter, and the door was opened just an inch wider.

"It's a pleasure to meet you, Mr. Jamison. Would you do me a great kindness and ask Dr. Van Dorn if he would mind having a word with me?" Cheney asked graciously. Seeing his hesitation and confusion, she added, "I shall be happy to wait here, Mr. Jamison."

"Thank you, ma'am," he said with obvious relief. "I'll go ask Dr. Van Dorn."

He disappeared, the door closed, and Cheney stood still. For once she didn't fidget or fret. In fact, as she looked out over the tranquil lake, her eyes were soft, and she smiled a little to herself.

Thank you, Lord, for this beautiful blue morning and this beautiful blue lake. Between her hotel room and the front door of this hospital, all her uncertainty and irritability had melted away in the timid winter sunshine.

The door opened and Dr. Van Dorn stepped outside, closing the door behind him. He looked a bit wary, but he bowed and kissed her outstretched hand with his customary gallantry. "Good mornin', Miss Duvall. How may I help you?"

She dropped her eyes, took a deep breath, then looked back up at him. He was surprised at the depth of pain showing plainly on her face. "Dr. Van Dorn, I came here today for two reasons. First, I must apologize to you for my rudeness the other day. My behavior was inexcusable, while you behaved like an honorable, Christian gentleman. Please forgive me."

His dark eyes, so deep and penetrating, mirrored genuine surprise. "Why, Miss Duvall, I feel I have nothin' at all for which to forgive you! But of course, for whatever imagined slights you believe you have inflicted upon me, I assure you that I do most heartily forgive you."

"Thank you, sir," she said, nodding gracefully, a very slight queenlike tilt of her head. "The other reason I am here is to let you know that I still need to speak to Captain Allan Perry." She raised her hand, a gesture both imperious and pleading at the same time. "No, please, Dr. Van Dorn. I have no intention of forcibly breaking into your hospital. I understand your rules, and I intend to abide by them."

"Well—thank you, ma'am," he said, smiling very slightly.

"So I shall just come here and wait until I may see Captain Perry." Her voice was steady, but her shoulders stiffened in a tiny, almost imperceptible defensive movement.

Dr. Van Dorn looked blankly around the porch, the small, quiet street, the grounds, the entire outdoors. "What . . . what exactly do you mean, ma'am?"

Again she took a deep breath. "I mean, Dr. Van Dorn, that I shall come here and wait until I may see Captain Perry," she repeated, but with no rancor. "Just that. I just wanted you to know. Now, I will not keep you from your work any longer; I'm certain you are a very busy man, and that your patients need your attention much more than I. Good morning."

She smiled brilliantly at him, turned, and untied her horse. She led Stocking across the street and simply dropped his reins. The horse lowered his head and began to graze on the short winter grass contentedly. Dr. Van Dorn watched, dumbfounded, as Cheney walked slowly down to the water and sat on one of the stone benches underneath a live oak tree. The great sweeping branches were bare, but thick and strong, and they seemed to arch protectively over the woman in black who sat, her head bowed slightly, alone at Colonial Lake.

★　★　★　★

Cheney stayed on the grounds of the lake across from the hospital all morning. The day grew warmer as the sun lazily rose higher, and Cheney was vaguely surprised that she actually grew more comfortable and stronger as the day wore on. Her weariness from the strain of the long night and the mere three hours of sleep she had had seemed to fade away with the fog wisps of the morning. The early breeze across the lake was bitter, and the stone benches were cold and hard. But somehow Cheney didn't notice any of this, particularly. She sat and read her Bible until she grew uncomfortable, then she walked slowly around the pretty little lake, then she sat and read some more. She was vaguely surprised when she took out her watch and saw that it was two o'clock. It was dinnertime in Charleston, and she was hungry. She knew that the Lord was telling her she had done well, and now she should go home and eat all she wanted, and then take a long nap. Tomorrow was Sunday, and she would come back here after church. Jauntily she made a mental note to bring a quilt to put on the stone bench, so that she might sit and read for longer periods of time.

She returned to the Planter's Hotel, smiled brilliantly at Mr. Barlow—making him drop his pencil—and lightly flew up the stairs. When she reached her door, she thought at first that she must be at the wrong room, or perhaps on the wrong floor; her door was ajar, and someone was weeping, loudly, somewhere.

Suddenly the door to Cheney's left was jerked open, and the crying immediately became louder. Cheney started, still not certain she was in the right place. But Shiloh took one half step out of the room—Rissy's room—and motioned to her, an awkward, tense gesture that immediately made her feel a small chill of fear.

"What? What is it?" she said, hurrying to him.

"Where have you been?" he demanded harshly.

"What? Who is that?" she said, trying to push past him.

"Doc," he said, grabbing her arm, "where have you been? I mean it!" His eyes were raking her from her head to her feet, accusing, suspicious.

"I . . . I was at the hospital . . . I . . . Who—" Cheney's voice was thin and quavery. She strained to see past Shiloh, and he clenched his jaw and blew out an angry puff of breath between gritted teeth.

"Wait," he ordered, then pulled the door shut behind him. The piteous grieving was muted somewhat.

"Who ... who is that in Rissy's room crying, Shiloh?" Cheney pleaded.

"Are you all right?" he demanded, still angry. "There's big trouble down at City Hall! Didn't you even see it?"

"N-no. I ... I told you, I was at the hospital ... I rode in from the north. . . ." City Hall was two blocks south of the hotel.

Shiloh's shoulders sagged, and he shut his eyes with relief for a few seconds. Then he stepped close to her and rested his hands on her shoulders, and his voice was so gentle Cheney could hardly hear him. "Doc, that's Rissy in there crying."

"What!" She put her hands on his chest and leaned close to him. "Rissy! What's happened? Is she. . . ?"

"She's not hurt," he said, anchoring her frantic gaze with his calm, steady one. "But she's—I'm glad you're here, and you're all right." He took a deep breath. "Vess Alexander is dead."

★   ★   ★   ★

Charleston, South Carolina, it was widely believed, was the "kingdom by the sea" referred to in Edgar Allan Poe's famous poem "Annabel Lee." Indeed, the city did retain a secret air, a separate, aloof, regal entity. She was considered to be the birthplace of the slave trade and the mother of rebellion against the United States. The armies and navy of the United States repeatedly, desperately attempted to capture, defeat, and humiliate her. Yet she stood, bloodied but unbowed, surrounded but defiant, for four years of war that completely ravaged all of her sister states. On February seventeenth, 1865, her 16,000 guardians in gray left her to face Sherman's hordes as they turned toward the state's capital, Columbia. On February eighteenth, 1865, Union troops landed at the foot of Broad Street near East Bay Street, established headquarters in The Citadel, declared martial law, and ordered the stars and stripes hoisted over all public buildings and fortifications. After the great war it was often said that the South was overpowered but never conquered. Certainly this was true of the South's shining jewel, the "kingdom by the sea," Charleston, South Carolina.

Yet the death of one Negro man nearly engulfed her.

225

Even though Vess was a Negro, he had been a freedman, the only freedman in Charleston for many years. He could read, obviously, and no one ever questioned this breach of law. Any freedman was required to have a white guardian, and all of Charleston seemed to be Vess's guardian. Charleston had come to regard him as special, as unique as the city itself, and as such he occupied a singular niche—more than property, certainly, less than a son, maybe. Vess simply belonged to Charleston.

When he was murdered, the white citizens of Charleston were horrified and outraged, and darkly whispered in the privacy of their homes that only renegade darkies, jealous of his status, his near-equality with white people, must have killed him. The Negroes were convinced—for exactly the same reasons—that white men had killed him.

Vess was killed on Friday night. By Saturday morning City Hall was besieged. General Hatch's martial forces that patrolled the city streets were doubled. The provost marshals went on twenty-four-hour alert and were detailed both to control and to guard the hundreds of Negroes who surrounded City Hall and refused to leave. Finally the marshals allowed them to camp in the small park across the street—most of them had no home, anyway—and they packed there, a seething mass of barely controlled fury.

White citizens of Charleston attended church on Sunday morning in groups of at least four men, and no woman ventured out unless she was accompanied—surrounded—by at least six men. All the men of Charleston, in direct violation of martial law, armed themselves when they went out. They were discreet, but defiant.

Vess's funeral was on Sunday afternoon, and the little African Methodist Episcopal Church north of town was packed, with hundreds of Negroes outside weeping. Dozens of whites attended the graveside service at the little cemetery beside the church, and though the two groups—black and white—stayed strictly, physically segregated, a riot nearly broke out.

Alexander Dallas was a pallbearer, disdaining the implied disapproval of many white citizens, and the outright anger of some of the colored citizens. Dallas solidly maintained that Vess was his closest friend, and he was Vess's closest friend, and Dallas would honor him in this way if he had to carry Vess's coffin alone. Some Negro men—Caleb Blood Roddy seemed to be the ringleader of these—took exception to this and threw a rock at Dallas as he stood, swaying and weeping, at Vess's grave. White men surged toward Dallas; Negroes moved to stop them; soldiers moved in, fired over the heads of the crowd, and forcibly broke up the small but intense fight. Caleb Blood Roddy and another colored man were slightly injured; Alexander Dallas was kicked savagely and had bruises on his face. Dr. Langdon Van Dorn was also kicked and shoved while trying to reach and attend him.

Vess's widow, Miss Ona, collapsed. Luke Alexander, Vess's eldest son, brusquely dispatched Rissy Clarkson home with his mother. Then he gathered up his two younger brothers and returned to City Hall with Caleb Blood Roddy and some of Roddy's men. The provost marshals were going to make an arrest, and Corporal "Teach" Case had invited Luke to accompany the marshals so that he would be there to see that justice was meted out to his father's murderers.

19

FULL DARK

The room had grown dark and cold. The sky was low and threatening. A gray mist, so fine it did not fall but floated with every aimless wisp of air, covered the city. Suddenly Cheney realized that she didn't know what day it was.

"Friday . . . the Knights' parade . . . and Rissy and I went to Moody's," she muttered almost incoherently. She really was disoriented.

Vess was killed.

"Yes," she went on, distractedly answering the confusing buzzing in her head. "We only slept a couple of hours that night . . . after we got back from Mr. Moody's . . . then . . . Saturday . . . I went to Van Dorn's. Luke met Rissy on the road and told Rissy . . . about his father."

Vess was murdered Friday night.

Luke met Rissy when he was coming in. She was on her way to Moody's.

Cheney shook her head slightly, trying to impose order on her flitting, erratic thoughts. It seemed that she was missing something, but then the past few days had been so kaleidoscopic, so catastrophic, that Cheney decided that her mind was strained almost to incoherence by lack of sleep.

"When I got back . . . Rissy was here, crying. . . ." she went on with stubborn weariness, her eyes vacant as she stared outside, "Shiloh was here then, but he left. . . ." She hadn't seen Shiloh since then—when was it?

"That was Saturday afternoon," she nodded to herself with relief. "Rissy and I stayed up all night—that was last night. Today's Sunday," she finished with satisfaction. Then she closed her eyes and rested her forehead on her hands sadly. *Today was*

Vess's funeral, and Rissy didn't want me to go with her. . . .

That morning, as soon as the sun rose, Rissy had suddenly calmed down and become almost like her old self again, only without the merriment that Cheney now realized was such a major part of Rissy's warmth. Rissy had simply, quietly, asked Cheney's permission to go to the funeral with Luke, and to go home with his mother afterward, and perhaps stay the night with her. Of course, Cheney had said yes.

So Cheney had stayed alone all day in her room, reading and praying and sometimes weeping. Now Cheney realized that she had felt an overwhelming burden, and had prayed without ceasing all day for Rissy and Luke Alexander. She had prayed hard and long for Vess's widow, whom she had never met—Cheney still could not remember her name—yet she prayed with knowledge and understanding of the widow's grief and shock. She prayed for Shiloh, and Shadrach Forrest Luxton, and Logan Manigault, and Maxcy Roddy. Why she prayed for them she did not know, but she did know how to pray; she earnestly sought God's mercy for all four of them.

Suddenly Cheney knew she was finished—released—peaceful. Rising from her chair, shocked by the stiffness in her legs and arms, she stumbled to the bed and fell into a deep, dreamless sleep.

She saw a light far, far away, and she thought that it must be the first light of morning. Her legs and arms seemed heavy, but she made them move, to take her toward the light . . . the dawn . . . warm, and good, and Shiloh was there. . . .

"Hi, Doc," he said.

Cheney opened her eyes all the way, blinked, and focused. Shiloh sprawled in one of the chairs at the little table, his tall, muscular figure backlit by big golden flames in the fireplace behind him, making his long blond hair form an aura around his head.

Cheney threw aside the thick coverlet, jumped straight up, and stood looking stupidly down at her bare feet. "My shoes . . ." she mumbled, then looked accusingly up at Shiloh. "Did you take off my shoes?"

" 'Course," he shrugged. "Guess since Rissy's not here, you didn't know you're not supposed to lie across a bed with your feet and head hanging off the sides, and your shoes on, and no cover over you, in a cold room."

Cheney's eyes glinted furiously for a moment, then suddenly, like a distracted little kitten, she yawned enormously and stretched. Grinning sheepishly at Shiloh, she went to stand close to the fire and hugged herself. "I'm cold," she said petulantly and yawned again.

"Here, Doc, sit down." He maneuvered a chair close to the fire for her, then went to her armoire, opened it, and bent down to rummage around in the bottom of it.

Cheney yawned achingly again and said lazily, "I should be mad at you, and fuss at you for a long time, for coming in here and—"

"Taking care of you?" he interrupted, returning to kneel in front of her. Cheney was so surprised she couldn't reply. He was putting on her shoes. In confusion she thought, as he buttoned each tiny button, how delicately his fingers moved, though they seemed much too large and coarse to be able to close the small silk-covered buttons into the tiny loops.

He finished, then went briskly over to the bed, retrieved the coverlet, and wrapped it around her. "Better?"

"Y-yes," she said, then sat up straighter. "Stop fussing. I'm fine. I just took a nap." She looked around uncertainly. "What time is it?"

He took out his watch and listened to the tune for a few moments, his eyes far away, before answering. "Four-twenty-eight." Closing the watch with a snap, he shoved it back in his breeches pocket.

Cheney smiled to herself. Ever since she had given Shiloh that watch, he always quoted the exact time, down to the minute; he never said, "About half past four," or "almost four-thirty." She started to tease him, and then, for the first time, noticed the tension in his shoulders and the grim line of his mouth. "What's wrong, Shiloh?" she asked.

He turned to face her. "Shadrach, Logan Manigault, and

Maxcy Roddy have been arrested for the murder of Vess Alexander."

Cheney caught her breath, and her eyes grew round with shock. "What?" she gasped. "What did you say?"

"Yes," was all he said, turning to look out the window. It was full dark.

"What . . . how? Did they . . . are they . . . what's—" She stopped and took a deep breath. "Just tell me everything that's happened, please," she said more calmly. "I haven't left this room since . . . since—yesterday, when you left me with Rissy."

Shiloh remained motionless, his elbows on his knees, his hands clasped together, his face turned away from her. Cheney saw his hands clench, the knuckles whiten, then relax, then clench again. When he finally spoke, his voice was so distant, so cold, that he barely sounded like himself. "The whole city's gone lunatic. I've heard so many scary stories and ugly rumors that I don't know what's happened. I don't think anyone really knows."

He dropped his head, and Cheney watched his jaw tighten over and over again. She knew and recognized this danger signal. Shiloh was angry, deeply angry, and he was barely keeping it under control. She waited without speaking, and finally he continued, "All I know for sure is this: the provost marshals— all twenty of them—went to the Citadel to arrest them, and they let about twenty Negroes come with them. Luke Alexander, and Caleb Blood Roddy, and a coupla his men I been tryin' to keep my eye on. . . ."

The danger signals were more intense now. Shiloh's nostrils flared white, and his full mouth clamped into a thin line. "Looked to me like they had trouble when they arrested those three boys. Some of the marshals had black eyes, cuts, bruises. I don't know about the rest of the cadets."

Now he turned to Cheney, and she flinched slightly from the scalding heat of his anger. "They hooded Shadrach and Logan and Maxcy, and tied their hands behind their backs, and made them walk to City Hall. The nigras shouted at them and threw stones at them and shoved them, all the way to the Hall. When they got there, the other hundred or so that are camped out joined in, and they turned into a lynch mob. At least the blue-bellies put a stop to that. But those boys got hurt. Shadrach was limping bad. And I saw Caleb Blood Roddy—spit on him!"

He jumped up, and Cheney recoiled, now more in horror than shrinking from him. "Oh, Shiloh . . . how horrible! How beastly! What . . . what can we possibly do? How can we help?"

He put his hands on the French doors and leaned far over, shaking his head. Cheney was afraid for a moment, when she saw the violence in his hands, that he might break the small windows out. But she felt helpless and sat in awkward silence, waiting.

Shiloh shook his head twice more, as if to clear his mind. He took several deep breaths, then slowly—Cheney could see it was with a conscious effort—he relaxed the tension in his shoulders. After a few more moments he turned and sank back into his chair. His movements lacked his usual slow grace, but at least he no longer looked murderous. He just looked tired.

"I don't know, Doc," he finally said in a quiet voice. "I've been so mad I haven't been able to think. I gotta calm down," he added almost to himself, then grinned up at her. It was far from his usual warm, easy smile, but it was certainly a triumph over the last few minutes. "It's just so confusing," he drawled, "'cause I can't decide who to kill first."

She looked warily at him, then smiled weakly. "Yes, if you do that you would at least be keeping the three cadets company."

"Yeah." He dropped his head and sighed deeply.

"Shiloh, did you talk to Shadrach?" Cheney asked thoughtfully.

"No." Again he clasped his hands together and looked out the window. "I've been hanging around City Hall since—well, never mind that," he said hastily. "Anyway, I was there when they brought Shadrach and the boys in. Word musta got out fast, because Logan's and Maxcy's parents got there pretty quick. But the marshals said they weren't letting anybody visit them. Orders of Judge Garth Granger. Dr. Van Dorn tried to get in, and even he got into a scuffle with one of the marshals—a smart-mouthed bluebelly sergeant who musta got a pretty good whack himself. He was limpin' bad. Worse than Shadrach. Hope Shadrach's the one that nailed him," Shiloh finished with contempt.

"Good heavens!" Cheney exclaimed. "What a horrible mess!" She thought for a moment, then said dully, "You said . . . Shadrach and Mr. Manigault and Mr. Roddy were hurt? And they wouldn't even let Dr. Van Dorn in to attend to them?"

"No. They aren't letting anyone in, and Dr. Van Dorn knew that too. But he was mad, and he went up and hollered at that sergeant, and tried to push his way in, and stomped on that sergeant's foot, the one he'd been limping on." Shiloh's eyes lit with fierce amusement.

"Good," Cheney muttered, and Shiloh's eyebrows flew up in surprise. "I'd do the same thing if they were my patients!" she declared. "Well—maybe not quite the same thing—but I would try to make them let me in to attend them. That's not allowing a parade of visitors in—that's just simple, humane treatment!"

Suddenly Shiloh's eyes lit up, and he was looking at Cheney in a most peculiar way. Immediately she got wary and drew back from him slightly. "What?" she asked suspiciously.

"Y'know, Doc," he said slowly, "Shadrach said once that he'd want you to be his doctor if he needed one."

"He did?"

"Ye-es," Shiloh went on, studying her closely. "And so, that kinda means that you're like, appointed to him, huh?"

"Well—yes—I suppose."

"What I'm getting at is that you wouldn't be lying if you went to them and said that you were his doctor, huh?"

Cheney watched him, her face a mask of caution, but her sea green eyes lit with interest. "No, if Shadrach clearly told you that, then I wouldn't be lying. But, Shiloh, what makes you think that they'd let me in to see them?"

He sat up straight and grinned at her. Now he looked like the Shiloh she knew so well. "Doc! I had forgotten a couple of little details here!"

"What? What do you mean?"

"I mean," he said, shooting up, grabbing her hands and yanking her out of the chair, "I forgot! You're one of *them*! And for sure your father is!"

★ ★ ★ ★

Thirty minutes later Shiloh and Cheney stood on the street in front of City Hall. It was enclosed with a solid line of soldiers in blue, their rifles cradled close in their arms. Across the street in the park, ragged tents had sprung up, and dozens of campfires were lit. Several colored men lined the fence, lounging on it and watching across the street. Cheney could hear dark murmurs and an occasional surly shout behind her, but she paid no attention and prayed fervently that Shiloh would choose to ignore them, too.

Stepping up close to a young private in the line she asked, "Who is in charge here?"

"Captain Hawkins, ma'am," he answered, careful to keep his eyes straight ahead and his tone courteous. From the looks of the tall man looming close behind her, the private figured he'd never see the blow coming if he was insolent to this pretty lady. "He's inside, ma'am."

"Go get him, please," she said firmly.

He hesitated, his eyes cutting up to Shiloh's face.

"*Now*, private," Shiloh growled. "I'm gonna get unhappy if this lady's kept waiting."

The private wheeled and ran across the courtyard and down a flight of stairs that led to a below-ground level of the building. Within moments an older man marched across the courtyard, followed by the nervous young private. The older man walked directly up to the hole in the line left by the private and stuck out his hand to Cheney. "I'm Captain Riley Hawkins, ma'am. You wish to speak to me?"

Cheney was relieved; this man was perhaps fifty, with a firm, no-nonsense handshake. Though his uniform was worn casually, as with long-time usage, he was well-groomed, his brown hair combed neatly. He carried his rifle with unconscious ease, a grace of long familiarity. His gaze, as he looked at her, was thoroughly professional.

"Sir, I am Dr. Cheney Duvall," she said calmly. "I am Shadrach Forrest Luxton's physician. I understand that he was injured when he was arrested and requires medical attention."

Captain Hawkins' eyes narrowed. "His physician?" Now he looked carefully at Cheney: her rich gray cashmere mantle, the hood framing her strong, exotic features, the expensive kid leather gloves—the businesslike black leather doctor's bag she held.

"That's right," Shiloh said in a deceptively soft voice. "The lady *said* she is Captain Luxton's physician."

Hawkins' eyes went up to Shiloh, and he nodded imperceptibly. "Yes, all right. But Judge Granger has stipulated that the prisoners will have no visitors. Sorry, ma'am."

"You a marshal?" Shiloh asked with apparent casualness.

Captain Hawkins stiffened slightly. "No. I am not. I am the Captain of Company D, Chandler's Battalion, Hatch's Brigade. But that doesn't matter; I am here to guard the prisoners, and I have been instructed to allow them no visitors."

Cheney smiled at him and said dryly, "I understand that, Captain. But I am a special case, you see."

"Oh? And why is that, ma'am?"

"Because I am not making a social call upon Mr. Luxton," she said, her voice growing tight. "I am his physician, and I believe it is the policy of the United States government to allow even prisoners of war medical attention if it is needed. It seems that policy would extend to prisoners under martial law. Is that correct, Captain?"

He wavered, but only slightly. "But, ma'am, I am under orders."

Now Cheney drew herself up to her full height. "Captain, I truly did not want to be obliged to resort to this, but it appears that I must. If you continue to refuse to allow those men medical attention, I intend to march straight over to the telegraph office and send a telegram to my father. His name is Colonel Richard Duvall." She saw with satisfaction that while the captain's jaw didn't exactly drop, his mouth opened slightly as his eyes widened with surprise. "I shall report to him that these men are being treated inhumanely, and I shall ask him to forward my complaint to—"

"His long-time friend, General Ulysses S. Grant," the captain finished for her, his mouth now twitching. The privates on either side of him started, and the first private Cheney had addressed peeked around Captain Hawkins' shoulder—and his mouth *was* wide open. Shiloh had to control his own grin.

"I see you have heard of my father," Cheney smiled, graciously now.

"Yes, ma'am, I have," he replied, and bowed, very slightly. "I even met him once, in the field, under quite adverse circumstances. It was a pleasure to meet him, just the same. Please, Miss—pardon me, I mean, Dr. Duvall—come with me. I have decided I'm going to allow the prisoners to see a physician," he said in a voice suddenly loud and belligerent as he led Cheney across the courtyard. Shiloh followed her doggedly, his arms crossed and his booted footsteps hard and determined. Both of them noticed that three men lounging on the landing of the steps that led up to the main entrance of City Hall jumped up at Captain Hawkins' belligerent yell.

"If any of you provost marshals have any trouble with that," he bawled lustily as they passed, "you can come talk to me! Have I got some news for you!"

When they reached the steps that led down to the basement level, Captain Hawkins suddenly turned and stepped behind Cheney, directly in front of Shiloh. "Wait a minute," he said firmly. "The doctor can go in, but you can't."

"I'm her nurse," Shiloh growled.

"Uh-huh," Captain Hawkins nodded his head up and down. "And I suppose *your* father is General William Tecumseh Sherman?"

"Yes," Shiloh said, staring at him coldly and taking a step closer.

"Wait a minute," Cheney said, stepping around Captain Hawkins and laying her hand on one of Shiloh's arms, which were still crossed. She could hardly believe how tense the corded muscles were, and she reflected wryly that he must be keeping them tightly crossed to keep from hitting someone. "Captain Hawkins, this is Mr. Shiloh Irons. He is my nurse, and has been for almost two years. May he assist me?"

"Sorry, Dr. Duvall," Captain Hawkins said, not unkindly. Very, very slowly he reached out the tip of his rifle—Shiloh's eyes did not even flicker downward, away from Captain Hawkins' face—and with it, Hawkins pushed aside Shiloh's duster and nodded. Shiloh was wearing his gray Confederate breeches with the yellow stripe down the side. A .44 Colt was stuck butt-out in the waistband of these same incriminating breeches, but Captain Hawkins appeared not to notice that and dropped his rifle to point at the ground. "*Sergeant* Irons, is it?" he asked coolly.

"Was," Shiloh said tightly. "Now it's *Nurse* Irons."

Captain Hawkins shrugged. "Sorry, Sergeant. Just the doctor." With that he spun around—neither Cheney nor Shiloh could see him flinch expectantly as he turned his back on Shiloh—and went down the stairs.

Cheney squeezed Shiloh's arm lightly and whispered, "I'm sorry, Shiloh. Wait for me, please." Then she turned and followed Captain Hawkins.

Charleston had a prison north of town that could house eighty inmates, which currently had only fifty-six. But Judge Granger had ordered that these three prisoners be held at City Hall, where they could be guarded vigilantly for their own protection. Unfortunately, the only prison cells at City Hall were down in the basement, and normally they served only as temporary holding cells for prisoners awaiting hearings in the courtroom upstairs.

Too kind to call them "cells," Cheney thought dismally. *"Cages" is what they are.*

And they were, simply two small cages enclosed on all four sides by iron bars. Shadrach was in one, and it contained one cot and one chamber pot. Logan and Maxcy were in the other, and it had two cots squeezed in and one chamber pot. Their only light was from a kerosene lantern sitting just out of reach of the cages.

The basement was huge, a sublevel room the size of the entire City Hall. It was not partitioned by walls, but by hundreds of boxes of documents, stacked to the ceiling, and forming mazes with narrow walkways in between. It was a dark room, with desolate echoes, and it was cold and dank.

Directly across the large room from the stairwell entrance where Cheney stood was a door into a stairway leading up to the first floor of the building, and there was a narrow hallway between the two entrances. The holding cells were close to the door leading into the interior stairwell. Also in the narrow passageway formed by the rows of anonymous boxes was a large wooden table, close to the cells, with a single kerosene lantern sitting on it, and three chairs on each side of it. A soldier jumped out of one of the chairs when Cheney entered, and—obviously in great confusion—first half raised his rifle at her, then snapped to attention and saluted her.

"Settle down, lieutenant," Captain Hawkins said gruffly. "This is my responsibility."

"Yes, sir!" he grunted, keeping his eyes straight ahead as Cheney hurried past him to the cells.

Shadrach was pressed up against his cell, holding on to the bars with both hands, watching her in stunned disbelief. Behind him, in the other cell, Cheney saw Logan Manigault helping Maxcy rise from his cot. Logan's face was such a mess that he was totally unrecognizable. Both of his eyes were swollen so tightly that Cheney wondered if he could see at all. Maxcy leaned heavily on him, sharply cutting off a groan when he rose, clutching his right side. His face was the color of old parchment.

Cheney took a deep breath, touched Shadrach's hand, smiled at him, and held up her medical bag slightly.

His eyes flamed. "Finally," he said coolly, "my doctor's here."

Captain Hawkins stepped in front of her, jingling keys, and opened an ancient padlock that, with a ring-and-hasp arrangement, secured the simple door formed of iron bars in a frame. Then he unlocked Logan's and Maxcy's cell. From inside Shadrach's cell Cheney turned to smile at Captain Hawkins. "It's all right, Captain. You may lock the door behind me if you wish."

He nodded slowly but said, "Thank you, ma'am, but I don't think that will be necessary if these men will give me their word they won't try to escape while you're attending them." Without even waiting for Shadrach, Logan, and Maxcy to do that, he turned on his heel and went to sit at the desk, turning his back pointedly to the cells. "You can go get some coffee, lieutenant," he muttered, and the lieutenant scooted gratefully out the door.

Shadrach Forrest Luxton was a mess. His white dress breeches were filthy, especially at the knees. Two buttons were missing from his tunic, and one of the sleeves was almost torn off. His bandoliers and belt had been taken away, along with his sword. His boots were muddy. There was an angry red abrasion high on his cheekbone, with an open raw gash oozing blood. He stood with difficulty, and Cheney saw him grimace with pain and push against his left leg with his hand.

"Sit down, everyone," she ordered and waited until the three cadets obeyed. Then she turned to Shadrach. "What hurts?"

"This doesn't," he mumbled, touching a corner of his mouth.

Cheney's mouth twitched. "That's good. So let me rephrase the question. What hurts worst?"

He looked up at her, and Cheney moved close to him. She was relieved to see his blue-gray eyes were clear, not at all shocked or feverish. "To tell you the truth, I think Maxcy's hurt the worst. Will you attend to him first, please?"

"No ... you first, Captain ..." Maxcy Roddy gasped and turned weakly on his side on his cot.

"Be quiet, Private," Shadrach said quietly, still looking up at Cheney.

"Yes, of course," Cheney said decisively. "But you take a swallow of this right now, Shadrach, to ease some of the pain. Start with one small swallow, and we'll see how you're doing in fifteen minutes." She handed him a small cobalt blue bottle, waited until he had taken a drink, then hurried around to Logan's and Maxcy's cell. Logan again jumped off his cot, and

Cheney frowned. "Mr. Manigault, I insist that you stop hopping up and down. I am—now—your doctor. Forget I'm a lady."

"Impossible, Dr. Duvall," Logan said, bowing deeply to press his swollen lips to her hand. "You are, under any circumstances, a courageous, and most gracious, lady. I will never forget that, or you."

"You can aim all that devastating charm elsewhere, Mr. Manigault," Cheney said briskly, though her cheeks colored slightly with pleasure. "As your physician I am ordering you to sit down and stay seated!"

Logan sat.

Maxcy didn't even try to rise from his cot, though he looked distressed. "Dr. Duvall, please forgive me . . . I . . . I . . ."

Cheney knelt by him. "Nonsense. Here, take some of this—more—that's good. Now let me see—here?" Though her touch was light, Maxcy gulped in a deep, harsh breath, but managed not to cry out. One of his ribs was broken, and another was cracked. Cheney was relieved, however; his pulse was strong, though rather elevated, so he had no internal injuries. Probably.

"I'm going to cut off your tunic and undershirt," Cheney said matter-of-factly, reaching into her medical bag.

"No, ma'am, you can't do that," Maxcy said between gritted teeth.

"What?" Cheney's hand, gripping a large pair of bandage scissors, was stopped in midair.

"This is my Citadel uniform, ma'am," he said, struggling to get up, his breath coming in harsh, painful bursts. "You can't cut it. I'll take it off."

Cheney started to disdainfully overrule him, but she saw the light in Shadrach's eyes as he stared at Maxcy, and the smile that played on Logan's lips, and suddenly understood. "All right, Mr. Roddy," she said, smiling a little. He smiled back weakly at her, but with gratitude. "I will allow this, but only if you let me help you."

Although it must have been a jarring, shocking pain, Maxcy managed to take off his tunic without uttering a single sound. Finally he lay back on the cot, gasping. Cheney handed the tunic to Logan, who fumbled a bit as he reached for it, then folded it reverently and placed it at the foot of Maxcy's cot. In his cotton undershirt, Maxcy shivered suddenly.

Cheney frowned darkly, then said in a pointedly loud voice, "It's very cold in here. You should all have more blankets and heavier clothing." Everyone turned to look at Captain Hawkins' back. He stayed motionless, giving no sign that he had heard.

Cheney blew out an exasperated breath. "When I leave, I will go get you all an extra blanket for tonight. Tomorrow, when I return, I'll bring you some clean clothes. And food. And water to wash with!" she finished in a loud, angry voice, then threw herself down by Maxcy's cot again.

She wrapped Maxcy's ribs, then applied iodine to the cuts and scrapes on his face. The knuckles on his right hand were swollen and raw, and she applied carbolic acid to those, then an arnica liniment to his hands and all of his bruises.

Logan Manigault insisted he had no injuries to his body, only his face, and Cheney reflected angrily that someone seemed to resent Logan's smooth, aquiline good looks. Both of his eyes were horribly bruised, almost swollen shut, and his mouth was cut, the bottom lip swollen. His face was covered with bruises, which were slowly turning blue. Cheney considered him, and he turned his swollen mouth up in a mocking smile as she lightly touched his face.

"I'm glad there's no mirror in here," he said thickly, but waving his hand with affected grace. "I have been told, once or twice, that I am a handsome man, but I think the sight of my face right now would make little children cry."

"It would make you cry harder," Maxcy grunted painfully.

"Possibly," Logan replied as airily as he could with his mouth so swollen. "But I do think, Dr. Duvall, that my injuries are more ugly than they are serious. Please go ahead and attend to Captain Luxton first."

"No," Shadrach grunted.

"Yes," Cheney said decisively and went back to Shadrach's cell. Kneeling by his cot, she laid her hand gently on his thigh and ran her fingers down to his knee. A large, hard knot was forming directly on the first quadricep, on the outside of his knee, all the way up to mid-thigh.

"Shadrach, how did this happen?" Cheney asked in a low voice, running her hand over the big knot. His leg was not broken, but the huge, powerful muscle was bruised, perhaps even torn. She could feel the heat of inflammation in the swollen limb.

His eyes narrowed as he glared at Captain Hawkins' back. "I don't know, Dr. Duvall. It felt like someone was chopping at my leg with a dull ax. It could have been the edge of a rifle butt, but it was hard to tell, since I had a black hood thrown over my head, and my hands tied behind my back."

Captain Hawkins visibly stiffened in his chair.

Cheney swallowed, hard, her fingers probing lightly, trying to determine if the muscle was indeed torn. Shadrach was difficult to read; his face remained expressionless, though she must have been hurting him, and his voice stayed cool and even. He still stared at Captain Hawkins' back.

"How many times were you struck?" Cheney asked clinically.

"Until I fell to my knees," Shadrach replied levelly.

The room was thick with silence. Suddenly Captain Hawkins' chair screeched horribly as he jumped to his feet and, without looking back, stalked across the room and savagely threw open the door. Clearly they heard him bawl, "You, Sergeant! No, not you, you idiot! That Johnnie Reb sergeant! Get over here!"

Cheney looked up at Shadrach and smiled. "I'm going to have to apply cool compresses to this leg, Shadrach. But since it's so chilly I think we'll wait until Shiloh gets back. He'll bring blankets and all of you some clean clothes."

"Please, Dr. Duvall," Shadrach said quietly, "go ask him if he'll bring my Bible."

"I'll get it for you," Cheney said soothingly. "But right now—"

"You don't understand, do you, Cheney?" Shadrach interrupted. "They're going to hang us. Maybe tonight."

Cheney shot to her feet, laid her hands on Shadrach's wide shoulders, and stared down at him. "No, no! They are not going

242

to hang you, Shadrach! You haven't even had a trial yet!"

He smiled up at her, sadly, as if he didn't wish to distress her. "Cheney, Judge Granger has already taken the evidence of Vess Alexander's wife—widow. On the strength of that evidence he ordered our arrest. Now all that's left is sentencing, which I expect he'll do—at any time."

Cheney backed away from him and looked at Logan, and Maxcy, and then around the cages with horror. "But . . . but . . . you must have a lawyer, and there must be . . . a trial, and—" She broke off and suddenly stared at Shadrach, her eyes wide and dark. "Did you . . . did you . . . already plead guilty? Is that what you're telling me?"

Shadrach jumped up, his smooth face distorted with horrible pain for a moment. Still he took two long strides and put his hands on Cheney's shoulders, gripping them hard. "No," he said sternly. "No, Dr. Duvall. We did not kill Vess Alexander."

He stared down at her, his eyes cold and proud. Cheney searched his face for long moments, and then she dropped her eyes. "I'm sorry, Shadrach," she said quietly. "I truly didn't think you did. I just don't understand."

Shadrach dropped his hands abruptly, then turned slowly and went back to his cot, limping painfully. "No, no, I'm the one who's sorry, Cheney. I shouldn't have—put my hands on you like that. Please forgive me."

"I will forgive you," Cheney whispered, coming to stand close to him again, "if you will forgive me."

He smiled a little. "All right."

Logan had jumped up, tense and watchful, and stood gripping the bars between the two cells, pressing close up against them as if he could give his support to Shadrach by his nearness. "You must understand, Dr. Duvall," he said, his voice as hard as Shadrach's hands had been on her shoulder. "Judge Garth Granger is the provost tribune, and we're under martial law."

"But what does that mean?" Cheney demanded. "I thought the law was the law!"

"The only law in Charleston is Judge Garth Granger!" Shadrach retorted angrily. "That means that accused persons in his court can be tried and convicted without benefit of jury or rules of evidence. Judge Granger can consider—or disallow—any evidence he chooses. He can, at his sole discretion, pronounce guilt or innocence. He can pronounce sentence and have it executed immediately upon his order." He lifted his chin defiantly, though his voice stayed level. "And there is no appeal."

20

AND SO HE CAME

Rissy was moving around in the next room.

The slight rustles and creaks woke Cheney up.

This was so unusual and unsettling—Cheney could not recall ever hearing Rissy making noise when she walked or worked—that she threw back the covers, ran across the room, and burst into the connecting room.

"Rissy! Are you all right?"

"You done gone crazy?" Rissy demanded, propping her fists on her hips. "If I'd-a been standin' on t'other side of thet door you woulda knocked me to Savannah!"

Cheney smiled, then rushed across the room and threw her arms around Rissy. "You are all right!"

Rissy, paralyzed for a moment, finally hugged Cheney back, hard, then pushed her away and frowned darkly. "Go git back in there an' put somewhat on! Runnin' up and down in yore bare feet and gown-tail! My mama'd have my head! G'wan!"

Cheney flounced back to her room, leaving the door open. She washed up, put on her prettiest morning dress with the matching satin slippers, and was trying, and not succeeding, to brush out her hair when Rissy came into her room.

"Heah's yo' coffee an' some . . . somethin's," she said with heavy disdain. "I ast for some o' them sweet rolls of Miz Philomena's, but whut I got was some . . . somethin's." Setting a tray down at Cheney's table, she carried on her steady monologue in the same wrathful tone. "This here's called a fireplace, Miss Cheney, and this here's a poker. It's for pokin'. In the fireplace. It makes the fire work better. Thass what makes the room warmer. An' quit messin' with that hair. It takes me twice as long to fix it when you been tanglin' it up."

245

Cheney reflected, with some surprise, how warm and nice her mornings were when Rissy was taking care of her, and how much she had missed her the one day she was gone. "I missed you, Rissy," she murmured, obediently laying the brush down. "Won't you sit down with me? Have some coffee with me?"

Savagely Rissy poked the fire until the bed of coals flared up, keeping her face averted from Cheney. Finally she straightened, folded her hands primly in front of her spotless white apron, and replied quietly, "Why, thank you, Miss Cheney. The coffee—at least—smells good. I b'lieve I'd like some, at that."

They sat down, fixed their coffee, and Cheney took Rissy's sturdy brown hand for a moment. "I prayed for you and Mr. Alexander—Luke—and . . . and . . . his mother all day yesterday."

Rissy squeezed Cheney's hand. "Thank you, Miss Cheney. We all needed it for sure. And her name's Miss Ona. You'd like her a lot, and she'd like you."

"I really am so sorry about Mr. Alexander. How . . . how are you, Rissy?" Cheney asked gently.

Rissy took her coffee cup in both hands and stared, unseeing, into the depths of it. "He was a fine Christian man, was Mr. Vess. He's with the Lord Jesus now, an' that means he's a whole lot better off than we all are. An' happier." She sighed deeply, then looked back up at Cheney, her liquid chocolate eyes filling with tears. "I guess I'll tell you this, Miss Cheney. I was fallin' in love with Luke. And I know he loves me."

Cheney sat back in her chair. Though she had suspected this, Rissy's plain declaration caught her unprepared. She simply couldn't think of what she should say.

Fiercely Rissy blinked back the unshed tears and went on, "I'd almost decided not to say anything to you 'bout Luke, Miss Cheney. 'Cause ain't nothing gonna come of it. But—we all done got so tangled up with them Alexanders! It seems like since we first rode into this town we all been bumpin' up agin one of 'em somehow!"

"Wait, Rissy," Cheney said, shaking her head slightly. "First—what do you mean, nothing's going to come of it?

What's wrong? Aside from the obvious, I mean?"

Rissy again dropped her eyes. "Ever since I was a young girl, I allus knew that when the Lord wanted me to fall in love, I would. And I was fallin' in love with Luke Alexander, and I really thought that he was the man the Lord wanted for me."

"You've never been in love before, Rissy?" Cheney asked hesitantly. "I know there have been other young men in your life."

"Yep. An' as soon as I knowed 'em, I knew they wasn't right for me," Rissy said sturdily. "But I thought as soon as I started knowin' Luke that he was the one." She shook her head vehemently. "But he ain't."

"But . . . but . . . why, Rissy?"

Now Rissy looked up and met Cheney's gaze, unflinching. "He never was too fond o' white people, Miss Cheney. I knew it, but I knew, too, that he's a Christian man, and I thought that the Lord Jesus would heal him of all that."

"Oh—yes—I think I see, Rissy," Cheney said slowly. "You mean, since his father was . . . was . . ."

"Murdered," Rissy said evenly. "By white men. Luke ain't never gonna forgive them, I know. And now I don't think he's never gonna even try to git healed of the hate in his heart. And I know the Lord Jesus don't want that kind of husband for me. I just wisht I hadn't started lovin' him."

Cheney, her face stricken, stared at Rissy, and Rissy's face suddenly grew gentle and warm. She even smiled, the tiniest bit, at Cheney.

"Oh, Rissy!" Cheney's face crumpled, her eyes filled up, and tears began rolling down her face.

"Well, blue tarnation!" Rissy burst out.

A knock sounded on the door. "Doc? You all right?"

"She sure ain't!" Rissy called out on her way to the door.

"D-don't let him in!" Cheney sniffed.

Rissy threw open the door. "You might as well c'mon in, 'cause I know you're gonna c'mon in anyways, Mistuh Arns."

Shiloh, astounded both by Rissy's invitation and Cheney's tears, hesitated in the doorway. Rissy rolled her eyes and went to Cheney, wiping her face with a corner of her apron. "You hush thet cryin' now, Miss Cheney. I done cried enough to full up an ocean. The time for mournin' and weepin' is over now."

"Can I come in?" Shiloh asked belatedly and needlessly.

"Oh, for heaven's sake, come on in. You're going to anyway," Cheney declared, scrubbing her face roughly with Rissy's apron.

"Thought I done said that," Rissy grunted. She squinted down at Cheney's upturned face.

"I'm all right now, Rissy," Cheney murmured, smiling woefully.

Rissy nodded briskly, folded her hands in front of her apron, and glided toward her room. "If you ain't a-comin' in, Mistuh Arns, quit dancin' in the doorjamb and shut thet door. If you *is* a-comin' in, leave it open." She sailed into her room, pointedly leaving the connecting door gaping.

"You okay, Doc?" he said anxiously, crossing the room to stand over her.

"Yes. It was girl stuff," she retorted, "and you don't need to know."

"Okay," he said with undisguised relief. "I got some good news."

"Yes? What?"

He grinned with boyish delight, pulled a crumpled piece of paper from his pocket, and waved it triumphantly. "He's coming! General Forrest is coming. He'll be here at two o'clock Wednesday."

★   ★   ★   ★

Cheney considered whether to unhitch Stocking from the buggy, but decided to leave him in the harness for a little while. For some reason, she had a feeling—strong and distinct—that she and Rissy would not be there very long. Cheney was cautious about saying or even thinking to herself such things as "The Lord told me this-and-such ..." She had heard His Voice, clearly, once, in Manhattan—at, of all places, a Vanderbilt party. She had not heard with her ears, but she had *heard* it just the same. That was the only time she could truly have said, "The Lord told me ..." After that, she resolved never to say it lightly again. Now she contented herself with just knowing that Dr. Van Dorn would come out of the hospital—soon—to speak with her.

"This is right pretty," Rissy murmured as they walked slowly toward the lake. She gave Cheney a puzzled look. "Don't misunnerstan' me, Miss Cheney—I ain't fussin' 'bout comin' here with you—but what are we doin' here?"

" 'By long forbearing is a prince persuaded . . .' " Cheney replied softly, looking out over the lake.

" '. . . and a soft tongue breaketh the bone,' " Rissy finished, her voice deep and warm. She glanced back at the hospital, then nodded with complete understanding.

They stopped and stood close together. The lake was a calm mirror of the steel-colored sky. It was chilly and damp. Cheney could feel tiny droplets of moisture in the wind and thought about how the small bits of water had swirled and danced in the amber glow of the streetlights as she and Shiloh had stood beneath them at City Hall last night. She said a quick prayer for Shadrach and Logan and Maxcy, and then—somewhat to her surprise—she found herself praying for Shiloh and General Nathan Bedford Forrest, who was right now on his way to Charleston from Rome, Georgia.

"Good mornin', Miss Duvall."

Before she turned, a knowing, grateful smile flitted across Cheney's face. Rissy smiled to herself, too.

"Good morning, Dr. Van Dorn," Cheney said.

As he kissed her hand, Cheney was distressed to see that Dr. Van Dorn had a gash on his cheek, a raw gash, and it was inflamed. He was pale, and she saw that he was leaning heavily on a cane.

"Would you come over here and sit with me for a few moments, Dr. Van Dorn?" Cheney asked politely. "It is so lovely here, even in wintertime. If you have time I would enjoy your company for a little while." She threaded her arm through his, and though Cheney could see he tried not to, he leaned heavily on her as they turned and walked up the slight incline to the stone bench beneath the great oak tree.

"You are a very tactful lady, Miss Duvall," he sighed.

They sat down, and Rissy stood close behind Cheney. "Not at all," Cheney protested. "I really meant it."

He smiled wearily at her, and his normally flashing dark eyes were a dull, muddy brown. "Actually I have been looking for you this mornin', ma'am. I thought you might come, and I hate to admit it, but I was lookin' forward to it."

"Oh?" Cheney was truly surprised.

"Yes, ma'am," he replied, his eyes lighting up just a little. "It appears that you're not just another pretty lady, you're an important lady. And a well-respected doctor."

"No, no, that's not true," Cheney protested, blushing. "I . . . I'm . . . I just—"

"—faced down the whole U. S. Army and doctored three of the most important men in this city that no one can even get in to see, and"—now his smile was wide, and his eyes kindled—"called General Nathan Bedford Forrest in for reinforcements."

"Oh, dear," Cheney said in great confusion. "It's not like that at all, Dr. Van Dorn—really—I . . ."

"Well, what is it like, ma'am?" he teased.

Cheney suddenly giggled. "Maybe it is kind of like that. Except that it was my nurse, Mr. Irons, who actually did it all."

Dr. Van Dorn grew serious. "That's not what I heard, Miss Duvall. And that's not what I see." His eyes roamed out over the lake. "I came out here to tell you that Captain Perry is doing fairly well. He still has a fever. His scalp wound is healing all right, but the St. Anthony's fire . . . it's not spreading . . . but . . ." His voice dropped, and he lowered his head and sighed deeply.

Cheney chewed on her lip for a few moments, fighting back the impulse to jump up and start shouting at Dr. Van Dorn. In the space of a few seconds she suddenly knew exactly what to say, and knew that the Lord was giving her words as fast as she could say them. "Dr. Van Dorn, I respect you, both as a man and as a physician. I tell you this, from my heart. I am concerned, not only for Captain Perry, but for you. I am certain that you know that erysipelas almost always invades open wounds on the head or face." She motioned gracefully toward the cut on his face. "Therefore, you are at grave risk. If you contracted it, it would be a terrible thing for you and for your patients."

His hands, white, clean, blue-veined, tightened on the head of his cane. Slowly he turned his head to stare at Cheney. "Miss Duvall," he said quietly, "I know you mean no disrespect to me. I know there is no spite in you, none at all. You are a gracious and gentle lady."

"Thank you, sir," Cheney said quietly.

"You are most welcome, ma'am," he responded with his usual gallantry, then asked in a firm voice, "But—are you a good doctor?"

She looked straight into his eyes. "Yes, Dr. Van Dorn, I am. A very good doctor. The Lord has blessed me exceedingly, abundantly, above all that I have ever asked or thought."

"Ephesians," he murmured absently.

He turned to look straight ahead, and Cheney searched his profile. He was still a very handsome man, even now, with the ugly gash on his cheekbone and the pallor of his face. He had fine aristocratic features, but fire and passion burned in his eyes. *He has a young man's eyes*, she thought, *and he will until the day he dies.*

Finally he spoke, quietly and thoughtfully. "Ma'am, there is something you must understand. My men"—he motioned toward the hospital—"are all widowed, or single men. My rule about women—ladies—in the hospital is not just because I'm old and set in my ways." He looked at her then and smiled. "During the war we heard that the ladies of Richmond were actually doing some nursing at Chimborazo, and everyone in Charleston—men and ladies—was absolutely horrified. It's not that the men here in Charleston think that it's shameful, you see; it's that they can't abide a lady to see them in a weakened condition. It . . . distresses them."

"Yes, I noticed that," Cheney said dryly.

"That is why I cannot allow you in the hospital, ma'am."

"All right, Dr. Van Dorn. I understand, and I will abide by your decision," Cheney said evenly, though her heart sank.

"But, Dr. Duvall—"

"Yes, sir?" Cheney interrupted eagerly, her eyes lighting up. It was the first time he had called her "Doctor."

He smiled again. "I would like to ask advice from a colleague, from a doctor that I respect. Do you know of any way I can prevent the spread of St. Anthony's fire? And are you aware of any particular treatment that might effect a complete cure?"

"Thank the Lord!" she exclaimed, jumping up from the bench. "Finally!"

Dr. Van Dorn threw back his head and laughed. "You want to explain that to me, young lady?"

"Oh yes, sir, I will!" Cheney cried. "But first, let me tell you about Ignatz Semmelweiss!"

"Blue tarnation," Rissy muttered from behind them. "I better find me a place to set down."

★ ★ ★ ★

The telegraph operator told everyone he saw, for two solid days, that General Nathan Bedford Forrest was coming, and would arrive at the Planter's Hotel at two o'clock on Wednesday afternoon.

Mr. Barlow told all the people who came to ask—and there were many—that, yes, Mr. Irons had reserved a room for him, and the Planter's Hotel was pleased to accommodate him in the Planter's Suite, which had a generous sitting room, a well-stocked bar, two bedrooms, and a private bath.

Shiloh told Captain Riley Hawkins, who received the information expressionlessly but grinned widely when he informed Company D, Chandler's Battalion, and Hatch's Brigade. Captain Hawkins laughed out loud when he related the news to Provost Marshal Corporal "Teach" Case and saw the expression on his face.

Caleb Blood Roddy stood on top of a makeshift table in the park, announced it to all the Negroes, and reminded them, with great passion and heat, that Forrest was a former slave trader who beat slaves every day with a trace chain and then doused them with salt water, and that he stole Negro babies, and that he burned Negro soldiers alive at Fort Pillow. At the news of Forrest's descent upon Charleston, fourteen of the Negroes left the camp at City Hall Park, and, in fact, were never seen in Charleston again. Some of the Negroes who stayed in Charleston swore that Forrest had probably met them on the road out of town and killed them and burned them or buried them alive.

Judge Garth Granger had not reported to his office in City Hall since his interview with Ona Alexander. In fact, he was not seen at all by anyone, except his closest aide, Corporal Case. On Monday afternoon, three orders of the provost tribune were issued. They were first posted on the doors of City Hall, and then were printed the next day in the *Charleston Record*.

One tribunal order was that any member of the secret society known as the Knights of the White Rose was thereby ordered to report to the provost marshals for questioning concerning the murder of Vess Alexander.

No one reported.

The second was that the secret society known as the Knights of the White Rose was judged to be an order dedicated to sedition and treason, and membership in such order was thereby declared a martial offense, punishable by arrest and imprisonment.

The citizens of Charleston reflected that perhaps it was a good thing that no Knights of the White Rose had reported for the first tribunal order.

The third order of the provost tribune stated that applicants who wished to address a complaint to the provost tribune concerning Freedmen's Bureau matters must make an appointment with the provost tribune's office. Such appointments would be scheduled at a minimum of two weeks in advance.

An anonymous, but nevertheless daring, artist drew a cartoon and somehow managed to post it underneath the third tribunal order on the door of City Hall. It only stayed there for two hours, until a provost marshal tore it down. The *Charleston Record* received a copy of it but dared not print it. Mysteriously, however, the cartoon was reproduced on four-by-six-inch pieces of paper that were strewn on all the streets from Calhoun Street down to the Battery.

The cartoon depicted an unmistakable and skillfully drawn likeness of Nathan Bedford Forrest standing with his booted foot propped up on the body of a man whose face could not be seen, but who was wearing a judge's black robes. Forrest's arms were crossed, and a smoking six-shooter stuck out from under one elbow. In the background was a line of three Citadel cadets, all with carefully drawn faces that looked like no one, and everyone. The caption—of General Forrest's words—was: "I done him a favor and decided not to make him wait two weeks."

After the distribution of this little bit of merriment, not one of Judge Granger's four favorite provost marshals was seen at City Hall.

★　★　★　★

And so he came.

Cheney was extremely irritable when he arrived.

First she was impatient with Shiloh because he was so openly eager to see General Forrest again. Her resentment was completely illogical, she told herself peevishly, which did not make her feel the least bit more charitable.

And it was aggravating because even the weather seemed to be dramatizing his arrival. The day was gray, the sky was lowering, with occasional far-off thunder rumbling, and a light, wet fog swirled and danced in the air currents created by anything that moved.

Mostly she was mad at herself. *Here I stand, out here on the street, in this . . . this . . . air made out of cold water . . . waiting for him, as though he were the king of the world, or something!* Naturally Rissy had insisted on being with her, and she and Rissy were the only women in sight.

Of course, Shiloh had asked her to be at the hotel when General Forrest arrived. Dr. Cheney Duvall was, after all, the only person besides Union soldiers who had seen Shadrach since his arrest. Shiloh had also had the effrontery to ask her to wear a riding habit, in case General Forrest wanted to interview her from horseback; and then Shiloh had had the unimaginable impudence to ask her to wear "that pretty purple-blue-black outfit."

And here she stood in her lapis lazuli riding habit, fuming and fretting, switching her riding crop back and forth in the air. Once she actually popped the back of Shiloh's leg—she told herself it was an accident—muttered, "Excuse me," and waited for him to turn around. He didn't seem to notice either the swat or the apology.

And Shiloh did try to make you wait inside, she told herself severely, and then argued with herself. *But by the time he makes it through all these people I would have probably had to wait three or four hours!*

At least a hundred Union soldiers lined the street around the Planter's Hotel, waiting; some men of Charleston—all white— were dotted up and down the street, but stayed distant from the knot of soldiers crowding in front of the hotel. Cheney was surprised to note that most of the soldiers were as excited as if he were a famous Union general—Sherman, or Meade, or even General Grant. Then she realized that there might have been twice, or maybe three times, that many soldiers, if the patrols hadn't been doubled in the last week. It also occurred to Cheney that none of the provost marshals—their uniforms had red piping and buttons—were on hand. All of the soldiers were General Hatch's men.

Standing directly in front of her, Shiloh took out his watch and popped it open.

When Johnny comes marching home again, Hurrah! Hurrah!

The tune sounded clear but oddly faraway, the music curiously swept away in the swirling fog. Until Cheney heard the music, she had been unaware of exactly how quiet the street was. "Well?" She nudged Shiloh's broad back sharply. She still thought it was ridiculous to expect General Forrest to arrive on the minute, even though Shiloh swore that if he said he'd be there at two o'clock, he'd be there at two o'clock.

"It's almost two," Shiloh answered.

Long moments passed.

"That's him," Shiloh said in a low tone, pulling himself up straighter.

Nathan Bedford Forrest sat tall and wide-shouldered in the saddle. His hat was high-crowned and broad-brimmed, with the front of the brim turned slightly downward, shading but not hiding his eyes. He was wearing a canvas duster, pushed back away from his legs and chest. One gauntleted fist rested on his thigh, and the only movement he made was the horseman's slight motion of the hips accommodating a horse's natural movements. The fog danced around him. His eyes did not move to the right or left, but he seemed to see everything. When he was still far down the street, he nodded, a quick, slight motion of his head, and somehow everyone knew that he was looking at Shiloh. Shiloh stood up straighter. The soldiers pressed a little closer.

Beside Cheney, Rissy shrank back.

THE

PART THREE

MANSLAYERS

And among the cities which ye
shall give unto the Levites
there shall be six cities for refuge,
which ye shall appoint for the
manslayer,
that he may flee thither....
And they shall be unto you cities
for refuge from the avenger;
that the manslayer die not,
until he stand
before the congregation
in judgment.

Numbers 35:6, 12

21

BROTHERS IN ARMS

"That's King Phillip," Shiloh murmured, his voice suffused with recognition and pleasure.

"Who?" Cheney exclaimed.

Two soldiers suddenly sifted themselves out from the crowd and hurried to huddle up against the wall of the hotel. They were very close to Cheney, and she saw with puzzlement that they actually seemed to be hiding behind Shiloh.

Suddenly one of the younger soldiers in the crowd took a tentative step forward and looked around the crowd of men. "Well, I wanna see him," he said with great bravado. "C'mon, let's go!"

"I wouldn't do that if I were you," Shiloh drawled, nodding toward the horseman. "That's King Phillip."

But now—since one had had the audacity to lead them—all of the soldiers stepped out into the street and began hurrying toward the rider. Cheney stepped up to Shiloh's side to watch Forrest curiously; again, he gave no sign as the crowd of soldiers in blue hurried toward him. He kept riding, slowly, fist on thigh, his eyes straight ahead. Cheney had finally understood that "King Phillip" was the horse, and to her, he looked weary and sluggish. She thought he was probably an old horse. But he was handsome, likely over sixteen hands, a light "Confederate gray" with charcoal mane and tail and points on his legs.

The soldiers rushed down the street—some of the younger ones now running—shouting Forrest's name. They engulfed him, and the only move Bedford Forrest made was to casually take King Phillip's reins in both hands.

As the soldiers crowded around, King Phillip suddenly threw up his head, screamed long and loud, and reared furiously.

When his front hooves hit the ground again, he stamped up and down, fast and mean. His ears were as flat as a mad tomcat's. Tossing his head, he managed to knock down one bluebelly who'd grabbed at his headpiece. Fortunately King Phillip did not stamp the fallen warrior, but another soldier tripped over him, and another, and a pile of three soldiers made a great blue hump in the street. King Phillip, his mouth pulled back in a grimace, his teeth snapping, rushed the others, who were running everywhere. Only then did Forrest guide the horse, turning him in the general direction of the hotel. Two soldiers were headed that way, and though Cheney could see that Forrest had the horse well under control, it looked to the two fleeing men as if the horse were chasing them—and gaining on them. They rushed by the small group still standing in front of the Planter's, the whites of their eyes showing, throwing desperate glances behind their shoulders.

One of the soldiers who was standing close to Cheney—and close behind Shiloh—was an older man with a corporal's stripes and a brown-and-gray beard almost to his waist. He looked up at the other, a cherub-faced private, first class. "You done met him before, too, huh?" he asked.

The young private nervously replied, "I've never met General Forrest before, in person. But I've met King Phillip." He kept his eyes fixed on the horse and rider.

"I heard that General Forrest surrendered," the corporal ruminated, "but I see King Phillip ain't."

At a rebellious, furious, kicking trot, King Phillip came reluctantly to a stop in front of Shiloh. The big horse still seemed to eye the fleeing soldiers longingly. The two soldiers behind Shiloh shrank back even more but held their ground.

Nathan Bedford Forrest dismounted. Shiloh came to attention stiffly and saluted. Forrest's eyes glittered, then he gave Shiloh a casual, dismissive salute and held out his hand. "Irons, good to see you again."

Shiloh grabbed his hand, first with one, and then with both hands. "Sir. It's awful good to see you again, sir."

The two men stood motionless, and the small group around

them neither moved nor spoke. Shiloh had his back to Cheney, and she wished fervently she could see his face. She could see Forrest's face, however, and to her great surprise he looked warm and kind as he looked at Shiloh, who clung to his hand.

Nathan Bedford Forrest was a big man. Cheney thought he was much bigger than Shiloh; she found out later that, at six two, he was actually two inches shorter. But even after she knew this, Nathan Bedford Forrest still seemed *bigger* than Shiloh. His shoulders were the widest Cheney had ever seen on a man, though he was not barrel-chested, not thickly muscled. Neither was he a slender man. He just seemed hard-packed, tightly knit, like the handle of a bullwhip. And he moved like the crack of a whip, with fast, decisive ease.

After long moments Shiloh released Forrest's hand, stepped back, turned, and motioned toward the breezeway by the side of the lobby. "Jubal! C'mon out here!"

The little colored man who always took care of the hotel guests' horses stepped out of the alleyway, then stopped, staring at Forrest with great black-and-white eyes.

"Don't be scared, Jubal," Shiloh said, not unkindly. "Nobody's going to hurt you."

"Well, now, Mistuh Arns, I know you ain't," he called in a squeaky voice, "an' mebbe Gen'ral Forrest, he ain't—mebbe—but I sho' dunno 'bout that devil-horse!"

"C'mon and get this horse, Jubal," the thick-bearded corporal called out. "He's gonna see us in a minute!"

All eyes turned to General Forrest, who surveyed the scene, his arms crossed, his booted feet wide apart. His shoulders were thrown back proudly, the set of his head was disdainful, the expression on his face arrogant—but his gray eyes flickered with amusement.

"Here, boy," he finally called out, and Cheney started at the sound of his voice. With her eyes closed, she would have sworn it was Shadrach Forrest Luxton's well-modulated tenor that carried so clearly through the air. "Git over here and take care of this critter. He ain't gonna hurt you. It's just bluebellies he don't like."

Shiloh nodded encouragement. Jubal, who was wearing his old Johnny Reb overcoat, suddenly squared his shoulders and swaggered up to take King Phillip's reins. The horse, though he honestly did seem to be hungrily eyeing the two men behind Shiloh, was docile when Jubal took the reins from Forrest. With a shaking hand Jubal touched the horse's massive neck, then began to stroke him. The horse tossed his head slightly and made the soft blubber with his lips that all horses make when they're pleased.

Forrest stepped back and started untying a huge blanket roll behind King Phillip's saddle. Shiloh hurried to help. "Your room's all ready, sir."

"Good. Thanks."

Jubal turned around and spoke with newfound courage, and in the aura of his new ally who was successfully cowing two Union soldiers. "Gen'ral, I'll tend to them saddlebags an' thet blanket roll afore I take King Phillip down to the livery, if'n you want me to."

"I'd be obliged," Forrest replied quickly, flipping a coin through the air. "You take real good care of this horse, now, boy. He's been rode hard the last two days. There'll be two more of those for you if I see King Phillip's restin' good tonight."

Crossing his arms, he turned to Shiloh. "Where's my brother?"

"In City Hall, sir," Shiloh answered, standing almost at attention.

"Where's that?"

"Two blocks south, sir." Shiloh nodded down the street.

Forrest turned to look back, and Cheney saw again that when he moved it was not jerky, but smooth and quick. Instead of craning his neck around, he turned his upper body to cautiously scan the distance and the street just behind him. His eyes came to meet Cheney's, and he studied her. She met his gaze solidly.

"Sir, I thought you would like to meet this lady, and speak with her. In a way, she knows more about Shadrach's situation than anyone," Shiloh said quietly.

"That right?" Forrest said, still looking at Cheney. Then he flowed forward, removing his gauntlets, sweeping off his hat, and bowing deeply.

"Dr. Duvall, may I present to you Lieutenant General Nathan Bedford Forrest," Shiloh said clearly. "General Forrest, it is my honor to present to you Dr. Cheney Duvall, a well-respected physician from New York, and a friend of mine, and Shadrach's."

Cheney was surprised; this was the first time she had ever known Shiloh to observe the formal rules of introduction. But she merely smiled and extended her hand, which literally disappeared into Nathan Bedford Forrest's huge, long-fingered fist. But the kiss he brushed against the tips of her fingers was so light Cheney could barely feel it. Holding her hand for a moment, he looked up at her. "Dr. Duvall, it is my great honor, and pleasure, to meet you."

His eyes were gray, the color of shattered steel, with none of the genial blue tinge of Shadrach's, and they were slightly hooded, mysterious, secretive. His hair was coarse, thick, coal black, with silver streaks, but his neatly trimmed mustache and chin-whiskers had no trace of gray. He had a high, broad forehead, and his cheekbones were so sculpted they looked as if they'd been hammered out by a metalworker's cold chisel.

"General, it is my pleasure to meet you," she said quietly, "though I regret that we meet under such unfortunate circumstances."

"I'd appreciate it if you'd tell me some of them circumstances," he said, dropping her hand and fixing her with an intense stare.

Cheney knew the pleasantries were over, and it was time to get down to business. She took a deep breath. "I am your brother's personal physician, General Forrest. And as such, I have been the only person allowed to see him since his arrest."

"Yes?" He took less than one second to assess this. "He hurt?"

"Yes, sir. Not seriously."

"How?"

263

"His leg was injured. The vastus lateralis was bruised but not herniated, and . . ."

General Forrest turned to glare at Shiloh. "Doctors! What the deuce does that mean, Irons?"

Cheney, her eyes sparkling, stepped up and with her riding crop tapped General Forrest's left leg, twice, just above the knee, on the outside. "This muscle right here, General Forrest."

His head swiveled back toward Cheney, and Shiloh's eyebrows flew upward. Then General Forrest grinned, and Cheney, smiling gamely back, noted with interest that his teeth were straight, even, and very white, and his two upper canines were long and pointed.

"You got some grit, ma'am," he said softly, watching her face with narrowed eyes. "And I don't mean no disrespect by that, Dr. Duvall. None at all."

"I understand that, General," she replied calmly. "And I thank you for the sincere compliment. Now, Shadrach's leg is injured, and he has bruises and some contusions. But the damage is not serious or permanent."

General Forrest turned to look up the street once again. A line of people still loitered up and down Church Street, obviously looking for Forrest, but the men of Charleston would consider it unforgivably rude and ill-bred to crowd around him on the street and gawk. All of the Union soldiers had disappeared— except for the two determined soldiers who still stood on the other side of the hotel door, motionless and at attention, obviously eavesdropping, but looking straight ahead. They could have been invisible, however, for all the attention Forrest paid them. He turned back to Shiloh. "We'll walk, and you fill me in while we go, Irons."

"Yes, sir!" Shiloh said smartly, saluting. Old habits die hard.

Forrest turned back to Cheney. "Ma'am, did you say you been the only one they'll let in to see those boys?"

"Yes, General. They are not allowing any visitors in at all, not even the families of the other two cadets, who live here."

"That 'cause you're his doctor?"

"No, that is not the sole reason, sir," Cheney replied honestly. "But that is one reason."

Forrest's eyes again seemed to be taking in the whole world, and, somehow, everyone knew that he was now including the two Union soldiers in the conversation. "Dr. Duvall," he called clearly, "would you do me the honor of being my personal physician while I am in Charleston?"

"Certainly, General Forrest," Cheney replied calmly, her eyes twinkling.

"Thank you, Dr. Duvall," he said, still addressing the public in general. Then he grunted to her and Shiloh, "That way, if anybody in Charleston drops dead whilst I'm in town, and I end up in jail, I reckon at least I'll have one visitor." Then in a normal tone, "I'm going to City Hall to see my brother, Dr. Duvall. Would you come with me and check up on those three boys?"

"General, I would be honored." She went back to Rissy, who had stayed flattened against the hotel wall, watching Nathan Bedford Forrest with the vigilance of a mongoose eyeing a cobra. Cheney whispered, "Rissy, you go on back up to the room, please. Thank you for staying with me, but I'm fine. I'll be back soon."

"Well, I guess he ain't gonna kill us all outright," Rissy muttered direly. "An' he ain't got horns an' hoofs an' a tail, even though he do have them big white fangs. All right, Miss Cheney, I'll wait for you." She went into the hotel without glancing back.

While Cheney and Rissy were talking, the brown-bearded corporal had stepped forward slightly, and though he did not dare address Forrest, he looked up at Shiloh expectantly. Shiloh looked amused, then stepped close to him and turned back to General Forrest. "Sir, I have never met these two soldiers, but I understand that they have met King Phillip, and would like to meet you."

Forrest focused on them and thrust out his hand. "I'm Nathan Bedford Forrest."

"Gen'ral, it's a real pleasure," the corporal said, saluting snappily before shaking Forrest's hand. "I'm Corporal Benjamin Baker, and this here's Private, First Class Francis Todd."

The men shook hands all around, and Shiloh introduced himself, though the two soldiers already knew his name, his rank, and that he was one of "Forrest's boys." Cheney rejoined the group.

Private Todd took a slight step forward to announce proudly, "I was at the garrison outside Decatur, sir, and I was *trying* to surrender to you. But I got too close to King Phillip, and he bit my arm and I fell down, and he stomped me. Only time I got wounded in the war!"

Corporal Baker pushed forward and eagerly offered, "You took me prisoner, Gen'ral Forrest! Twice! Once when you ran us plumb down into the dirt with Sookey Smith, and the other time was when you beat us all to kingdom come at Brice's Cross-roads!"

Forrest's slate gray eyes sparkled like a tinderbox. Shiloh grinned, then started chuckling, and suddenly all the men burst out laughing. Cheney, while smiling politely, thought the Union soldiers' reactions to General Forrest were quite odd, and couldn't see what was so funny. She decided to ask Shiloh about it later.

When everyone stopped laughing, Forrest nodded to the two soldiers and said, "Nice to meet you men." It was a dismissal, and they stepped back politely, but did not leave.

Forrest turned back to Cheney. "Are you ready, ma'am? Do you mind walking?"

"No, General, not at all."

"General Forrest, sir." Corporal Baker again stepped forward and snapped to attention. "Private Todd and I request permission to escort you and your party to the Hall."

Forrest nodded curtly. "Thank you, I'll accept your escort. Lead off."

Forrest, Cheney, and Shiloh followed the two soldiers in blue. Cheney was between the two men and felt dwarfed by them. It was a pleasurable feeling for her—at five ten, she loomed over many men—and she was surprised at how nice it was to walk with two men without feeling obliged to round her shoulders and slump. Though Shiloh and Forrest walked quickly, and both had long legs, Cheney kept up with them easily.

Forrest was careful to be gallant to Cheney, insisting on carrying her medical bag, stepping behind her and putting his arm up protectively when bystanders crowded the three of them, taking her elbow lightly to step up and down on the curbs, careful to shield her from the street. But he kept up an intense interrogation of Shiloh over her head, and Cheney thought that she might be the only woman ever to witness what amounted to a council of war by General Nathan Bedford Forrest.

"What's the situation, Irons?" he demanded.

"They're in—cells—in the basement of City Hall, sir."

"Cages," Cheney muttered darkly. Forrest's eyes flashed on her, then immediately he looked back up at Shiloh.

"What are the arrangements?"

"A company of Hatch's men guarding them at all times, sir," Shiloh answered grimly. "Four provost marshals around the clock. Negroes—anywhere from eighty to a hundred—are camped in a small park across the street."

Forrest stared ahead at the soldiers' backs. "Hatch's entire brigade here?"

"No, sir. Two battalions."

"Provost marshals?"

"Only twenty, sir."

"What rank commands the guard company?"

"Company captains are present at all times, sir."

"Provost marshal ranks?"

Shiloh's head swiveled around, his eyes suddenly lit. Forrest watched him intently. "Sir, I believe the highest ranking provost marshal is a sergeant."

"That so?" He searched up the street impatiently but muttered, "That's good, Irons. You done good."

Shiloh's face positively glowed, while Cheney began to wonder if General Forrest and Shiloh were preparing to attack City Hall.

"Tell me about the provost tribune," Forrest growled.

"He's a lawyer from Ohio, sir. Served in the Washington

Quartermaster's Office. A colonel—breveted," Shiloh said with disdain.

"Brevets!" Forrest growled. "If a man deserves a rank, they oughta give it to him. If he don't, then leave it."

"Yes, sir!" Shiloh heartily agreed. "That's all I've been able to find out about him. I've never met him. I tried to see him, but my appointment is in two weeks."

Cheney smiled at the heavy sarcasm in Shiloh's voice and glanced up at General Forrest. He had not seen the cartoon, she knew; they had all disappeared from the streets of Charleston within hours. But a wicked glint in his eyes told her that he understood exactly what Shiloh's words implied.

They were across the street from City Hall. Forrest grunted, "Halt," and stopped. The two soldiers in front of them stopped cold without looking back. Shiloh and Cheney jerked to a standstill, and, unseeing, Forrest thrust her medical bag back in front of her, and she took it back silently.

Forrest's eyes hooded to slits. Cheney watched him curiously; he was a most compelling man. His eyes did not dart, as Shiloh's did, as he seemed to be assessing each man in the scene separately. Forrest stood motionless, not moving at all except for breathing. First he took in the two Citadel cadets standing at a meticulous parade rest on the near corner of the courtyard. Shadrach's great white horse grazed quietly behind them. Israfel was unsaddled and had no bridle or headpiece, but was hobbled by one hind foot to a long, heavy iron chain attached to a rude stake hammered into the hard winter earth.

Forrest slowly turned toward Shiloh, and his eyes, already dark and full of anger and passion, smoldered like the heart of a blacksmith's hottest fire.

"The cadets got permission to set an honor guard for their captain, sir," Shiloh said without looking back at the general. "They change every two hours." Forrest looked back, and Shiloh continued in a low, charged voice, "There are seventy-six cadets at the Citadel, General Forrest, and they actually fight to be in Captain Shadrach Forrest Luxton's honor guard. Major Phil Chandler of Battalion One, Hatch's Brigade, was obliged to schedule the Citadel Honor Guard detail."

Forrest nodded slowly, then his all-encompassing gaze returned to the business at hand. Now he took in the street and, across from the hall, the park and the crowd of Negroes. They had seen him and knew him and were crowding along the fence, shouting and shaking their fists. A detail of soldiers lined the fence on the street side, rifles unslung but not at the ready. Forrest's unlimited gaze swept over them disdainfully. He ignored them to the point of annihilation.

Then he took in the soldiers crowding the grounds of City Hall. It appeared that the bluebellies who had been vanquished from the Planter's Hotel had come here. Forrest looked at the steps leading up to the main entrance. Four soldiers, in blue uniforms with red piping and red feathers stuck in the front of their kepis, lounged negligently on the steps. He studied the entrance to the stairway leading down to the basement.

"Corporal," he said quietly, pushing back his coat, "come back here and take charge of this for me." Pulling out a Colt .44, he slapped it hard into Corporal Baker's hand, then looked up at Shiloh. "Yours too, Irons." Without hesitation Shiloh gave Private Todd his Colt.

The two Union soldiers exchanged delighted grins and stuck the guns in their waistbands, butt-out, as Shiloh and Forrest had worn them. "Wish there was a photographer around here," Baker mumbled through his beard as they headed across to the Hall.

"Boy, me, too," Todd agreed. "You think he'd sign something we've got?" He looked down, plaintively trying to find something in his clothing and accouterments that a general might possibly consent to write on.

"Way I figger," the stolid Corporal Brown noted, "we're lucky he don't tattoo our heads. An' it don't look to me like everybody's gonna be as lucky as us."

Cheney was thinking along these lines herself as Forrest grew silent and walked. His tanned face darkened to the color of heated bronze, and she noted clinically that his respiration was increasing, though the breaths certainly did not get shallow. His nostrils flared as he sucked in great lungfuls of air, then breathed out.

Cheney, in spite of herself, tensed up.

Forrest began to take long harsh strides, passing up his two escorts. He marched up to the two Citadel cadets, who instantly, simultaneously, snapped to attention and slowly, with great ceremony, saluted. Forrest, who already stood with shoulders thrown back and head held high, drew himself even taller and saluted beautifully. He held the salute for long moments, then turned on his heel. Cheney watched; the two cadets held their salute until Forrest disappeared into the great crowd of men in blue.

He plowed through the crowd of soldiers on the lawn who were not in formation, and who quickly stumbled back to make a path for him. Shiloh was following a single step behind Forrest. Cheney, with the lagging escorts who came to walk on either side of her, struggled to catch up.

A cordon of soldiers was drawn in a tight circle all around the Hall, but Forrest did not walk up to the private who stood at attention directly in front of the steps leading downstairs. He marched up to the man who stood in front of the line. "Captain!" he called out and thrust out his hand. "I'm Nathan Bedford Forrest, and that's my brother in there. I'm gonna see him."

Shaking Forrest's hand firmly, the captain replied formally, "It's a pleasure to meet you, General Forrest. I am Captain Riley Hawkins. I regret that I cannot allow you in. I am instructed that the prisoners may have no visitors."

"Instructed?" Forrest barked, and several of the nearby privates jumped. "Instructed by who?"

"By the provost marshals, sir." Riley Hawkins looked puzzled, and his eyes cut to Shiloh. Shiloh nodded, so slightly that no one else noticed except Hawkins.

"The provost marshals," Forrest repeated. "This marshal who gave you these instructions, what is his rank?"

Riley's eyes opened wide with surprise. "Why . . . why . . . he was a sergeant, sir."

"Then of course he cannot issue *orders* to you, Captain,"

Forrest said, watching Riley Hawkins' face closely.

Captain Riley Hawkins was not a stupid man, and suddenly he saw clearly General Forrest's strategy. He sneakily admired it and wished he'd thought of it himself. "No, sir, no sergeant ever tried to give me an order, sir!" he shouted gleefully.

Now Forrest studied the private who stood in front of the steps leading down to the basement. That private, and the two soldiers on either side of him as well, looked extremely unhappy. But they stayed at attention, their rifles slung, and looked straight ahead.

Forrest's high, clear call rent the air like lightning. "Is there anybody here who's got direct orders not to let me in to see my brother?"

At last the four provost marshals, all buck privates, got to their feet. Three of them slouched down to stand in front of the steps, their rifles slung carelessly, their hands propped on their hips. The other one stood behind, his face strained.

The tallest and most arrogant marshal stepped forward. "Listen, *Forrest*, I got direct orders from the provost tribune not to let anybody in to see these prisoners!"

General Forrest wrenched off his duster, threw it to the ground, yanked off his tie, threw it down, and began unbuttoning his waistcoat. The three marshals in front looked disconcerted. The leader looked at Captain Riley Hawkins accusingly, but Captain Hawkins merely crossed his arms and shrugged. "What . . . what are you doin', Forrest?" the tall marshal asked with sudden alarm, standing up a bit straighter.

"I'm gonna do you boys a favor," Forrest replied, and ignored the loud groans that accompanied this remark, "and keep you from disobeying your orders." Throwing off his waistcoat, his voice made the air sizzle. "I'm gonna beat you senseless!"

The tall marshal's eyes grew round, and he looked again at Captain Hawkins. "He can't do that! Can he?"

Captain Hawkins considered Forrest, then looked back at the marshal. "Sure he can, you dummy."

"No!" the marshal yowled. "I mean, you ain't gonna let him, are you?" He fumbled for the rifle strap across his chest.

"Stow that rifle, private!" Hawkins barked. "No deadly force unless the situation is life threatening! This man is unarmed!"

Implacably Forrest rolled up his sleeve, his eyes as dark and deadly as a viper's, his jawline a tight muscle and thick bone. He never took his eyes off the marshals.

Even in her uneasiness—almost fear—Cheney observed that Nathan Bedford Forrest did not seem to need to blink.

The provost marshal behind the other three—the smallest, and the youngest—stepped around to hide behind Captain Hawkins. "No siree, huh-uh, not me! I'm turning myself in for disobeying orders, Captain Hawkins!"

"Smart boy," Hawkins muttered over his shoulder.

The three remaining marshals looked at one another.

General Forrest began to roll up his other sleeve and watched the marshals.

Shiloh Irons, watching the general, looked as if he were readying for a spring, his arms held slightly out from his sides, his leg muscles twitching.

Captain Riley Hawkins watched everyone.

Cheney held her breath, her fingers in a death-grip on the handle of her medical bag. Her shoulders and neck ached.

The tall marshal gritted his teeth and then dropped his eyes. He took one long side step, away from the entrance to the Hall's sublevel. Then he growled an obscenity under his breath.

The next few seconds were very confusing for the young marshal. One moment he was flat on the ground, staring blankly up at the spiky stars that whizzed around in a red sky, his jaw shrieking with pain. In the next moment Nathan Bedford Forrest grabbed his collar with one hand, hauled him back upright—his feet actually cleared the ground by an inch—and shook him like a Jack Russell terrier shaking a rat. "Don't you never, never say no word like that in front of a lady agin, you little piece of dirt!"

Forrest's mighty arm shook; the marshal's head popped forward and backward, and his teeth made loud clicks. "Y . . . Y . . . Y . . ." sounds were coming out of his mouth.

"Wonder what he's trying to say?" Hawkins asked in an aside to Shiloh.

"I dunno," Shiloh replied, cocking his head at an angle. "But it's peculiar. That's the same funny noise I heard the last man make that said that word in General Forrest's presence."

"General Forrest kill him?" Hawkins asked with interest.

"Naw," Shiloh replied. " 'Course, there was no lady present that time."

Now Hawkins frowned and looked slightly uneasy, but at that moment Forrest let go of the marshal's collar, and the man fell to the ground in a sodden little heap, gasping and choking. "Y-yes, sir, Gen . . . Gen . . . eral F-F-Forrest, sir," he sobbed.

But Forrest had already gone down the steps. Shiloh followed him, expecting Captain Hawkins to grab him. He sensed the man right behind him. But Captain Hawkins didn't touch him.

Shadrach stood, gripping the bars of his cage, his face pressed up hard against them. When Forrest drew near, Shadrach snapped to attention and saluted. In the cell behind him, Logan and Maxcy stood side by side, at stiff attention, saluting. Maxcy's face was filled with dread and was as white as clean ash. Logan's face was solid blue and purple, his eyes two round humps with narrow slits. Shadrach looked stricken, and he, too, appeared almost frightened.

Forrest walked up, grabbed the iron bars, and shook them viciously. Both of the "cages" clanged deafeningly in the expanse of the room. "Open this door!" he thundered.

Hawkins pushed forward, rattling keys. Shadrach stood at attention, holding his salute, his eyes riveted on Bedford Forrest. Forrest stiffened as if he might strike Captain Hawkins down, but finally the door swung open. Forrest took one stride, then threw his arms around Shadrach Forrest Luxton. "Boy," he muttered, "drop that salute. I'm your brother."

Shadrach threw his arms around Forrest and squeezed his eyes shut tightly, fiercely, so that the tears could not escape.

Shiloh blew out a relieved breath, then moved quietly to stand outside the cell, his back to the men, so he could watch the doorway. Cheney hovered nearby, her pale face glimmering in the gloom, watching General Forrest and Shadrach.

Captain Riley Hawkins unlocked Logan's and Maxcy's cell, then—averting his eyes from everyone—headed toward the door, muttering dourly to himself. "I better go see about General Forrest's clothes before some of those fools set up a booth and start an auction."

Slowly Shadrach and General Forrest stepped back, though Forrest kept his hand on Shadrach's shoulder. He looked past him and saluted Logan and Maxcy. "At ease, boys," he said softly. "Be at ease." He looked closely at Shadrach, then nodded. He seemed not to notice Shadrach's uncanny resemblance to himself. "You've grown up, Shadrach. You're almost as tall as me. Handsome fella, too, ain't you?" he said ingenuously. "C'mere and sit down for a minute. What kinda hole you boys dug and jumped off into?"

Shadrach waited for Forrest to sit down, then sat close to him. Forrest put his arm around his shoulders, and though Shadrach didn't actually lean on him, he drew closer. "Sir, they've accused us of murdering a colored man," he said evenly.

"I know that," Forrest nodded. "Irons sent me a telegram that said that, and that you was in trouble."

"That's the truth, sir," Shadrach sighed. "Deep trouble." He jerked upright and looked his brother straight in the eyes. "They're going to hang us, Bedford."

Forrest smiled. "You kill that nigra, Shadrach?"

"No, sir!"

"You with the man that killed him?"

"No, sir!"

"Then I'm swearin' to you, right here, and right now," Forrest said in a low voice, "nobody's going to hang you, Shadrach. Nobody."

Shadrach's shoulders sagged with relief. Then he straightened again and cast an anxious glance behind him at Logan and Maxcy, who sat close together on one cot, watching and listening. "Sir, these two men were with me when Vess got killed. They are innocent, too. And," he swallowed hard, "they're my men."

Forrest looked at Logan and Maxcy, then back at Shadrach. When he spoke, his voice was rich and warm. "I'm right proud of you, brother. You're gonna be a good officer, prob'ly a good general, someday." He stood up, propped his hands on his hips, and looked around the room. "Irons!"

Shiloh managed to jump to attention and whirl around at the same time. "Sir!"

"Go lead that boy—and help that one—what's your name, boy?—Mr. Roddy—git over there to that table and sit down. Now I'm here," Forrest declared wrathfully, "ain't nobody gonna stay in these cages for another minute!"

22

ONCE YOU'VE BEATEN A MAN

Lieutenant General Nathan Bedford Forrest clasped his hands behind his back, bowed his head to stare at the floor, and paced.

Shiloh got Cheney, Shadrach, Logan, and Maxcy seated at the table—facing the stalking general, for no one could bear to turn their back to him—and then, walking quietly in a wide circle, Shiloh slipped around Forrest to stand between him and the door.

Once, Captain Hawkins came through the door. Shiloh jumped, his hands tensed, and he almost charged. But Forrest never looked up, or blinked, or stopped his relentless march. Captain Hawkins hurried up to Shiloh, holding out Forrest's hat, duster, waistcoat, tie, and gauntlets at arm's length. Then he turned and walked—with deliberate slowness, his shoulders stiff as steel—back outside, closing the door softly behind him.

In the waiting silence Cheney reflected that Nathan Bedford Forrest seemed even more imposing in just his denim breeches, his plain white shirt with the sleeves rolled up, and his knee boots. The violence in him was plain, uncloaked, revealed.

Bedford stopped and looked at Shadrach, who jumped up straighter in his chair. "What's the evidence against you three, Shadrach?"

"I don't know, sir. None of us do."

Forrest merely looked at him, and Shadrach swallowed, hard. "Sir, when they came for us, the provost marshals just said that we were being arrested for the murder of Vess Alexander. That's all they've told us—except for when they've come down here to tell us that Judge Granger's going to hang us."

Forrest paced forward two steps, wheeled, back another two

steps. He stopped. "What was you doing when this man was killed? Where was you at?"

Shadrach looked helplessly at Logan and Maxcy. Logan's bruised features twisted even more with distress. Maxcy looked as if he was about to topple over. Cheney's mind whirled; she had no clue as to why the cadets were so hesitant, and she looked to Shiloh for help. Shiloh was frowning, watching Shadrach, uncomprehending.

Forrest's eyes blazed, and he took a long step, too close to the table. "Speak up, boy! What's the matter with you! You tell me, right now, where you was at!"

Shadrach looked up at Forrest expressionlessly. He met his gaze, refusing to be beaten down by the furnace blast of Forrest's nearness.

"Sir . . . wait . . . wait a minute, sir," Shiloh said softly, easily. Forrest whirled, and Shiloh stood straighter but did not flinch. He closed his eyes, touched his forehead, then rubbed it for a moment. "I'd forgotten—with everything that's happened—that Vess was murdered Friday night."

Cheney's mind took on an annoying buzz, but she was so enervated by the events of the last few days—and particularly by the last few hours—that she was unable to analyze the tangled, hot-colored visions and memories snarled up in her head.

Shiloh went on quietly, "Friday night. The Knights of the White Rose paraded, sir."

Forrest whirled back again to look at Shadrach, who remained impassive and bore his brother's scorching stare. Cheney admired Shadrach exceedingly for this.

"Well?" Forrest thundered.

Shadrach blinked. "Sir, the provost tribune has declared the Knights of the White Rose a seditious and treasonable organization. All members of this organization are to be arrested and imprisoned," he said clearly and slowly.

The room grew silent, and Forrest grew very still. No one looked at Cheney—as a matter of fact, all the men kept their eyes carefully trained far away from her—but even in her foggy weariness she comprehended exactly what Shadrach was saying, and not saying. If the three cadets admitted to, or indicated in any way, their connection with the Knights of the White Rose, and Cheney were questioned about it, she would be forced to admit knowledge of their membership. Undoubtedly General Forrest and Shiloh would refuse to cooperate with any such questioning, regardless of the consequences.

But Shadrach Forrest Luxton understood that Cheney Duvall would—must—tell the truth. She knew, very well, that it was strictly for her benefit, and her comfort, that these men were treating this matter with such delicacy. She was extremely grateful to all of them, and by subtle body language drew back away from them, to signal her acknowledgment of the situation.

Forrest's eyes were still focused on Shadrach, but everyone saw the sudden comprehension in his expression. Then the color of his face began to heat up. Cheney couldn't help but notice that his neck, his chest where the top button of his shirt was unbuttoned, and, even his hands, seemed to fire up.

"Irons, where's that judge's office?" he snarled without turning.

Shiloh said placatingly, "Sir, Judge Granger's office is upstairs, but . . . sir . . . sir . . ."

But Forrest had already stampeded into the stairway, his heavy boots pounding hard and loud. He was taking the stairs two at a time.

The people left in the basement were silent for a few moments. Shiloh, Cheney, Shadrach, Logan, and Maxcy all took turns staring blankly at one another.

Overhead a loud, raucous commotion commenced. Everyone looked up at the low wooden ceiling, as if they could see through it to the tornado on the first floor. Thumps, crashes, boot steps, and Nathan Bedford Forrest's thunder filtered clearly down to the sublevel.

Shiloh blew out an exasperated breath and ambled over to sink into one of the chairs at the desk. Maxcy sighed and laid his head down on his folded arms. Shadrach's eyes were still turned upward. Logan closed his swollen eyes and took long, deep breaths.

Cheney asked uncertainly, "Do you . . . do you suppose you ought to go tell him that the judge isn't here, Shiloh?"

"No!" all four of the men shouted.

"No, I suppose not," Cheney agreed.

The sound of doors being kicked in and Forrest's roar of challenge made the ceiling vibrate slightly. Sounds of heavy furniture being suddenly shifted—then perhaps tossed—were plainly discernible.

Shiloh commented, "Probably a good thing the Doc can't hear the words. Bet the climate up there's a lot hotter than it is down here."

"Boy, that's the truth," Shadrach declared.

Cheney said in a small voice, "But . . . but . . . that man, outside, that marshal . . ."

Shiloh looked at her indignantly. "He can't stand vulgarity, Doc. Not a whiff of it. And outright obscenities—" He shrugged expressively.

"Bedford often does show considerable disregard for the Third Commandment," Shadrach sighed, "but it's true, he hates any words or behavior that are . . . unseemly."

This pronouncement of Nathan Bedford Forrest's delicacy suddenly struck the four of them as funny, particularly since the spectacular ruckus upstairs was steadily continuing.

Logan, grinning painfully, asked, "How did he get in here, anyway?"

Shiloh smiled back at him. "Typical Forrest tactics. He—"

Cheney interrupted, "He demanded their surrender, to prevent the further effusion of blood. And two hundred of them surrendered to him and Shiloh, to prevent this terrible effusion."

Again Shadrach and Logan laughed, while Maxcy smiled weakly and laid his head back down. Cheney said contritely, "Mr. Roddy, why don't you go lie down? You look—"

"No!" he cried, jerking upright, then wincing. "General Forrest said not to go back into the cage!"

Cheney said impatiently, "But he didn't mean . . ." Suddenly the shouting upstairs increased in volume; they could hear a lower-pitched shout answering Forrest, then the crackling smash of a window breaking. Cheney trailed off into silence.

"I'll take the cot out of the cage," Shiloh said hurriedly and brought it out for Maxcy to lie down on. He did, reluctantly, but turned so he could watch the stairwell. Lieutenant General Nathan Bedford Forrest was not going to catch him lying down unless he was a dead cadet.

Shiloh sat back down, and Shadrach looked at him moodily. "I wish he hadn't . . . had to . . . see me like this."

Cheney ventured, "You shouldn't be ashamed of being in jail, Shadrach."

"It's not that, Dr. Duvall!" Shadrach declared indignantly. "Bedford's been in jail . . . uh . . . three times, I think! He was just acquitted of one murder last October! But Bedford really did kill *that* man, you see!"

Cheney was first astonished, and then outraged as Shiloh and Logan nodded solemn agreement to this preposterous argument. "Oh, you mean that if you'd actually killed Vess, like your brother killed someone, then you wouldn't be so embarrassed?" she shouted, almost as loudly as the thumps and crashes upstairs. "Yes, certainly, now I understand!"

Shadrach frowned darkly, Logan gave her a sharp look, but Shiloh almost smiled. "No, Doc," he said quietly, so she had to strain to hear. "General Forrest caught one of his servants beating his wife to death and went into the cabin and stopped him. The nigra drew a knife and attacked General Forrest, who was unarmed. General Forrest was wounded, but the nigra was killed."

Cheney stared at him.

"Based on the wife's testimony, and another of the servants who witnessed the event, General Forrest was acquitted of murder on the grounds that he was acting in self-defense," Shiloh went on calmly.

"Oh," Cheney said.

"And what I think Shadrach's saying is that if something like that had occurred, then they would not be ashamed of getting themselves into this stewpot," Shiloh said heavily. "But getting into it because they were skylarking around and showing off is different."

"Exactly," Shadrach muttered and looked upward. Loud thumps began: a rhythmic pounding against the wall. Cheney hoped fervently that it was General Forrest's iron fist, and not someone's head.

"That must be the fella that had to tell General Forrest the judge ain't here," Shiloh drawled.

Suddenly the noise upstairs stopped. The quiet, it seemed to Cheney, was even more ominous than the crashing and banging had been. Then they clearly heard the even rhythm of heavy boots pounding back and forth.

Cheney, her eyes wide and filled with dread, looked at Shiloh. "Do you think he's going to kill Judge Granger?"

Shiloh shifted uneasily in his chair and looked at Shadrach, who stared down at his clasped hands. The hesitation of the two men filled Cheney with horror. Finally Shiloh muttered, "I don't know, Doc. Maybe."

"Lord Jesus, I pray not," Shadrach whispered. Logan gingerly touched his face, staring toward the door that led outside.

"But . . . but . . . do you think . . . he wouldn't . . . shoot him, or anything, in cold blood, would he?" Cheney beseeched Shiloh.

Shiloh looked over Cheney's shoulder, obviously seeing something none of the rest of them could. He spoke calmly, almost indifferently. "Hard to say. Best I can see of General Forrest, he can get mad as a cornered grizzly, and look like he's going to kill everything, but he doesn't, and he's actually pretty cool and calculating. Other times—he crosses a line, somewhere, somehow—and that's when he's really dangerous."

Shiloh glanced at Shadrach for affirmation, but Shadrach looked bemused and halfway answered Cheney's question. "No one but Bedford knows. He might."

Cheney recoiled and gasped, her hand going up to her neck. General Forrest's boots sounded on the stairs. Maxcy groaned, stopped abruptly, and clambered up. Shiloh bounded to his feet.

Shadrach and Logan got up a little more slowly. Cheney found she was unable to rise.

Forrest rushed in and filled the room as soon as he entered. "Irons, come on. We're goin' to find that judge." He moved like a shadow across the darkening room, pulled on his duster, grabbed his hat, and picked up his gauntlets.

He came back to stand by Cheney and bowed slightly. His voice became courtly, gentle. "Ma'am, would you stay with my boys, here?"

"Cer-certainly, General," Cheney stammered.

"Don't let them put them back in there," he said quietly, entreating her.

"I . . . I . . . won't, General."

"Thank you, ma'am," he said, and smiled at her.

★ ★ ★ ★

Forrest had sent word for Jubal to bring King Phillip, Sock, and Stocking, and give them into the care of the cadet honor guard. The soldiers stood in a circle—a wide circle—around them, considering King Phillip, who snorted and pawed the ground as he considered them.

Corporal Benjamin Baker and Private, First Class Francis Todd stood in the middle of another circle of soldiers. They refused to let anyone touch Forrest's and Shiloh's guns; indeed, they even refused to take them out of their waistbands. They allowed soldiers to step close and look down at them, but that was all. There was much discussion and speculation as to just how many men those two well-worn Colt .44 six-shooters had killed.

Forrest and Shiloh appeared, and the entire crowd jumped alertly. The two men hurried over to their horses, leaped into the saddles, and thundered away. Two hundred men watched them, and no one said a word.

Forrest didn't speak as they rode straight south, down to the Battery, right to Judge Granger's house. They tied up the horses to a painted iron lawn jockey and walked up to the massive front door. Forrest, disdaining the brass door-knocker, banged on the door and shouted, "Granger! I am here!"

While Shiloh was reflecting that this was probably the exact method of guaranteeing that they would *not* gain entrance, the door silently opened. Juliet Granger looked up at Forrest and then Shiloh, and then she smiled sweetly. "Good evening, gentlemen," she said, taking a step backward. "Please come in."

Shiloh was completely taken aback and tense. The two men stepped inside, and Shiloh said hurriedly, "Miss Granger, this is Lieutenant General Nathan Bedford Forrest. General Forrest, this is uh . . . Miss . . . uh . . . Granger."

"Juliet, Mr. Irons," Juliet said softly. "It's a pleasure to meet you, General Forrest." Shyly she extended her hand, and Forrest bowed deeply and kissed it, his movements slow and graceful. Shiloh watched him with ire; how could this man of war suddenly seem so gentle and so kind?

"You are here to see my father, General?" Juliet asked politely.

"Yes, Miss Granger. I hope he is in this evening, and receiving guests." Forrest's voice was respectful. But in spite of this, and in spite of the confusion Shiloh felt as to who—or what—Bedford Forrest actually was, Shiloh sensed—could almost smell—the fury emanating from him. He watched Juliet Granger curiously to see if she could truly see Forrest.

If she did, she gave no indication whatsoever. Inclining her head slightly, her voice musical, she said, "Please allow me to show you into his study, General Forrest, Mr. Irons." She led them through the foyer and down a hall. "He is, I believe, in conference with Marshal Case, but I am certain that he would like to see you, General."

Shiloh had no idea if this was ignorance on her part, or blindness, or deafness—considering Forrest's menacing announcement of his presence—or perhaps it was a gentle form of rebellion against her father. Briefly he considered the puzzle of Juliet Granger, then all such thoughts vanished from his mind.

He looked ahead at the door they were approaching, a tall rectangle of yellow light outlined clearly at the end of the long, dark hallway. Oddly, the hallway was lined with gas lights, but none of them were lit. He looked at General Forrest's broad back and considered what to do if Forrest simply entered the room, walked over to Judge Granger, and broke his neck. Shiloh didn't think he could move fast enough to prevent Forrest from doing this. He also considered the very real possibility that General Forrest could—and would—hurt him badly if he tried.

Shiloh knew that his was a hopeless mission, because he—Sergeant Shiloh Irons, of Lieutenant General Nathan Bedford Forrest's renowned escort—could never raise his hand against Bedford Forrest.

But Shiloh Irons made his decision even as they reached the doorway. He would try to prevent General Forrest from killing Judge Granger. He reflected that he probably could not; he knew that if this was what Forrest intended to do, it would be done, even if it was over Shiloh Irons' dead body. But Shiloh, too, had made his decision, and he stepped as close as was possible behind the general without actually walking up his bootheels.

Juliet threw the door open wide, stepped aside, and looked in at Judge Granger and Teach Case. "Father, Marshal Case," she said with only the faintest tinge of dryness, "Lieutenant General Nathan Bedford Forrest and Sergeant Shiloh Irons are here to see you." She waited, her eyes lowered, until Shiloh had passed her. Then she closed the door soundlessly.

General Forrest walked into the study. Teach Case leaped out of the chair and stumbled over behind the judge's desk. Judge Granger sat, unable to rise, his eyes wide with alarm. Shiloh slid up behind Forrest and breathed with immeasurable relief when Forrest crossed his arms and looked around the study with deliberate slowness and casualness.

Teach, behind the judge's chair, was pale, and transparently afraid. The judge seemed to have stopped breathing and looked like a statue made out of gray marble.

Still Forrest did not speak. Shiloh now assessed Judge Garth Granger's study and thought that it was such a lifeless room that it looked like a tomb.

"This room looks like a tomb," Forrest announced loudly.

He looked down at Judge Granger. "You don't wanna die in here, do you?"

The judge's face went slack with shock. "Wh-wha-what?"

"Niver mind." Forrest sat down in the chair Teach had just vacated. Shiloh backed up a little and moved to Forrest's left so he would be within the general's peripheral vision. Though Forrest did not look around, Shiloh sensed his approval.

"Granger, I ain't a man for long-winded conversations and arguments," Forrest said with disarming honesty, in a surprisingly subdued voice, considering his eyes were like augers drilling into the judge's brain. "I want you to let my brother and those two boys loose."

"But . . . I . . . but . . ." The judge simply could not regain his mental balance.

Behind him, Teach gripped the back of the judge's chair so tightly his knuckles turned white, but he summoned the courage to speak. "General Forrest, your brother and the other two cadets—"

"Shut up!" Forrest shouted suddenly and savagely. "I don't know who—or what—you are, but I ain't talkin' to you!" His gaze burned a path back to the judge. "You talk to me, Granger," he said quietly, and this was more frightening to the judge and Teach than his former shout. "Right now."

The judge stiffened in his chair. His face turned an alarming shade of red, and his eyes started burning with an intensity of hatred that was almost demented. "You! You . . . you come in here, into my home, and make demands on me! I am the provost tribune of Charleston, a duly appointed judge, with a charge entrusted to me by the United States government! You will show some respect to me, sir!"

Forrest's chiseled features remained set, and the judge, even in his righteous tyranny, hesitated. But Forrest said nothing, merely watched and waited, and the judge swallowed hard, then went on, "Your brother, Forrest, has been arrested for a vicious murder! I will not release him!"

"Why not?" Forrest asked silkily.

The judge had, truly, lost his senses. He jumped up, slammed the desk with his hands, and shouted, "Because I know you! Oh, I know you! General Sherman said you were the devil, the very devil! And you are! I had to worry about you, and make excuses for myself because of you, and humble myself to lesser men because of you! For four solid years! You are nothing but white trash, a filthy slave trader, a murderer, a common thief—"

Forrest uncoiled. He backhanded Judge Granger hard, viciously, across the face. It knocked the judge to the floor.

Teach threw himself down, trying to help the judge to his feet. Granger was stunned, senseless, for long moments.

Forrest crossed his massive arms and waited.

Shiloh crossed his long arms and waited.

The judge moaned, then with Teach's help pulled himself up by holding on to the arm of his overstuffed chair. Blood ran down one side of his mouth, and his eyes still bore the dullness of shock.

"You have insulted me beyond repentance," Forrest said, now as cold as a Cumberland winter, "and I demand satisfaction, sir. Postings will be done tonight, and I will insert a card of notice in the *Record* tomorrow. Mr. Irons will be my second, and he will be in contact with you."

Forrest turned on his heel and stalked to the door. Shiloh followed.

"W-wait," the judge groaned. "W-wait . . . stop . . ."

Forrest turned. His hand was on the doorknob.

The judge hesitated, but with a sinking heart realized that he had no place to hide this time. Dueling was perfectly legal and widely accepted as the correct settlement of disputes among gentlemen in the state of South Carolina.

Forrest had beaten him again.

"I . . . I . . . apologize, General Forrest," he whispered and collapsed into his chair.

★　★　★　★

Nathan Bedford Forrest and Shiloh Irons returned to City Hall and handed an order of the provost tribune directly into Captain Riley Hawkins' hand. The order informed the provost marshals and the City Hall guards that the status of the prisoners, Shadrach Forrest Luxton, Logan Drewe Manigault, and Maxcy Cooper Roddy, had changed; although the three were still under investigation for the murder of Vess Alexander, they were to be released to the custody of the acting president of the Citadel, Brigadier General John Hatch. The order directed that the former prisoners be confined to the buildings and grounds of the Citadel, but were not to be restricted from any commerce with any persons within those grounds.

Shadrach insisted on riding Israfel back to the Citadel and denied Logan's and Maxcy's request that they be allowed to escort him. He ordered that Lieutenant Manigault and Private Roddy be taken back by carriage, and he and the honor guard would escort them.

Nathan Bedford Forrest shouted instructions, directed and abused a number of Union privates who couldn't find a place to hide from him, arranged for transports, and issued several expressive and loud orders to the three cadets as they sorted out the carriage and horses and gathered their scanty belongings to return home. Shiloh Irons was Forrest's shadow, close, silent, attentive at all times.

When the Negroes across the street learned what was happening, they rioted. Captain Hawkins sent another squad to reinforce the troops already surrounding the park. Fifty soldiers cordoned it and refused to allow the Negroes to leave until the cadets were back at the Citadel and General Forrest was safely away. Blood-curdling yells and curses and shouts continually carried across the courtyard through the shreds of fog. As darkness fell, the Negroes lit torches; some of the men threw them over the fence, and the soldiers fired guns over their heads. The torches landed harmlessly in the street and soon spluttered out. Shadrach and Bedford Forrest never looked across the street or seemed to take any notice of the epithets or obscenities screamed at them.

But Shiloh Irons did take notice. Cheney saw him looking across the street, his lips a small line, his eyes spitting sparks. But he never left General Nathan Bedford Forrest's side.

In the midst of the maelstrom, Shadrach rode up to his brother and bent down to speak in his ear. Cheney, watching from the steps, marveled that Israfel was so obedient, though he had no bridle or headpiece, not even a rope around his neck. She knew that, considering Shadrach's painful injury, he could not possibly control or guide him by pressure from his legs or kicking. Shadrach seemed to direct Israfel by pulling lightly on his silky mane—something most horses completely ignored if one pulled too softly, and took great exception to if one pulled too hard.

She watched as the younger brother, the thirty-year-late twin, spoke earnestly, his head so close to the older brother's. They were both stroking Israfel's neck absently, with the same length of stroke, the same long, bony fingers, the identical absorbed expressions. It was uncanny.

General Forrest nodded once and wheeled around to charge toward Cheney, with Shiloh following close behind. The soldiers surrounding them parted hastily, and he came to stand in front of her, his arms crossed. His expression was completely unreadable.

"Shadrach tells me you sent a message to Langdon Van Dorn," he said evenly, "releasing the cadets from your care and notifying him that he was their doctor agin."

"That's right, General," she replied.

"Shadrach tells me Van Dorn won't let you in his hospital," Forrest said bluntly.

"No, he won't, but he has always treated me with the utmost respect," Cheney said with spirit. "Anyway, that has nothing to do with all this, General. Dr. Van Dorn is the Citadel physician, after all, and he will be allowed to attend them now."

Forrest was quiet for long moments, studying Cheney's face. This habit of his—among others—was particularly unsettling. Cheney began to fidget. Behind General Forrest, she saw Shiloh watching her with sympathy and a touch of amusement.

Finally Forrest's eyes softened, and when he spoke his voice was warm and slow. "Ma'am, I gotta admit it's a pleasure to meet a lady of such honor and nobility."

"I beg your pardon?" Cheney asked, genuinely puzzled.

"Yes, ma'am," Forrest said with emphasis. "Once you've beaten a man, be as generous to him as you can. This, and only this, is the way of honor. You're an honorable woman, Dr. Duvall."

23

A Conspiracy in General Nathan Bedford Forrest's Room

After the cadets were safely on their way to the Citadel, Shiloh, Cheney, and General Forrest rode back to the hotel. An immense crowd of soldiers and men still hovered around General Forrest, and he spurred King Phillip to a reckless gallop as he led Shiloh and Cheney. But it was useless. The crowd followed, some at a run, some at a more sedate pace, for they knew exactly where Forrest was going.

Jubal was waiting for them and dashed up to take the horses as they hurried inside. Both the Planter's restaurant and bar were overflowing with men and women. Many of them pressed into the lobby as Forrest entered, and the crush and the din were enormous. Shiloh put his arm protectively around Cheney's shoulders, but as he doggedly stayed close behind Forrest, he dragged her along at a rapid pace. They fought to get to the stairwell. Suddenly Forrest stopped, swept his broad shoulders around like a wet grizzly throwing off water drops, and roared, "Git back!"

After a second of silence, the deafening noise renewed, some women screamed, and the crowd surged backward as if from an imminent explosion. One man fell down, and it looked to Cheney as though he might have been trampled. Forrest charged for the stairs, with Shiloh and Cheney close behind. He bounded to the landing, which was out of sight from the lobby, and waited for Cheney and Shiloh.

"Please, Dr. Duvall," he said, motioning for her to go first.

Cheney shook her head as she passed him and wearily climbed the steps. "General Forrest, I had never considered that one might feel sorry for a person who had gained fame. But I assure you that you, sir, have my greatest sympathies."

"You're a smart woman," he rasped behind her. "But bein' famous ain't the problem. Bein' IN-famous is."

They reached the second floor. Shiloh went to the corner suite, inserted a key in the lock, and looked up at Forrest before opening the door. "Sir, would you allow me to check this room before you go in?"

Forrest looked at him and suddenly grinned. "No."

"Didn't think so," Shiloh muttered, then threw open the door and handed him the key. General Forrest watched Shiloh, baiting him, but he quickly, smoothly stepped in front of Cheney. Forrest stepped inside the room, looked around, then turned back to them. "I'm fixin' to git cleaned up. Irons, I want you to have supper with me." He looked down at Cheney, and she marveled at how his features—indeed, all his sharpened saber-edges—softened when he addressed ladies. "Dr. Duvall, would you do me and Mr. Irons the very great honor of having supper with us?"

"General Forrest, it would be my pleasure to have supper with you and Mr. Irons," Cheney replied, matching his formality, then added mischievously, "But I do have a suggestion, sir. No, I have an urgent request."

"Yes? And what is that?"

"That we do not dine downstairs in the hotel restaurant," Cheney declared, "or in any other restaurant, as I am certain that you will be mobbed unmercifully no matter where you go."

"Dr. Duvall, I'm awful sorry for the ruckus," Forrest said with exasperation. "But you saw the only thing I kin figger to stop it. And that never works but for long enough to make a getaway."

"Please don't concern yourself on my account, General," Cheney replied. "I just wanted to suggest that we have a cold supper sent up here. Your suite has this nice sitting room and dining area, and I find the idea of some quiet conversation—and also some food that we can eat in peace—very tempting. My companion, Rissy, can accompany me, which will, I believe, be adequate to chaperone us."

Forrest looked greatly relieved. "Dr. Duvall, that's the best idea I've heard since I rode into this town. You two come back in half an hour. And, Irons, don't loiter around in front of this here door. Escort Dr. Duvall to her room, and go to your own room and wash up."

"Yes, sir," Shiloh said, although reluctantly.

Forrest closed the door, and Shiloh and Cheney walked down the hall. "Doc, you look awful tired," Shiloh admonished her. "Are you sure you don't want to just have supper in your room and go to bed?"

"Shiloh, being in the same room with that man is the most exhausting experience I've ever had," Cheney declared, "but I wouldn't miss it for the world." Rissy opened Cheney's door, and over her shoulder Cheney called, "We'll be ready in half an hour exactly!"

★ ★ ★ ★

Cheney wore her emerald green velvet dress. The dress had an off-the-shoulder neckline for evening wear. Rissy overruled the glamorous emerald-and-diamond necklace that Cheney always wore with the dress, though she did approve the earrings. The dress was form-fitting through the waist and hips, and was drawn into a small bustle with a gathered, short train in the back. The neckline and hem were trimmed with a fine cream-colored Maltese lace. Cheney did not wear the above-the-elbow satin gloves that matched the dress, as they were too formal for a cold supper. Rissy piled Cheney's hair on top of her head and managed to arrange the tangle of curls into a graceful crown. Cheney thought she looked passable, considering she felt as though she'd been run through a laundry mangler. Shiloh didn't seem to notice one way or the other.

"Ready, Doc? Rissy?" he asked as Rissy opened the door.

"Yes," Cheney said.

"Hmph," Rissy grumped.

"What's the matter, Rissy?" Shiloh teased as they went down the hall to Forrest's room. "Don't be scared of him. I'll protect you."

"Oh, good, I feels so much better now," Rissy asserted. "One of Forrest's boys is gwine to protect me from Forrest."

Shiloh nodded, apparently with great thoughtfulness, and said regretfully, "Yeah, that's true, Rissy. I'll probably just have to let him kill you as soon as we walk in." Then he knocked on Forrest's door.

Rissy only had time to grunt, "Prob'ly."

Forrest opened the door, and Cheney was so amazed at his appearance that she didn't enter the room until Rissy poked her sharply in the small of her back. The general was dressed in a superbly cut suit of fine wool, with a double-breasted waistcoat and long frock coat. The suit was severe, but with a modest reminder of his exalted former rank: the double row of gleaming gold buttons on his waistcoat were in vertical sets of three, as were the Confederate generals' uniforms. His dress, shoes, and grooming were immaculate.

His hair, freshly washed, had a blue-black sheen in the soft light, the shots of gray gleaming like liquid silver. It was combed back from his broad forehead, but the coarse mane refused to be completely tamed. Cheney noted with pleasure that Forrest—like Shiloh—disdained the smelly, greasy, macassar oil to tame it. Nathan Bedford Forrest was a strikingly handsome man, she decided, but that was probably the very last thing anyone—man or woman—ever noticed about him.

"Please, c'mon in, Dr. Duvall, Irons. And you are—"

"Rissy Clarkson, suh," Rissy said before Cheney could introduce them.

"Nathan Bedford Forrest," he said easily, shaking Rissy's hand. "C'mon in, all of you."

The sitting room was sumptuous in size and decor. A comfortable fire, with a three-inch bed of red coals, glowed in the white marble fireplace on the left. On each side of the fireplace were two spindly-legged French empire sofas, with a mahogany tea table between. In the corner, two sets of French doors led out onto a wrap-around balcony. A round dining table with four chairs was set in front of the doors. Cheney reflected sadly that the exquisite wrought-iron set, similar to the one in her room but larger, must have been made by Vess. She glanced at Rissy and saw that she was looking at the table and chairs, too, but her expression was guarded.

Rissy immediately went to the bar and began pouring lemonade from an immense crystal pitcher. Cracked ice tinkled temptingly into the fine crystal glasses. Shiloh, Cheney, and Forrest seated themselves at the table, which was already set with a selection of sliced cold meats, bread, cheese, sliced tomatoes, fruit, a pound cake, and candied pecans.

"Dr. Duvall, would you say a grace?" Forrest asked.

"Why, yes, of course, General," Cheney said, then: "Dearest Jesus, we take this food from Your hand, as You know that we hunger and thirst. You alone, Lord Jesus, give us our daily bread, as You give us our very breath of life, and we thank You. Amen."

"That there was a good grace," Forrest said approvingly as he began to pile food onto his plate.

"Thank you, sir," Cheney smiled. "It's really very simple. I can teach you how to do it, if you'd let me."

Forrest grinned at her. "You got some grit, Dr. Duvall."

"As do you, General Forrest."

"Guess I do, at that," he admitted. "But my wife, Mary, is the one with real heart, like you, Dr. Duvall. She's in charge of saying the graces and doin' all the prayin' for me." His voice was soft, caressing.

"Then your wife must indeed be a strong and faithful Christian," Cheney said with a smile.

"She's a saint," Forrest said calmly, "and she's the best friend I ever had. I dunno why God give me a gift such as her. I ain't never talked to Him much, but I do thank Him for my Mary."

With this small, humble speech, all of the doubts Cheney had about Nathan Bedford Forrest's basic character disappeared. In this age of husbands speaking of their wives at best as housekeepers and hostesses, and at worst with open contempt, Cheney viewed a man who openly and unashamedly declared his love and respect for his wife as a real man and a true gentleman. Richard Duvall, without fail, treated Cheney's mother, Irene, this way, and Cheney had often thanked the Lord for her father's love for his wife, and his obedience to the Lord.

The Duvall household had always been a place of peace and joy.

Rissy brought over a tray with three tall glasses and silently set them down by the diners' plates. "Thank you, Rissy," Forrest said politely.

Surprise lurked in her eyes, but she recovered quickly, as usual. "You're welcome, Gin'ral Forrest." She retired discreetly back to stand by the bar.

"Your wife sounds like a lovely person, General Forrest," Cheney said softly. "I wish I could meet her."

"If you're ever around Memphis, ma'am, you be sure and call on us," Forrest ordered. "Mary sure would take to you. And it seems to me you're kinda like her—you know how to handle yourself with a bunch of heathenish men." He cut his eyes slyly to Shiloh and popped a grape into his mouth.

"I guess I am a heathen," Shiloh remarked, blandly taking a huge bite of a pear. "But don't flatter me, General Forrest. I'm not in your league. You're the very devil, you know."

Forrest sat up straighter, and his eyes began to glint. "Huh! What was all that jawin' about, anyway? You know, Irons?"

Shiloh crunched reflectively. "I knew General Sherman called you the devil, yes, sir. But I don't know about all of those personal problems Judge Granger has."

Cheney looked uncertainly first at Shiloh, then Forrest. No one had told her what happened at Judge Granger's, but she gathered, since no one had arrested—or shot—Shiloh and Forrest that the judge must, at least, still be alive. Also, it appeared the judge was able to speak when Shiloh and Forrest were there. That was a good sign.

"I don't neither," Forrest was grumbling. "I ain't never met that man, ain't never heared of him. But it sure does look like he tripped up on me somewheres. He have a field command?"

"I don't know, sir," Shiloh replied with exasperation. "I haven't been able to find out anything about him."

Cheney looked down at her plate, pushing a grape in a circle with her fork. "Um . . . General Forrest, sir . . . Captain Hawkins came in while you and Shiloh were gone to . . . call on Judge Granger and told me and Shadrach and Mr. Roddy and Mr.

Manigault some . . . facts about the judge. Captain Hawkins and also the other three captains of the guard companies—in fact, many of the Federal soldiers—seem to feel great sympathy for the cadets. It was very odd. Captain Hawkins simply walked into the basement and started reciting certain facts about the judge's past." She poked holes in the grape with one tine of her fork.

"You ain't much of one for tellin' tales, are you, Dr. Duvall?" Forrest asked shrewdly.

"I hate gossip," Cheney muttered. "But . . . if Judge Granger . . . has a complaint against you, and he . . . insulted you . . ."

"Oh, the judge insulted him, all right!" Shiloh declared, his mouth twitching. "General Forrest made sure he did!"

"Wasn't as hard as I thought it was gonna be, neither," Forrest said, stretching out his jackal's smile, but he addressed Cheney with gentle formality. "Ma'am, I don't ask that you defame Judge Granger, but if you have any information about his military career, it might be very helpful to me in figgerin' how to get my brother outta this here mess."

Cheney considered her massacred grape, then said firmly, "I shall repeat to you exactly what Captain Hawkins said. It is not slander, as I see it. In fact, I don't understand the import of it at all, though the cadets seemed to—that is, they laughed quite loudly. And rudely."

Forrest and Shiloh, amused, glanced at each other, but stayed silent. Cheney looked up. "Captain Hawkins said that Judge Granger was appointed to the Quartermaster's Office, Washington, Army of the Cumberland. He wanted a field command, but it was repeatedly denied him. He particularly wanted to be assigned as adjutant to a colonel or two generals, but none of them . . . er . . . requested him. He was, however, assigned as Chief Quartermaster of their commands."

"Who were these men?" Forrest demanded, his eyes glittering.

"Colonel Abel D. Streight," Cheney answered, watching Forrest closely, "and General William Sooy Smith, and General Samuel D. Sturgis."

Forrest and Shiloh looked incredulously at each other. Forrest grinned widely—Shiloh grinned back—then they began to laugh, raucously and roughly.

"That's exactly how Shadrach and Mr. Roddy and Mr. Manigault reacted," Cheney muttered to herself. "And Captain Hawkins appeared about to burst himself and turned and marched out of the room."

"Poor Granger *was* jinxed!" Shiloh groaned.

"I don't understand," Cheney complained. "How could he be jinxed? He was breveted to colonel for his expert procurement of supplies and ordnance for Colonel Streight's regiment!"

Forrest and Shiloh again shouted with laughter, while Cheney looked up at Rissy, and the two women shrugged helplessly.

Finally, when Shiloh had calmed down somewhat, he took a long drink and told Cheney, "Doc, that poor judge musta had a tough military career. See, General Forrest ended up capturing or destroying everything those three men had.

"Abel Streight was a good soldier, and when we were chasing him we all felt kinda sorry for him, 'cause some genius in Washington had procured mules for his command instead of horses, thinking they'd be better for the rough country we were in."

Forrest, his voice barely under control, said, "I sent out my brother Captain Bill Forrest and his independent command to scout out Streight. But"—here his voice shook so much he could hardly continue—"turned out we didn't need to scout out Streight. Them mules announced long and loud where they was at every mornin' at breakfast time!"

"Oh, dear," Cheney murmured. But her eyes glowed with laughter.

"Colonel Streight was obliged to surrender unconditionally," Shiloh declared, "to prevent the further effusion of blood—of his two thousand men—by General Forrest's five hundred!"

"He sure was mad when he give up and found out I'd fooled him," Forrest said, shaking his head. "I made sure we got betwixt them and their stands of arms before I let him see it was barely five hundred of us. Then he still tuck back his surrender and wanted to fight it out!"

Now Cheney was giggling, and Shiloh's eyes began to glow. "Then we went on to General 'Sookey' Smith. That was a running fight for four days. With two thousand men, General Forrest whipped Smith and his seven thousand into the dirt."

"That was a tough battle," Forrest murmured.

Shiloh glanced at him and grew somber. "Yes, sir." He turned to Cheney. "We lost Major Jeffrey Forrest in that fight. General Forrest had two horses killed right out from under him, and then he had King Phillip brought up. Both General Forrest and King Phillip got shot. But General Forrest killed four men in that battle."

Forrest, whose gaze had focused on the bloody and war-torn past, now roused himself. "You keep sayin' I did this and I did that, Irons. You put two men down, right in front of me, in that fight," he said proudly, turning to Cheney. "Me an' my escort got ahead of our support and got all tangled up with five hundred of the enemy." He frowned at Shiloh. "Hardest fightin' I had to do was to keep from killin' Irons, here. He was always up in my face, seems like. Hard to shoot around him."

Shiloh told Cheney blandly, "I just didn't want General Forrest to get shot. He's the meanest man in the world to nurse when he gets shot."

Cheney stammered, "Well . . . goodness . . . how many times have you been wounded, General Forrest?"

"Uh . . . you mean, in the war, ma'am? Or in all?" Forrest asked, his eyes glinting. "And do you just mean shot, or stabbed, or whacked with a saber?"

"Well . . . well . . . for heaven's sake!" Cheney blustered.

Forrest and Shiloh glanced at each other and grinned, but Shiloh nodded imperceptibly and smoothly changed the subject. "Then there was General S. D. Sturgis, Judge Granger's last hope." He took a deep breath, his eyes began to shine again, and he looked straight at Forrest. "General Forrest defeated Sturgis at Brice's Crossroads. Sturgis had eight thousand men, and our forces numbered thirty-three hundred. This was a pitched battle, an infantry battle, not a raid, not a pursuit and capture. General Forrest's victory over General Sturgis has been recognized as one of the classic beatings of the Civil War."

Forrest stared at him, then frowned. "What are you talkin' about, Irons? It was just another battle. Richmond didn't hardly know it happened."

Shiloh watched and listened and kept his gaze trained on General Forrest with an odd intensity. For a moment he didn't answer, then he seemed to come to a decision, and spoke quietly but firmly. "No, sir. Richmond didn't notice and still hasn't. But I want to tell you, sir, that every Union field commander from General Ulysses S. Grant on down took a hard look at all of those battles, and a lot of people in Washington—including President Lincoln and Secretary of War Stanton—took a good deal of notice of what you were doing."

Forrest's eyes narrowed. Without looking down, he pushed his plate carefully away. "It appears to me that you know an awful lot about what General Sherman says and what General Grant done and what Washington thought, Irons. Just 'zactly how is that?"

Shiloh looked at Cheney and smiled. "Dr. Duvall's father is Colonel Richard Duvall of the U. S. Army."

Forrest's head swiveled, and his gray eyes bored into Cheney. He didn't look startled, but Cheney thought uneasily that he did seem irritated. "Duvall! Grant's aide? And I didn't connect it up? Blast me," he muttered, now almost smiling. "I'm losin' my edge!"

"No, sir, you're certainly not," Cheney said with relief.

"And, sir, Colonel Duvall and I have become good friends," Shiloh went on, now showing his eagerness. "When he found out I was one of your boys, he made me tell him about everything we did. They spent a lot of time trying to figure you out during the war, and Colonel Duvall said General Grant might give him a bigger pension if he could get you figured out and explain you to him."

"Boy, don't you be tellin' such lies," Forrest scoffed.

Shiloh went on, "General Sherman did call you the devil.

Several times. He put a price on your head, General Forrest."
Forrest gazed at him with open disbelief, and Shiloh nodded
vehemently. "General Sherman said—in the same dispatch
when he first called you the devil—and I quote, 'I will order a
force to go out to follow Forrest to the death, if it costs ten thousand lives and breaks the Treasury! There will never be peace in
Tennessee until Forrest is dead!' "

Forrest frowned. "We sure didn't know about all this dust-
up, did we, Irons?"

"Sir, you have no idea," Shiloh declared. "In late '64 and '65
Sherman sent about thirty thousand men to look just for you."

"Huh! And we thought we was out huntin' them!"

"How in the world did you keep from getting hounded to
death, General Forrest?" Cheney asked.

" 'Cause," he replied, his eyes glinting, "I was at that place
they were not looking for me."

Cheney laughed with delight. "Oh? And where is this wonderful place?"

"Well, Colonel Duvall said they were always looking for that
devil Forrest somewhere in general and nowhere in particular.
We musta been close around that place." Shiloh grinned.

Forrest's eyes sparkled with rich humor, and his fangs
flashed.

"And that's not all, sir," Shiloh went on. "Sturgis promised
General Sherman he'd bring him your hair."

"My hair!" Forrest roared and reached up to smooth down
the coarse, springing locks. "Well, now I'm glad I beat the boots
offa him at Brice's! My hair!"

"Yes, sir. General Sturgis didn't know, I guess, how proud
you are of your hair," Shiloh said slyly.

"Huh! That rascal Sherman! If I woulda knowed he was so
personally anxious to put me away, I woulda give him the
chance to do it hisself!"

Shiloh shook his head. "Don't think so, sir. You'd never have
gotten close enough. Sherman said—he told Colonel Duvall—
that when you charged . . . uh . . . those two thousand men at
the Fallen Timbers"—Shiloh was laughing so hard, he was hav-

ing difficulty talking—"Sherman said, 'I and my staff ingloriously fled pell-mell through the mud.'"

Forrest began to grin.

Shiloh told Cheney, "General Forrest ordered a charge, you see, and three hundred and fifty of us charged with him and captured or killed the forty-three men in the skirmish line. Then we galloped back up the rise, chirpin' like little birds at our victory. But General Forrest"—his voice deepened and grew louder—"then he was Colonel Forrest—kept charging, alone! And I tell you, I stood up on that rise, with my jaw hangin' open, and saw two thousand men breaking up and running off! It's the truth, Doc!"

Cheney was speechless. She knew Shiloh was telling the truth, but she simply couldn't conceive of such things as they'd been speaking of—so lightly—for the past half hour.

"They shot me for doin' that, though," Forrest grumbled.

"Only once," Shiloh retorted arrogantly. "That bluebelly you yanked up by the scruff of the neck and threw up on the back of your saddle to use for a shield got shot a whole bunch of times!"

"Good heavens!" Cheney said in a choked voice.

"Oh. Sorry, Doc," Shiloh said unrepentantly.

"Sorry, ma'am," Forrest said, equally unrepentant.

"It's . . . all right, I guess—gentlemen," Cheney managed to say. "It's just that . . . my father was just on General Grant's staff, as an aide, you see, and so—I—he never talked about such things. He—my father—never had a field command."

Shiloh and Bedford Forrest exchanged a glance so quickly Cheney almost missed it, but so intense that the air between the two men's faces seemed to crackle. She was shaken by this unspoken, rapid communication between the two men—and knew, obviously, that it must have had something to do with her father—but she couldn't recover quickly enough to phrase a question or leading comment to them.

The moment passed, Shiloh and Forrest looked at her, and Shiloh smiled warmly. "Yeah, Colonel Duvall said that the entire staff had a running joke about General Forrest. General Ulysses

S. Grant always said that the safest place he could think of to put a piece of paper where he'd find it again was in an aide's pocket. So they had an aide they called 'Forrest Pockets.' His pockets were responsible for keeping up with all the dispatches about that devil Forrest."

"And there I was, in that place they were not looking for me, with all my hair." Forrest grinned.

Rissy, forgotten as she stood silently listening at the bar, now glided up to the table and began to clear it. "If you'uns would like some coffee or tea, I'll serve it to you over there by the fire."

"Thank you, Rissy," Forrest said politely, rising and hurrying to hold Cheney's chair. "That does sound good. Coffee, black for me."

The three settled into the couches, Shiloh lounging on one couch by Cheney, facing General Forrest. Rissy served them and quietly finished clearing the table, making no sound of clinking dishes. Her footsteps were silent.

Forrest watched her for a few moments, then turned to stare into the fire. "Well, I guess now we know about the burr Judge Granger's done got under his saddle," he muttered. "Shame he's got it in his head that Shadrach is Forrest, though. I dunno what them boys were doin' last Friday night, but I know they didn't kill that man." He settled back, stuck his long legs out in front of him, and sipped his coffee. "I couldn't even find out what kinda evidence he's got agin 'em."

Rissy, Cheney noticed, silently set down the dishes she was holding, turned, and watched General Forrest's profile intently. Cheney asked hesitantly, "General, you mean you got him to release Shadrach and the others, but you didn't—couldn't—"

Forrest shrugged carelessly. "I believe in the law, ma'am. I know it don't seem like I'm a man that does—but Granger is the law here. He says he's got evidence agin them boys, and he had to arrest 'em. But they ought to be charged, and indicted, and then tried, fair and square. So Judge Granger agreed to that, and I talked him into lettin' them boys outta them cages. He give me that much."

Though Forrest spoke casually, his eyes flamed, and Shiloh's jaw clenched as he spoke. Cheney was burning with curiosity to find out what had really happened at Judge Garth Granger's house. But she would not intrude upon these two grim men; they did what they felt they had to do. If Shiloh wanted her to know, he would tell her later.

"Then—I suppose—Judge Granger refused to tell you what the evidence was against Shadrach, if he agreed to a formal indictment," Cheney said quietly.

"Yep. All he said was that the man's widow give evidence agin 'em." Forrest's voice dropped. "I ain't got no notion of what that means. How bad it is."

The three had virtually forgotten about Rissy, and her voice startled them when she spoke up. "Gin'ral Forrest," she said quietly.

Though he looked surprised, he turned smoothly to look across the room at her. "Yes, Rissy?"

"I know what Miss Ona told Judge Granger," Rissy said, her mouth set. She folded her hands in front of her apron. "I've decided I'll tell you, if'n you want to know."

Forrest sat up straighter and searched Rissy's face for long moments. "Yes? Why would you do that?"

Rissy's shoulders stiffened. "Miss Ona—she ain't got nobody to tell about it, 'cept Judge Granger. But the last thing she'd want—or Mistuh Vess hisself would want—would be for somebody to git accused of killin' him when they didn't."

"My brother and them two boys didn't kill that man, Rissy," Forrest said firmly but gently. "I don't know who done it, but if I could find out I swear I'd hand 'em to Judge Granger on a platter."

"Alive or dead?" Rissy asked acidly.

Forrest stiffened, and his eyes blazed, but then he almost grinned at Rissy as she watched him so calmly and severely. "Alive, if'n they'll allow it," he shrugged.

She nodded, then glided over to stand in front of the fire, and watched Nathan Bedford Forrest grimly as she spoke. "Miss Ona and Mistuh Vess heared a ruckus outside. It was early of the mornin' but not sunrisin'. He jumped up outta bed and looked out the window. 'It's jist some o' them boys from the Citadel, out skylarkin',' he said. He told Miss Ona to stay inside, and he got dressed real quick and went out."

"Wait," Forrest barked. "You mean, the man said it was Shadrach and them other two boys?"

Rissy shook her head vehemently. "No, suh. He jist said boys from the Citadel." Her face became hard, chiseled, and she went on, "Miss Ona looked outen the window, and it was three men, dressed in them Knights of the White Rose sheets, carryin' torches."

Forrest, Shiloh, and Cheney exchanged sober glances. "So she never saw the men? Their faces, I mean?" Cheney asked.

"No, ma'am. And neither did Vess. He jist knew some o' them boys at the Citadel been dressin' up like that, ridin' round the country, and scarin' colored folks, 'cause they thinks they's haints."

Forrest gritted his teeth and muttered incoherently under his breath, then turned back to look at Rissy. "What happened?"

Rissy met his gaze squarely. "Miss Ona couldn't hear, but she watched. Vess jist called out to 'em, not ugly, like he would tell boys to move on and let folks git a night's sleep. Then them men jumped off their horses, stobbed them torches, and started beatin' on him. Vess fought 'em back, but they was three of 'em, and he was havin' a hard time of it. He grabbed up an ax, and Miss Ona saw he was still tryin' to swing the flat of it, so he wouldn't chop nobody, you know. He give one of 'em a good bust in the leg, and he went down, and Vess raised the ax. Then one of 'em shot him."

Profound stillness weighed heavy in the room. Rissy sighed and closed her eyes. "They never said nothin', not a word. They gathered up that one what Mistuh Vess had knocked down and went back to they horses. The one what got knocked down shook hisself loose and limped back to lay somethin' down on Vess's chest. It was one o' them White Rose signs, you know. That they stick on them sheets."

"Blast it to kingdom come!" Shiloh muttered fiercely. "This doesn't look good, not good at all. . . ."

"What, Irons?" Forrest demanded.

Shiloh looked sideways at Cheney, then turned back to speak in a careful monotone to Forrest. "Sir, the Doc and I don't have any personal knowledge at all about the Knights of the White Rose. Unfortunately, however, our horses were conscripted by two members of the organization, and they joined up." Even Rissy's eyes sparkled a little at this, and Cheney started. She had completely forgotten about Shadrach and Logan—then she mentally corrected herself violently—two men riding Sock and Stocking in the parade.

"Our horses did take part in the parade, sir," Shiloh went on, his voice still dull. "And I'm sorry to say they were out until daybreak Saturday."

Forrest digested this in less than two seconds. Then he looked up at Rissy. "This lady, this man's wife, could she identify the horses the killers were riding?"

Rissy hesitated. "I dunno, suh. She said even the horses was swathed in them sheets, like they do. An' it were pitch dark, 'cept for the torches."

"Blast!" Forrest swore.

Sternly Rissy said, "Suh, they is one more thing I think I oughta tell you."

"Yes?" Forrest said curtly.

Rissy took a deep breath. "Caleb Blood Roddy said that the Knights of the White Rose came to their camp after thet parade Friday night. Afore your brother and them other two boys was arrested, Caleb Blood Roddy said that it was them three that was leading the Knights, about twenty of 'em. Then"—Rissy's face settled into lines of distaste—"after your brother was arrested, Caleb Blood changed his story and said nobody knew who any of them Knights was."

Bedford Forrest glared at Rissy, his face flushing to a dull copper. Then he jumped up, clasped his hands behind his back, and began to pace in front of the couch. He came perilously close to Rissy but did not look up.

Rissy gathered up her skirts and moved hastily back to the safety of the bar. Cheney swiftly followed her. "Thank you,

Rissy," she said softly, taking both her hands and clasping them gently. "I know that couldn't have been easy for you."

"It surely was not!" Rissy bristled. "But I hadda do it. It was the right thing to do."

"It was," Cheney whispered, "and the Lord will bless you for it."

"He done has," Rissy sighed. "I feel better 'bout Mistuh Vess already. Somebody needs to pay for killin' that man, but it don't need to be the wrong somebodies."

"You're right, as usual," Cheney smiled. Rissy smiled back.

Shiloh had jumped up and stood by the fire as General Forrest paced. Cheney had started back to her seat on the couch when a loud, imperious knock sounded at the door. Shiloh was suddenly beside her and grabbed her arm, hard. Then he looked back at General Forrest. But Forrest seemed not to notice any of them, or the knock, or even, indeed, where he was. He was staring down at the floor, glowering and pacing.

The knock became a pounding, and Shiloh started for the door when suddenly it burst open, and a most extraordinary woman swept into the room.

She was tall and gaunt. Her thin brown hair was parted in the middle and pulled back so severely it appeared to be yanking the skin of her face up into her hairline. Her eyes were filled with outrage. In her left hand she carried a Bible, and in her right hand she carried a large umbrella. She rushed toward General Forrest, and Shiloh attempted to step in front of her. But with a swift movement she rapped Shiloh above the knee with her umbrella. He mumbled, "Ouch!" then faltered to the side.

She advanced to General Forrest and came to a stop so sharply in front of him that he almost rammed her. He looked up.

Waving her umbrella with menace, she demanded in a loud, grainy voice, "Are you the Rebel General Forrest, and is it true that you murdered those dear colored people at Fort Pillow? Tell me, sir; I want no evasive answer!"

The general rose up to his full height, and his hair positively stood on end. "Yes, madam! I killed the men and women for my soldiers' dinner and ate the babies myself for breakfast!"

The umbrella stopped waving, and the lady's jaw made a popping noise as it fell down. Then she turned and fled, and a steady, keen wailing began at Forrest's doorway and steadily increased as she retreated down the hall. "Oooohhh nooooooo . . ."

General Forrest kept on glaring, at the world, at Shiloh, at Cheney. Suddenly, in the ominously silent room, a stifled giggle sounded—from Rissy. Forrest transferred his glare to her, and she guiltily pressed her hand to her mouth. But it didn't help.

Soon all four of the conspirators in General Nathan Bedford Forrest's hotel room were dissolved in helpless laughter.

24

HIS HEART WAS RENT

"Please accept my humblest apologies, Dr. Duvall," Gard Granger said, though he did not sound the least bit humble. "But I must speak with you for a moment." He bowed stiffly.

Cheney, in a frothy pink and white morning dress, with a white ribbon holding back the tangle of her hair, looked incredulously at him. Behind her Rissy stood, arms crossed, staring at him suspiciously.

"Oh ... yes ... of course, Mr. Granger. Please come in," Cheney managed, attempting to sidestep for him to enter. She bumped squarely into Rissy, however, who stood unmoved.

"That won't be necessary, Dr. Duvall," Granger replied, humor glinting in the hidden depths of his eyes. "I will be brief. First, here is a message we just received for you. As I wished to speak with you anyway, I decided to deliver it myself."

Cheney took the envelope out of his hand without looking down. She was staring at him, quite strangely and rudely, and Gard Granger marveled that her gaze had not traveled the usual course down to his blighted right hand. She was avidly searching his face, her eyes narrowed. She looked thoroughly perplexed.

Accordingly, Gard Granger was perplexed but did not show it. "The reason I wished to speak to you is to offer you my abject apologies, Dr. Duvall, for the unfortunate—incident—that occurred last night, as you were in the party dining with General Forrest. I'm certain you were distressed and shocked as an unwilling witness to such ill-mannered and rude behavior."

Suddenly Cheney smiled, and her eyes sparkled. "Quite the contrary, Mr. Granger. I was not at all distressed; neither was I in any condition to be shocked, in the light of all the events that occurred yesterday. Nor was I an unwilling witness. If the truth be told, I shall treasure the memory for the rest of my days."

Deadpan, Granger replied, "Yes, I do envy you, Dr. Duvall. I heartily wish I might have witnessed the incident, instead of only hearing the aftereffects. I must assure you, however, that such an incident will not happen again in my hotel. Would you happen to know where I might find General Forrest, Dr. Duvall?" He frowned darkly. "I must apologize to him and offer to make amends."

"No, I'm sorry, I haven't seen or spoken with General Forrest this morning," Cheney said thoughtfully. "Have you asked—oh, never mind. I know he's shadowing him, wherever he is."

"Yes. Mr. Irons is not in the hotel at this time," Granger agreed. "Thank you so much for your time, Dr. Duvall." He turned, then looked back at Cheney, his expression severe. "I should inform you that I have arranged for guards for the hotel while General Forrest is in residence. They will attend all the stairwells and will only allow guests and servants of the hotel to visit the rooms."

During this calm speech Granger watched Cheney with obvious bafflement. Cheney's color was rising, her eyes were widening, and she was growing more and more agitated as he spoke.

"Guards . . . Gard! Rissy! Oh, where has my mind been!" she cried. "Mr. Granger . . . Mr. Granger . . ." In her excitement she reached out—he had turned his right side to her—and grabbed his right arm. Granger stiffened, his dark eyes burned, and he pulled back violently.

Cheney didn't notice. She kept a grip on his arm and looked back at Rissy. "Rissy! Vess lives up past where Moody and Lalie live, right? Moody and Lalie! 'Gard's Rangers!' "

Rissy's eyebrows shot up, her eyes widened, and then she swooped aside. "You kin come in," she ordered, "Mistuh Granger."

Cheney hauled him bodily inside her hotel room. As Granger could not think of any possible way to make this woman unhand him—short of striking her, which, to his credit, he only considered momentarily—he followed, and savagely yanked out a chair for her to sit down.

She did, and he hurriedly pulled out the other one, seated himself, and bit off, "Yes, Dr. Duvall! I am at your disposal! How may I be of assistance to you?"

Cheney ignored him and looked up at Rissy. They stared at each other, both of them obviously perturbed. "Rissy! How could I have forgotten about Gard's Rangers! And Moody, and Lalie!"

"Prob'ly 'cause youse head's been all full up with them two Forrest-is," Rissy pronounced scathingly, "jist like mine! I can't even 'member who I am, tryin' to skitter aroun' and stay outta Gin'ral Forrest-is way fer one minute and holdin' my breath to stand up an' talk to him the next!"

"Yes, yes," Cheney agreed, "and I've been so terribly tired since . . . since . . . ever since that night! I haven't been thinking!"

"I'm sorry you ladies are so tired," Granger snapped, "so I'll take my leave now—" He began to rise.

"Sit down!" both women said, though Cheney quickly added, "please, Mr. Granger," and Rissy said, "Please, suh."

Granger sat, fury in every line of his body.

Finally Cheney turned to him, took a deep breath, and spoke calmly. "Mr. Granger, you must pardon me . . . us . . . for our horrid rudeness. It's just that we remembered something that may be very important to the investigation of the murder of Vess Alexander."

"Oh? And how may I help you with this?"

Cheney leaned over, placed her hands on the table, and tightly entwined them. "Sir, we—Rissy and I—were out that night, or rather, that dark morning. We had been called out to attend a couple who were ill. They live out on the Cooper River, off the turnpike, on one of the side roads that follows the swamp."

"Yes?" Granger asked frigidly.

"Yes," she said, nodding her head with excitement. "And when we were returning, it was almost dawn. On the turnpike we heard three of your rangers."

Granger said nothing, merely looked at her.

Cheney didn't notice his aloofness. "They stopped on the turnpike while we were still on the side road, and we heard them talking. Don't you see? They were riding in from some patrol farther up north! And they might have heard or seen something! Something about Vess's murder!"

Granger studied her, and his voice was carefully neutral. "Do I understand that you did not see these men, Dr. Duvall? You only heard them?"

"Yes, that's right!"

"Then may I ask how you happen to know they were"—his handsome face twisted with unmistakable aversion—"some of the harbor master rangers?"

"Because we heard them talking, Mr. Granger," Cheney replied with a touch of impatience. "We heard one of them say . . . um . . . something about 'Gard's Rangers.' Didn't we, Rissy?" Cheney finished with uncertainty, looking up at Rissy over her shoulder.

Rissy frowned. "I cain't 'member 'zactly what he said. But they was talkin' about you, Mistuh Granger."

Granger propped his elbow up on the table and rested his forefinger on his chin as he considered Cheney and Rissy for long moments. Cheney was struck again by his smooth, fine features; she looked at his right shoulder, set lower than his left, and recalled the warm strength of his right arm as she had so unthinkingly grabbed it. His arm and wrist had moved independently—so he had no prosthesis. Cheney stubbornly made up her mind that if he gave her the slightest opportunity at all, she would ask him about his right hand.

"Dr. Duvall, I have decided that I will relate this to the proper authorities for investigation," he said evenly.

"That would be your father, yes?"

"Yes."

Now Cheney studied him critically. "Do you know of these three men, Mr. Granger? Weren't you aware that they were patrolling the Cooper River that night?"

"No." He met her gaze squarely, with no trace of emotion, betraying nothing.

Cheney went on stubbornly, "Then how will you find out who they are?" A thought jolted her, she frowned, and went on, almost to herself, "But—they know who they are, of course, and they—surely they—have already come forward if they have any information. . . ?"

"Perhaps not. You did not," Granger said curtly.

Cheney frowned at him.

"You, Dr. Duvall, an intelligent woman with a composed mind, an organized mind, didn't connect all of these events, times, and places together until just now," he countered. "Perhaps these men simply are not as incisive as you are."

"Why, thank you, sir," Cheney said, now smiling at him.

He didn't smile back. "Dr. Duvall, as I said, I will pursue this matter. But I would like to ask you something, as I am very curious."

"Certainly."

"Who *are* you?" he asked, now showing a hint of his exasperation. "What are you doing here in Charleston? And how in the world did you become so entangled with these events and all these people?"

Cheney laughed, and even Rissy chuckled. Cheney, with obvious delight, replied, "Why, Mr. Granger, I am, as you know, Dr. Cheney Duvall, from New York. I came to Charleston partly for a vacation, and partly to see to some family business matters. And as to how I've become embroiled in all of this—" She laughed, richly, expressively, and waved one white, long-fingered hand. "I suppose the Lord just blesses me! I certainly have not been bored!"

Granger's arched eyebrows winged up, and he shook his head with incomprehension. Then, rising, he said cautiously, "Now, ladies, if you will excuse me—that is, if you will allow me to leave—I will attend to these matters we've discussed, right now."

Cheney stood up, and her face grew sober. "Mr. Granger, you have reminded me of something else . . . there is one—no, perhaps there are two—more things. . . ."

"Oh no," he muttered, almost inaudibly. But his face was

lightened with unreleased laughter, and Rissy and Cheney could see it clearly now.

"Sir, I came to Charleston—initially—to look into a problem with my father's business, Duvall's Tools and Implements. That problem has been almost forgotten because of everything that's happened to me—to us," Cheney amended, glancing back at Rissy. "But since you are here—at my disposal—do you happen to know anything about the Guardian Bank?"

He shrugged. "I've seen their notes, of course, and I know where their office is located. But it is a private bank, I believe, Dr. Duvall, because I've never seen any individual's drafts drawn on it, and I don't know of any individual depositors."

"Hmm. Where is their office, Mr. Granger?"

"It's located up on Columbus Street."

"Thank you." Cheney was assessing him again.

"Was there something else, Dr. Duvall?" he asked with exquisite politeness. "Of course, I am, and remain, your obedient servant."

Cheney bit her lip, but suddenly she knew—it was not the time to mention his hand. "No. Thank you again, Mr. Granger, for everything," Cheney murmured and held out her hand—her left hand.

He stared down at it, then took it with his left hand. Then, swiftly, he bent and pressed a fervent, lingering kiss to it, turned on his heel, and left the room without another word.

★ ★ ★ ★

The message Gard Granger delivered to Cheney was from Dr. Langdon Van Dorn. It said simply that he requested the pleasure of her company that afternoon at one o'clock and would call for her at the hotel.

"You're a-wearin' thet navy blue," Rissy announced.

"Yes, that's good," Cheney agreed. The navy blue suit had a narrow skirt, only slightly flared at the hem, a tight-fitting jacket with gold buttons, and a saucy little hat trimmed with navy blue net. Gold piping around the cuffs and collar of the jacket and the hem of the skirt gave the outfit a crisp, rather military look.

"Aren't you coming, Rissy?" Cheney asked when it was time.

"No, Miss Cheney." Rissy smiled at her. "I got a feelin' youse goin' to work. An' I ain't gotta do no chaferonin' for no doctah."

Cheney went downstairs at precisely one o'clock, just as Dr. Van Dorn walked into the hotel lobby. She noticed that the restaurant and bar were filled to capacity with people, but they never even looked up as she breezed through. Cheney was immensely relieved; she had told the truth to Nathan Bedford Forrest last night. She had decided, unequivocally, that she never, ever wanted to be famous, for any reason.

Dr. Van Dorn had an old, shabby, but comfortable two-seater buggy, and he had driven himself. Cheney settled in beside him and breathed deeply of the thin, cold air. At least today the sun was out, and the sky was a mild, far-off blue.

After exchanging pleasantries, which included Dr. Van Dorn's effusive and outrageously gallant thanks and inquiries after her well-being, he looked straight ahead and smiled. "Dr. Duvall, General Nathan Bedford Forrest paid us a call at the hospital this morning."

"Oh?" Cheney said politely.

"Yes, ma'am," he said, humor warming his deep voice even more. "I'm acquainted with General Forrest, you see, but he was kind enough to insist upon meeting, and speaking with, all of my patients when he made his personal call upon me."

"General Forrest is a . . . a . . . he's . . . he's . . . certainly . . ." Suddenly Cheney had no idea what she was trying to say; as Rissy had often commented, "her mouth had done took off ahead of her brain." Cheney was outrageously embarrassed, and her face flamed.

"Yes, he is," Dr. Van Dorn agreed dryly, not looking at her. "I've been acquainted with him for five years now, and I can honestly say I know him now quite as well as you obviously do."

"Exactly," Cheney said with great relief, if not great logic.

"When he and Sergeant Irons arrived, I went out on the portico to greet them, of course," Dr. Van Dorn went on, his eyes crinkling with amusement. "He spoke with me for a few moments about Earl, offering me the most sincere condolences in person, though he had sent me the kindest and warmest letter I have ever received when Earl was killed. Then, when that was done, he yanked off his hat and said, 'I wanta meet your boys. You go on in there, Van Dorn, and tell all the layabouts to git outta them beds and hitch up their britches, 'cause I'm a-comin' in.'"

Cheney pressed her hand to her mouth and turned away slightly, her shoulders shaking.

"So," Dr. Van Dorn went on imperturbably, "since everybody's got their britches on, I decided to invite you to tour the hospital, Dr. Duvall."

When Cheney could speak, she turned back to Dr. Van Dorn, and her eyes were a brilliant, sparkling, lively, sea green. "Thank you, sir," she said warmly. "I deeply and sincerely appreciate your consideration."

"You are most sincerely welcome, Dr. Duvall," he said, nodding to her.

They rode along Broad, and Cheney looked idly up at the huge, graceful mansions that lined this famous street. Many of them had earthworks in the yards, but none of them had any scars of war. "Dr. Van Dorn, I don't wish to intrude into your personal life, or to bring up a painful subject, but since you mentioned it, I would like to hear about General Earl Van Dorn. Was he your son?"

"No, ma'am. He was my second cousin." He sighed deeply, but he did not look grief stricken, merely regretful. "We were close, though. He was almost like my son; my wife and I have no children, you see. Earl spent several summers here with us as a young boy, and he visited us often after he was grown. He grew into a courageous, valiant man . . . a good soldier, a fine and able leader of men. He was a cavalryman, Dr. Duvall."

"Like General Forrest . . ." Cheney mused.

"No, not like General Forrest," Dr. Van Dorn demurred, shaking his head. "There was—and is—no one like him, cavalryman or not, Union or Confederate. Forrest is brilliant. He was never defeated until he was simply overrun by forces more than ten times his own."

"Overpowered," Cheney sighed, "but never conquered."

"Yes," Van Dorn said quietly. "But Earl . . . Earl . . . he was very handsome, one of the handsomest men you've ever seen, Dr. Duvall. Some men thought he was a dandy, but he was not. He was a fine figure of a man—and he knew it. He was arrogant, and could be downright cocky."

Cheney waited as Dr. Van Dorn searched the distance with his dark, flashing eyes, and wondered if his eyes—those young man's eyes set in a sixty-five-year-old man's face—were like Earl Van Dorn's before they were forever closed when he was but forty-three years old.

"Earl had an acidic sense of humor, and he was man enough to laugh even at himself. He wrote me once," Dr. Van Dorn went on, "and told me that he had insulted General Nathan Bedford Forrest to his face. Earl bragged that he was the only man who'd ever done that—and lived long enough to apologize profusely."

Cheney smiled as Dr. Van Dorn turned to her, grinning wickedly. Then he looked ahead, and his face slowly grew somber. "Ladies loved Earl. They swarmed all over him, ever since he was sixteen years old. A man—a doctor, as a matter of fact, with a pretty wife—shot Earl in the back, and then fled behind enemy lines."

Cheney gasped and groped for something to say. But she could think of nothing.

"We don't know what happened to Dr. Peter's wife," Van Dorn went on dully. "No one's ever seen her again, that I know of."

"That must have been a very difficult time for you, Dr. Van Dorn," Cheney said quietly.

"It was, for me, and my wife too," he replied. "But we both know the Lord Jesus, Dr. Duvall, and He helped us. I don't know how anybody got through that terrible war without the Lord Jesus Christ. I couldn't have. Still couldn't."

"Me, either," Cheney agreed fervently.

They had almost reached the hospital, and Dr. Van Dorn looked at Cheney appraisingly. Then he turned back to look straight ahead and said in a lecturing tone, "I'm going to tell

316

you about Captain E. Allan Perry, Dr. Duvall."

Cheney held her breath and said nothing.

"He came to Charleston in 1860, from where, I don't know. He went down to the docks and got a job with an old fisherman named Navvy Downs." Dr. Van Dorn smiled briefly. "Navvy Downs is—was—a fixture of Charleston. In 1860, Navvy was already older than I am now. He'd been all over the world, I guess. When he was young, he'd hop on board any ship that would take him on and sail off. But he'd always come back to Charleston. When he got older, he stayed here and made a good living as a commercial fisherman. He had a nice steam trawler, with a captain's and first mate's cabin, and he took on Allan Perry as soon as he wandered down to the docks."

They reached the hospital. Dr. Van Dorn muttered, "Ho, there," and pulled up on the reins. The horse stopped, but Dr. Van Dorn looped the reins around one of the roof uprights, turned to face Cheney, and continued, "Allan Perry made a pretty good fisherman. But Navvy, who knew every rock and sea oat along this coastline, found out that his mate could do something even better than fishing. Allan Perry could make maps. Accurate maps, clear maps, detailed maps that looked more like works of art than exercises of science."

"Really!" Cheney exclaimed. "I didn't know that! Actually, Dr. Van Dorn, I know very little about Captain Perry."

"I know that, Dr. Duvall," he said sternly. "And, as I am about to relate to you, I know very little else about him; most of this story I learned only recently, from General P. G. T. Beauregard. Captain Perry stubbornly refuses to talk at all about himself, but he is my patient, and General Beauregard was kind enough, and concerned enough for him, that he told me much about Captain Perry's past. I still do believe, however, that a man's life is his own business, so I would ask that you keep what I am about to relate to you to yourself, ma'am."

"I assure you I will do that, Dr. Van Dorn," Cheney replied with dignity.

"Yes, I know," he said easily. "When the war started, Allan Perry joined the Secret Service. Even though I was General

317

Beauregard's personal surgeon, I knew very little about the Secret Service. They dealt only with the commanders of the armies, you see, and those commanders never discussed the Secret Service, not even with their aides. At any rate, that is how Captain Perry got his rank. He—along with Navvy Downs—also became the most daring blockade runners that Charleston was fortunate enough to have."

"Goodness," Cheney muttered. She began to wonder if she and Shiloh were mistaken; could this man, this dashing blockade runner, this captain in the Rebel Secret Service, actually be the same gentle, sad Allan Blue from Manhattan?

"We heard that he got caught twice," he said, his dark eyes now heavily intent. "And at the time we had no idea how he got away. After the war we found out he had papers, Union papers, and even a Union captain's uniform. His papers said he was a cartographer in the service of the Signal Corps of the United States Army. His papers identified him as Captain Allan Blue."

Cheney's eyes grew enormous.

"But Captain Allan Blue of the Signal Corps of the Union Army died," Van Dorn said steadily. "He died during a rescue attempt after the *C.S.S. Hunley* sank the *U.S.S. Housatonic.* Oddly enough, Navvy Downs also perished that night."

"Wait . . . wait . . ." Cheney pleaded. "This is—I'm confused. This fisherman, that Allan Perry knew, died in that action? And Captain Blue, of the Union, died?"

"That's correct," Van Dorn asserted.

"But Captain Allan Perry, the Rebel Captain Perry, lived?"

"He did."

Cheney stared at him. Van Dorn smiled, very slightly, then expanded just a little. "That was in February of 1864, ma'am. The Union had already tried three times to invade Charleston; each time our forces knew their exact plan of attack, the time of their attack, and their strength, and each time we easily repulsed them. After Captain Blue died, you see, the flow of information to General Beauregard stopped. Later the Union suspected that Captain Blue had been a spy—but it was immaterial then. Captain Allan Blue was dead."

"Oh . . . oh, my gracious heavens," Cheney stammered. "He was a spy? He . . . he . . . blue skies! I can hardly sort it out myself! How did he actually live it? And manage to live through it?"

"Captain Perry is possibly the only man I have ever met, Dr. Duvall, who truly does not seem to care at all whether he lives or dies," Van Dorn said in a distant, sad voice. "He is utterly fearless and reckless and careless, though he is not a man of violence, not at all. I cannot imagine how he lived through the war. It certainly was not because he was cautious."

His voice quickened. "Somehow, some rumors have gotten started that Captain Allan Blue was a man from Charleston and is not dead. I've asked Captain Perry if the attack on him pertained to these rumors, but he flatly refuses to discuss it. He said he didn't see anything or anyone, that they came up behind him, and the first blow knocked him unconscious. And," he added with a deep sigh, "Navvy Downs' boat was torched that same night. It sank in the harbor."

"Dear Lord, is this war ever going to end?" Cheney sighed.

"I don't know, ma'am," he said quietly. "We must pray that it does."

"Yes, I will. I do. Dr. Van Dorn, have you said anything to Captain Perry about me?"

"No, ma'am," he replied with a mischievous glint in his eyes. "After I was rude enough to question you about it, and you were impertinent enough to tell me to mind my own business, I recalled that it was none of my concern anyway, and left it alone. Now, are you ready to visit my hospital?"

"Oh yes, sir," she responded eagerly. "I've been ready for a long time."

★   ★   ★   ★

The men were lined up alongside their beds, at attention. Cheney was certain that they had presented themselves, as if for inspection, to General Nathan Bedford Forrest exactly in this manner. She stopped and spoke to each one of them, and they smiled and were extremely courteous to her. But Cheney reflected wryly that, no matter how professional and competent she was, it would be very difficult for these men to forget she was a lady and think of her as a doctor. Shadrach, Logan, and Maxcy had done so, on her first visit, when they were in such extremities. But on her second visit, the next day, they had reverted to being gentlemen—acutely ashamed of their weaknesses, horrified at their crude surroundings, awkwardly embarrassed for her.

Cheney thought it likely that every gentleman in Charleston would, forever, be the same.

Dr. Van Dorn insisted on properly introducing her to each man, and it took a long time for them to work down to the end of the ward. Finally they came to the doorway, which was curtained off.

"In here are the men with erysipelas," Dr. Van Dorn told her in a low voice. He stopped, his hand on the curtain, and smiled at her. "I read Dr. Devlin Buchanan's study, Dr. Duvall. I won't say I agreed with all of his conclusions—" He pulled aside the curtain, and Cheney's eyes fell on a washstand set up along the wall, just on the other side of the partition that led into the ward. The strong disinfectant smell of carbolic acid rose from the yellow liquid in the basin. "But I can see no harm in this," Van Dorn finished.

Cheney gave him a brilliant smile, then eagerly looked around. There were eight men, all standing by their beds. Dr. Van Dorn unhurriedly introduced Cheney to all of them, and in spite of her impatience, she took care to speak to each one of them for a few moments.

Captain Perry was the last one.

"Dr. Duvall, may I present to you Captain Allan Perry," Dr. Van Dorn said. "Captain Perry, I have the honor of presenting you to Dr. Cheney Duvall, a colleague of mine, a physician from Manhattan."

She shook his hand and hungrily searched his face.

He was the same height as Cheney. His face was swollen and blistered with the erysipelas, but underneath it his skin, and the skin of his hands, was a glowing golden tan. His eyes were clear, a green-glass hazel color, large, with thick, curly brown lashes. His hair had been washed and was parted on the side. It was very long, wandering down over his collar. It was an unusual, rich color. When Cheney first set eyes on Laura Blue, she had dubbed the color "honey gold."

He watched her with only mild curiosity as she studied him so ardently. When he spoke his voice was heavy with weariness and almost devoid of inflection. "I'm very pleased to meet you, Dr. Duvall."

"Captain Perry," she said, smiling, "you have no idea how very pleased I am to meet you."

"Dr. Duvall wishes to speak to you privately, Captain Perry," Dr. Van Dorn announced in a no-nonsense tone. "Both of you follow me, please." He led them to the back of the hospital, into a large, comfortable office, obviously his own. It was sun-washed, light, with windows that overlooked the lake. Books and papers and medical supplies were cluttered comfortably all over the desk and wall-to-wall bookshelves. Cheney and Allan Perry seated themselves at the two chairs in front of the desk, and Dr. Van Dorn closed the door behind them.

Cheney considered him. He looked back at her, so neutrally that Cheney wondered for a moment if he was actually seeing her at all.

"Captain Perry, I have a message for you," she said simply.

"Oh?" he asked noncommittally.

"Yes. It is from Jane Anne Blue."

He started violently. But he said nothing.

"She asked me to tell you that she forgives you, for everything, now and always," Cheney said clearly. "She asked me to tell you—and I can also tell you this with personal knowledge— that you have two wonderful children. Your son, Jeremy, has grown to be a fine young man. He has a great deal of courage and honor. Your daughter, Laura—" Cheney's voice lowered to velvet, and she felt her face soften and her eyes crinkle with warmth. "She is absolutely beautiful. She has your green-gold eyes, your wonderful hair—she looks just like you. And when Laura Blue laughs, Captain Perry, it lifts your heart to the heavens, right into the presence of the Lord Jesus himself."

Captain E. Allan Perry stared at her—through her. Then, suddenly, his hazel eyes filled with tears, he bent his head, and he wept as if his heart were rent in two.

25

THE SAVING OF CAPTAIN E. ALLAN PERRY

Cheney had not expected such a strong, immediate, emotional reaction from Captain Perry. She sat motionless for a while as he wept with great tearing sobs that shook his slender body. She stared out the window at the cool blue beauty of the lake.

It's odd, she thought. *I, too, was acting as if Allan Blue—the sad, gentle Allan Blue from Manhattan—was dead. When I saw this man, this man with strength in his hands and a clear eye, even in his illness, this golden young man, I immediately saw Captain E. Allan Perry. Dear Lord, how can we ever know the hearts of men?*

Captain Perry's sobs finally came to an end. He placed his elbows on his knees, clasped his hands, and stared down at them. "Jane Anne. She's not here, is she?"

"No. She is still in New York."

"How is she? Is she doing well?"

"She's fine. She is the head of the Behring Memorial Orphanage in Manhattan—"

Captain Perry's head jerked around and he stared at Cheney almost angrily. "I beg your pardon? What did you say?"

"I . . . I . . . said she's the head of the Behring Memorial Orphanage—" Again Cheney's words were cut off by his reaction.

He looked back down, shook his head, and chuckled, an arid, desert sound. "I don't know why God doesn't just strike me dead." He sounded as if he were quite irritated with God for this.

Cheney was shocked speechless. Captain Perry took no note of her; he looked up and out the window and began speaking as if he were talking to someone who was not only not in the room but did not exist at all. He simply talked to the air. It gave Cheney an odd, uneasy feeling, but she listened carefully.

"And all my days are trances . . . and all my nightly dreams . . . are where thy dark eye glances . . ." He nodded grimly to himself, or to his unseen, unknown listener. "I told Navvy I had been brought up in the Behring Orphanage—a harmless, silly lie—and it has haunted me ever since. Strange—considering the many great, dark lies I've told, and the innocent blood I've shed, and the criminal damage I've done in my life . . . and that one little lie, leering at me from dark corners, shambling like a wraith, waits for me, and slyly slips in front of me. . . ."

He sat in the sunny, cheerful room, in his great darkness, and looked unseeing out the window. Cheney prayed hard for the Lord to help her think of what to say to this tortured man. She didn't notice the moments as they swept by, and neither did Captain Perry. When he spoke again, he looked at her and seemed to have put aside his near-dementia. He was polite and detached.

"Laura?" he asked. "How is she?"

"She's beautiful," Cheney declared. "She laughs, she cries. She recognizes Jane Anne's and Jeremy's voices, and she always hears anyone laughing." Cheney smiled warmly at him. "Jane Anne says she is a true blessing from God; Laura is never rebellious, never disobedient, never gives her a moment's worry."

"Never gives her a moment's worry," Perry repeated. "Then she is healthy?"

"Oh yes. She requires special care, of course. But she is well and strong."

He looked back out the window. "And Jeremy?"

"He looks very much like Jane Anne. Jeremy works hard and is an extremely intelligent boy. He has great courage, as I said, and has a man's sense of honor."

He stared back down at his hands. They were thin, delicate hands for a man, but now they were bronzed, hard-bitten, calloused. "Dr. Duvall, you just said that both of my"—he had to swallow hard before continuing—"children are strong. This is such a difficult and cruel thing for a man to face. My children are strong and courageous, and I am weak and a coward."

"Dr. Van Dorn says that you are fearless."

He looked at her, his hazel eyes red-rimmed and dull. One corner of his full mouth turned up with disdain. "Fearless? Maybe I am, if walking around not caring whether you live or die is a lack of fear. It is not courage. It is certainly not strength."

Cheney watched him, listened to him, and knew with pity that this man was telling the truth. He looked life-hardened, but he had no strength, no hope, and he was alone. Her eyes fell on Dr. Van Dorn's large, well-worn Bible, almost hidden under a pile of papers on his desk. Cheney picked it up, opened it, turned a few pages, and began to read slowly, with emphasis.

"For when we were yet without strength, in due time Christ died for the ungodly.

"For scarcely for a righteous man will one die: yet peradventure for a good man some would even dare to die."

"Wait," Captain Perry said abruptly. "What is that Scripture?"

"Romans, chapter five, verses six and seven."

"How did you know to read that Scripture? What—do you know about me?" His voice was raw and rough—almost afraid.

Cheney said quietly, "Captain Perry, what I know about you has nothing to do with it. I was just praying for you, and the Lord brought this Scripture to my mind, to read to you."

He stared at her, his face hard, set in disbelief. "Then you did not know that Navvy Downs, the best friend I ever had, a righteous and a godly man, died—for me? Instead of me?" His voice rose. "He died—willingly—for a worthless cur like me!"

Cheney was surprised, and her face was open, honest. "No, Captain Perry. I knew nothing of this. But if what you say is true, then your Heavenly Father knows that this Scripture is exactly what you need to hear."

His eyes widened. Then he dropped his head again, and his shoulders sagged. "Then read," he mumbled.

Cheney continued, "But God commendeth his love toward us, in that, while we were yet sinners, Christ died for us.

"Much more then, being now justified by his blood, we shall

be saved from wrath through him."

Cheney closed the Bible.

Captain E. Allan Perry did not move or speak for a long time.

Then he stood. Cheney looked up at him. To her surprise, he crumpled to his knees and put his head down onto his clasped hands on the chair. Quietly she slid to her knees beside him. "Tell me how to pray," he said in a muffled, broken voice.

He could not see her, and she smiled. "Allan, do you believe that you are a sinner?"

"Yes."

"Do you understand that God, the Mighty Jehovah, the Creator, Who is from everlasting to everlasting, sent his only begotten Son, Jesus Christ, here, to die for you?"

"Yes . . . yes . . ."

"Do you know," Cheney said with wonder, as if she were just realizing it herself, "that Jesus died instead of you? And because He did, your sin was washed away, gone forever, cleansed in His blood?"

"Oh, God! Yes!"

"Then, Allan, all you have to do is ask Him to forgive you for your sins, and ask Him to be your Lord, and to come to live in your heart, forever. He will wash you clean and make you a new man, and you will walk with Him, unashamed."

"Oh, Lord Jesus!" Allan cried. "Please, please forgive me— forgive me for my sins . . . and, Lord, please, take what is left of me, my heart, and make me clean, and make me whole, and make me new . . ." The anguish slowly faded from his voice, and after a time he finished quietly, ". . . and make me strong. I thank you, Lord Jesus, and I love you."

After a long time of quiet, Cheney and Allan rose. Allan immediately grabbed the Bible that Cheney had laid back on Dr. Van Dorn's desk, opened it, and began to fan the pages. "I need to read this . . . let me see . . . how long. . . ?"

"The rest of your life, I think," Cheney ventured.

He looked up at her and grinned. His face was terribly swollen, flame red on one side, but he looked boyish and happy.

"Yes. Yes. For the rest of my life." Suddenly he became intent. "I'm going to live forever, aren't I?"

"Oh yes," Cheney said softly.

"And does this mean, Dr. Duvall, that I'll see Navvy again? And be able to thank him?"

Cheney laughed with delight. "It so happens, Captain Perry, that the physician Luke tells us in that book that there is great joy in heaven over one sinner that repents. And I tell you that if your friend was a Christian, he is rejoicing for you right this minute and already understands exactly how grateful you are to him."

Captain Perry sat, gazing at the open Bible he held. He ran his thin hand down the center of the book and then caressed a single page between his fingers. "Navvy . . . I'll see him again." He looked at Cheney, and his eyes filled with tears again, though they shimmered and did not fall. "You didn't even know what he did."

"No, I didn't. I still don't."

"He died, saving my life. It was when the *Hunley*—the Confederate submarine—sank the *Housatonic*, you see." He spoke with great earnestness, and Cheney nodded encouragement to him. "I—we—knew, about the *Hunley* . . . when it happened, no one realized at first . . ."

His hazel eyes searched the tranquil setting outside the window. "Navvy and I were waiting. We were hidden in a little inlet on James Island watching for it, and when it happened we set out in the dinghy. There were plenty of rescue boats out for the survivors of the *Housatonic*, but Navvy and I were the only ones who knew that she'd been sunk by a submarine. There were nine men in that floating coffin. . . . We flew out there, to where we knew the sub must be . . . and, like a stupid fool, I jumped in."

He faced her then and said quietly, "It was February seventeenth, 1864. The water was freezing. I didn't see anything, but I kept floundering around out there, trying to . . . anyway, in a matter of minutes I couldn't move my arms or legs, and I started going down. I remember that, and then it seemed as though I was in fog, a dark, cold fog . . . but then I kind of woke up, and I knew Navvy had me, so I relaxed, because I knew I was safe. Then ... I ... woke up, in the dinghy. Alone. And Navvy was gone."

Cheney smiled at him. "Yes, he's gone to heaven, Captain Perry. But you're not alone now. You'll never be alone again, and you'll see your friend again, and you will both be rejoicing."

Allan sighed, but now he was not melancholy, not a tragic figure. "Navvy was a good Christian man." He made a face. "That lie, that little lie I was blathering about, I told it to Navvy, you see, when I first met him. And it caused me no end of grief and heartache after I got to know him. That was the only thing he ever questioned me about, asking me about my past, and I kept stumbling around and had to make up more lies."

Suddenly he started, jolted bolt upright in his chair. "Because it was about the Behring Orphanage—and he had the most peculiar connection with it. And now you sweep in here and announce to me that Jane Anne is at the Behring Orphanage in New York?"

"Yes. One of the Behring sisters moved there and started a new work. She died last year, and Jane Anne is the head of the orphanage now." Cheney's eyes crinkled in bewilderment. "You're saying that Navvy Downs was connected in some way with the Behring sisters?"

"Yes. I mean no. The orphanage. Or rather, one of the orphans." Allan blew out an exasperated breath. "It's a rather odd and complicated story ... about a baby that Navvy found on James Island after a terrible accident at sea. He took this baby boy to the Behring Orphanage but never knew anything of him after that."

Now Cheney jumped up abruptly and stopped breathing. The blood hammered against her eardrums so loudly she could barely hear her own voice when she whispered hoarsely, "Dearest Jesus, dearest Jesus—can it be? What ... what year ... when was this, that Navvy found this baby boy?"

He was startled by her intensity. "Why ... why, it was in 1843, Dr. Duvall. In November of 1843."

26

THE GRAY RIDERS

"Shiloh! Shiloh!" Cheney shouted, beating furiously on his door. "Open this door! I have to talk to you!"

Rissy came chugging down the hallway, a veritable iron horse with a red-hot stack. Her eyes were round, her mouth a straight line, and her sweeping skirts almost made smoke rise from the carpet. She never said a word. She just grabbed Cheney Duvall, M.D., around the waist, did an about-face, and steamed back south. After she had hauled Cheney into her room and released her, she closed the door quietly; then, gliding, turned to face her. Ever so slowly her strong brown hands crept up to rest on her hips.

"Hullo, Rissy," Cheney said in a very small voice.

"Mistuh Arns ain't in, Miss Cheney."

"Oh."

Rissy didn't say a word.

Cheney fidgeted with her reticule and shifted from one foot to the other. "I have something really important to tell him, Rissy."

Finally Rissy moved, and Cheney was horribly relieved, even though Rissy was shaking her head with alarming violence from side to side. "Miss Doctah Cheney Duvall! I cain't even think of anything—I cain't even holler loud enough—I cain't hardly think of what—!" She stopped shaking her head and gave full vent to her outrage. "Yore mama would just sink down into the flo' and die!"

"Yours would too, I think," Cheney gulped. "Let's don't tell them, all right?"

Rissy threw her hands in the air, then banged them back down to her sides. "I've allus been a strong woman, but I need some mo'!" She glared at Cheney again, but the glare was turned down to her normal heat. "Where you been all day an' night?"

"Why, I've been at the hospital, of course. You knew that."

"Does you know what time it is?"

"Why, yes, it's . . . um . . . it's . . . dark."

"Does you know what day it is?"

Cheney grinned and grabbed both of Rissy's hands in hers. "Yes! It's a wonderful, miraculous, blessed day!"

Rissy's strong, honest face melted into a warm smile. "It is?"

"Yes! Oh, where is that Shiloh?" Cheney whirled, threw herself into the chair in front of the dressing table, and tried to snatch the hatpin out of her hat. It was terribly tangled up in her hair, and Rissy moved up and slapped her hand lightly.

"Now you know where he's at. He's 'bout two foot behind Gin'ral Forrest. And don't you get to thinkin' you'll just sashay down the hall an' bang on Gin'ral Forrest-is door and screech for him to come out, Miss Cheney Duvall. Not whiles I'm still livin' and breathin'." Gently Rissy worked the long hatpin out of Cheney's thick hair. "'Sides, Gin'ral Forrest ain't been heah all day. I knows 'cause iss been too nice an' quiet roun' heah. 'Til you got heah."

A faint knock, almost a quiet scratching, sounded. Cheney and Rissy looked at each other. "That's your door, Rissy," Cheney said unnecessarily.

"I know dat," Rissy said indignantly as she headed into her adjoining room. "You mean you ain't gonna jump up and knock me down tryin' to answer it?"

Cheney heard Rissy open the door, and quiet murmurs. Rissy reappeared at the connecting door. "Miss Cheney—could you c'mere?"

Cheney hurried into Rissy's room. Moody stood at Rissy's door, his head bent, crushing and crumbling a shabby brown hat between his gnarled fingers.

"Moody! What's wrong?" Cheney asked gently.

"My . . . my . . . Lalie. She's sick." He didn't look up.

"She is? Did she have a relapse?"

Moody didn't answer, didn't look at Cheney, just kept nervously torturing his hat.

Cheney softened, recalling how intimidated Moody was by her presence, and stepped a little closer to him. "It'll be all right, Mr. Moody. Don't be afraid. I'll come."

"Thank you, ma'am." He turned and walked soundlessly down the hallway.

"But . . . wait . . . Mr. Moody . . ." Cheney called. But he had disappeared.

She shrugged and hurried to her room. "Rissy, we have to get some more fruit juice and soup stock. Will you go down to the kitchen, please? And go find Jubal and tell him to bring me a cart."

Rissy followed her, her arms crossed, frowning. "I'm goin' with you."

Cheney shrugged. "All right, if you wish. It's not necessary, though." She jammed the hatpin back into her hat, then rummaged in her medical bag. "Hmm . . . I'm out of codeine . . ."

"It sho' is." Rissy frowned, then said stubbornly. "I'll go do all them things, but I'm a-gonna see if I kin find Mistuh Arns and ast him to go with us."

Cheney stopped mining in her bag and looked up at Rissy. "Rissy, we don't have time. There is absolutely no telling where those two men are. I want to leave as soon as possible. Poor Mr. Moody—he's probably already halfway back home, and he'll be waiting for us." Her face twisted, and she looked back down into her black bag. "And this is all my fault, anyway! I should have gone back out there long before now to check up on them!"

Rissy wavered indecisively for a moment. Then she nodded slowly, stalked over to the armoire and opened one of the drawers. "All right, Miss Cheney. I'll go git everything. But while youse packin', you pack this." Next to Cheney's medical bag she set down Cheney's gun case, a long, flat box covered with fine black kid leather. Then she hurried out of the room.

Cheney looked blankly down at the gun case. Her face changed, and she considered it for a while. Then she sat down, opened the case, and began to load the gun.

★ ★ ★ ★

The two women rode out of the glow of Charleston and into the deep night. They did not speak for a long time, as they searched around them and willed their night-eyes to reveal to them what was real and what was shadow in the dark woods. The moon was old, nearly gone, with only a thin crescent of time left. But the night was clear, and the stars were vibrant and shimmered with their sweet light of life.

Cheney thought of Allan Blue, and then of E. Allan Perry, and then of Edgar Allan Poe. Staring up at the heavens, she said softly:

> "In Heaven a spirit doth dwell
> 'Whose heartstrings are a lute';
> None sing so wildly well
> As the angel Israfel,
> And the giddy stars (so legends tell)
> Ceasing their hymns, attend the spell
> Of his voice, all mute."

Rissy threw her head back and breathed deeply. "That sho' was pretty, Miss Cheney. An angel . . . named Israfel . . ."

"Shadrach named his horse after that poem," Cheney murmured. "And Allan Blue gave him that book of poems by Edgar Allan Poe."

Rissy jolted upright and grabbed Cheney's arm, hard. "What is that?"

Cheney stared straight ahead, straining to see.

The road ahead was straight, but with slight rises and dips that fooled the eyes. First Cheney and Rissy only saw a big moving shadow—then it disappeared—then it appeared again, blotting out more stars—and then the shadow separated into three—

"Those are riders, coming fast," Cheney muttered. She yanked hard on the reins, and Stocking came to an obedient quick halt.

Cheney and Rissy both turned, searching around them desperately. No side roads were close. Here the deep cypress woods were thick and seemed to crowd up to lean over the narrow turnpike.

They turned back around and looked; the shadows were close, and the pounding of their horses' hooves grew loud. The riders came into focus as shapes of men—but distorted and strangely glimmering.

The horses were dark shadows. But the riders were wearing tall white hoods and long white robes.

Rissy turned to Cheney. "I'm scared, Miss Cheney. You . . . you know they . . . they's comin' for me. Not for you. For me."

"I know, Rissy." Cheney swallowed, hard, and took one last look around, even though she knew there was no place to run.

I'm scared, Lord Jesus, I'm scared, please help me, I'm so scared. . . .

Her mind became clear, the chattering little voice in her head stopped, and her hearing became overly sensitive. She could hear the horses pounding toward them, and she could hear Rissy breathing hard beside her. She picked up one of Rissy's hands, thrust the reins into them, and ordered, "Here. Hold these. Don't let Stocking move an inch. Keep them tight, but don't jerk on them."

Rissy took the reins, slid one hand partly up to get a double-good grip, set her mouth, and stared ahead.

Cheney reached down, yanked her medical bag out from under the seat, opened it, and pulled out her gun. Then she stood up and waited.

They rode in fast, one in front, two slightly behind. Cheney waited until they were about twenty feet away. Then she pointed the Colt to the stars and fired. The explosion tore the quiet night to tatters, and from the barrel of the gun a spout of angry flame flew upward.

The three ghost-men reined up hard, their horses kicking and plunging. Cheney slowly lowered the gun, clasped it tight with both hands, and held it out at arm's length, just below eye level.

The horses calmed down, separated, and the three white

hoods turned toward her. The eye-slits were like black holes. Cheney kept the gun steady and pointed toward the man who had ridden in front.

"Wait a minute," he called. "Don't shoot, lady! I'm unarmed!"

Cheney did not move.

"Okay?" he said. "Don't shoot anybody . . . just calm down."

"You . . . you—" Cheney swallowed and began again. "You get over here. Over here to my right."

The mask was curiously, bizarrely, anonymous. He was looking at her and didn't move, and she couldn't tell if he was frightened or rebellious. Well, it was his own fault for wearing the dumb thing.

"Now!" she shouted.

He jumped, lightly tapped his horse's sides, and moved close to the cart and to Cheney's right.

"Lady, I'm unarmed," he pleaded, holding up his hands.

"If anybody moves, or if anybody's horse moves, I'm going to shoot you," Cheney muttered between gritted teeth.

"Nobody move!" the leader ordered. The two behind stayed motionless. Rissy was still. Cheney was still. Only the leader moved, and that was to put his hands back down, very slowly and carefully, to rest on the saddle horn. He waited, but somehow, even though he did not look human, Cheney knew he was growing impatient. He flexed his fingers slightly.

"Now what?" he demanded.

Cheney honestly didn't know, so she didn't say anything.

"Lady, you've got it all wrong," he said reasonably. "We were just riding, out on our own business. We got nothing to do with you and your nigger. So why don't you just put that gun down and let us ride on, and you go on about your business?"

"He's lyin', Miss Cheney," Rissy whispered as lightly as the flutter of a moth's wing.

But the men heard her, and the leader spat, "You ain't gonna listen to your nigger, are you? We're white men! We ain't gonna hurt you, lady!"

"Be quiet," Cheney said in a calm but unmistakably firm tone.

And so they were quiet and still. The moments stretched out. But silence, and waiting, was not the way of these men.

"The man behind you, the last man, is reaching inside his robe," Cheney called out harshly. "You! Don't move!"

"Listen, you idiot! She means it!" the man in front shouted without turning around.

"But Sarge—"

"You . . . shut . . . up!"

Rissy gasped, Cheney started. They'd heard that man say those exact words on this same road once before. Cheney tensed up, and the gun jerked. The man under the gun jumped. The second man, on the left, growled an animal sound. The last man, the man behind, yanked up his long robe.

"No!" Cheney shouted. "I'll shoot him!"

"No!" he shouted, still fumbling with his robe.

Cheney cocked the hammer of the gun; the man in front started shouting; the last man called out in his eerie, bloodless voice; and the man in the middle turned to face behind him, growling gutturally.

The tension, the fear, the confusion, turned the scene chaotic. Cheney kept the gun inexorably pointed on the leader of the men, but her mind was sluggish, wallowing in disbelief and a feeling of unreality. They were all shouting, and Cheney couldn't exactly see what the two men on her left were doing— she kept her eyes straight ahead, on the one man.

They didn't hear the horses coming up hard behind the cart until they were already very close. All three of the men shut up as if their voices had been sliced away.

"Rissy! Turn around and look!" Cheney muttered.

"Wha-what?"

"Turn around and look! You have to see if they—if it's— more of them! Now!"

Rissy jerked her head around and squinted her eyes.

"Wait . . . wait . . ." the leader implored, and now his voice was tinged with fear. "Lady, I . . . that's . . . there's nobody else! Don't shoot! Just don't shoot!"

"I'm really nervous!" Cheney complained loudly. "So everybody just stay still, so I'll calm down!"

Rissy turned back around and stared straight ahead. "Iss two men. Big men, an' big horses. They ain't wearin' white."

The tableau hung in space, frozen in time.

The Gray Riders were a blur as they passed the cart. Then they split in two, and one stopped directly in front of Cheney, by Stocking. It was Shiloh and Sock. But the other Gray Rider kept riding, and, as he passed by, the men in white—one, two, three—took sudden flight, then crashed to the ground.

Nathan Bedford Forrest wheeled King Phillip around and pounded back to the middle of the scene. He jumped off the horse and went to the man who lay to Cheney's right, a white bump on the side of the road. Cheney thought crazily, *That is a curiously small bump.*

Forrest put his heavy boot on the bump and shoved it. "Git up!" A gun appeared in Forrest's hand, and he shot the roadside, directly behind the white bump.

"No! No! You'll kill me!"

Forrest tossed his gun over his shoulder. It flew through the air and made a small thumping sound out in the darkness. "Now git up!"

"No! You'll still kill me!"

"That's right!" Forrest roared. "Now git up!"

One of the two white humps in the road behind Forrest started moving. Shiloh jumped off Sock and made the distance in three strides. Forrest, a blur again, was there before him. He reached down, snatched up the white lump, made a quick grabbing movement, came up with a gun, and threw it far into the deep woods. He drew back his fist—then he threw the small ghost down, and he became a shapeless lump in the road again.

Cheney, who had carefully eased down the hammer of her gun and lowered it to her side, was still standing, ordering her knees to stop trembling. She saw the man to her right move very slightly. She raised her gun back up. "Go ahead. Take out your gun, and . . . and . . . throw it away—somewhere."

Shiloh and Forrest turned, looked, and both of them unconcernedly turned back around. The leader pulled out his gun and flung it over his shoulder, making a loud hissing noise as he did.

Forrest stepped in front of the other man, the middle man. He looked up and raised his hands above him, in supplication. "I got a gun," he said clearly. "You can have it whenever you want it, General Forrest."

Forrest stalked off, growling. He went up the road, grabbed up in one hand what could have been called either a small log or a large branch, and savagely hammered it against a tree trunk. It broke, and splinters flew into the air. Forrest stalked farther up the road and was swallowed up in the night.

"Y'all made him real mad," Shiloh sighed. He backed up until he felt Sock and Stocking at his back and waved his gun casually. The gesture was still, however, quite meaningful to the men sitting on the ground. "Anyway, you better get up and take off your dresses. I'm pretty sure that's the next thing he'll want. And since he didn't kill you, I think you better do what he wants from now on."

"You're real funny, pretty boy," the leader rasped.

Shiloh turned, and his gun ended up pointing at the man's nose. Suddenly he did not look nearly so languid and good-natured. "I may be funny, you little grub worm, but you'd best listen to what I'm telling you. Stand up, strip off those sheets, and start talking. Right now."

The three men stumbled to their feet. Slowly they pulled off their hoods, which were separate from the robes. Their faces meant nothing to Cheney; she had never seen them before. The leader—the man she had been pointing a gun at for what seemed like hours—was a man of about thirty-five with heavy, dark features, a mustache and beard, and black eyes. The man in the middle was dark, with a long, unkempt beard and a big belly. The last man—or boy—had colorless hair, colorless eyes, and a blank expression.

"You," Shiloh said softly. "I know who you are."

Sergeant Sonny Micari glowered at him.

"Take the rest of that stuff off!" Forrest shouted from behind the three men. All three of them jumped high.

"Sarge," the boy said in a toneless voice, "The Guard ain't gonna like this."

"Shut up, Billy!"

Forrest muttered something dark under his breath, took one step, and ripped the sheet off of Billy Rand.

He was wearing a uniform, blue, with red piping and red buttons.

"The Guard!" Cheney cried. "They're provost marshals!"

"Everybody shut up! Don't say nothin'!" Micari croaked.

Forrest, his catamount's fangs bared, was in his face before he finished the choppy sentences. Quietly, calmly, Forrest reached up and wrapped his long, bony fingers around the man's neck. His grip was soft, barely touching. "They ain't gonna have to say a word, Sergeant. Because you're gonna tell me everything."

And so he did.

27

THE OLD GUARD AND THE NEW GARD

"I love to watch the Gullah women weaving sweetgrass baskets," Juliet Granger mused. "They mingle sweetgrass strips with strips of leaves from the palmetto tree and with pine straw from longleaf pines. They call it 'coiling,' or a word that, as best I understand it, means sewing. It is done with the handle of a spoon, but it is not winding it into a coil, nor is it sewing. It is mystical, and no matter how many times I watch them, I can never understand how the pile of leaves and grass are transformed into a single tightly woven unit." Suddenly she blushed painfully. "You all must think I am odd, blithering on about such nonsense."

"No, ma'am," Shiloh protested. "I like to watch the Gullah women coil, too. I never thought about it like that, though. Like life." Juliet glanced at him gratefully, then quickly dropped her eyes.

"Oh yes, Miss Granger," Cheney said quickly. "I think that is quite an insightful allegory for how our lives got so interwoven."

"Do you?" Juliet asked with surprise. "You are so quick, so intelligent, Dr. Duvall, it surprises me that you would think this of me."

"Juliet, you must, starting now, begin to understand something," Gard Granger said sternly. "You, too, are quick. You are intelligent, and you are clever. Get used to it."

"Yes, Brother, sir," Juliet replied with a sly glance at him. Granger pretended not to notice and nimbly managed to gather up a fat shrimp, some corn, and a chunk of sausage all in one spoonful of his Beaufort stew.

Three days had passed since the night meeting of the two

women, the ghost-men, and the Gray Riders on the hard turnpike. Judge Garth Granger had been arrested by Brigadier General John Hatch and had been returned to Washington to face a military tribunal for charges including, but not limited to, conspiracy to commit murder, fraud, and theft of United States property. Asher "Teach" Case faced similar charges. Sonny Micari, George Wynn, and Billy Rand were all charged with the murder of Vess Alexander, though Billy Rand had actually been the one to fire the shot.

Although no one had requested it, Gard Granger had quietly resigned as Charleston Harbor Master. He and his sister were leaving in two days to go to Washington and be with their father. They had asked Cheney and Shiloh to dine with them in Gard's suite; he lived in the last suite on the second floor, which was another "Planter's Suite." It was identical to the room where Nathan Bedford Forrest had stayed, except it was a mirror image. The fireplace, couches, French doors, and balcony were on the right, with the bar on the left. Cheney felt odd when she found out Gard Granger lived in this room, just two doors down from the hotel room where she had lived for the last month. She never knew he lived on the second floor, never saw him coming and going. He was such a solitary man, it seemed, that all of his paths were hidden from curious eyes.

"*Interwoven*," Gard Granger repeated thoughtfully. "Yes, that is apt. It is a most extraordinary story, when you step back and look at it."

"We all know the end of the story, Mr. Granger," Cheney said, watching his face closely. "But I am curious about the beginning and middle."

Cocking his left eyebrow, Cheney thought for a moment that he was offended. Then he almost—not quite—smiled. "Yes, well, that is one reason I asked you and Mr. Irons to join us for dinner, Dr. Duvall. Juliet and I"—he glanced at his sister with warmth—"have made many apologies and explanations in the last three days. We certainly owe one to you and Mr. Irons."

"No, you don't," Shiloh asserted. "He is your father, but you and Miss Granger had nothing to do with any of his crimes. Everyone knows that."

Cheney added stubbornly, "I agree. And I do not intend to parry any more apologies from you, Mr. Granger, for telling your father about my inquiries and questions about Vess's murder, and Guardian Investments, Limited. Again, you were merely acting—conscientiously—in accordance with my own request. None of us—not even Shiloh and General Forrest—had any idea of the consequences it would entail, and besides, everything turned out just fine. So I want to hear no more about it."

Granger looked rebellious, but Juliet said softly, "Thank you for your generosity, Dr. Duvall. We accept your wishes, and will say no more about that." She gave Gard a stern look, then turned back to Cheney and Shiloh. "By the way, one thing I still have never understood is how you, Mr. Irons, and General Forrest, magically appeared on that terrible scene."

"Moody couldn't stand it, after he'd sent the Doc out. The Guard had threatened him and his wife, and made him go ask her to ride out to his place. He tried to just go back home and forget it, but he couldn't." Shiloh finished in a gentle voice, "He was afraid to come tell me, because I was with General Forrest. We had returned to the hotel shortly after Cheney and Rissy had left. But Moody told Jubal, and Jubal came and told us."

"It's a miracle," Juliet whispered.

"Yes, it is," Cheney agreed heartily. "The Lord was watching out for me and Rissy. He took care of us."

"Still," Granger replied firmly, "there is one man responsible for all of these tragedies—our father. We must make amends as best we can." He searched Shiloh's face, then Cheney's, for long moments. Then he turned to Juliet, who smiled at him, her rich brown eyes warm and sympathetic, and nodded slightly.

"It did all begin with Duvall's Tools and Implements," Gard said. "An honorable and generous man, Richard Duvall made a kind offer to Alexander Dallas. The trouble was that my father and John Pride Rounds were the owners of Dallas Farm and Supply, and they—as we know—are not honorable or generous." Gard stopped, frowned darkly, cleared his throat, and continued. "They crossed the line between honor and dishonor, and from there it must have been easy to take one more step into crime."

"Yes, it seems that is so often the way," Cheney sighed. "But Mr. John Pride Rounds"—she glanced quickly at Shiloh—"who is he, Mr. Granger? We know he is the lawyer for Guardian Investments, but we don't understand his connection."

Gard shrugged. "He and my father have been law partners for twenty years. They were never very successful until the war, when my father began cultivating, as best he could, clients and connections in Washington. Mr. Rounds, who is sixty now, kept their law practice going."

"This Rounds," Shiloh asked, his eyes gleaming, "does he by any chance have a son?"

"Yes." Gard shot a cautious glance at Juliet.

"Oliver Cromwell Rounds," she sighed. "My father . . . tried to make me . . . but . . ."

"Oliver Cromwell Rounds is a conceited, spoiled, overbearing, skirt-chasing little pip," Gard maintained with disgust, "and has been ever since we were children. And my father always considered him a model son—unlike his own—and thought him a fine figure of a man."

"Oh, yeah?" Shiloh asked, mischief making his eyes an innocent cornflower blue. "Well, last time I saw him I thought the same thing. He was a fine figure of a pip, riding around backward on a horse in front of his busted cavalry, with his nightshirt flappin' in the hot Tennessee wind."

Gard Granger looked surprised and then smiled with cold satisfaction. Juliet Granger stared at Shiloh. But then, as she always did, her face and eyes softened in a telling manner, and she dropped her gaze.

"I wish I could've been there to see that," Granger rumbled. "But the mental picture is quite satisfactory. Forrest?"

"General Forrest nailed him," Shiloh drawled, "and then got real busy someplace else and let his boys take over the terms of Captain Rounds' surrender."

"Knew I liked Forrest for some reason," Gard commented.

"I liked him, too," Juliet asserted with the beginnings of defiance.

"See there? You are smart," Shiloh said, grinning.

"Thank you, Mr. Irons," Juliet managed to say with dignity.

"Welcome. Anyway, we know about the deal with Duvall's—but what about Vess? Sonny Micari just said that Vess had found out too much about The Guard, and he tried to contact General Hatch, and—" Shiloh stopped abruptly at the identical jolts of pain that crossed Gard's and Juliet Granger's faces.

"It's all right, Mr. Irons," Juliet whispered, but she was looking at Gard. "My brother and I are . . . appalled . . . and . . . ashamed, but together we have seen that the guilt is not ours to bear. Together we have determined to learn to deal with our father in the most generous way we can."

She turned back to face Shiloh and Cheney squarely. "Vess was in Father's study, waiting to see him. Evidently there were some incriminating papers on Father's desk—concerning the fraud with the Freedmen's Bureau—and Vess saw them. So The Guard knew that Vess must be . . . dealt with," she finished with difficulty.

"I never quite understood that scheme," Cheney said carelessly. "What, exactly, were they doing with the Freedmen's Bureau?"

Gard Granger appreciated Cheney's matter-of-fact tone, and he matched it. "It was actually a simple plan, but required complex paper shuffles. My father and I are expert paper shufflers," he said dryly. "They simply doubled the counts they reported to Washington on the goods distributed on draw day. That left exactly one-half of the Freedmen's Bureau goods here, in Charleston. The Guard shuffled receipts, shipping orders, and warehouses, and ultimately established ownership to these goods. Then Guardian Investments, Limited, shipped them out and sold them."

"And Vess found out. . . ." Cheney murmured.

"Yes. And they killed him," Gard said harshly, then took a deep breath. Juliet closed her eyes tightly for a moment, then looked back up at Cheney. Cheney smiled at her sympathetically.

"Well, I gotta say this much," Shiloh drawled. "When Micari was tellin' us this story, see, he swears that none of The Guard really set out to kill Vess. They were just going to scare him, like, by tellin' him that General Hatch, or nobody else in the world, cared about him or his little complaints, and he better mind his own business."

"It is kind of you, Mr. Irons, to mention this, for mine and my sister's comfort," Gard said stiffly. "But they did kill Vess. And, of course, that little strategy would not have worked with Dr. Duvall. Yet, there they were—three men, with guns, riding after two women alone. What do you suppose would have happened if you and General Forrest had not gotten there?"

"The Doc woulda shot 'em," Shiloh said lazily.

"Shiloh!" Cheney cried, appalled.

A smile lurked in Gard Granger's dark eyes, and Juliet Granger looked properly shocked.

"I didn't say you woulda killed 'em, Doc!" Shiloh said indignantly. "You coulda winged 'em, easy. You know. One arm, one leg, one arm—"

"I need more practice," Cheney said icily. "Your arms and legs are long and would make excellent targets."

"Oh, my," Juliet Granger whispered, her big brown eyes traveling back and forth from Cheney to Shiloh.

But Shiloh refused to be deterred. "Naw, Doc, you don't need any more practice. I promise. Besides, I'm attached to my arms and legs, if you get my meaning. Both of them. Meanings, I mean. 'Cause I'm actually attached to all four of them. Two arms, and two—well, one of my legs I'd consider trading for another without a musket ball groove in it . . . but . . ."

Here he had to pause, because Gard Granger was chuckling, Juliet Granger was giggling, and even Cheney's fury abated, and she laughed at his nonsense. Shiloh finished airily, "And if you think her shootin's good, you ought to see her with a scalpel!"

"Oh, dear!" Juliet said, but this time her eyes were alight, and her smile was warm.

Cheney sniffed disdainfully, though her eyes sparkled. "Which proves my point. I've had plenty of practice on you with a scalpel, Shiloh. I've decided to move on to target practice."

Shiloh grinned at her, and Cheney made a small face at him. Gard and Juliet Granger watched them closely; Juliet looked wistful. But Gard suddenly looked grave and intent.

"Are you a trained surgeon, Dr. Duvall?" he asked with elaborate casualness.

Cheney was startled and hesitated. Shiloh looked straight at Gard Granger and became serious. "She is one of the best surgeons I've ever seen. And, Mr. Granger, I've seen dozens of them."

Now Cheney turned to look at Shiloh, her eyes wide. "Thank you, Shiloh," she murmured. "It is very . . . satisfying to me to hear you say that."

"Welcome." He turned back to Granger, considered him critically. "You need a surgeon, Granger? Because if you do, you couldn't do better than the Doc."

Gard Granger dropped his eyes, and his jaw clenched. Juliet's eyes glistened with tears, and she leaned over and put her hand over her brother's. "Gard . . . let Dr. Duvall look at it. It can't possibly hurt."

"Oh yes," he rasped, "it could."

"Mr. Granger," Cheney said firmly, "I am a physician. To me, it is the most satisfying, the most rewarding, the most exciting work in the world. It is my life, and I love it. Please consider what I am telling you."

The room grew quiet. Gard Granger didn't move, except for the muscle in his jaw that tightened occasionally. Cheney studied him, his handsome features, his compact build, his right shoulder set lower and smaller than the left, and the hand that was always hidden.

A single tear slid down Juliet's smooth cheek. Shiloh watched her with pity.

Granger looked up, his face hard. "I suppose you've seen deformities before."

"Yes," Cheney answered.

He looked back down.

But her heart sank. If he had a bone deformity, she could do nothing about it. If he had a birth defect, she could do nothing about it. If his hand was withered from an injury that blocked the blood supply to his hand, she could do nothing about it. In fact, even as her mind catalogued these things, she began to cast desperately about for something she *could* help. And she began to doubt. She glanced at Shiloh, and he was watching her. He smiled.

"Please, Gard," Juliet whispered.

He jumped to his feet. "All right. Dr. Duvall, would you please take a look at my hand?"

"Yes," Cheney answered calmly. Shiloh held out her chair and lightly brushed her hand as she rose. He touched her fingertips, squeezed them lightly, and let go, without looking at her.

The four of them went to sit on the couches, Cheney and Gard on one, and Shiloh and Juliet on the other. Shiloh lounged casually, leaning back, throwing his arm loosely along the back of the couch, crossing one booted leg over the other. Juliet leaned forward tensely. Gard sat as abruptly as he had risen and began pulling off the black leather glove that was his constant uniform. It took some time, as it was quite form-fitting.

Finally he yanked it off and thrust his hand toward Cheney. Then he turned his face away. Cheney took his hand in both of hers and leaned closely over it.

His four fingers were close together and slightly bent. His thumb was attached to his palm. The hand was withered, small, a deadly white from lack of exposure to air and light. It was, however, meticulously clean, and Gard evidently kept it well coated with talc to counteract the continuous close wear of the glove.

Cheney didn't speak for several moments. The silence in the room was heavy, tense. Neither Shiloh nor Cheney was affected, or seemed to notice. Shiloh watched Cheney with interest, and Cheney looked at Gard Granger's hand with interest. She turned it up, then palm down, studying it. She pulled the fingers upward, then apart, and her face almost touched his hand as she leaned closer. Gard turned back then, with an awkward jerk, because he could feel Cheney's breath on his hand. It was the first time his right hand had felt another human being's warmth.

"Mr. Granger, your hand has been this way from birth, correct?" Cheney asked in a curiously guarded voice. She didn't look up.

"Yes."

"You have never consulted a physician about it?"

"No. My father . . ." he began, then swallowed, hard. "No. I never thought it would help. I still don't."

She looked up, sharply, angrily. "You're wrong! This should have been corrected long ago! It could easily have been corrected at birth! Why have you—"

Juliet Granger clasped her hands to her breast and cried out in an anguished voice, "Oh, Gard! Oh, Gard!"

Gard Granger's face drained of all color. His features took on a slightly gray look, and his nostrils pinched, and his eyes dulled. Cheney suddenly realized he was either going to faint or go into shock, or both.

"Shiloh—" Cheney began. But Shiloh had already jumped up, moved across the room to the bar, and was back, thrusting a squat glass under Granger's nose.

"Drink it, Mr. Granger," Cheney urged.

He drank the small amount of brown liquid, then coughed. But his eyes cleared, and the color came back into his face. "I . . . I beg your pardon," he said, pulling himself up straighter. "This . . . this . . . is quite a shock to me."

Cheney relaxed as Shiloh moved back to the bar and brought Juliet Granger a glass of water. "Here, Miss Granger. You look thirsty," he gently urged her. For once she didn't look at him. She took the water and sipped it absently, her eyes locked on her brother's face. Suddenly she jerked, and some of the water splashed out, and Shiloh reached over and slipped the glass out of her hand. "My . . . father!" she spat. "Our . . . father! He . . . he . . . he's—"

Gard shook his head. "No, Juliet. Don't." His voice was calm and without rancor.

347

Juliet stiffened, then seemed to crumple. "You're right, Gard. He's our father."

Cheney was still holding Gard's hand, lightly, in both of hers. Now he searched her face, took a deep breath, and looked down at his withered right hand, his eyes narrowed. "All right, Dr. Duvall. Please explain to me about my hand."

Cheney said evenly, "Many children are born with webs between their fingers or toes. In the womb, you see, all babies have these webs, and sometimes they don't degenerate completely as the digits form. It's . . . it's a very simple procedure to—"

She stopped, uncertain of how to tell this man that this deformity, this terrible handicap, and all his suffering, had always been needless. She still couldn't imagine how this had happened; even the most ignorant midwives generally knew to cut away the tiny, fragile webs from a newborn's hands.

"Go on, Dr. Duvall," he ordered. "I have already assimilated the fact that I've been walking around with this deformity for the last thirty years, needlessly. I understand that, I accept that, and now I'm ready to move on. Can you fix it? Can you make it—right?"

Cheney smiled. "Yes. It's a fairly simple procedure."

His indrawn breath was sharp, almost a gasp. "Are you certain?"

"Yes."

He stared at her for a long time. Cheney waited, watching him expressionlessly. Suddenly he grinned, a wide, untrammeled, devilish grin. She never thought she would see Gard Granger's severe features so full of open joy. "Then do it! Now!"

"What? Now?"

"Sure, Doc," Shiloh said, rising to his feet. "This is gonna be a whiff for you. You can get this done easy, right here, before dark. I'll go get your bag."

"But I'm not certain this is the best way, and the best place—"

"I don't know about all that either, Dr. Duvall," Gard Granger said imperiously, "but I do know this is the best time. The best in the world. Right now!"

* ★ ★ ★ ★

Shiloh returned with Cheney's medical bag and a large wash-basin from his own room. The servants had cleared the table, and he laid a clean sheet over it, smoothing it carefully. He considered the French doors with narrowed eyes, then rearranged the chairs so that Cheney would have the best light. He took out a huge, forbidding brown bottle of carbolic acid, poured some into the basin, then scrubbed it carefully. Then he poured it out, and poured more of the yellow, acrid-smelling disinfectant in. With care he selected three scalpels and two needles, placed them in the basin, and left them. While they were soaking, he ordered Cheney and Gard to come to the table and instructed them where to sit. As Cheney was questioning Gard, and still examining his hand, Shiloh was scrubbing his own hands, then Cheney's, and finally Gard's.

Juliet was watching and listening to Cheney and Gard, but her eyes kept wandering to Shiloh Irons. For such a tall man, with such long legs and big hands, he was graceful and quiet. His movements were sure, with no hesitation and no faltering. She thought, *He is the most handsome, the warmest man. . . . But it's more than that . . . languorous . . . sensual. . . .* Juliet's face flamed, her eyes widened, and she dropped her head quickly. No one noticed.

"Look away, Mr. Granger," Cheney ordered, then made a small sign to Shiloh. Juliet Granger couldn't imagine how Shiloh knew what she wanted, but he did. He went to the basin, pulled out a long needle, and handed it to Cheney, making certain that Gard couldn't see it.

"I want you to tell me if you feel this, Mr. Granger," Cheney said. Gently she began pricking the narrow strip of skin between his fingers at intervals with the needle. Once, twice, three, four times, and Gard Granger was silent.

"You feel nothing?" Cheney asked intently.

"I can feel a slight pressure on the insides of my fingers," Gard replied. "But no pain."

"Good," Cheney murmured. She turned his hand over and

repeated the pricks on the strip of skin forging his thumb to his palm. "And this?"

"Yes, I feel it. But no pain."

Cheney frowned and looked up at Shiloh, who bent over and looked. "Vessel?" he asked.

"Yes. But no nerve endings." She looked up at him.

"I can do it with cocaine," Shiloh said confidently.

"Good," Cheney said. "Have you got it mixed?"

"Yes, but what about the extraneous ridge? You gonna dip into the epidermis?" Shiloh asked.

Juliet was awed; she knew that Shiloh was not a doctor, not even a trained nurse. But he certainly seemed to know a lot, and Dr. Duvall consulted with him as if he were an equal, a colleague, instead of her assistant. *Which,* Juliet reflected, *he certainly seems to be, no matter what his title.*

Cheney said, "Mr. Granger, you may turn back around now. I want to explain this very carefully to you, so that I may make a decision concerning this surgery according to your wishes."

His eyebrows shot up. "Oh yes? I never knew a doctor before that gave a—that cared about my wishes, or anyone else's."

Cheney smiled. "Oh, there are some out there who do. At any rate, I want you to understand exactly what we're going to do. I'm simply going to cut away this skin between your fingers, and between your thumb and palm. Now, you still have muscular control in all of your fingers, and that is good. That is excellent. You do have one connective blood vessel, from your thumb to your palm, so it will bleed when I cut it. But to the best of my knowledge, the connective tissue growth—the webs—have no musculature and no nerve system. That means that you should feel absolutely no pain when I cut them."

"Yes, that's probably right," he agreed. "I've had those webs for a long time, and I'm sure I've never had any sensation in them."

"Good. But now, you must understand two things." Cheney looked hard at him.

"Yes. Go on."

"This surgery will not magically make your right hand—or

your right side—look exactly like your left. All of the muscles in your fingers, your hand, your arm, and your right shoulder have deteriorated from nonuse. Only exercise—painstaking exercise, repetitive exercise—of each finger, your hand, your wrist, your arms—will make them as strong as your left side."

"And this is a bad thing?" Gard grinned.

"All right," Cheney relented, smiling slightly. "The other consideration is the cosmetic effect of the surgery—what your hand will look like. You have two choices. One is, when I cut away the webs, I can leave a small layer of the extraneous skin around your fingers and thumb, trimming them as closely as I can to the skin of your fingers. This will leave small ridges around your fingers, and along one side of your thumb."

"I understand," Gard said quickly. "Will these ridges be permanent?"

"I honestly don't know," Cheney said. "They could deteriorate and slough off. Or they could harden and become permanent, like raised, tough scar tissue. I have no way of knowing which would happen."

"How wonderful!" He laughed. "It's so refreshing to have a doctor who is confident enough to admit she doesn't know something!" Cheney, Shiloh, and Juliet all smiled back at him. This new lightness of his was quite infectious. He continued, "So what is the other choice?"

"I could cut the web tissue all the way into your epidermal layer—that's the top layer of skin. It could hurt. If I'm good enough, you won't require any stitches, and you will have almost no scarring. But if I'm not, it's possible I might have to stitch some, and that could, possibly, be very painful; you would have light scarring, which would, however, disappear with time."

Gard considered this, and Cheney went on quietly, "I want to tell you, Mr. Granger, that Shiloh will be applying a local anesthetic—that means a powder that will numb your skin—and he's the best I've ever seen at attending to a patient, and being almost uncannily sensitive to their needs. He will know, before you do, if you are going to feel pain. And he will, most likely, be able to prevent it. But I want you to know that there is a chance you will feel some pain, should you choose to have this completely cut away."

Gard hesitated no more. "Cut it. All of it. And I personally believe, Dr. Duvall, that I won't feel a thing."

Shiloh nodded, Cheney smiled, and Juliet Granger beamed. Gard Granger settled more comfortably in his chair, laid his head back, and closed his eyes. For the first time in his life, he felt completely unafraid and totally relaxed. He was reflecting how odd this was—considering that a woman he barely knew was cutting on him with a very sharp knife—when he drifted away and went to sleep.

28

A PEARL OF GREAT PRICE

White Point Gardens, pockmarked and pitted by the afflictions of war and muted in its winter sleep, was still a tranquil place, with its own subdued beauty. Oak trees and palmettos gestured slightly, answering the sea wind. In the harbor, Fort Sumter's ragged outline was benevolently lit by a sleepy morning sun.

Shadrach Forrest Luxton and Cheney Duvall walked slowly down one of the manicured paths toward the gently lapping water. Cheney's arm was threaded through his, and she glanced surreptitiously up at him. He was slender and proud, splendid in the full-dress uniform he had worn when his and Cheney's eyes had first met on that dreary day when she arrived in Charleston. He walked slowly, in deference to Cheney. His head held high, his shoulders thrown back, his stern expression, were all indeed the Forrest mark.

At a discreet distance behind them walked Rissy Clarkson and Luke Alexander. Rissy was dressed in a maroon skirt and jacket, with a fetching new hat, and Luke could hardly keep his eyes off her. Rissy's eyes, however, never left the couple ahead of them. Rissy appeared to be doing most of the talking, and Luke appeared to be satisfied with this arrangement. Rissy made a gesture of cutting the air with one brown hand. Luke nodded, squared his broad shoulders, and moved up behind Shadrach and Cheney.

"Mistuh Luxton," he said in his deep, rich voice.

Shadrach and Cheney turned. "Mistuh Luxton, I've come to believe I owe you an apology." He stuck out his hand and waited.

Shadrach's eyes narrowed, and he considered Luke's face for

a few moments before slowly reaching out to shake his hand. "Do you?" he asked noncommittally.

"Yes, suh, I do," Luke replied, standing up even straighter.

Their hands clasped. Shadrach's expression was set, proud, almost arrogant, but his melodic tenor voice was kind. "Though I do not understand the necessity, Mr. Alexander, I accept your apology without question."

"Thank you, Mistuh Luxton," Luke said with great dignity and returned to Rissy, who was waiting for him and smiling. Their arms intertwined, they turned and went to sit in a small lacy gazebo down one of the side paths.

Shadrach and Cheney turned and walked on.

Cheney reflected that Luke Alexander must, indeed, have changed. Rissy had confided to Cheney that the proud young man had finally admitted that he needed healing from the hate in his heart. Together Luke and Rissy had prayed that he would learn to forgive. Luke's apology to Shadrach Luxton was visible evidence of God's redeeming and healing grace.

"I expect Rissy and Luke will be married soon," Cheney said bemusedly to Shadrach. "At first I couldn't believe that she wanted to stay on here in Charleston. In fact, I considered forbidding her to do it. I'm glad I came to my senses. But it was a hard realization for me, to think that somehow, down deep inside, I thought of Rissy as my personal property, to do with as I pleased." Cheney sounded pained.

"These things are hard for all of us to come to terms with," Shadrach said. "I know that I, too, would have the same problem if Abel wanted to leave me. Bedford gave him to me when I was eight years old. Of course, Bedford manumitted him, along with the other eighty or so slaves he owned. But twenty-two of Bedford's slaves stayed with him, as employees. Abel was one who decided to, so I never really had to deal with losing someone who was so much more than just a slave. I did—and, I suppose, still do—consider, deep in my heart, that he belongs to me."

"Yes," Cheney nodded. "Rissy pointed out to me, when I confessed to her, that it was really no more than the selfishness that many people feel when they lose a close, dear friend." She smiled. "At least, that was the gist of it."

"Yes, Bedford mentioned that she is quite eloquent," Shadrach commented, his voice deepening with amusement.

"Is that what he really said?" Cheney teased.

"No. You know I cannot repeat to you what he really said," Shadrach replied, "but it was, I promise, said—or growled—respectfully." He glanced at Cheney's profile. "I wish Bedford could have stayed longer. But he's hard at work in Rome, trying to get a railroad built, so he hurried straight back there. I'm going to miss him."

"He is a remarkable man," Cheney said quietly, "and though I didn't know him long or well, I can see how you would miss him very much."

They reached the end of the path, which was on a slight rise overlooking the harbor. Shadrach looked down at Cheney and smiled. "Cheney, I want you to know that I wish you were staying here, in Charleston. And if I had not come to understand your situation so well, I would do everything in my power to get you to stay. For me."

He spoke so calmly that Cheney, at first, did not understand the weight of his words. When she did, she was speechless. He met her gaze without flinching, his stern features unchanged. His gray-blue eyes, however, flamed and darkened into a deep indigo. Cheney suddenly understood that though Shadrach Forrest Luxton was seventeen years old, he was, in many ways, like his beloved "twin" brother. Nathan Bedford Forrest had become a man at fifteen, and Shadrach had the same passion, the same strength. But Shadrach also had a man's understanding, and yielded to God's reins. He deserved a man's respect.

"I am flattered, sir," she said formally. "And I consider it an honor for you to make this declaration to me so truthfully, and with such delicacy. I thank you, and I assure you that I treasure your friendship, Shadrach." Her arm was still intertwined with his, and she squeezed it lightly.

His eyes flickered. "I treasure our friendship, too, Cheney, though it is my second choice. So be warned; I will graduate from the Citadel in another year. Look for me."

She smiled at him, honestly, openly. "I shall, with great pleasure."

They looked out over Charleston Harbor in a companionable silence for a while. Then Shadrach said quietly, "I have a request to make of you, ma'am."

"Yes?"

"May I have a lock of your hair, please?"

Cheney blushed but said quietly, "Of course you may."

He produced a tiny pair of scissors and turned to her. Cheney worked a shining auburn curl loose, pulling it over her shoulder. He stepped close to her, caressing the lock of hair for a brief moment, then snipped a length of it. He pulled out a white silk handkerchief, gently placed the hair in the center, and folded the handkerchief with great care. Then he politely held out his arm for Cheney, and she took it, and they looked out toward the endless sea.

★　★　★　★

The heavens were incensed and flung watery javelins at the earth. Enraged, the Atlantic smashed herself relentlessly against the gentle sands of the barrier islands.

Navvy Downs stood in the lighthouse on James Island with the harbor master and watched the two ships desperately trying to thread the narrows, into the peace and safety of Charleston Harbor. They did not speak, and both men were taut, leaning far forward, as if they could by their will move the two pitiful vessels more rapidly, more surely.

The minutes passed. The inside of the lighthouse had become a miniature eye in the world of a vengeful hurricane.

The two ships—one a chunky, sturdy freighter, the other a slender, graceful reed of a clipper ship—danced their fateful dance as they desperately tried to escape the savagery of the sea. They drew close, then fought apart, as they rounded the prominent tip of Morris Island.

And then a multitude of great water-fists picked them up and smashed them together as if they were a child's unwanted toys.

Navvy Downs ran down the spiral staircase, flung open the door, and launched himself out into the tempest.

★　★　★　★

Two hours later Navvy walked along the storm-littered sands of James Island, alone, in the sudden peace and tranquility of the night.

"Herself is not a cruel mistress," he told a million stars. "She is a hunter, and she were triumphant this night." The sea was, indeed, Navvy's love and breath of life. He knew no other sailor who cared nothing at all for ships. He did, in fact, resent his forced ties to clumsy earthen vessels in order to be always with Herself.

Four sailors had made it to the farthest point on Sol Legare Island, struggling to the hope of the lighthouse. But three of them had died before they could say anything, and the third had only lived for a short time. Once he had whispered the word: "Daydreams . . ." The harbor master had grunted that it was more like nightmares, and these four men were likely the only survivors to be found.

But Navvy Downs had not given up hope, and would not, until he had covered every inch of coastline that might conceivably be reached by the lost souls.

"And Herself is strangely kind sometimes," Navvy murmured, his salty breath steaming before him. "She has, a time or two, given back those she's already taken and conquered."

And then he saw her, and even before he reached her he had named her Pearl.

She was dressed in white, a ghostly shimmer watched curiously by the stars' crystal eyes. Lying on her side, turned away from him, her pose was one of ease and grace. Navvy covered the last few feet quickly and bent over, touching her, and only then realizing that she was gone.

She looked to be asleep and even had a very slight smile on her face. Her shift was frozen, the thin white material turned to a garment of translucent ice. Her hair was wet and stiff with cold but did not look matted or tattered. It fell to her waist, a smooth, un-

357

broken curtain of black satin. Her closed eyes made a straight dark line, and her brows were straight above them. Navvy had thought she was a child, but when he saw her up close, he realized she was a young woman, tiny and flower-delicate. She was Oriental.

Her arms were gracefully arced into a circle. In the center of the circle was a crate, and in the crate was a baby. He—for Navvy somehow knew instantly that it was a boy-child—looked up at Navvy with big, round blue eyes. He made no sound. He was swaddled tightly in a flame-colored cloth.

Navvy reached out one sea-scarred hand to touch him—and then Navvy Downs, who feared nothing in or on the earth—drew back in sudden fright.

For the baby, and his cloth of flame, were warm and completely dry.

First he carried Pearl up to the grove on the rise directly behind them. He gently laid her on the cold earth beneath the trees and crossed her tiny little hands in a natural manner beneath her breasts. "I'll be back, Pearl," he said solemnly. "I promise ye I won't forget ye."

Navvy Downs took the baby straight to the Behring Orphanage. He rode an old broken-down horse, bareback, and he kept the baby in the box under one giant arm. It took two hours, but Navvy's arm never grew weak. The baby never cried, or went to sleep, and Navvy kept glancing down at him with concern. Whenever Navvy's eyes rested on him, the boy seemed to return his gaze with knowledge.

Navvy left him on the porch and whispered, "Here, now, boy. From this night ye'll have your Bearings." For though Navvy knew all times and tides, he could not read, and thought that the Bearing Sisters would be a good-luck charm for this baby who had escaped the grasp of Herself.

In two hours he returned and carried Pearl to the lighthouse. Navvy stayed with her through the remainder of the night and through the procession of ponderous officialdom the next day. And then, disdaining all orders from all men of consequence, he insisted that Pearl was his charge and he would take this last care of her.

Though Pearl wore a small gold cross around her slender neck, she was not white, and she could never be buried in any of the churchyards in Charleston.

So the next day Navvy Downs, alone, buried Pearl in the grove of trees on James Island, looking to the East, whence she had come.

★ ★ ★ ★

Shiloh, Cheney, and Allan Blue stood in the small grove of trees, grown so closely together and leaning toward each other so willingly that they formed a small private room. Spanish moss trembled above them in the slight breeze, and the sunlight was searching with the last of her golden fingers through the open branches above.

Cheney looked at Shiloh. He stood, his hands clasped in front of him, his head bent, as he considered her resting place and her simple marble cross. The only engraving on it was "Pearl."

Cheney tried to read his face but could not. He seemed to be absorbed, thoughtful, unaware of his surroundings. Cheney had wiped tears from her cheeks, and even now her hands were trembling from the power and vision of the story that Allan Blue had told so beautifully. But Shiloh showed nothing, and Cheney looked away.

"Doc? Would you say a thanks?" he asked. His voice revealed the awkwardness and vulnerability that his face did not.

"A . . . a . . . thanks? You mean a parting prayer?" Cheney stammered.

He looked at her and smiled, and Cheney's heart was rent. "No, Doc. Just say a thanks for me, please."

New tears glistened on Cheney's face, but her voice was steady. "Oh, Lord, Shiloh and I thank you for Pearl. We thank you for answering our prayer and granting us this knowledge of Shiloh's life. We thank you for your everlasting love and your unending care of us. Amen."

"Amen," Shiloh and Allan repeated. Shiloh stepped forward and laid a single white rose on the grave. Around the thorny stem was tied an old, faded black velvet ribbon.

★ ★ ★ ★

"So you're the one who burned all the harbor records," Shiloh grunted.

Captain Allan Blue shrugged, no mean feat for a man rowing a boat with three grown people in it. "I wasn't the only one who was burning all the records, Irons. We only had one day and one night, you know, after our men moved out and the Yanks marched in. Even the ladies of Charleston helped."

"Captain Blue, are you certain that Navvy never said anything about the two ships? Have you thought carefully over all your conversations?" Cheney pleaded.

"As I said, he said one was a freighter and one was a clipper. I think Navvy just didn't pay much attention to the logistics of the accident. It was a mystical experience for him, as deep and inexplicable as . . . as . . . *Herself.* It changed his whole life."

Allan rowed steadily and breathed easily. He had a wiry strength, and his recovery from the erysipelas had been so quick as to be almost miraculous. His face bore no trace of swelling or redness; it was again the color of dull gold. Shiloh sat facing him, his long legs stretched out as far as possible in the small dinghy, with his arms crossed, frowning. Cheney sat in the stern seat, glowing in royal blue, a lacy white parasol trimmed in the same rich color shielding her from the teasing winter sun.

"How did it change his life?" Shiloh finally asked curiously.

"He never forgot Pearl or what she did for you," Allan said quietly. "Obviously you were not her child, but she died for you, you see, and Navvy saw her, and knew that she had died happily. Fifteen years went by, and while Navvy sailed his beloved seas, he thought of the ways of men and their time upon earth. He finally came to understand that his Pearl was a picture, a type, of perfect love."

Shiloh turned his face aside and watched the wide stretch of lonely beach on James Island disappear. Allan studied his profile a few moments, then continued, "Navvy said that one night, on a freighter bound for Borneo, he finally understood what Pearl was to him. He climbed up to the crow's nest and leaned out as far as he could, so that all he could see was the sky and the sea. And he spoke aloud, and prayed for the Lord Jesus Christ to come into his heart and save him from his sin, and told Him that he wanted to know that kind of love."

Allan sighed deeply. "And he did come to know Jesus' love, too; what he didn't realize was that he would become a man with the same kind of love that his Pearl had in her heart. When he asked to be the recipient, he also became the giver."

"That's how it works," Cheney said with wonder. "That's exactly how *He* works. "

Shiloh turned back around, whipped off his canvas duster, and thrust out his hand toward Allan Blue. "Gimme those oars," he grunted. "I'll take a turn at 'em."

"Glad to," Allan grinned. "You shoulda been doing this all along anyway. You're bigger than me."

"I just want you to save your strength," Shiloh retorted. "You better take good care of Sock and Stocking."

Allan sat back, crossed his arms, and thrust out his own legs in much the same pose as Shiloh assumed so often. "What do I need strength for? I told you, the S.S. *Darnley*'s a good freighter, clean, solid, with a tough captain. I won't have to do anything but pet them."

"You *pet* puppies, Blue," Shiloh declared wrathfully. "You *groom* horses. Especially Sock and Stocking. Twice a day. And give 'em grapes once a day. And you exercise 'em every day—separately—and . . ."

Cheney had gotten distracted watching Shiloh's back and shoulders as the corded muscles smoothly worked beneath his cotton shirt. Her thoughts and observations had nothing whatever to do with review of the science of human functional anatomy, or with the theory of hypertrophy of existing muscle fibers that occurs with muscle training. When she realized what she was doing, and where her thoughts were, she suddenly blushed, and—for some reason—got irritated with Shiloh.

"Oh, that's marvelous, Shiloh," she interrupted. "Yes, Captain Blue! You be certain and ride those two horses around that freighter every single day!"

Shiloh grinned, then winked at Allan Blue. "See? You got the easy job. All you gotta do is escort the horses to New Orleans. I gotta escort the Doc and try to keep her out of trouble."

Solemnly Allan repeated, "I got the easy job."

"Men!" Cheney fumed.

"Yes?" they both asked at the same time.

Cheney opened her mouth to reply, her green eyes fierce— but then she closed her mouth, pressing it tightly closed to keep from smiling. "Never mind," she said primly. "My Tante Marye and Tante Elyse will put you two in your proper place."

Allan and Shiloh exchanged glances, each with a hint of un-certainty. "I . . . I . . . kinda figured your great-aunts were . . . um . . . gonna be like your mother," Shiloh mumbled, rowing harder as if in repentance.

Cheney smiled. "Did you? You just wait, Shiloh Irons." With that threat still pending, Cheney leaned forward slightly so she could see Allan more clearly. "Captain Blue, I wish to stress to you, again, that my aunts would be most happy for you to stay as long as you wish, after what is bound to be"—here she poked Shiloh's back sharply with her forefinger—"an extremely tiring trip."

Allan Blue's clear hazel eyes softened. He looked away, to the horizon, and murmured, "No, Dr. Duvall. I intend to take the first ship I can get back to New York."

Shiloh frowned slightly, and though Cheney couldn't see his face, she sensed it and lightly touched his back reassuringly. His shirt was slightly damp from the exertion, and for a fleeting moment she observed, with no trace of embarrassment, how won-derfully and curiously wrought his fight-hardened muscles were, how miraculously they worked. Then she smiled at Allan Blue, though he wasn't looking at her. "Jane Anne will be so happy."

"Jeremy might not," Shiloh said distantly.

Allan looked back at him, and his features, though sensitive and almost delicate, seemed firm and sure. "I understand that, you know, Irons. And Dr. Duvall has, quite tactfully and kindly, made me understand that Jane Anne is making no promises to me. But I'm going back, and I'm going to stay there. And I am going to try to win back my wife's love, and my son's love, and my daughter's love, if it takes the rest of my life."

"I guess it's none of my concern," Shiloh ventured, "but for what it's worth, I think that's the right thing to do, Captain Blue. And I think it takes a strong man to do it."

"Thank you," Allan said with great dignity.

"Besides," Shiloh growled, "every bluebelly in this city is looking for you, *Captain Allan Blue*. You better turn tail and run, since you've been dumb enough to take back that name."

"It's my name," he said mildly. "And Allan Blue has risen from the dead and is a new man." Then he grinned. "Besides— to quote Navvy Downs—there b'ain't nothing wrong with knowin' when to run like a school of spooked fish."

"Captain Blue, you're a smart, educated man, huh?" Shiloh asked with great seriousness.

"Educated, yes. Smart is debatable."

"Okay, give you that," Shiloh drawled. "But this 'School of Spooked Fish' principle you've got there. Would you please expound on that to the Doc? About the turnin' 'round and runnin', you know—like, for instance, when three ghosts with big guns are chasin' you on a dark road in the middle of the night?"

Now Cheney poked Shiloh hard, and he jerked. "You, Mr. Forrest's Boy Big Man, have a lot to talk about." She sat back, twirled her delicate parasol complacently, and reiterated, "Just wait, sir, until Tante Marye and Tante Elyse get hold of you."

Three soldiers on the wharf, stout men of General John Hatch's Brigade, watched curiously as the modest dinghy pulled up to the pier. They were, as were all the Yanks in Charleston, burning with fervor to catch the daring and reckless seaman, the fearless spy, Captain Allan Blue, who was reportedly still alive. Everyone wondered and speculated about all the men of Charleston. These three alert soldiers lined the edge of the wharf and squinted in the bright sunlight to observe the occupants of the dinghy.

They recognized Sergeant Shiloh Irons, one of Forrest's boys, who was rumored to have been in Forrest's legendary escort. Dr. Cheney Duvall, the beautiful, talented lady doctor from Manhattan, they knew well, as she had been a leading player in the city-wide drama of the last month.

The slight, slender man who had accompanied them out to James Island they did not know, and barely considered. He looked too mild and sensitive to be the fearless, reckless, and still triumphant Captain Allan Blue. They turned away with disappointment. A renegade sea gull, its cries of raucous mockery echoing around them, circled for a while, and then wheeled and flew out to sea.

NOTES TO OUR READERS

LIEUTENANT GENERAL NATHAN BEDFORD FORREST, C. S. A., has become more and more famous as time has passed since the great and terrible War Between the States, though the nature of his fame has changed since the nineteenth century. Forrest's battles have been studied and taught by educated men of war such as Field Marshal Viscount Garnet Wolseley, General in Chief of the British Imperial Forces; Sir Douglas Haig, commander of British Forces in World War I; and Erwin Rommel, the famous "Desert Fox" of World War II.

Forrest, through his own great common sense, worked out for himself and applied surprisingly "modern" methods of dealing with time, space, men, and materials—methods by which he was able with meager resources to accomplish major results. His logistical and logical methods are still recognized as a model today. In addition, as Forrest employed his cavalry as mounted infantry, his basic tactics proved sound for the kind of mobile warfare that was fought by tanks and motorized infantry in World War II.

But as Forrest remarks to Cheney Duvall within the pages of this book, ". . . bein' famous ain't the problem. It's bein' INfamous." And so he was, and so he still is.

Organized at first as a social club, the Ku Klux Klan became a powerful political organization in the early years of Reconstruction. Nathan Bedford Forrest, who had been dubbed "The Wizard of the Saddle" during the war, became the first Grand Wizard of the Ku Klux Klan in 1867. In the course of our research, we consulted six historical texts, and each of them concludes that Forrest attempted to make the order into a respectable, patriotic organization.

To summarize and condense the various sources, it appears that the original Klan was formed for three reasons: first, to encourage and assist ex-Confederates who were disenfranchised to apply for pardons and get their rights to a vote lawfully restored. The difficult Reconstruction years must be considered here; Nathan Bedford Forrest was indicted for treason twice (though after he posted a $10,000 bond each time, no action was ever taken), as were many of the prominent leaders of the Confederacy. The secret nature of the organization therefore appears to be justified.

A second reason for the forming of the Ku Klux Klan was to unite and empower a voting bloc. The first Democratic National Convention after the war met in New York on July 4, 1868, and Nathan Bedford Forrest was a delegate from Tennessee (although he did not receive his pardon from President Andrew Johnson until July 17). At that time, he was once more a citizen of the United States, although under the Tennessee state law disenfranchising Confederates for a period of fifteen years, he was not yet, technically, a voting citizen. Still, he was elected, and he went; and although he took no vocal part in the proceedings, he dutifully cast his electoral vote. This event in Forrest's life is an excellent example of the double standards that existed at the time, both in the laws and the politics of the land.

The third goal of the Ku Klux Klan appeared to be to render aid and assistance to poverty-stricken ex-Confederates, or their widowed families. Nathan Bedford Forrest, whose fortune was estimated to be around $1,500,000 at the onset of the war, gave liberally to many public charities of this order and to countless private, unpublished ones. He was poor at the time of his death, but his wife, Mary, continued to give unstintingly for the fifteen years she survived him, until, at her death, the estate of Nathan Bedford Forrest was practically worthless.

Regardless of all of these high and noble intentions, the Klansmen increasingly resorted to violence and intimidation in their efforts to suppress their foes, and they suffered as well from crimes committed in their name by outsiders. Though Forrest was a proud Rebel, when the great war was over, he vocally and visually became a law-abiding citizen and abhorred the corruption of the society by the vigilante factions. In 1869 Nathan Bedford Forrest resigned as leader and ordered the Ku Klux Klan to disband. Shortly thereafter, Congress passed legislation restricting Klan activities and ultimately declared the organization illegal. It maintained a covert life, however, until the late nineteenth century. The modern Ku Klux Klan, founded in 1915, has no direct link to the Reconstruction order.

★　★　★　★

It has been said, in this book and in other Southern times and places, that the South was overpowered but never conquered. This bit of defiance seems to be embodied in the life of Nathan Bedford Forrest.

He was, however, finally conquered; not by force of arms, but by the love of the Lord Jesus Christ.

In 1875 Forrest encountered one of "his boys," Raleigh R. White, on the streets of Memphis. Forrest asked White what he had been doing since the war, and White replied, "Preaching the Gospel of the Son of God."

The answer surprised General Forrest, and he began to diligently inquire about White's work. Mr. White eagerly began to relate to him the Old, Old Story, which so many men know by heart, but cannot say that their hearts know it in truth.

General Forrest listened avidly to Mr. White, then asked him to step into a bank parlor, where they could escape the noise of the street. White continued to expound with his former commander the principles of the saving grace of God and His Son, Christ Jesus. Finally Forrest asked White to pray for him. Then it must have been Raleigh R. White's turn for great surprise, because the proud general, the man who could not be envisioned by anyone who had ever met him bending his knee to any force, got down on his knees in that bank to pray and accepted the Lord Jesus Christ as his Savior.

On November 14, 1875, Nathan Bedford Forrest attended church with his wife. The preacher spoke on the man who built his house upon the sand. When he finished, Nathan Bedford

Forrest jumped to his feet, crossed his arms, and strode forward. The preacher, though he was slightly addled, went to meet him. Forrest stuck out his hand. "I am that man," he said quietly.

With his wife at his side, Nathan Bedford Forrest publicly announced his final surrender—to the saving grace of the Lord.

To judge by his activities, and the surviving photographs of him, Forrest appeared to stay strong, his frame steel-tempered, his demeanor arrogant (though after he was saved, he did outwardly and obviously change to a kinder and more tolerant man). Suddenly, in the spring of 1877, he simply broke down. His body wasted away, and as it did, he grew softer, gentler, and more loving in both his expression and his spirit. On October 29, 1877, he died at the age of fifty-six.

We believe that he and King Phillip ride still, though now as simple soldiers in the presence of the Great King.